Christmas on Primrose Hill

Karen Swan was previously a fashion editor before turning her hand to writing novels. She lives in East Sussex with her husband and three children.

Visit Karen's website at www.karenswan.com, or you can find Karen Swan's author page on Facebook or follow her on Twitter @KarenSwan1

Also by Karen Swan

Players
Prima Donna
Christmas at Tiffany's
The Perfect Present
Christmas at Claridge's
The Summer Without You
Christmas in the Snow
Summer at Tiffany's

Christmas on

PRIMROSE HILL

KAREN SWAN

PAN BOOKS

First published 2015 by Macmillan

This edition published 2015 by Pan Books
an imprint of Pan Macmillan
20 New Wharf Road, London N1 9RR
Associated companies throughout the world
www.panmacmillan.com

ISBN 978-1-4472-8013-2

5 7 9 8 6 4

A CIP catalogue record for this book is available from the British Library.

Typeset by Ellipsis Digital Limited, Glasgow
Printed and bound by CPI Group (UK) Ltd, Croydon, CR0 4YY

Visit **www.panmacmillan.com** to read more about all our books
and to buy them. You will also find features, author interviews and
news of any author events, and you can sign up for e-newsletters
so that you're always first to hear about our new releases.

For Vic and Lynne,
who also understand the joy
of a good cup of tea

Prologue

November, three years earlier

The note lay on the table in a sunspot, dust motes spinning in the air above like dancing sprites. All around it was silence. A coffee cup to the side was half full, but a skin had formed across the top and it sat, now, below the tideline inside. The chair stood at an odd angle, the newspaper smooth and unread, fruit quietly over-ripening in the fruit bowl.

She had stood in the doorway, staring at it like a set piece in a Dutch painting – that was what she would always remember of that moment as her instincts absorbed the narrative laid out before her.

It had taken several moments to move from the spot and intrude into the scene, to become a player on the stage. But her feet had done their job, and her eyes, on the note, did theirs.

And that was how it had begun.

Chapter One

December, present day

'I am a giant blue bunny. A blue freaking bunny. Of course I am. Of *course* I am,' Nettie muttered, her voice muffled beneath the outsized plush-furred rabbit's head, one long ear dangling down and obscuring her already compromised vision.

'On the plus side, your bum looks cute,' Jules grinned, flicking at her white pom-pom tail.

'Yeah?' Nettie twisted, trying to catch a glimpse of her large moulded rear end in the mirror, but her ear kept getting in the way.

'Yeah.' Jules grinned devilishly. 'All the better for Alex to grab next time you get back to—'

'There won't *be* a next time,' Nettie said furiously, turning on the spot and stamping her foot – well, paw – on the ground. 'Not this time. We are over. Completely over . . . What?'

Jules had collapsed against the wall like she'd been thrown against it. 'Do that again.'

'Do what?'

'Stamp your foot.'

3

'You mean like this?' Nettie stomped her foot on the ground again.

Jules cackled with laughter. 'My childhood just flashed before my eyes! You know you're just like Thumper when you do that?'

'Oh, well, as long as you're amused by all this . . .' She tried swatting the ear back with her paw. 'You get to look gorgeous, while I have to endure the ritual humiliation of wearing this thing.'

'Aw, it doesn't matter – no one will know it's you in there,' Jules said, trying to stifle her giggles as she too tried to manipulate the ear into staying back. 'Besides, it's all for a good cause.'

'But I still don't get why I have to be a giant blue bunny! It's not like it's a toddlers' tea party out there. Who's going to want to give money to me? Look at you. You look cool dressed like that. They'll all wait for *you* to go round with the bucket.' Nettie looked on enviously at Jules's sexified, micro Swiss traditional dress costume, her breasts in the scooped blouse offered up like peaches on a plate. She'd look good in it too, she knew, given half the chance. OK, maybe not as good as her glamorous colleagues – she didn't have legs up to the ceiling or a washboard tummy, for starters – but her gentle curves and almond eyes (both in shape and colour), and crowning glory, a sleek hazelnut mane that was both swishy and shiny, deserved better than to be mummified in this monstrous get-up.

'Yeah, maybe, but it was a closing-down sale and there were only three of these costumes left.' Jules nodded in agreement, tugging her top down a little lower. 'The only other thing they had was a giant banana, apparently. I think Mike figured he'd done you a favour.'

4

'He'd be doing me a favour if he could point out to me where exactly in my job description it says anything about dressing up in costumes? We are professionals, for heaven's sake.'

Jules shrugged helplessly. 'Well, look on the bright side – at least you get to be warm in that thing. It's flipping freezing out here.'

'I'll happily swap,' Nettie said quickly.

'Nah, you're all right.' Jules winked, her light brown eyes dancing with mischief. 'I rather like the look of that Canadian racer – what's his name?'

'Cameron Stanley?'

'Yeah, him. I reckon this might help my cause.' She fiddled some more with her neckline and tucked stray wisps of her hair back into her short, stubby plaits; her dark, curly hair fell to just below her jawline and they had had a devil of a job weaving it back. 'Do you reckon he's got a girlfriend?'

'No idea,' Nettie muttered, glowering that she'd have no chance of pulling in this outfit. Not that she'd want to go out with any of the guys here. They were mad, the lot of them. Certifiable, in fact. Why else would anyone willingly throw themselves down a steep and winding ice track on skates?

On the other side of the screens where they were standing, the lights strobed red, pink, blue and green, the roars of the crowd getting louder as the DJ whipped them into a frenzy. It was more like a rock concert than a sporting event, although the sponsors (and her marketing agency's star clients), White Tiger, had carved a niche for themselves supporting the hard-core, extreme sports that were practically uninsurable, attracting a radical, die-hard crowd, and this annual event had become the fans' favourite fixture.

And here she was, in the thick of it, dressed as a giant blue bunny. Nettie picked up her collection bucket. The first heats were completed and they would be ready at any moment for the second round to begin; then they could go round collecting money for Tested, the testicular cancer charity currently benefiting from White Tiger's corporate social responsibility (CSR) beneficence.

'Honestly, why are they taking so long?' Jules tutted, peering round the White Tiger sponsor's board to the race-track, warming her bare arms with her hands. 'I'll die of exposure if they carry on like this.'

Nettie came up behind her and wrapped her furry arms around her friend – at five foot three, she was usually three inches shorter than Jules, but was currently two feet taller thanks to her giant head. 'Don't say I never do anything for you.'

'Ah, that's so nice,' Jules sighed as she watched a couple of the engineers talking in a huddle at the top of the ramp. They were wearing pensive expressions and talking intermittently into their headsets, occasionally rattling at the starting gates beside them. 'Hmm, that doesn't look good.'

But Nettie's attention was elsewhere. She wasn't great with heights, and the ice-skinned course, built upon specially adapted scaffold towers, rose sixty metres above ground level. Narrow spectator aisles flanked the run on either side, and Nettie could see the long-haired, goateed supporters beginning to get restless, their gloved hands starting to pound the boards. Most of them looked just like the gnarly guys all padded up behind the gates, helmets and skates on and ready to go, punching their hands into their fists as they kept their adrenalin and aggression levels up. Ice cross downhill racing wasn't a sport for the faint-hearted – in fact, it made ice hockey, famous for its punch-ups, look positively limp by comparison – and the title given to this event was apt: Ice Crush. So far there had already been one broken wrist and a dislocated shoulder, and there were still six rounds to go.

One of the engineers walked in their direction; from the expression on his face, he was being bollocked in his ear-piece.

'Hey,' Jules said to him as he walked past. 'What's going on?'

The guy, clocking Jules in her provocative costume, seemed happy to stop, pushing the microphone of his headset away from his mouth. 'Technical difficulties. The gate mechanism's jammed.'

Jules pulled a cross-eyes face. 'Urgh, but I'm *frozen*. The sooner I can get out there with this bucket, the sooner I can get back into some proper clothes.'

The engineer didn't look particularly incentivized to make that happen.

Nettie looked across at the competitors trying to keep warm and psyched behind the gates. 'How long till you fix it? They look more like they're going to pick a fight than have a race.'

'Could be hours. We need to get to the circuit board underneath, but some daft idiot's built the ramps over the access hatch. If we can't find another access point, we'll have to cancel.'

'Oh great,' Nettie groaned. 'We came all the way to Lausanne for nothing.'

'Not nothing. Wait till we hit the bars later.' Jules grinned, burrowing back into the rabbit fur to keep warm.

'Mike's going to be on the warpath if we go back with just this for the pot.' Nettie shook the yellow bucket despondently and a few coins rattled.

'Well, it was a rubbish idea anyway,' Jules said. 'I keep telling him nobody collects donations by shaking a bucket anymore – well, except the Foreign Legion and the Salvation Army. If he wanted us to do this, we might just as well have gone and stood outside Tesco.'

Nettie looked back at the engineer. 'Is there really nothing you can do? Because if not, I'm taking this stupid costume off. It stinks and it weighs a ton.'

The guy shrugged. 'Well, there's no race if the riders can't even get out of the gates.'

'Why can't they just stand in front of the gates?' Jules asked.

'The gates are too low when they're behind them, meaning they'd be on the back foot. The riders need to start with their weight low but forward, on the front foot, to get the explosive power they need to blitz the course.'

'Oh.'

Nettie would have thought a seventy-degree slope and blade-encased feet were more than enough to get blitzing. 'So then why don't you get people to stand in front of each gate and the riders can hold on to them? That way, they'll be able to put their weight forward.'

'It's a bit . . . crap.' He frowned.

Nettie shrugged. 'Well, they did it for the snowboarders at the Winter Olympics.'

'Yeah, I guess . . . I guess that's a thought.' The engineer frowned, holding up a finger to listen to his boss on the one hand, while considering Nettie's proposal on the other. He spoke quickly into his headset.

'*We* should go out there and do it,' Jules hissed.

'What?'

'Yeah. It'd be great exposure. Everyone would see us up there before we go into the crowds.'

'It'd be great exposure all right – everyone would be looking straight up your skirt!' Nettie laughed.

The engineer overheard and looked back at Jules again. 'How many others are there like you?' he asked her, a quick – appreciative – flick of his eyes indicating her costume.

'Two more dressed like me,' Jules said. 'And then our big bunny here.'

'Yeah, four . . .' the engineer said into the headset again. 'It's about the only option we've got . . . I know,' he murmured. He looked back at the girls and a few moments later gave them a thumbs-up. 'OK, then. Get the others over here.'

'Yo! Daisy! Caro! We're up!' Jules yelled.

Daisy – six feet tall with legs that came up to Nettie's armpits and blonde hair as soft as swansdown – sauntered round the corner looking like Heidi Klum playing Heidi. Caro, a skinny strawberry blonde with freckles and a serious gum addiction, followed after her.

'Time to head into the fray, is it?' Daisy asked wearily, pocketing her phone inside her dress. 'About time. I've got plans after this. My second ever boyfriend's best friend lives here now and we're meant to be meeting up after.'

'Yeah, well, there's been a technical hitch, so we're helping out,' Jules said as the engineer told them all to follow him.

9

'Uh, sorry, what's going on?' Caro asked as they lined up at the side, along the top of the track.

'Pick your rider, girls. We're gonna get to hold their hands,' Jules winked. 'But I'm taking number three. Cam Stan is gonna be *my* man,' she laughed, trotting off friskily towards the snowy ledge.

'What's she talking about?' Daisy demanded, squinting to see past the bunny's eyes and decipher who was inside. 'Nettie?'

'Yeah, it's me,' Nettie sighed. 'And we've got to stand in front of the gates so the riders can hold on to us. The gates are jammed.'

'Oh great!' Caro tutted, chewing exaggeratedly on her gum so that her jaw looked like it was on springs.

The crowd erupted as the girls filed out – their tanned legs, plattered bosoms and kinky plaits highlighted in the spotlights, buckets still over their arms as they waved to the crowds below them. Gingerly, being the most cumbersome of them all with an eighty-inch waist, Nettie followed slowly along the ledge that topped the ice ramp and a ripple of laughter accompanied her entrance, as though she was deliberately intended as a joke. The riders – having been told of the solution – were already clambering over the gates, seemingly unencumbered by their bulky padding and very obviously anxious to get going.

'Hi,' Nettie smiled at her rider in lane four, an Austrian called Juls Frinkenberg, who had once been in the world top three.

'Oh really? I get the bunny?' he said irritably, stepping out of the way while she wedged herself past him to squeeze into the space in front of the gate.

'That's exactly what I said,' she replied, grabbing hold of

the gate with one paw and holding out her other arm for him. She swallowed at the sight of the near-vertical ice drop, just a metre in front of them. How could this guy be so desperate to go down it? Every instinct in her body was telling her to get the hell back.

'Link arms!' the engineer shouted across to them all. Nettie saw Jules giggling as she proffered her arm to Cameron Stanley like it was the prelude to a seduction. Cameron seemed more than happy to link up with her, and nowhere near as keen as Juls to hurl himself down the slope, not when he had his very own milkmaid standing at the top.

Juls linked his arm round hers just as Nettie noticed that the bucket was still swinging from it.

'Oh—' she said, going to remove her arm, but the first of the three race bells sounded suddenly and everyone went still, the riders crouched low in their starting positions like wolves ready to hunt. Nettie bit her lip – sod the bucket – and tried to tighten her hold on the gate, but it was hard to get a good grip with her padded paws and she could feel Juls straining away from her, pulling her outwards too.

The second bell blared and she felt herself begin to tremble from the strain of trying to counterbalance against Juls's weight as her paws failed to grip.

'Oh . . . oh . . .' she wailed, panicking as the seconds dragged like weeks. She couldn't hold on; she was going to drop him . . . Oh God, she was going to drop this rider down the ramp . . .

The third bell sounded and like a rope snapping he was gone. Just like that, to a whip-crack of cheers, the tension was released and she staggered backwards into the gate, her ear falling in front of her eyes again so that she couldn't see, only hear the riders race away, the crowd's accompanying

KAREN SWAN

roar following them like a Mexican wave, down and away from her.

Relief arrowed through her – she had felt fear, real fear, in those few moments when she'd thought he might pull her over with him. 'Close one!' she muttered as she straightened herself up, the long, wide, padded paws of her feet slippy on the ice. Wasn't there a scene in *Bambi* in which Thumper went flying along a frozen pond? she wondered as she turned to get the hell off this ledge and back to the safety of the race meet area.

But the bucket . . . she'd forgotten about it as she scrabbled against Juls's weight, and only as it slid off her thick, furred arm and rolled onto the ice with a thud did she remember it again.

'Oh! Shit!' she said, scrambling down to pick it up before it too headed down the ramp. If that hit a corner and went flying into the crowd, there could be an injuries lawsuit before she got this costume off. She didn't think, though, to calculate for the greater weight of the rabbit's head, and as she leaned forward, her paw just grasping the bucket's handle, she felt herself begin to tip. The ice drop stretched out in front of her, vertigo-style, and she over-corrected, lurching up to standing again, but her paws slipped, and as she moved her front foot wider, trying to plant herself solid, she stepped over the lip of the ledge and immediately began to slide down the ice sheet.

'*Nets?*'

Jules's voice was immediately far away and becoming smaller, the crowd speeding towards her as she rushed down the first drop, too shocked, too terrified even to breathe, much less to scream. The crowd were doing it for her anyway – screaming and laughing and cheering as she

12

sped past them, arms outstretched, ears flying behind, her wide, flat paws steady but speedy on the ice. What . . . ? No . . . No . . . No . . . She'd never experienced speed like this before, never anticipated what it does to your body when fear activates the survival instinct. She couldn't breathe; she couldn't draw in a breath to let out a scream. Instead, her body froze as she sped down the ice – immobile and yet more mobile than she'd ever been.

She was going to die.

She was definitely going to die.

The first bend came at her before she could even process it. Her body was rigid inside the giant suit and she couldn't steer, stop, see . . . She hit the first corner, then the second almost immediately, but rather than fall, she ricocheted off the walls, the bunny's moulded round tummy seemingly rebounding her like a pinball. Left, right, left, right . . . She felt the hits, but it was like taking body blows in a sumo suit at a school fete – faint and distant.

OK, not dead yet, then.

But . . . suddenly the course was running straight again. There was no relief in that, quite the opposite, in fact, and Nettie felt her heart almost leap clean out of her body as she knew what that meant – after the chicanes came the bumps, the ramps . . . and that meant she was going to . . . going to catch some . . .

She flew through the air like a cannonball, her arms still outstretched and flailing like cartoon wings. Something – muscle memory, perhaps, from a childhood ski-school lesson – made her bend her knees, ready for the impact, and amazingly, somehow, she got over the first and the second; she was barely aware of the crowd or their roars of delight as she sped past; but the third . . . She knew the riders called it 'the Giant Killer'. It was what made this event such a big ticket, built especially for this competition, and as she soared higher than any bunny should ever soar, she knew she wouldn't land this one.

She wasn't sure at which point up became down – while in the air or when she hit the ice again? – but the world tumbled, and for a course that was all white, she could see only black as her head was knocked about in the giant rabbit's head as she rolled and bumped and skidded and collided until . . .

It was a moment before she realized she had stopped moving. It was a moment before the clamour of the crowd came to her ears. It was a moment before someone carefully pulled off the rabbit's head and the world rushed at her in a warp weave of colour and sound, brightness and cheer. It was a moment before she found she was standing again, two padded men – the visors of their helmets pushed back – draped beneath her arms as they slid her from one corner of the finishing square to the other, hailed as a legend. And it was a good few moments before she saw that the yellow bucket was being passed round the crowd and was rapidly filling up.

Chapter Two

Nettie eyed the custard creams. They were the safest place for her to rest her eyes while Mike prowled in front of the whiteboard with an excitement that was all the more alarming because it had been aroused by her.

'Well, I think we can say that was a successful event, don't you?' he asked, nodding his own agreement with himself. 'Certainly, the costumes worked.'

'Totes,' Jules grinned, nodding back, one of the custard creams halved in her hands, and Nettie knew her friend was just waiting for Mike to turn his back momentarily before she licked the filling. 'They lapped it up, especially the bunny – it was hard-core *and* cute.'

'It was not cute,' Daisy said, looking up from filing her nails. 'That thing freaks me out. I mean, who's ever seen a blue bunny?'

'Who's ever seen a *seven-foot* blue bunny, you mean,' Jules chuckled.

'Exactly. It's like a mutant.'

'Tell you what, then – next time you can wear it. That way, you don't have to look at it,' Jules said helpfully, earning herself an arched, beautifully threaded eyebrow from Daisy.

'There won't be a next time,' Nettie said curtly. It was

two days later and she still had the bruises on her arms and torso to show for her misadventure; plus her neck felt like she'd slept with her head on a brick.

'Well, that combination is clearly what we need to tap into again,' Mike said, beginning to prowl once more, clicking his fingers rhythmically. Nettie stared at the patch of thinning hair on the back of his head as he stopped and surveyed the up-down zigzags on the chart. 'Donations were up seventy-six per cent after Nettie's stunt. It really engaged the audience and caught their imagination.' He spun on his heel and pointed at Jules intently. Nettie could imagine him practising the move in his bedroom mirror, perhaps imagining he was Clint Eastwood and with a pistol in his hand rather than a remote control. 'Hard-core and cute, you say?'

'Yep.' Jules looked back at Nettie, who was sitting beside her. 'You did look adorable whizzing down the ice like that, your little arms flailing about, ears flying.'

'Yeah, it was the ears I loved. They were hilarious,' Caro snorted from across the table. 'Honestly, you couldn't have planned the whole thing better.'

'Ha! No chance Nettie would have signed up for that in advance. You've got a thing about heights, haven't you?'

'*And* speed,' Nettie mumbled, quite sure she had a borderline case of PTSD.

'Well, the good news is, you survived,' Jules said, patting her on the hand. 'Another bicky?'

'Thanks.' Nettie nibbled at the edges of the custard cream. She needed the sugar. She wasn't sleeping well at the moment.

'Ladies, if we could focus on the matter in hand, *please*.' Mike had put on his sarcastic voice, but it only served to make him sound needy and Daisy resumed filing her nails. 'I'm sorry I missed the stunt. It would have been good to see. We need to come up with more ideas like this.'

'I can show you,' Caro said, tapping quickly on her iPad and then picking up the Apple TV remote on the table. As their IT and data analyst, she was the go-to person for anything technical (and spare charging cables). 'I already asked White Tiger for the footage . . . There. I've sent it to your inboxes,' Caro said with customary boredom. Her higher intellect meant she rarely engaged below a certain interest level.

'Oh, right . . .' Mike said, his face brightening as the screen on the wall was switched on. 'Righty-ho, well, let's see what we've got here, then.'

He straightened up and Nettie swivelled her chair a little, to get a better view of the white screen as 'Titanium' began pumping through the speakers, Mike nodding his head in time to the beat. The camera angle was wide, panning over the crowds, their heads flashing red, pink, white and blue in the strobe lights. Nettie felt sick, actually sick, as the lens picked out the menacing white ice wall that meandered between them all, the riders already shooting down it in a clash of flashing skates and jutting elbows.

Then she saw it. The blue blob that looked like a glob of Blu-tack from the wide-angle camera, tipping over, heavy-headed, at the top of the ramp, its padded paws as frictionless and unsteerable as if a pillow had been thrown down. Nettie felt her heart catch as she watched the blue bunny rapidly pick up speed; within three seconds she must surely have been doing sixty miles per hour, her arms flailing – the bucket dangling uselessly at her elbow – and ears flying, just as the girls had said. Her hand clapped over her mouth in aghast horror as she watched the bunny ricochet off the chicanes like a cartoon character – up one moment, doubled over the next. It was so hard to believe it was her in there, even though her body still all too clearly remembered the sensations, and adrenalin fizzed in her hands and feet and stomach.

Vaguely she was aware of the girls laughing – it seemed, from the corner of her eye, that Caro had her head on the desk – but she couldn't tear her eyes from the screen. The ramps were coming up, and in the next instant she watched open-mouthed as she flew through the air, belly up, the huge paws at least creating some drag, before she landed with a teeth-clattering thud and slid in spinning revolutions all the rest of the way down the slope.

The crowd were going wild for it, almost falling over the barricades to applaud her, as the riders – who'd seemingly been watching with the same horror she'd felt, for no one unwittingly went down that course – rushed over, pulling her to her feet and taking off the rabbit's head.

Instantly the cartoon-like illusion was broken. Her head seemed dwarfishly small in the outsized suit, and her long dark hair, matted from the heat in there, stuck to her pale cheeks in limp strands; even her full lips – usually rosy – were blanched. A shriek of laughter pealed through the conference room as her head actually reeled a little, her stunned, slightly cross-eyed expression seemingly as funny as the rest of it. Nettie watched her own legs buckle, her paws sliding everywhere on the ice as the two riders – one of whom was Jules's latest conquest, Cameron Stanley – grabbed her under the arms and jubilantly presented her to her adoring public.

The cheers grew yet louder still.

'Hear that? They reckoned it was a bloke in that suit,' Jules said. 'What a surprise for them seeing a pretty little thing like you in there.'

'They probably assumed it was another of the riders,' Daisy added. 'Who else would be *able* to go down there like that?'

'I can't believe I'm alive,' Nettie muttered, her eyes wide as she watched her wan self, trying to smile, to stand. 'Honestly I can't. It's a miracle. My dad must never see this.'

Mike pressed 'pause' – freeze-framing the short on an image of Nettie being held up, her head lolling to the side – and perched himself on the corner of the conference table, his arms crossed loosely over his thigh as he leaned in slightly towards her.

'Well, Nettie, I think we can all see for ourselves there the incredible response to your . . . uh, slide.' He smiled. 'How would you feel about repeating the success?'

'Terrible.' She shook her head firmly, reaching for another biscuit.

'No, no, don't make a rush decision. One thing you must bear in mind is that it would never be as bad as the first time. You've done it already, remember, mastered the course.'

Mastered the course? *Mastered the course?* She had slipped and crashed and bounced her way down a sheet of ice! How did that constitute mastering the course? There had been no technique, no free will involved at all. 'I could have died, Mike.'

He gave an earnest shake of his head. 'I think the bunny saved you, Nettie.' His forefinger stabbed onto his own leg. 'You were as safe in that costume as a kitten in a drum.'

KAREN SWAN

There was a pause. 'That's not very safe,' she said, flummoxed.

He looked at her for a long moment, before inhaling sharply and pulling back. 'Well, far be it from me to force you to do anything you don't want to do. I'm merely looking for ways to help you.'

She frowned. 'Help me?'

'Well, yes. You're in charge of charitable donations. It's no secret that when Jules was doing the job two years ago, she exceeded her targets by forty-six per cent, whereas you are down fifty-one per cent. The clients keep asking me if there's a problem.' He threw his hands in the air. 'And what am I supposed to say, huh? That my head of CD has personal problems? Is that *their* problem?'

'Of course not, but . . .'

He nodded repeatedly, and the 'but' rippled into the room like a big, fat excuse. 'You see what I'm saying here?'

'Um . . .' Nettie hesitated, keeping the biscuit to her mouth, as though for protection rather than ingestion.

'I can't carry dead weight. Everyone has to earn their place on the team.' He pointed towards the window. 'I've got people queuing up to sit in that chair you're sitting in right now. Young graduates, hungry for the exposure, the experience . . .'

Nettie wasn't sure that was true. She opened the post every morning. He got five CVs a week at most.

'I know your personal circumstances have been difficult, Nettie, but I think you need to take some time to think, really think, about whether or not this is the industry for you.' He slammed his fist into his palm. 'It takes drive, commitment, hunger, passion. You used to be so . . . so . . . hungry, Nettie.'

To her surprise, no one cut in that she still was. Nettie eyed the girls on the team. There wasn't much evidence of drive or passion in any of them, and the only hunger in the room had been just about sated thanks to the plate of biscuits. Daisy was checking her hair for split ends. Caro had the iPad secretively tipped towards her, which meant she was playing solitaire. Only Jules was paying full attention, resentment burning her eyes black.

'What happened to you? Where did you go?'

Nettie wanted to slap him. He knew exactly what had happened.

'From what I was told by my predecessor, you used to be first in, last out every day. You knew if we were low on tea or needed to order more print cartridges. You answered every phone on the first ring. But now?' He frowned. 'Now . . . ? I know things have been difficult for you, but I want you to take a long, hard look, Nettie, at where you're going with your career. Is this still right for you? Because if so, we need to start getting some results, and fast. The bunny worked. Don't dismiss it out of hand. You should be thinking how to make it work for you again. Make it your USP.'

'What, Giant Flying Bunny?' Jules grinned, leaning forward and squeezing Nettie consolingly on the shoulder.

Mike shrugged. 'Why not? Think big. You could become White Tiger's mascot.'

Caro frowned, momentarily ceasing chewing her gum. 'Well, if they were to have a mascot, wouldn't that be a . . . white tiger, then, Mike?'

Mike straightened up irritably. 'You know what I mean.' He clapped his hands together, looking round at the lethargic, now completely demotivated team. 'Right, well, on the *plus* side, the Ice Crush event brought in more than two thousand pounds in total. I don't have the exact figure here, but let's take heart from that.' He punched the air feebly and everyone sighed collectively as he tried to rally them, as though his comments to Nettie had been a mere pep talk and not thinly veiled threats about losing her job.

'Next week the Christmas countdown begins in earnest, so I want you all in on Monday and working at high revs. You don't need me to tell you it's our biggest week next week, so rest, take it easy and come in refreshed and good to go. Have a good weekend, everybody.'

Mike had barely got the words out before the women were scraping back their chairs and showing more energy than they had at any other point in the day. Caro already had her phone to her ear, finalizing the arrangements for her evening plans. Nettie watched as Jules grabbed the last two biscuits and slipped them into her pockets 'for later'. Everything was always 'for later' with Jules – the crumbs on her shirt, the cake in her bag, the cheeky chappy standing by the bar.

'Ignore him. Tosser,' Jules said under her breath to Nettie as they walked back into the office.

Nettie hugged her papers closer to her chest. 'He's right, though. I'm terrible at this job.'

'No, you're not. He's just a bad leader. He couldn't organize a piss-up in a brewery and he expects you to coin it in for the charities?'

'Well, you managed it.'

'Only because I was going for his job and trying to impress the bosses,' Jules groaned.

'You should have got it. It's a travesty that they gave it to him. We all know he only got it because his wife's father knows the Middletons and they're hoping to wheedle an introduction.'

It wasn't just Jules who'd been disappointed by the decision. With no obvious career progression at the agency, Nettie had been mentally bracing herself for the news that, any day now, Jules would be leaving. She knew head-hunters contacted her on a regular basis but her friend always stopped them in their tracks and Nettie suspected the only reason she was still working there (apart from tor-menting Mike whose inept people skills meant he was clearly vastly out of his depth in the job) was to keep an eye on her.

It was a suspicion that she couldn't articulate, not least because Jules would deny it and Nettie didn't want to face the guilt, because she didn't care about the job like Jules did. Sure, she liked the team, the commute was fine and the hours were pretty regular, but this wasn't where she had thought her career would end up – shaking buckets at sporting events, begging for spare change in the name of big business charity. Not to mention wearing grotesque fancy dress costumes for a living.

No, in her previous life, she had wanted to be in adver-tising, giving people added narratives in their everyday lives and sprinkling happiness over the prospect of pur-chasing car insurance or washing powder. She would come to the rescue of ailing giants like Tesco and RBS, and single-handedly rewrite the public's perception of them before setting up her own company. She'd graft for a few years and then sell at a great profit to Ogilvy & Mather. This was her plan; this had always been her plan, ever since she'd fallen hard for the Diet Coke guy in the Noughties and mended her heart after her first proper breakup. Only, the dream job in advertising hadn't materialized in time – too many graduates, not enough jobs – and she had settled on this one as a short-term stopgap, justifying it as a lateral move into marketing, which everyone knew was inextricably linked with advertising. One and the same really.

But then she hadn't ever anticipated the schism that would one day rip through her life like a tear in a sheet of paper, and ever since then, new rules had had to apply: six months had turned into almost six years, life twisting away from her at all the pertinent moments so that this was all she could cope with, anyway – something low-level, doing just enough to get by. Jules's arrival on the team nearly five years ago had undoubtedly helped make this office and those meetings bearable – the two of them had connected immediately, Jules buying her first flat just around the corner from Nettie, and they worked and played together as a team – but was Mike right? Was it time to move on? Were she and Jules actually holding each other back, clinging to each other like bindweed, their grip too strong for the other to grow?

Jules was quiet for a moment. 'Yeah well, bygones and all that. No point in dwelling on it. Far more importantly, what are you up to tonight?'

'I was supposed to be seeing Em, but she's doing another double shift,' she groaned. Emma was Nettie's best friend from university, a Titian-haired, porcelain-skinned willow wand with a brilliant brain, luck on her side and men at her feet, and who was on the fast-track to becoming a consultant obstetrician. Subsequently, she cancelled their plans a lot.

'Well, I want to check out that new vodka bar on Prince Albert Road. Come with.' Jules dropped her iPad, jotter and pens on their shared desk. Jules's side of the desk looked like it had been raided by the police, with skewed sheets of paper scattered everywhere, coffee rings on the only visible bits of grey veneered desktop, the paperclips linked together in an industrial daisy chain – testament to the amount of staring out of the window she did – and sitting in the corner, a bug-eyed lemur toy she'd been given by her ex and couldn't quite part with yet.

Nettie's side, by contrast, was neat and tidy, with everything in its place and a motivational placard that read, 'Your breakthrough is just beyond your breakdown', which never failed to amuse Jules, who joked that the lot of them were fast heading towards one – now that Mike was running the show.

'I really shouldn't. I need an early night,' she said, filing her paperwork into her top right desk drawer. She didn't need to look up to know the expression that would be on Jules's face at her words. 'And before you say it, Em and I had promised to have a quiet one – she's strung out, and I'm all bruised from the other day. She says I need a hot soak to bring it out properly. Bath salts. Doctor's orders.'

'Pah! What does she know? A night on the tiles is what you need. It would help you unwind properly. You've got to relax, Nets. Have some fun and go nuts. It's much better for you. Blow off the cobwebs.'

Nettie arched an eyebrow but didn't reply. Ever since Jules and her Big Passion ex had broken up, Jules's answer to everything was a Big Night – promotion, engagement, winning a tenner on the lottery . . .

'Would it hurt you to come for one drink? It's on the way home anyway.'

'But it's never just one with you – that's the problem.'

Jules slapped her hand over her ample chest. 'I promise, just one. On my life.'

Everything hurt. That was all she knew.

Hitting ice walls at sixty miles per hour had been bad. But this was worse. So much worse. So, *so* much worse.

Her head was falling off, for one thing. Well, that had to be what it was. It was the only possible explanation for the throbbing above her neck.

And she must have been punched in the stomach for it to feel quite so battered.

And who knew her *tongue* had a pulse?

Downstairs, she could hear the sounds of Radio Four already blaring in the kitchen. That meant her father was up; it also meant pigs everywhere were running for their lives as the fat hit the pan. Should she go back to sleep? If she could just doze till, say, a week Tuesday, she'd get through the worst of this.

But John Humphrys wouldn't be denied, his voice carrying through the gaps in the floorboards like water running through the pipes, and she stared at the wall for what seemed like an epoch, but according to her clock was only eleven minutes, before attempting verticality.

She had just managed it – her hands actually holding her head, like it had come loose – when she heard another voice vibrating through the floorboards of the draughty house and knew Saturday was well and truly underway. She sighed.

A few minutes later she was being propped up by the kitchen doorway. She stared at the familiar scene. Both her father and Dan were standing in the middle of the kitchen, working on her father's bike, which was upside down in the middle of the room, the front wheel spinning.

'Ah! It awakens!' her father boomed – or so it seemed to her, anyway.

'Dad, please?' Nettie winced, simultaneously holding her hands up as though trying to push back the sound waves while marvelling at her own voice: seemingly it had grown hairs overnight.

'Sorry, love,' he chuckled, his eyes twinkling at the sight of her, bedraggled and broken. His Saturday mornings were never like this. He didn't drink, never sat still; the man radiated busy-busy-busyness, always doing something, and everything about him suggested bonhomie: the bosky beard, sparkling hazel eyes, the rounded tummy that paid testament to his great love of French cooking and none whatsoever to his second great love, cycling.

Dan turned round to face her, just as bad as her father, a laugh already on his lips. 'Oh, it is you. I thought Barry White had come back from the dead.'

He laughed freely at his own joke. Nettie had always thought it would be a lot easier to hate him if he didn't bear more than a passing resemblance to Damon Albarn – both of them tall, cheeky-chappy types with round blue eyes and mousy hair, scruffy (perpetually wearing jeans, Pumas and hoodies), heads always hung low, usually from avoiding ex-girlfriends or irate customers. Currently, Dan was without a girlfriend, but she expected that to have changed by Friday night.

'Not funny,' she said testily, massaging her temples again as she grudgingly staggered into the kitchen, her white towelling robe tightly belted round her waist, her long dark hair hanging in a tangle down her back. Her foot caught in the handle of her mother's handbag, kept in its usual place between the wall and the table, and she stumbled, falling awkwardly onto the back of the kitchen chairs.

'Oh, for Chrissakes!' she cried, her temper flaring from the fright. 'That thing is a bloody liability there! Why can't we move it?'

'Love,' her dad said sympathetically, pushing the bag against the wall and tucking in the handles, 'you know your mother likes it there. Look, just sit down. I'll get you a cup of tea. You know she always says there's nothing a good cup of tea can't remedy,' he said, pulling out the orange Arne chair – each one round the unpainted table was a different colour of the rainbow – and gently pushing her into it. She gave him a sullen look, which he either ignored or, more likely, genuinely didn't notice. 'So, out with Jules again, were you?'

'I hate her,' Nettie muttered, just as Scout, Dan's beloved Norfolk Jack Russell, trotted over to her for a cuddle. She looked down at him sadly, not sure she could bend that far right now.

'And yet every week . . .' Dan went back to spinning the wheel again, pressing the brakes on the handlebars and testing the ceramic discs, her father stopping to tweak something on his way back from switching the kettle on. Nettie watched with slack-jawed apathy as the two men began consulting each other again, heads together, the tea forgotten.

It had once been her Dan would come to see. They had first met when he'd been thirteen and she was eleven; she'd been coming out of the house as he walked up the path on his newspaper round, delivering their daily copy of the *Guardian*. He was two years above her at school, but

28

it was the first time they'd spoken, and the following week she saw him from the upstairs window lingering in the corner of the square until their front door opened, whereupon he'd leaped to his feet and raced over, falling into a casual stroll just as he got to their path – and promptly ran into her mother.

After that, Nettie had made a point of opening the door at the same time every Saturday, and their chats on the doorstep were soon held over mugs of hot chocolate in the kitchen as her mother fretted over his cold hands in the wintry temperatures and deplored that his own mother had never thought to give him some gloves. So she had knitted him some for Christmas, which Nettie had found mortifying; but shortly after, when Dan had been fired from the paper round (on account of his persistent lateness for all the deliveries after number 91 Chalcot Square), he would still be found in their kitchen at the same time every Saturday. Her mother was convinced he felt more at home in their house than in his own, and as Nettie had advanced into the long, bleary sleeps of teenagedom – sometimes not waking before lunch – her father had spent more and more time with him, so that Nettie was now quite convinced he considered Dan a surrogate son, irrespective of the fact that the boy already had four stepfathers and counting.

Nettie slumped face first on the table as the two of them continued to spin and test and frown and tweak, used to being ignored on a Saturday morning. The kettle had boiled, but no one else appeared to have noticed. She rose, gingerly, and made the tea herself.

'Oh, sorry, love!' her father said distractedly, realizing his oversight as she noisily plonked herself back down at the table and reached for the half-closed laptop at the other end. 'So . . . I take it you girls had fun last night, then?'

'Yep,' Nettie mumbled, wishing he'd stop pretending to be interested in her night out. He was too absorbed in his own special projects – cycling round Regent's Park every day, gardening at the community orchard in St George's Terrace, gathering a 'Town Team' to petition for a farmers' market, model building – to pay too much attention to hers.

In truth, she remembered precious little about last night anyway. What was the point in having such a great time that you wiped all memory of it from your consciousness and had only pain as a memento in the morning?

She retrieved the laptop, which was, as ever, completely hidden beneath her father's papers on the table – a children's author and illustrator who had enjoyed some early success in the 1980s, he was currently working on a modern-day reimagining of the Pied Piper of Hamelin and there were at least forty drafts of the Piper scattered across the tabletop, some of them scrunched from when he'd thrown them against the wall in frustration. His most recent publisher had politely declined to renew his contract when it had expired a year last spring and he was writing this on spec, which was why – he kept saying – 'It had to be perfect.' Nettie privately suspected it was taking so long to complete because he spent most of his working days staring, lost, at the walls. The mortgage on the house had been paid off long ago, but she knew he was troubled by his diminishing royalty cheques, and the peppercorn rent she gave him, which he wouldn't hear of increasing, didn't cover their outgoings.

She tapped the keyboard with one lethargic finger and opened up her emails, sipping her tea and vowing some sort of revenge on her friend who thought that toffee vodka on a Friday night after a bad day at work was a good idea.

'So where did you go?' her father asked.

She didn't want to think about it; a wince skittered across her features at the very thought. 'Just some new vodka place opened on Prince Albert Road,' she grumbled, closing down the line of conversation.

She frowned as the 'loading' icon circled continuously on her screen and drank some more tea. She looked out of the window towards the grey sky. It was the colour of an old bra, bedraggled and overused.

She looked back at the screen. Come on. Come on. Why was it taking so long?

She slid out her arm along the table, her head resting heavily on her hand. 'Dad, is the Wi-Fi down?'

'Don't think so, pet. I was on an hour ago and it was working then. Why?'

'It won't load. The little blue circle thingy's just going round and round.'

'Sounds like there's a big file coming through,' her father said helpfully. 'Just give it a minute.'

'I've already given it three.'

Dan chuckled. 'Nothing if not patient, you.'

She pitched a glare in his direction.

'Are you expecting any photographs? They usually jam the feed,' her father offered again, trying to temper her black mood.

'Oh no. Don't say you've sent yourself a load of selfies again?' Dan teased, and she groaned, hiding her face in her dressing gown. Would she ever live that down?

Dan, recognizing that she had no reserves this morning and knowing she would be soon descending into an

Official Grump, got up from his position on the floor. 'Oh, come on, then, let me have a look at it.'

'Oh. It's working!' she said brightly just as Dan was halfway across the floor to her, and shooting him a sarcastic grin before taking a noisy slurp of her tea. It was his turn to groan as he turned back to the bike again, used to her taking out her hangovers on him.

The screen – after its unusual dormancy – had sprung into life, the emails ticking down through the inbox like pages being flicked in a book. They loaded more quickly than her eyes could scan, but there was one word she did pick up on, one that was repeated over and over again so that it read almost fluidly off the rapidly uploading screen: Twitter.

'What the hell . . . ?' she whispered as the screen continued to scroll down. 'You have a new follower . . .' was repeated over and over and over and over.

She stared open-mouthed. This had to be some sort of technical glitch, or a computer malfunction. She checked the keyboard for a sticky key, but everything appeared normal, and after a few more minutes it finally and suddenly stopped.

Hesitantly – wondering if she was, in fact, still drunk – she began tabbing down individually with the arrow keys, but after several pages, she switched to the 'pg dn' button – and still they came, supposedly all these new followers and not a single name she recognized.

'What is it?' Dan asked, intrigued by her unusual silence.

But Nettie didn't reply. She didn't hear. She still couldn't process what her eyes were showing her. This couldn't be right. She was drunk. Hallucinating. She had to be.

She leaned in closer to the screen.

'Nets?'

Still nothing.

'I just don't . . . I don't believe this,' Nettie murmured, frowning at the unintelligible cluster of letters and numbers of a shortcut link some – many, in fact – were re-tweeting.

The doorbell rang and her father straightened up. 'Ah! Now, that should be my new carbon wheel,' he said, pleased, as he trotted down the hall to the front door.

Dan sauntered back over to Nettie, curiosity getting the better of him and even surmounting the mystery of why the new brakes didn't work. 'Fine, then the mountain shall come to— Holy crap!' He leaned a hand on her shoulder.

'I know!'

They were quiet for a long while, both trying to make sense of it. 'Well, how many are there?'

'I don't know. I haven't counted yet. There's too many.'

'Duh! Just go into your home page,' Dan said, tutting again as Nettie's hung-over fingers failed to synchronize and she dropped her head, already defeated.

Dan reached for the laptop and turned it to face him, his fingers flying easily over the keyboard as he logged in to Twitter. 'How many followers did you have before?'

There was a pause. 'Thirty-seven? I think?'

Dan stopped typing. '*Seriously?* I mean, I know I'm pretty much your only mate, but—'

'Shuddup. It's not my thing.'

Dan chuckled but didn't argue back. His eyes were fixed on the screen, his fingers moving swiftly and making little tap-taps. She slid her arm further along the tabletop so that she was lying fully flat and rested her head on top of it. Her eyes closed.

'It's just gonna be some weird mix-up,' she mumbled. 'You know, like when a bank accidentally wires a million pounds into your account because they got one digit wrong.'

'Yeah, because that happens *all* the time,' Dan replied, his eyes widening as the Twitter page came up. He laughed out loud suddenly. 'Jesus, Nets! Take a guess how many you got now?'

'I can't,' she protested, her voice still thick and bleary.

'Twenty-two.'

Nettie's eyes opened again and she raised her head an inch. 'You mean I *lost* some? Oh, come on!'

'Thousand, you numpty. Twenty-two thousand!'

Nettie sat upright. 'What?' Was she hearing things? 'Did you just say . . . ?'

Dan nodded, his eyes bright.

'But *why*?'

'How the hell would *I* know?' he laughed, sitting down on the table, arms folded over his chest. 'Come on, Nets, out with it. You don't get twenty-two thousand followers overnight and not know why.'

'But I don't!' she cried, her hands to her mouth. 'Why are all these strangers following me? What do they want? Oh my God, Dan, what have I done?'

Dan watched her, his smile fading as he saw the truth on her face. 'You honestly don't remember?'

She shook her head.

'Would Jules?'

'Jules?' she repeated, a glimmer of fear creeping into her eyes like a stealthy cat.

'Well, it's got to be something that happened yesterday, and given the sorry state you're in, I think we can probably narrow it down to something that happened last night. Let's face it, where Jules goes trouble usually follows.'

Memories of toffee vodka swam behind her eyes again and she pulled her hands down over her face, only the vaguest impressions of light and dark, and much laughter, flashing through her mind in distorted images, like the world seen through a teardrop.

Oh no. Oh no.

Dan handed her the phone. 'There's only one way to find out.'

Chapter Three

The kite-flyers were out in force today. Scores of dads running with their kids as kites bumped and fell and soared and got caught in the trees. The sky was still dirty, with grubby clouds scuffing the London skyline, and she watched as the pigeons and blackbirds strutted and hopped by her feet, pecking at the hard, frosted ground. Nettie shivered on her park bench – actually her park bench: she and her father had paid for it – as she waited for Jules to arrive with the hot chocolates. It was a long-held agreement between them that this was how it would be for the rest of the day – as penance for leading her astray last night, it was Jules's duty to monitor her blood sugar levels more closely than a diabetic.

It was bitterly cold, but Nettie was grateful for that. It sobered her, the wind like stinging smacks on her cheeks, her nearly dry hair flying like little whip-cracks around her face. Her bobbled beanie had sagged low on the back of her head, and she was regretting the designer rips in her jeans, which were now responsible for her thighs and knees turning blue.

London sat before her at the bottom of the hill, laid out like a picnic blanket. In the distance, the BT Tower pointed like a finger into the sky, and she could imagine the hordes of Christmas shoppers bustling at its base along Oxford Street. How many of them, she wondered, had 'liked' her or followed her? Were they laughing, even now, as they disembarked from buses or sat in the coffee shops at the hilarious sight of #bluebunnygirl – yes, she had a hashtag – skidding down the ice?

'Here you go. Get that down you.' Jules plonked down on the bench beside her, looking irritably chipper and perky. 'What's it saying now?'

Nettie glanced at her iPad. It was still on the YouTube page Jules had opened, where the number of views for the video kept rising in front of their eyes. It had been 77,193 when Jules had gone off to get the drinks a few minutes ago; now it was 77,587. No—

'Seventy-seven thousand, five hundred and eighty-eight.'

Jules shook her head in disbelief. 'I just can't believe it. You're an internet sensation. *You* are. The girl who can't set her own phone to aeroplane mode and needs help getting the Wi-Fi code in Starbucks. How can *you* have gone viral?'

'Because of you!' Nettie half laughed, half wailed. 'It was your stupid idea to upload the damn thing.'

Jules slumped into yet more laughter. In spite of her own hangover, she was still able to function like a normal human being, moving easily, eating heartily and laughing lustily; in fact, she had laughed so hard when she'd taken Nettie's call earlier that she'd given herself the hiccups. 'But we had to! Oh, Nets, it had to be done. It was just too funny to leave malingering in some poky conference room, never to be seen again. And just look how many people agree with me,' Jules grinned, before taking a slurp of her drink and unwittingly sitting back with a chocolate moustache. Her hot breath fogged the cold air, her curly bobbed hair escaping like springs beneath her beret. 'Besides, you were well up for it last night. You thought it was a great idea.'

'Yes. And I probably thought jumping out of a plane with an umbrella for a parachute was a good idea last night too.'

'It was a great night. Remember that bloke . . . ?' Jules said distractedly, her eyes falling to a tall man striding across the grass, throwing a tennis ball for his dog as he spoke into his phone. She lapsed into silence.

'Jules?'

'Huh?' Jules couldn't wrench her eyes off the dog-walker as he leaned back, one leg counterbalanced in the air, and launched into a particularly impressive throw.

'A bloke?'

'I know – lasers are locked,' she murmured, watching as the ball flew through the air, the dog below it running at full stretch, ears streaming in the wind, a smile firmly fixed on its black lips. 'Damn, he's fit,' she murmured.

'The dog?'

'The bloke.'

'Tch.' Nettie sighed and, after a quick scan of the next crowd of people coming up the hill towards them, went back to looking at her YouTube page. Seventy-seven thousand, six hundred and thirteen.

Two hundred and sixty-eight people had given it a 'thumbs-down'. She felt surprisingly crushed by this. Was her exploit not daring or funny enough for these people, or were they sympathy votes, protesting against cruelty to bunnies, or at least girls in bunny suits?

She tabbed back to her Twitter page. She couldn't believe she had a 'k' after the number of her followers. As Jules had told her with great solemnity, she had now entered the social media stratosphere. If anyone had said to her yesterday afternoon – particularly as Mike laid into her – that she would become a member of the social-media elite within twenty-four hours, she'd have called them a loony.

But here she was, wrapped up in her beanie and wannabe-Moncler puffa, sitting on her bench overlooking London, with a fanbase to her name. The idea of it was so preposterous and yet . . . it made her sparkle inside. These people liked her. She'd made them laugh. They thought she was cool. Or brave. Or mad. Or all of the above.

'Where was I?' Jules asked, coming to. The dog-walker was almost out of sight now.

'No idea.'

Jules rested her chin on Nettie's shoulder and watched what she was doing. 'What you doing?'

'Reading my fan letters,' Nettie quipped.

There were a lot of emojis on the page as she scrolled down through the comments. Some of them were in foreign languages she couldn't even read, much less understand; some were seemingly following her for all the wrong reasons, leaving messages that bordered on the obscene – it would appear that finding bunnies attractive was a 'thing' – and instantly had her worrying about stalkers. But the vast majority were harmless – highly amused, in awe, sympathetic, asking for more . . .

'So weird,' she murmured, unable to process the sheer volume of people who'd sought her out and made contact. She would never be able to read them all, and there was no question of responding to—

'Wait! Go back!' Jules ordered her suddenly.

'What? Where?'

Jules jabbed the 'up' arrow, her eyes widening with unfettered delight at what she saw there. 'Holy *shit*! I don't freaking believe it!'

Nor did Nettie. Her mouth had gone dry, and it had nothing to do with the hangover.

'Wait, wait. Has it got the blue tick?' Jules demanded. 'It's only, like, official if it's got the blue tick. You get all sorts of nutjobs setting up accounts pretending to be the— Shit, it *does*!' Jules almost screamed with excitement. 'You jammy cow! Oh my GOD!'

Nettie stared back at her in stunned shock. Jamie Westlake was following her. The gorgeous singer-songwriter and truly one of the sexiest men in the world – as voted by the readers of *People* magazine and named *GQ* 'Man of the Year' too, so that meant it was official and true – was following her. *Her.*

'Nettie!' Jules shrieked, laughing and shaking her by the shoulders as though to rouse her from her stupor. 'Do you even know what this means?'

'What does it mean?' Nettie felt like she'd been zapped with a stun gun.

'You've got, like . . . a hotline to him now! You're one step away from getting his mobile number.'

Nettie laughed, roused from her stupor by the stupidity of the idea. 'I don't think so.'

'Yeah! God's truth. Why not? You can just reach him whenever you want now. You put something out there and *he'll see it*. And he obviously likes what he sees,' Jules cackled wickedly.

'Before you start planning the flowers, please try to remember that what he saw was me dressed as a seven-foot blue bunny. I hardly think this is some sort of calling card.'

'No, but it could be!' Jules breathed.

'Oh God,' Nettie groaned as the full impact of her own words boomeranged back and hit her. She slid a little down the bench. 'Jamie Westlake saw me dressed up as a seven-foot blue bunny. This is my worst nightmare ever. This is like dreaming you're on the Tube naked, only to wake up and find you actually are on the Tube naked.'

Jules frowned. 'Strange dreams you have, babe.' She shook her head, shifting position so that she was facing Nettie square on. 'Listen to me. This is not a nightmare. This is actually your Cinderella moment.'

'My what?'

Jules rolled her eyes. 'You shall go to the ball, dummy. Jeez, keep up.'

'Oh.'

'Listen, yes, the most gorgeous man in the world has seen you dressed as a mutant rabbit. However, this is not a disaster. *Au contraire*, it's an opportunity.'

'How? I'm a national laughing stock.'

'*Inter*national,' Jules corrected her, seemingly offended by Nettie's limited horizons. 'No, what I'm trying to say is, you've got his attention. Now you've got to keep it.'

The two friends stared at each other, as excited as teenagers.

'How?' Nettie asked after a moment. 'How do you keep the attention of a man like him?'

'Hey, how hard can it be? You've done it once already.'

Nettie's expression changed. 'I am not wearing that bloody costume again.'

'No, I—'

'And I am not throwing myself down any more ice walls either.'

'Of course not! But that man is following you. You've got to do something to keep him interested, something that keeps him coming back for more.' Jules looked pensive, which was always worrying. 'Oh, but what, though? How to keep the attention of the most gorgeous man on the planet in a way that doesn't involve dressing as a numpty or almost killing yourself?'

'Short of winning an Oscar or ... or streaking at Wimbledon, there probably isn't a way,' Nettie said, as her eyes resumed their familiar scan of the crowds walking by. 'Let's just count our blessings and rejoice in the knowledge that for a moment *I* amused Jamie Westlake.'

'No! Have some ambition, Nets!' Jules said, slapping her on the arm so that Nettie almost spilt her drink over her coat.

'You sound like Mike,' Nettie groaned, sipping her hot chocolate before there was an accident.

'Well, he wasn't completely wrong, then. Look, there is something we can do – I can feel it. I'm not sure what it is yet, but I will, I promise you. One way or another, we are going to get that man to more than just "like" you.'

It came to her in the shower. Or rather, Nettie was in the shower when Jules came to her with the idea.

She plonked herself down on the loo seat and called out over the torrent of steaming-hot water. 'So I've got it!' Jules shouted.

'Jules, bog off! Let me have my shower in peace,' Nettie shouted back, grateful for the frosted-glass shower door. She didn't share Jules's lack of inhibitions, even though their job meant they had been in many unorthodox situations together.

'I can't! It's brilliant, my plan. I've totally worked out how we're going to get Jamie Westlake to fall for you.'

It was a joke, but the kernel of truth nestled inside them hit her all over again: one of the most famous men in the world was following her. *Her.*

She put on a second application of conditioner, just in case.

A thought struck her as she rinsed – what if . . . what if he *un*followed her? What if she bored him? What if he had already realized she was too boring? Should she have given him some sort of reply to his 'follow'? She'd already been following him anyway, of course – most of the world did – but what if he wanted an acknowledgement of his attentions?

She stuck her head round the shower door, eyes wide with horror at the myriad potential faux pas she now had to negotiate.

'What are you looking like that for?' Jules asked in alarm. 'I haven't even told you what it is yet!'

'What if he *un*follows me?'

Jules relaxed, one arm slung over the cistern and knocking a loo roll to the floor, where it rolled and unwound like a gymnast's ribbon. 'Not gonna happen, hon. I just told you – I got it. The big idea.' Jules's arms had spread wide, like a circus showman addressing the crowd.

Nettie sighed as she reached for the towel on the hook, and wrapping it round her tightly, stepped out. She knew Jules wasn't going to give up – or go away – until she'd shared her grand plan. 'Fine. Go on, then. Sock it to me.'

Jules winced at the sight of her bruises from the race-track, still livid, across her upper arms.

Nettie – having forgotten about them – looked down, before giving a shrug. It was called Ice Crush for a reason. 'Yes, well, maybe "sock it to me" is the wrong phrase.'

'We're going to do a challenge a day.'

There was a long pause as Nettie dared to exhale. There were many, many things wrong with that statement. Where to start? 'We?' she asked finally.

'Well, you. You're the Blue Bunny Girl. You're the one with the hashtag.'

Another pause. 'A challenge?'

'Yep. Attention-grabbing stuff. Crazy stuff.' Jules held her hands up quickly. 'But safe, I promise. Totally safe. Some of it can be just funny stuff, others the best internet memes.'

There was a long pause as Nettie tried to work out what a 'meme' was.

'Ugh, word-of-mouth crazes,' Jules said, translating her baffled silence. 'Anything that's trended.'

'Oh. You said "a day"? How many days are we talking?' Jules winked. 'However long it takes to reel him in.'

'You make him sound like a trout,' Nettie said, grabbing another towel from the rail and bending forward to wrap her hair in it.

'Well, I'd pout for him,' Jules winked, picking up a bottle of Chanel No.5 body cream. She unscrewed the lid, sniffing the shell-pink mixture inside.

'Put that down – it's Mum's,' Nettie said, leaping forward and snatching it from her.

Jules shrank back and Nettie instantly felt guilty for her overreaction. 'Sorry, it's just … . expensive, that's all.'

Jules watched as Nettie replaced the cream on the glass shelf and secured her towel into a turban. Nettie stepped on the scales, her hands on her hips. No change, which was annoying. She had wanted to shift three pounds this past week in time for Christmas – five would have been a bonus – but the juicing hadn't worked out, and by Tuesday she'd switched to paleo, which had clearly been equally as unsuccessful. She blamed the custard creams.

Jules sagged dejectedly as Nettie chewed her lip and tried standing on one leg to make the dial move left. 'Is that *it*? You doing your best flamingo impression? It took me bloody ages to draw up this list.' She waggled the torn piece of jotter paper in her hand.

Nettie looked up. 'What's that?'

'The list of things you're going to do.'

'I'm not a lab rat, you know. I know what you're like, and I'm not going to do just *anything* to keep his attention.'

There was a stunned silence.

'You have remembered we're talking about Jamie West-lake?' Jules asked incredulously, leaning forward so that her elbows were on her knees. 'I mean, don't tell me you've gone all blasé about it because he's been following you for all of twelve hours now.'

Nettie rolled her eyes and stepped off the scales. She'd eat nothing but fruit today, she decided. 'No, but—'

'The man is six foot of pure, liquid sex appeal.' She closed her eyes, her hands wafting in front of her face. 'I mean, just consider the hair.' She opened her eyes and scowled to see that Nettie hadn't closed hers. 'Go on. Consider it.'

Nettie sighed and closed her eyes.

'Imagine running that silky brown hair through your fingers, those soft curls tickling your face—'

'He's had a haircut now, hasn't he?'

'Has he?' Jules opened her eyes, looking stern that she hadn't been notified of it before now.

Nettie peered at her through one open eye. 'Yeah. He's got it short again. Not many curls left.'

'Huh . . .' She closed her eyes again. 'Well, anyway, your kids might have curly hair – that's what I'm saying.' She slapped her hands above her heart. 'Imagine how *cute* they'd be.'

Nettie arched an eyebrow.

'And his eyes. Oh my God, the colour. No one has eyes like that. What would you call them?'

'Green?'

'Khaki, Nets! He has khaki eyes. So cool.'

'He has cool eyes?'

'Everything about that man is cool – in a red-hot way,' Jules sighed. 'I mean, just imagine it, Nets, those eyes staring at you – you might dive in and never get out again, like one of those flooded quarry pits.'

Nettie frowned. 'That's really not a very sexy analogy.'

'You're right. Scratch that. Scratch it from the record.' She waved her arms wildly and Nettie caught sight of the list in her hand again.

'Just tell me what it is you think I should do.'

Jules held out the list, biting her lip apprehensively as Nettie scanned it with a bemused expression. 'I don't even know what half of this means. What is all this stuff?'

'Just what I said – a round-up of the best Internet memes. Funny, random, bizarre stuff. Nothing dangerous.'

Nettie inhaled deeply, her eyes coming back to Jules's. 'So what exactly is horse . . . What does that say? "Horse-*manning*"?'

'Oh, that's one of the funniest,' Jules laughed. 'Always cracks me up.'

'Yes, but what *is* it?'

'You have to get someone to lie, like on a table or a bed, in a position where you can't see their head, and then you put *your* head – just your head; that's all they can see – a short distance away.'

Nettie frowned. 'So, like that scene with the disembodied horse head in *The Godfather*, then?'

'Exactly! Bloody funny.'

'If you say so.' She looked at the list again, puffing out through her cheeks. 'If this is what passes for fun on the Net, no wonder I'm a technophobe.' She frowned as she saw the last dare on the list. 'Oh my God! Are you kidding?'

Jules frowned. 'What?'

'I am not dyeing my eyebrows blue.'

'Not even for Jamie?' her friend wheedled.

Nettie chuckled. 'As if he'd want me after any of that anyway!'

'He'd admire you.'

'Thanks, but it's not his admiration I'm after.'

Jules looked pained.

'Forget it. I'm not doing it.' Nettie opened the bathroom door, plumes of steam escaping ahead of her into the narrow landing. Jules trotted after her.

'But that's why I put it at the end. It's the pièce de résistance. We'll work up to it.'

Nettie stopped at her bedroom door. 'No.'

'Well, let's keep it at the end for the time being; that way, you've got the chance to mull it over. Think it over at leisure?'

47

'I'm not doing it – *any* of it. I don't see how doing any of those things is going to attract someone like Jamie West-lake.'

'Because they're funny and that's why he followed you in the first place. The guy's obviously got a great sense of humour.'

'The answer is still "no".' Nettie closed the door on her. 'Now leave me alone. I'm getting dressed.'

Jules stood in the hallway for a moment. 'Tell you what, I'll go put the kettle on,' she called, making her way over to the stairs. 'And let's just say it's a "maybe".'

Chapter Four

'Get that down you, then – you'll feel a lot better,' Tom said, placing the steaming plate on the table in front of her.

'Thanks, Tom,' she said weakly, looking down at the heap of saturated fat. 'Tomorrow, definitely fruit tomorrow,' she resolved.

'Refills?' he asked, picking up their empties, knowing the drill.

Jules gave him a thumbs-up and a wink but couldn't reply – she was already eating.

Nettie watched him go with a stab of poignancy. She'd been like him once – working behind the bar here during the university holidays. Saving up to move on to bigger and better things. Now she was just another punter, one of the locals who spent as much time – if not more – here as at home.

'I know. Nice bum, right?' Jules said, watching her wistful gaze.

Nettie began to eat, her eyes roaming the room. It was too cold to sit outside. The wind was still meting out punishing smacks, and every table in the Engineer was taken, the log fire crackling and throwing out a drowsy heat that was already making the bushy Christmas tree in the opposite corner droop. The flamboyant designer wallpaper contrasted with the rustic waxed tables (theirs had all their initials carved in the sides), and coloured-glass light globes hung from the ceiling. As ever, they were sitting beneath 'their' lamp – the green one – at 'their' table. She knew almost all the faces in here. 'Heard from your Canadian fella?'

'Ha! What d'you think?' Jules asked with a roll of her eyes. 'He's in Austria now.' She chewed not so quietly for a bit. 'I'm not bothered anyway. He kept doing this weird—'

'Don't!' Nettie held her hand up in a 'stop' sign. 'It's hard enough trying to get my food down.'

Jules shrugged. 'Well, anyway, onwards and upwards.' She dunked a chip in the ramekin of ketchup, stabbing it thoughtfully in the air. 'Good body, though. I think athletes might be the way to go.'

Nettie pulled a face. 'Nup. They're always training all the time, and they can't drink. Disaster for you.'

'Oh yeah, true,' Jules agreed with a disappointed expression as she chewed on the chip. A sudden glint sprang to her eyes. 'Still, not a worry for you. International heart-throbs don't come with caveats like that. Yours is as hard-living as we are.'

Nettie smiled as she was reminded yet again of her extraordinary new status and she wondered whether people could tell just by looking at her. She felt as mysterious as she had after losing her virginity. 'He is not mine, sadly. I wish.'

'Hey, we should post something right now,' Jules grinned, leaning in over the table and getting ketchup on her jumper. 'Let's take a photo.'

'Of what? My lunch? Hardly thrilling stuff.' Tom came back with their virgin Bloody Marys and she took a sip.

'Unless, of course, we start a food fight that turns into a riot.'

Jules winked excitedly. 'You should go into the loos and take a photo with your top off. You've got lovely boobs. That'd make him sit up and take notice!'

Nettie spluttered on the drink. 'What? And post it to the thirty thousand other people following me? I don't think so.' She wrinkled her nose, looking at her friend. '*You* don't do that, do you?'

Jules shrugged.

Nettie felt shocked. 'But what if it got out somehow?'

'Why would it?'

'Uh, bad break-up? Boasting? Any number of reasons.'

Jules shrugged again. 'I've got nothing to be ashamed of. It's no biggie. You're just a prude.'

'I'm private – there's a difference,' Nettie tutted. 'Besides, you wouldn't be so relaxed about it if your mum saw. Or Mike—'

Jules grimaced. 'Eugh. Don't put me off my lunch.' She narrowed her eyes, leaning over the table to her. 'I bet he has sex with his socks on.'

'You girls talking about me again?' a male voice asked, stopping beside them just as something warm sat on Nettie's feet.

'Oh God, here's trouble,' Jules groaned, slumping back in her chair as the two spares beside them were scraped out and filled with a couple of tall, lanky frames.

Dan immediately nicked one of Nettie's chips as she bent down to pat Scout's head. He was the only dog allowed inside – a discretionary agreement that acknowledged and recognized Dan's lifelong, and practically daily, patronage of the pub.

'Hey!' she said, smacking his hand. 'Get your own. This is an emergency.'

He draped an arm round her shoulder and squeezed it fondly. 'And how are you feeling now?' He raised an eyebrow at Jules. 'You do *not* want to know what she looked like first thing this morning. Smelt like Stig of the Dump, and with hair to match.'

'Hey!' she said again, joshing him in the ribs with her elbow.

He collapsed with a laugh.

'Dan was telling me all about your new celebrity status,' Stevie said, ripping open a bag of crisps. 'I expected to find you sitting over there with David Walliams.'

Nettie stuck her tongue out at him. 'Ha, ha.'

'Actually, it's not so improbable,' Jules said, speaking with her mouth full. 'Our Nets has got her own celebrity following now.'

'Oh yeah?' Stevie laughed. 'Who? The Teletubbies?'

Dan laughed again, one hand cupped round his pint of lager, his long legs splayed in his battered jeans.

'Jamie Westlake, actually.' Jules said it with no small amount of pride.

'Yeah, right,' Stevie grinned. 'And I've just accepted a friend request from Selena Gomez.'

'See for yourself if you don't believe me,' Jules said, pushing her phone into the table, set to the exact spot on Nettie's Twitter page where Jamie had commented – '*Cool*' – exactly thirteen hours earlier. 'And before you say it's not him . . .' She pointed to the blue tick beside his avatar, tapping it with her finger. 'Official.'

Both men looked sceptical, then impressed.

'Get you,' Stevie grinned. 'I knew we'd graduate to top table in this place one day,' he laughed to Dan.

'See if he can get me a signed Gooners shirt, then, will you? You know, next time you see him. Ha! I can't wait to tell everyone about this.' Dan grinned, stealing another of Nettie's chips. '*What?*' he asked, his face an expression of innocence as she slapped him again.

'No! No one must know. You mustn't tell anyone, ' Jules said bossily.

'What? About Westlake?'

'Any of it. Strictly speaking, we didn't have permission to post the film, and Nettie's job is precarious enough at the moment. It's best that no one knows it was her on that film.'

The boys looked back at her sceptically.

'But who here's gonna care about Nettie's secret life as a thrill-seeking bunny?' Stevie laughed, cracking himself up.

'I mean it.'

Dan groaned. 'Yeah, fine.'

Stevie frowned. 'Obviously you don't mean Paddy, though?'

Paddy was the third spoke in the boys' wheel – an old school friend with more ambition than Stevie or Dan, currently flying by the seat of his pants as a broker at BarCap and usually the one picking up the tab on a Thursday, Friday and Saturday night.

'No one,' Jules said firmly. 'You won't be telling Em, will you, Nets?'

Nettie shook her head, wishing her other friend hadn't bailed on her last night; it would have meant today was so much less painful.

'Anyway, who's coming back to mine to watch the

match?' Stevie asked. 'I've got fresh Pot Noodles and everything.'

The girls guffawed, knowing he was quite serious.

'Might do,' Jules said. 'As long as I get a sofa to myself. I'm going to need to nap after this.'

Nettie's phone buzzed on the table and she jumped as she saw the name on the caller ID.

'I'm in. I'm knackered,' Dan said, yawning and stretching out further on the chair so that he was almost a six-foot-long line. His job as a plumber meant he often had late-night call-outs, particularly at this time of year, when boilers kept breaking down and pipes kept freezing.

'Surely . . . surely you don't mean to suggest you've actually been working, Dan?' Jules gasped.

He chucked a paper napkin at her, one eyebrow cocked.

'Nets?' Stevie asked.

It was a moment before she heard him, her eyes glued to the message, which, as ever, told her nothing. *Just checking in – nothing to report here. Hope you're well. Call me if you need to talk.*

'Sorry, what . . . ? Oh, uh . . .' She hesitated, keeping her eyes down. 'Yes, I'll drop by later maybe.'

Jules looked sympathetic. 'Oh crap, you're not working at the library today, are you?'

'No, but . . .' Nettie shook her head quickly, sensing the stares being passed round the table. 'I've just got some bits to do, you know.'

There was a silence. Then Jules reached suddenly for the phone and saw Gwen's name. She sat back in her chair like she'd been pushed.

'It's *Saturday*,' Jules said, irritation and concern bringing a scratch to her voice. 'You agreed to cut back. Sundays only, you said.'

'I know, but . . .'

Dan looked at her, folding in the middle slightly and bringing himself up to a more standard sitting position. 'You can't go out in this weather anyway. Even Scout doesn't want to go for a walk.'

'It won't be for long.'

'Nets, it's bloody freezing. The wind chill is minus five.'

'Which is why I won't be long,' she said again.

A silence began to bloom.

'Fine, well, then I'll come with you,' he said.

'We all will,' Jules said, prompting a panicky look from Stevie, who was in just jeans and a sweatshirt, and had obviously nipped in from parking his van outside. She took a deep breath and Nettie could detect the sallow, hung-over tinge in her skin, beneath her tinted moisturizer. 'I'm quite up for some fresh air.'

'Thanks, but . . .' Nettie inhaled sharply. 'Look . . . I'll just come by later, OK?' Her tone made it clear her wish was final.

It was a moment before anyone responded. Clearly it wasn't OK.

'Sure, yeah . . . whatevs,' Jules nodded, forcing a smile. It was the only time, all day, a laugh wasn't sitting on her lips or in her eyes.

'If that's what you want,' Dan said after a moment.

'It is. Thanks.' Her voice was quiet, her smile strained. The hangover made it harder to pull off her usual low-key languor. She looked at Stevie, trying her best to dissipate the tension. 'I might even bring some Ben & Jerry's.'

His brown eyes twinkled as his face softened into an easy grin. 'Oh right, we're going posh, are we?'

'Well, now that I'm friends with the rich and famous, I'll be getting freebies left, right and centre,' she said with affected nonchalance. 'Diamonds, dresses, expensive ice creams – they're all open to me now.'

Dan leaned in. 'I meant it about the Gooners shirt, you know. And a season ticket would be nice too.'

'I'll have to see what I can do,' she grinned, the pub door opening and her eyes darting to it as ever.

'So spill the beans, then – what was it like going down that racecourse?' Stevie asked, folding his arms on the table interestedly and clearly wanting all the gory details.

'Quick,' she quipped.

'You hit those corners at some speed.'

'Yep.' She pushed up her jumper sleeve and showed off the livid bruises along her upper arms.

The men both winced and groaned sympathetically, as Jules had earlier.

'Shit,' Stevie laughed. 'I bet you've never been so terrified, have you?'

'Nope,' she grinned, keeping the smile in place this time.

It was only half a lie.

Forty minutes later she watched them go, the three of them huddled and braced against the wind as they walked towards Stevie's van and headed for his flat in Chalk Farm, on the other side of the railway tracks.

Dan kept turning back to see if she was still there – still OK – but she just gave him a jaunty wave, forcing him to give reluctant nods and waves back. He knew her too well to know she'd be dissuaded otherwise.

They slammed shut the van doors, Jules sitting between the two guys on the bench seat, and after several phlegmatic turns of the ignition, trundled past her with concerned expressions before turning right, out of sight. She stood alone in the cold, her black Zara puffa doing its best against the biting temperatures, knowing that she had to put one foot in front of the other and do this. There was no other way. This was simply what she did.

She began walking to the bus stop, but she was wearing leather-soled boots, for once not her beloved Puma trainers, and the cold seeped through them, chilling her bones.

She tried keeping the hood of her coat up, but the wind blew it back and off with effortless gusts, and having left her beanie at home, she resigned herself to the onset of cold, throbbing ears. For a Saturday afternoon, the streets were quiet, the bitter temperatures driving everyone inside, and only the hardiest families with young kids were venturing out onto the hill.

Just ahead of her, a striped cat trotted along the pavement, its long, plush tail hovering above the ground as it moved with silent purpose for a hundred yards before springing onto a low, ivy-covered wall and disappearing into the hunting grounds of the garden beyond.

Nettie walked quickly with the same resolve, her eyes continually drawn to the leached sky, where clouds tumbled overhead. It was beginning to grow dark already, even though it was only just after two, and she knew she wouldn't have long today. Deep in her pockets, she dug her nails into her palms, castigating herself for having wasted so much time on her hangover this morning. It was precisely why she hadn't wanted to go out last night.

There were a couple of people at the bus stop and she

joined them, standing with an apprehensive expression as she stared along the empty road, willing the bus to appear. Every minute mattered; she was already on a countdown.

She blew out through her cheeks, impatient and increasingly agitated, stamping her feet and trying to keep the blood flowing. She'd been stupid, so *stupid*, indulging in her hangover when she had known – in the back of her mind, always – that this wouldn't be put off.

She turned, walking towards the few shops that dotted this stretch of the road. Maybe if she didn't look for the damned bus . . .

She stood outside the estate agent's window and listlessly scanned the details of the brick and stuccoed Georgian and Victorian houses that had been going for a song when her parents had bought, forty years ago, and were now far out of reach for normal people like her.

It was a moment before she saw that the man inside was waving to her. She held up a reluctant hand in greeting, protesting as he motioned for her to come in and trying to indicate she was waiting for the bus. Instead, he jumped up from his desk and came to the door.

'Hello there, Nettie,' he smiled, holding the door wide. His hair was wiry grey, and he was wearing a brown tweed suit with brogues that looked like conkers.

'Hi, Lee. How are you?'

'You're *just* the person I wanted to see,' he said, pleased, rubbing his hands together.

'Really?'

'Yes. I've got it this time, I know it. Come in and I'll show you.'

'Uh, well, the thing is, I'm waiting for the bus and I

really can't afford to miss it. I've got to stay out here, in case it comes.'

He was unfazed, his enthusiasm undimmed. 'Just a sec, then.' And he darted back inside the tiny office, typing something on his keyboard, before disappearing into a room at the back.

Behind her, Nettie heard the familiar low rumble of the bus. Typical!

'Lee! The bus is coming!' she called through.

'Coming!' he called back. 'It's just printing now.'

She turned again to find the bus pulling to a stop, the doors hissing open.

'Lee . . .' She saw the other passengers getting on and she began walking backwards towards the bus. She couldn't afford to miss it.

'Coming, coming,' he panted, running awkwardly through the office with a sheet of paper in his hands. 'Probate sale. Just through in the past hour. Perfect for you.'

'But—'

He thrust the particulars into her hand just as she stepped, sideways, onto the bus. 'I'm listing it on the market on Monday. I'm on viewings for the rest of today, but I can see you there tomorrow, about four-ish, and you can have an exclusive preview, OK? First refusal.'

'But—'

'I promise you, Nettie. This is the one.' He smiled at her, his cheeks thread-veined, his bushy moustache making up for the lack of hair on his head.

'Are you getting on or what?' the bus driver asked, prompting her to turn.

'Uh, yes, yes,' she said, pulling out her Oyster card and showing it to him.

'Not valid till it's scanned,' the driver said with impressive boredom, as though she'd never been on a bus before.

She turned back to Lee as she held the card to the reader. 'Fine. I'll see you there tomorrow, then,' she said as it beeped.

'Four-ish,' Lee called as the doors immediately closed and the brakes were released. 'Don't worry if I'm late!'

She gave him a thumbs-up sign as the bus pulled away and she swayed her way down towards the seats at the back. The bus was less than half filled and she sank into a seat by the window and stared out, her eyes up to the sky again; a gauzy tendril of violet was beginning to inch across now, backlighting the clouds. She calculated that with fifteen minutes to get there – depending upon the traffic, of course – she'd have an hour and twenty minutes, maybe slightly more, before the light went completely.

She bit her lip as the bus stopped at the lights on Prince Albert Road and pedestrians began to cross, deliberately slowly, it seemed. Two feet below her, she watched as cyclists passed by the bus and stopped right in front of it.

The lights stayed red. She sighed and looked impatiently down the aisle, out through the windscreen at the cyclists getting in the way. They were all just standing about lackadaisically, their bikes held up at odd angles, some with the pedals stopped in the wrong position and therefore holding the bus up further.

She could feel her pulse quicken and she looked away again, taking slow, deep breaths and digging her nails into her palms once more.

She would be there soon enough.

That was the problem.

Chapter Five

Lee looked back at her with hopeful eyes.

Nettie gave a wan smile, her eyes falling to a dead, upside-down cockroach in the corner by the radiator. Yes, this was what £350,000 bought in the area now. The influx of TV and music stars, models and Hollywood actors had driven prices through the roof so that it now sat on a par, price-wise, with Notting Hill and Chelsea, but being sought out by those multi-millionaires who liked a cooler, edgier vibe to their des res. Her parents' house – four floors including the basement, six bedrooms, decent back garden – had been bought for pennies back in the 1970s but was worth a cool £4 million now, even in its 'unmodernized' condition. Not that they would sell up now. Ever.

No, £350,000 scarcely bought a parking space in this neck of the London woods, but that was all she'd got – well, the deposit for that grand sum, anyway. She'd been saving up for nearly five years now, and provided the bank would green-light the mortgage their financial adviser had said she could afford, she was good to go.

There were so many reasons why it needed to happen. She was twenty-six. She was fed up with the bemused stares she got from dates when they found out going back to her place meant her parents' place. Funnily enough, none of them were particularly keen on the idea of drinking cocoa in the kitchen with her dad, and those few who did then had to get past Dan on a Saturday morning, and he was the toughest gate-master of them all – quizzing them on their financial stability, A-level grades and whether they owned their own colander.

Yesterday morning had been yet another case in point. If she wanted to wake up to her hangover in silence and feel sorry for herself, then she was going to have to move out.

She was going to have to. And yet . . . as much as she dreamed of the freedoms that came with having her own place – the ability to take a bath with the door open, keeping the thermostat at twenty-eight degrees and stocking the fridge only with Pinot Grigio, Nutella and cheese strings (her mother never allowed them), she was going to miss the slightly tired, bohemian house that had been her only home.

From the street, it was a standout, one of the square's 'painted ladies', in a bright canary yellow her mother had chosen when they'd moved in. The neighbouring houses on either side were green and pink respectively, but it was their cheery yellow one that fostered so much local affection. She could see it from the end of the street or the other side of the square and she had never, as a child, lost sight of her home.

The magnolia tree that had once dominated the tiny front garden was long gone, but the house was positioned exactly opposite the slide in the children's playground in the square. She couldn't see through the windows from that distance, but she always remembered standing and waving at the top of it, her mother's face appearing like a sun at the bedroom window and waving back.

Most of her childhood had been spent within the safety of its black iron railings, the horse chestnut and birch trees within standing like giants over the kids racing round their roots, playing tag and hide-and-seek in the bushes. She and all the other local children had grown up in the square's protective enclave – riding bikes, learning to skateboard holding on to the parked cars' wing mirrors as they glided by, holding fiercely fought running races, before graduating over the years to playing kiss-chase and sneaking cans of beer into the rhododendrons.

Those kids had all gradually moved away over time, of course – their parents changing jobs or climbing the property ladder, others simply moving out to their own places as childhood faded, so that she was the last one standing now and a new generation of kids had claimed the playground as theirs.

The interior of the house was every bit as idiosyncratic as the outside. The hall walls were hot pink – a colour Nettie herself had chosen when she was eleven. Perhaps not the best-advised age, she thought now, for dictating interior-design policy in the family home. But her parents had never seemed to want to change it. The woodwork in the sitting room, which led through a wide arch into the kitchen, was custard yellow, and a turquoise Murano glass chandelier hung from the ceiling, galleried ranks of paintings and portraits and framed prints filling the walls. Thickly piled, brightly coloured Moroccan rugs covered the draughts that came up (along with the mice) through the gaps in the pine floorboards, and her mother had run up new sets of loose sofa covers for the different seasons – a grass-green linen for the summer, orange velvet for the winter.

Music was always blaring through the house – usually Pink Floyd or Lou Reed – and the smell of bacon and black toast fragranced the rooms in the way that gardenia wafted from scented reeds in Jules's. The roof leaked above the landing – it had done so for eighteen years now, but not so badly that her parents had ever been impelled to get it fixed; they simply kept a saucepan in the airing cupboard and brought it out when storms were forecast. The wind also blew in through a thumb-sized gap in the spare-bedroom window, making ghostly noises, which had convinced Nettie for years that the house was haunted.

It had been a scruffy, bohemian, slightly oversized house to grow up in, which was precisely why she wasn't thrown by the sight in front of her. When Jules had been looking to buy, she hadn't considered anything that wasn't newly plastered, right-angled and whitewashed, with beech work-tops and a 'damned good' laminate floor. But Nettie wasn't fazed by the damp patch in the bathroom or the signs of mildew on the kitchen curtains. The lino floor looked level at least and would be easy enough to rip up.

She walked over to the window, which appeared to be painted shut. She was on the second floor of three, so there was a chance she could be disturbed if the neighbours upstairs were noisy, but on the other hand, it wasn't a base-ment or garden flat, which would please her father. It had been his one condition.

She looked out across Princess Road – the painted-shut windows seemed to do a good job of insulating the flat from road noise. From where she was standing, she could just glimpse Primrose Hill itself, and through the leafless canopy of beech trees, she watched the last of the day's walkers come down it with jaunty strides, dogs and children running ahead as they enjoyed the downward momentum.

'The view really is extraordinary,' Lee said, ignoring the mechanic's garage on the opposite side of the road and following her skewed eyeline to the Hill. 'If the flat wasn't so . . .' he hesitated and she knew he was looking for a euphemism for 'dilapidated', 'tired, this would be in the high six figures. I've taken you round enough properties to know this one's a prime development opportunity. No sweat, no diamonds, am I right?'

Nettie nodded. Lee, alone, must have taken her round over thirty flats, not to mention the other estate agents in the area. Jules had thought it was fun, at first, coming with her and looking for the 'potential' in the starter flats they were shown, but eventually the litany of reasons why they 'weren't right' meant she'd stopped coming and had asked simply to be notified by a change-of-address card.

'And three fifty's an *incredible* price,' he said again. 'If this goes onto the market, it'll go for five, five fifty no problem. Even if you did nothing structural to it and just painted the whole thing white, you'd still be guaranteed to make a profit on this.'

'So why would they accept three fifty from me, then?'

Lee smiled sympathetically. 'The trustee involved owes me a favour.'

And he was doing her one, she knew, spurred on by the pity that everyone in the area reserved for her family. She'd be practically robbing him to buy at this price. She had to do this. Grasp the nettle. It was now or never.

'I'll offer three thirty-five,' she said firmly, turning back to face him. 'Obviously, with the amount of work it needs . . .' she shrugged, glimpsing his shocked expression.

Lee looked uncomfortable. He was putting himself on the line for her. 'They won't take less than three fifty, Nettie. That's the rebuilding cost, the lowest they can go. Anyway, I know you can afford it. I've taken you round properties that cost significantly more than this.'

She shifted her weight, remembering the red-topped electricity bill that had landed on the doormat last week. 'Well, we're all feeling the squeeze, aren't we? I've had to revise my sums a bit. Three fifty is my top-out budget now, and there's no point in me getting this if I then can't afford to do anything with it. Let's be honest, it's uninhabitable in this condition. I'm sorry, but that's the highest I can go to.'

Lee looked disappointed. 'Well,' he said slowly, 'if that's your offer, I'll do my best, but . . .' His voice trailed off as he rooted around in his pocket for his phone.

'What will be will be. I'm a firm believer in that.'

'Of course you are.' He patted her arm, again sympathetically. 'Let me see what I can do for you.'

Nettie watched as he wandered towards the kitchen, phone clamped to one ear, his other hand jammed in his pocket. She absently leaned against the radiator, but of course it was as cold as bone and she shivered as she stared into the sky, a skein of ice threading through the fat, congested clouds, which carried more than the threat of rain now that the wind had dropped. The temperature had been falling sharply all week – ever since they'd come back from Lausanne, in fact – and the Topshop duffel coats and Isabel Marant donkey jackets that had been the postcode's autumnal uniform had long since been turned in for heavy-duty Canada Goose jackets and Prada mitts.

She watched as a battered Volvo estate parked on the street below, a Christmas tree tethered to its roof. A man jumped out, followed by two little girls in the back, clapping their gloved hands as he stretched to release the bungee ropes and lift down the tree. A woman came out of the house to help him, a tea towel flung over her shoulder, and Nettie watched intently as they stretched to carry it into the house, her breath fogging the glass so that she had to wipe it clear again.

She looked around for other signs of Christmas, realizing how many she missed at street level. The area's new 'heritage' Victorian-style lamp posts – which her father's local pressure group had managed to get the council to buy – had miniature Christmas trees secured on shallow ledges, and giant hoops like over-scaled door wreaths straddled the shopping streets. It looked bucolically pretty.

A bus crawled past, the top-deck residents at eye level with her, and she recoiled slightly as they glided past in the late-afternoon traffic, weary shoppers resting their heads against the steamed-up windows, bags pooled at their feet.

'Well, well, well, I never would have thought it.'

Nettie turned as Lee walked back into the room; her breath caught. They'd agreed?

'I've spoken to the vendor. It's not a complete victory, but . . .' he paused for dramatic effect, 'if you can go to three thirty-seven and a half, you've got yourself a deal.'

'D'you know what this is about?' Nettie asked anxiously as she caught up with Jules in the lift the next morning.

'No clue.' Jules yawned, gripping her double-shot coffee even tighter. 'He's probably just having another of his hissy fits.' She checked her hair in the copper-tinted glass just as the lift arrived and the doors opened.

They stepped in.

'But he's never called an emergency meeting before,' Nettie said anxiously.

'That's because there's no such thing. It's an ego trip is all.' Jules reached into her bag and pulled out a copy of *Grazia*. 'Much more important – did you see this? He's a bad boy. Really bad.' She winked. 'I like it.'

'Huh?'

'Lover boy!' Jules said, tapping the page. 'Looks like it's going to take a bit more than sliding down a wall of death to hold *his* attention.'

Nettie felt her stomach drop. 'He's unfollowed me, then?' She'd hoped for at least a week of kinship.

'No, I'm talking about her! Look!' Nettie looked down at the photo of Jamie Westlake and American starlet Coco Miller stumbling out of Mahiki together, his hand closed tightly around hers as they battled their way through the assembled paparazzi to their waiting car. 'Tough act to follow.'

Nettie stared miserably at Coco's LA legs – yoga-honed and tanned – emerging from a diaphanous pink silk negligee-dress and worn with high-tops for a bit of urban edge. A Chanel Lego bag dangled from her wrist (no yellow bucket for *her*, Nettie thought hatefully), and a punky (but still two-carat) diamond crescent followed the upper curve of her ear, her dark blonde hair swept back into a side ponytail and worn low at the nape of her neck.

'Ugh,' she groaned, thrusting the magazine back to her friend. 'I wish you hadn't shown me that.'

The lift doors opened and they stepped out into the bright whiteness of the office, the grey plastic-topped desks and blue nylon carpets tidied and cleaned for another week. The space itself was generous for such a small company –

Daisy and Caro's desks were a good paper plane's throw across the room – with light pouring in on two sides through bland plate-glass windows, and posters from the agency's various clients – White Tiger, Astra healthcare, Phoenix chemicals – Blu-tacked to the wall in an overt display of loyalty.

A red foam sofa was positioned by the water cooler, and the curling, out-of-date magazines on the coffee table opposite it were supposed to encourage the team to sit and relax occasionally, taking time out of their busy days to recharge; but given that it was set right outside Mike's office, the girls far preferred congregating behind the giant potted yucca plant by the photocopier instead – much to Mike's chagrin.

The slatted blinds showed that the team in the events management agency opposite had yet to arrive at work. Lucky things.

Caro and Daisy were already at their desks as Jules and Nettie trundled in. Daisy stopped applying her lipstick and cast them both quizzical 'WTF?' looks.

Jules just shrugged and threw her bag down on the floor beside her desk. 'Your guess is as good as mine.'

'Seriously? An eight o'clock meeting?' Caro demanded, offering them all a stick of gum. They declined. 'What the . . . ?'

'Ego trip. Ego trip,' Jules said again in her best bored voice, just as Mike's office door opened and he marched down the corridor towards them. It was as if he'd been waiting for them.

'Ladies. Shall we?' he asked without stopping, and making a beeline for the conference room.

The girls watched after him in open-mouthed amazement. What was going on?

They trooped in slowly and took their usual seats at the table. Mike was perched on the table at the far end – no custard creams, expression inscrutable – and Nettie felt her nerves gather. Friday's meeting had, after all, ended with a warning for her.

They settled into unusual silence, unusually quickly, and he clapped his hands together.

'You might be wondering why I've called this emergency meeting.'

No one responded. They didn't want to feed his ego with curiosity and questions.

'Well, I've been in crisis talks with White Tiger all weekend.'

'Crisis talks?' Jules echoed, but there was a slight quaver to her voice that Nettie immediately caught. White Tiger were the agency's star clients, the big tickets that had drawn them to the attention of their other accounts. It had also been a White Tiger event at which Nettie had . . . achieved a certain notoriety. 'Yes, that's right. Crisis talks.'

Mike puffed himself up, building the moment, feeling the power. 'It would appear,' he said slowly, 'that the clip we viewed of Nettie's accident on Friday afternoon, in this very room, has been leaked.'

'No!' Jules gasped with dramatic gravity. She was a truly brilliant liar. It was incredible to watch sometimes.

'So?' Caro asked, jaws pinging up and down.

'So,' Mike said, adding great weight to the word, 'it's gone viral.'

'Viral?' Daisy echoed. 'But who . . . ?'

'Who indeed, Daisy?' Mike said, swinging his gaze over

to Nettie. 'Of course, it was simple enough to work out. The thief didn't try very hard to obscure her tracks.'

Thief? Nettie swallowed at his choice of word. That was overstating it, wasn't it? She wouldn't have called it 'stealing' necessarily.

'*In fact*, the film was uploaded with a link to a Twitter account, @BlueBunnyGirl, which White Tiger's IT team had no problem tracing back to the linked email address.' He arched an eyebrow directly at her. 'Had any broadband difficulties this weekend, Nettie?'

She blinked back at him, seeing her career flash before her eyes. This was it. She was going to get fired.

'*Nets* did it?' Caro exclaimed in shock. 'Christ, I'm most shocked that you even knew how.'

'Actually—' Jules said, clearing her throat.

But Mike put a hand up to silence her.

'Naturally, White Tiger's board are highly concerned at this breach. They own the copyright to the event – and therefore of the film. This is industrial theft. Not only that but their branding is all over the footage. It is only by the grace of God that the accident ended fairly happily, but the fact remains that had it not, they would have been severely embarrassed, their reputation *damaged*, in fact.'

Nettie took a gulp of air. Theft? Damages? Oh God, what had she done? Why hadn't she thought of this on Friday night? Of course she couldn't just steal someone else's footage of someone else's event and get away with it. She closed her eyes, trying to stay calm. If they could just fire her and not sue . . . she'd take that; she'd be *grateful* for that.

'Mike—' Jules tried again, and yet again he stopped her. 'I'm sure you can see why they find it no laughing matter that something like this should have got out. They can't have a mole on the team who's going to compromise their reputation just because she thinks something dangerous is funny.'

Nettie opened her eyes. 'But . . . not that many people have seen it, not in the scheme of things,' she said timidly, a hopeful wince on her face.

He sat up and with a dramatic flourish clicked the remote for the whiteboard behind him. The screen came up blue, a small whirring coming from the projector in the ceiling. Then it suddenly flashed white, with a large black number printed across the middle: *105,665*.

'That's quite a lot, in my opinion. And that was as of half an hour ago. I think we can confidently say it will have gone up another few hundred, if not thousand, since then.' He shook his head, but his eyes never left her and she knew exactly what he was building up to. 'It was bad enough leaving things as we did on Friday afternoon, but this? What were you thinking? You must see that you leave me no choice. You've gone into a whole other league, Nettie.'

'Exactly.' Jules's voice was firm, triumphant even, as she gave a small smack on the conference table, demanding attention. 'It's all gone exactly according to plan.'

Everyone looked at her.

'Excuse me?' Mike asked, irked to be interrupted from his monologue.

'Well, I take it you've looked at the donations coming in?' she asked disingenuously. 'Oh, what am I saying? Of course you have – it's patently *obvious* that with the number of views the clip's now had, there'd be an upsurge in traffic to the charity link too.' She worked on her iPad quickly.

'Yes, twenty-nine thousand pounds,' she shrugged. 'Which clearly is a very tidy profit for a weekend's work and a big uptick from where she was last week.'

'Twenty-ni—' Mike echoed.

'And that's not including any monies that will be paid from YouTube too, if we decide to go ahead and register as associates. Naturally, that's your call, Mike – we didn't want to go ahead on that without your say-so.'

'My . . . You mean, you did all this deliberately?' he asked, thunderstruck.

'As a fundraising initiative? Of course! This isn't theft. This is phase one of a carefully thought-out campaign, Mike.'

'A campaign?'

'Mm-hmm. Nettie took everything you said on Friday so much to heart that we had a brain-storming session after work and she came up with the plan. The footage was there, of course, doing nothing, and much as the thought of her humiliation and pain being made public was *utterly mortifying* for her, she agreed that if it would benefit the charity in any way, then it was only right and proper to let it go ahead and be seen.'

Nettie blinked at her friend, wanting to hug her, desperately hoping the hysterical laughter roiling in her body wouldn't find a way out before they'd left this room.

Jules winked back.

Mike looked at her. 'Is this true, Nettie?'

She nodded, not quite trusting what might yet come out of her mouth.

Mike sat back, pensive, the wind quite taken out of his sails. 'Well, twenty-nine thousand pounds certainly is a lot of money to raise in one weekend.'

'And it hasn't finished yet. People are still viewing and sharing the clip. We can expect donations to continue going up,' Jules said confidently. 'As you said on Friday, this is the biggest fundraising week of the year. 'Tis the season of goodwill to all men – everyone's beginning to wind down and relax in anticipation of the holidays. We've given them some entertainment.' She grinned. 'And we could still give them some more.'

'More?' Mike looked like he would blow over from a sneeze.

'Mm-hmm. Only if you want, obviously.' Jules gave a lackadaisical shrug, seemingly oblivious to Nettie's sudden look of alarm.

'Like what?'

'Well, we've drawn up a list of so-called challenges that Nettie could do over the coming days. One a day till Christmas Eve, we thought. I'm not sure if you're aware, but there's actually twelve days left to Christmas, so we could hashtag it to "twelvedaresofchristmas"? It's a pun on . . . Yeah, right, you've got it. We thought of a hashtag to tie in with the charity too: "ballzup". Geddit?'

'Is this right, Nettie? Have you come up with a list?' Mike asked, catching sight of Nettie's frozen expression.

'Uh, well, yes,' she replied tentatively, trying to balance the anxiety about what Jules was signing her up for with the fear of losing her job.

'It's all her idea, this,' Jules said again, giving credit where it was not due.

Mike looked pleased. He pulled out the head chair and sank into it, his fingers pressed into a steeple. 'Elaborate, please.'

Nettie pointed to Jules in panic. 'She's got the list.'

Mike turned to Jules instead, an eyebrow raised, a sigh escaping him. 'Jules?'

Jules stretched, in her element to be running the meeting. 'So clearly things ended well after the Ice Crush stunt, but they *could've* gone badly wrong, as you just said yourself, so obviously none of us wants to repeat something on that scale and put Nets in any kind of danger.'

Mike pulled a so-so face, as if he thought it was still up for discussion. 'It was funny, though.'

'Exactly. What people were responding to was the comedy of the situation, not the danger per se – and I thought we could replicate that by doing a round-up, if you will, of the best Internet memes.'

Oh God. Nettie felt sick as she saw where Jules was heading with this. She desperately tried to remember what had been on that list. It was hard to get past the dyed eyebrows.

'Go on,' Mike said in an unconvinced tone, probably because he too did not know what a meme actually was. 'What would that entail?'

'Well, I've drawn up a list of the most popular ones, so it could include things like owling, money-facing, planking, Blakeing—'

'"Money-what"? "Blakeing"?' Mike echoed. He frowned, sniffing at the deception. 'Are you making these names up?'

Jules chuckled. 'No. Blakeing's actually my favourite. It's named after the US basketball player Blake Griffin after he watched the replay of a foul he got called on. He was holding a cup of water at the time, and he threw his hands in the air and tossed the water all over the poor sod standing behind him. It was an accident, but honestly, you should've seen the other guy's face. Put it this way – it's so funny I won't watch it on a full bladder.' She caught sight of Mike's expression and turned to the girls. 'Sorry. Too much?'

Mike cleared his throat. His inability to deal with an office full of women was a constant source of amusement for them all.

'Anyway, so that's what Blakeing is – basically chucking water over someone behind you. Or we could do an Ice Bucket Challenge—'

'Stop right there!' Mike instructed, his face set in deep concentration, one finger held mid-jab in the air. 'Ice Bucket Challenge. Now, I know that. Let's explore that.'

'Why?' Daisy asked. 'It's been done to death, and it's minus two degrees out there.'

'True. It has been done to death,' Mike agreed, clearly unconcerned about the other detail.

'Although that just means everyone already knows and loves it. What if we could put a twist on it to make it fresh?' Caro said.

Mike looked at her. 'Like . . . ?'

'Like . . .' She thought for a moment. 'Like we could get people to vote. "Retweet" and "follow" if they want it to happen, "like" and "follow" if they don't. Obviously everyone will want to see it happen, so they'll both join our consumer base and actively grow it for us too. It's a pyramid scheme for the charity's Twitter following, basically.'

'I like that, Caro.'

'Yeah, but is that too passive? Like you say, this is a well-worn meme. If we're going to make it feel relevant again, couldn't we be more dynamic with the concept?' Jules argued.

'I don't follow,' Mike said.

'Well, rather than post and wait for people to share and donate, why don't we turn it on its head and get them to bid for the next event?' An audible gasp zipped round the room at the idea. 'What do you think? Five grand for the next skit? And it's got to be raised in a day or the "offer"' – she raised her fingers in speech marks – 'expires. That way, we put the onus on the public to get the message out there. I totally think there's the appetite for it.'

Nettie liked the idea of it – at least it meant there was a possibility that she wouldn't have to go through with all these crazy stunts.

'We'll look a bit daft if there isn't,' Daisy sighed, examining her nails.

Jules shot her a warning look. 'Surely you've got something to contribute other than doom?'

Daisy dropped her hand to the desk as all eyes rested on her. 'Of course I do.' There was a long pause as they all – Daisy included – wondered what that was going to be.

'Tell me your thoughts, Daisy,' Mike said, sounding more like a therapist than her boss.

Suddenly a light switched on behind her eyes. She glanced at Jules smugly. 'Well, most people did it in the summer in their gardens or their pools – private places, right? Why don't we do it somewhere we can get an audience gathered? Let's make it a happening, like a flashmob thing.'

'Flashmob, yes . . .' Mike nodded, thinking how cool this sounded. 'That's a good thought.'

'Where, though? Time is of the essence. If we're going to make the "twelvedares" hashtag work, we need to get on to it today,' Jules said, batting back the challenge with a smirk. She loved these mini-battles with Daisy.

'Uh . . .' Daisy stared at the ceiling, willing inspiration to strike. 'Uh, well, it needs to be somewhere public where loads of people will see it, so . . . it could be Hyde Park, maybe? Beside the Serpentine or . . . ooh, Speakers' Corner?'

Mike pulled a 'not sure' expression as Nettie groaned and slid further down her seat.

'Or . . . on the steps of St Paul's?'

He shook his head. 'They might think we're protesting about something.'

Daisy began to look desperate. 'OK, how about . . . ?' The room fell silent. And then quite suddenly Daisy's expression changed, a satisfied smile growing on her lips, which literally reeled Mike forward from his chair. 'Oh my God, I've got it.'

'What is it?' Caro asked.

'It's genius is what it is.' She looked around the room, drumming her French manicure on the conference table, her eyes coming to a stop on Jules. 'Trafalgar Square. Fourth plinth.'

Even Jules grinned, leaning across the table for a celebratory hand-slap. Everybody was looking jubilant – everybody except Nettie, who was looking between them all rapidly, looking for signs that this whole thing was a joke, a fix-up. It had been one thing trying to save her job, but this . . . this was way beyond anything Jules had run past her. The blue eyebrows weren't seeming quite so bad after all.

'This is great. Pure marketing gold,' Mike said, smacking his palm on the desk. 'We might rescue this account yet, ladies. I'll get on to White Tiger right away, bring them up to speed with the concept, but let's start putting everything in place.'

There was a scraping of chairs as everybody jumped up.

'And, uh . . . who's going to do this Ice Bucket Challenge in minus two degrees on the fourth plinth in Trafalgar Square?' Nettie asked, throwing her biro onto the desk.

The team looked at her.

'Well, you, of course,' Daisy said.

'Why me? The hashtag is "bluebunnygirl". Anyone could put that suit on. I've already done my bit. At the very least, we should rotate it and take turns.'

Mike sat back down again. 'Lest you should forget, Nettie, your impetuousness this weekend very nearly lost us our star account. White Tiger wanted you out. This changes things, I grant you – your idea is solid gold – but the fact remains you should have never gone ahead with it without the requisite permissions in place. You're lucky I'm not giving you a formal caution, or worse. I would have thought you'd appreciate that following through on the campaign is the very least you can do.' He took a breath. 'Not to mention that everyone sees you at the end of the clip when they take the rabbit head off you. *You* are the person all those people are following.'

'You can't really see me, though,' she argued.

'You can,' Daisy said quickly. 'Well, they can definitely see you're not a blonde, anyway.' She held up a wisp of her own tousled blonde hair with a 'sorry, not sorry' expression.

'Or a redhead,' Caro agreed, twirling one of her strawberry-blonde plaits.

'It's important that we maintain the integrity of the project,' Mike said solemnly. 'I don't think your followers would be very pleased to discover they'd been duped by someone else. What would there be to stop any old Tom,

Dick or Harry just going out and buying one of the outfits and stealing your thunder?'

Nettie stared back sullenly. Let them steal away. 'Well then, let's ditch the costume and I'll just do it as myself. I don't want to wear that thing again. It's heavy and it smells.'

'*Branding*, Nettie. The hashtag, remember? Blue Blunny Girl, not crazy, mad, brunette girl.'

She glared at him, but her arrows didn't pierce his thick skin.

'Added to which, there is very serious money attached to this already. The charities are *relying* upon you to grow and move forward with this. Lives are at stake, Nettie. If Jules is right about this, then you've got an opportunity here that money literally can't buy. It'd be madness – not to mention career suicide – to let it slip through your fingers. Who knows how long the momentum will be with you? We all know from bitter experience just how quickly the winds of change . . . uh, blow.'

He paused for breath again, but his point had been made in the concise two-word term 'career suicide' and she sighed defeatedly.

'Right,' he said, seeing he'd won the point. 'Well, let's hit the ground running with this, everyone. Jules, if you can send on that list to me of the other dares, along with explanations, please. Damned if I've ever heard of "owling".'

'Sure thing, Mike,' Jules said, her eyes sliding over to Nettie, who was still seated.

Mike, Caro and Daisy darted off to make phone calls as Jules slunk back to the table, knowing she'd run too far with her victory.

'It'll be OK, you know,' she said, sitting back down beside her.

'That's easy for you to say when you're not the one doing it.'

'I promise we won't let it get out of hand. It's just going to be silly prank stuff. No danger.'

'I hate that fucking costume.'

Jules pulled a comical sad face. 'Well, you could owe it a little more gratitude. It has brought you a huge fanbase, not to mention the eternal devotion of Jamie Westlake.'

'Or not, as you so kindly pointed out in the lift earlier.'

'Pah, don't worry about her,' Jules said dismissively, shuffling her papers into a neat pile. 'That's only 'cos he hasn't met *you* yet. He's just killing time, waiting for you to float into his orbit.'

Nettie sighed and pushed back her chair. 'Sometimes I worry about you, Jules, I really do.'

'I've been reading up on him, by the way, which is far easier said than done. Did you know he never gives interviews?'

'What? Never?' She picked up her notebook and pen.

'Nope. I practically had to get a private detective just to find out that he's twenty-nine . . . and a Scorpio, which means he's excellent in bed. Generous lover.'

Nettie turned at the door, unable not to smile. 'It does not mean that.'

'Course it does. And he grew up in Canterbury; he was a choirboy – would you believe it? So that explains the wildness.'

Nettie chuckled, leaning against the frame.

'And I think he's left-handed. In all the photos he's . . .' Jules bit her lip. 'Which way do you hold a guitar?' she mused, holding her own hands up in the air and having a go.

Nettie gently pushed herself back upright, ready to go. 'Whatever. I don't care.'

'But you have to know these things. You've got to know some background for when you meet.'

'We are never going to meet, Jules.'

'He's following you, isn't he?'

'He's following thousands of people,' Nettie said over her shoulder as she walked out.

'Eighteen, actually!' Jules called after her.

There was a pause before Nettie reappeared. 'Eighteen?'

Jules was waiting for her, a satisfied grin on her face. 'Eighteen. He's even worse than you. Look.' Jules brought up the Twitter screen on her iPad and, finding his profile, held it up for Nettie to see. She gave Nettie a triumphant look. 'Huh? Huh? That puts a different slant on things now, doesn't it?'

Nettie didn't say anything. She met her friend's eyes for a moment before walking away with a shake of her head – and a smile on her lips.

Chapter Six

The pigeons loved her. Maybe it was the purchase their claws could grab in the fur or possibly the sheer bulk of the bodysuit, which allowed so many of them to roost upon her at once, but inside the bunny head, Nettie was freaking out. She had never liked birds since she'd seen the Hitchcock film on a sleepover when she was twelve and she had provided Jules with many amusing moments over the years, almost lying flat on the pavement as she dodged Primrose Hill's low-flying pigeons.

'Caro! Get them off me!' Nettie demanded, jogging on the spot and waggling her shoulders wildly, shaking the pigeons off only for a moment before they settled upon her again.

Caro, standing ten feet away and filming her on her phone, laughed. 'Yeah! That's great, Nets. Funky dancing – they'll love it!'

Caro was live-streaming shorts of the 'build-up' and Jules was hoping the hashtag might start trending. She was sitting on the steps outside the National Gallery, monitoring the social media activity with an intense expression and nibbling on her nails as Daisy lackadaisically tried to give parking directions to the men in the van who were delivering the ice. This alone made Nettie nervous. She had assumed they would just use a few cubes from a cafe or, at most, buy a bag from the nearest grocery store. Why did they need a *van*?

Apparently, the latest 'short' – whipping up public appetite for the 'soak or not' vote – was already at well over 2,000 retweets, and donations were at £4,100. Nettie was sending up small prayers that the outstanding £900 wouldn't come in time.

But for all the supposed frenzy online, actual support in the square was muted. Whoever these two thousand people were, sharing and spreading her adventure on the net, seemingly precious few of them were in the vicinity of Trafalgar Square right now. Only tourists and students mingled outside the National Gallery, taking selfies of themselves 'with Nelson', or else eating sandwiches on the steps. Nettie's giant blue bunny costume was attracting some curious stares, but no one seemed particularly aware, or excited, that they were in the middle of a 'happening'.

Doubtless this was because she had been ordered by Mike to stay – 'and not move' – at the foot of the giant Christmas tree, which had its lights on even at this time in the day, so no one understood why a giant blue bunny was trying to keep warm in the middle of Trafalgar Square. Mike, wearing a purple sash, was off shaking his bucket, enjoying being 'in the field'. He still believed in recruiting sponsorships and donations 'the old-fashioned way', handing out flyers to everyone who stopped to stare at the dancing blue bunny and not realizing he was actually chasing most of them away. He had even handed a testicular cancer leaflet to a little girl who had come over to feed the pigeons, telling her to 'give this to Daddy' and the little thing had run off in tears.

Nettie now stood motionless, granted a brief reprieve from the birds' attention as some tourists began throwing out crumbs from their sandwiches. She scanned the square, grateful to have insisted on wearing the rabbit head almost the moment they'd got out of the van. It was less embarrassing if no one could see her face. Mike came over, brandishing a clipboard.

'How are you feeling, Nettie?' he asked, trying to see her inside the suit by peering through the mesh-covered eyeholes of the bunny head.

'I'm frozen,' she said, beginning to jog on the spot again, even though the pigeons had been frightened off by Mike's proximity. 'How can I be the size of a bus and yet my puffa wouldn't fit under this?'

'Don't knock it. That internal padding is what kept you safe on the ice. Besides, we've got towels on standby for you.'

'And coffee,' Caro said, hot on his heels and holding out a flat white. Nettie went to take it, only to realize that even if she could hold the cup in her paw – which she couldn't – she couldn't get it anywhere near her lips. 'After, then,' Caro said, placing it on the ground at the foot of the tree.

Nettie shrugged and dropped her paw down despondently. This sucked. She automatically did another recce of the square, sifting the students and the tourists from the homeless and the city workers. 'I still don't get why we're doing this here. No one's even looking at me, and if you won't let me go round with one of the buckets, I may as well be in the back garden at home.'

'Holy mother!'

The shout made them all look back at Jules who was

suddenly on her feet, jumping up and down on the step and air-punching at the same time.

'What? What's happened?' Mike asked excitedly as Jules sprinted over, holding her iPad like it was the Holy Grail.

'Jamie Westlake's what's happened!' Jules shrieked, jumping up and down again so excitedly that they could barely make out the words on the screen. 'He's only just gone and donated ten grand!'

'Shut! Up!' Nettie shouted as she read the tweet. *'Let's get this party started. #ballzup #Tested.'*

'We are good to go, baby!' Jules laughed, holding up her hand for a high five.

The smile faded from Nettie's face as she realized what blitzing their target meant – there was going to be no getting out of this now.

'Ha!' Caro laughed, looking towards the fourth plinth where the delivery men were decanting the ice into a bath. *A bath?* 'Hope you didn't do your hair this morning, Nets.'

Nettie wondered if Caro would be quite so enthusiastic about all of this if the bath of ice was going to be thrown over her. 'Slight problem. How are you going to lift that bath when it's full of ice?'

'We won't,' Daisy laughed, overhearing her as she joined the group, intrigued by Jules's excitement. 'But White Tiger have sent a couple of guys they sponsor in the powerlifting arena. See?'

She pointed to where a pair of vastly muscled men in tight shorts and White Tiger-logoed muscle vests were now climbing onto the famously empty fourth plinth in the square, shaking their arms and feet out like boxers primed for a match. Even given the size of them, Nettie couldn't believe they were able to tolerate the low temperatures in those flesh-baring outfits. There had been a hard frost last night and the black Trafalgar statues glinted ever more coldly in the flat light.

Nettie watched as the ice delivery men ran to and from the van – hazard lights flashing – to the plinth, huge sacks of ice balanced on their shoulders. The musclemen were looking down into the bath as it was filled, shaking their heads and laughing. She could see that the activity on the plinth was beginning to attract attention. Anticipation grew on people's faces as they looked from the muscled men on the plinth to the giant blue bunny who was surrounded by a team of people with sashes and clipboards and buckets, and was now being hustled towards the plinth. Something was clearly about to kick off.

Nettie noticed a megaphone in Mike's hand. Daisy and Jules had shot off again, now herding curious passers-by towards the fourth plinth, and Nettie felt her nerves grow as the small crowd quickly stood several people deep, everyone staring up at the two men as Jules and Daisy began distributing information. Nettie jogged on the spot again, swearing profusely under her breath because Jamie had chosen now as his moment to make contact again. Did he like seeing her suffer? Being humiliated?

Mike leaned in to her as they walked towards the plinth. 'OK, Nettie, let's give the people a show. We've got a chance to prove to White Tiger what we're made of. They are lapping this up. This campaign idea of mine has really got them going, so let's not "balls-up" like last time.' He laughed at his own joke.

Nettie looked at him, one of her ears falling over her eye. His campaign idea?

'You get up on the plinth. I'll do the rest.'

Nettie, at the foot of the plinth – which was at least fifteen feet high – stared up at the flimsy ladder that had been propped against the side. It was one thing to climb it as a five-foot-three, nine-stone woman who did circuits once a week. It was quite another doing it dressed as a seven-foot bunny with the waist circumference of a small car.

It took six minutes to climb the ten rungs of the ladder, with two guys standing underneath and pushing up on her bottom, so that by the time she stepped onto the plinth to a crescendo of cheers, it wasn't just Caro's phone recording her every move.

Mike's voice began booming out of the megaphone. 'Wassup, London?'

To the side, Nettie saw Jules, Daisy and Caro all drop their heads in their hands. On the far side of the square somewhere, a cab tooted its horn.

'You wanted more, so we're giving you more!'

The crowd frowned in puzzlement, clearly not having a clue what he was talking about or why the strange assortment of characters – bunny, bath, musclemen – were assembled on the plinth.

Nettie went and stood between the two musclemen, holding out her paw for a fist bump with each.

'More than forty thousand of you have already taken Blue Bunny Girl to your hearts and, in so doing, helped waved the flag for a charity very close to our hearts, Tested, which is standing at the coalface in the battle against testicular cancer. So we're picking up the baton again today and we're going to keep picking it up every day for twelve days. Today, we asked you to vote – *and donate* – on whether Blue Bunny Girl should do the Ice Bucket Challenge, something I know many of you will be familiar

with. Well, ladies and gentlemen, you have spoken. And
we have heard you. The public has made its wish clear by
a majority of' – Mike glanced down at his iPad and quickly
did the maths, the murmurings of his mental arithmetic
carrying over the crowd – 'six thousand and twenty-four
votes, and with donations of nearly £15,000, smashing our
target of £5,000, Blue Bunny Girl *shall* do the Ice Bucket
Challenge.'

The bemused but steadily swelling crowd cheered – it
was a fractured smattering of noise; Nettie flapped her ear
out of the way and looked down at her audience, the overwhelming majority of whom, she was quite sure, had not
heard of Blue Bunny Girl till this moment. But they were
clapping. And filming. And clearly about to google her
when they got home.

'But we're gonna do this the White Tiger way,' Mike
said, ever aware of pleasing the client. 'Bunny, if you
would take your seat.'

With the help of the musclemen – for she couldn't see
where to perch herself when her bottom was easily four
times the width of the chair – she sat down, her paws on
her lap. Across the square, by the Christmas tree, she saw a
homeless man pick up her steaming coffee with extra
macchiato and wander off with it. Her eyes roamed the
square again, darting and quick.

'Hurry now, guys,' Mike said in a low voice, away from
the megaphone, as the musclemen rolled their arms and
expanded their dramatic chests with swinging arm move-
ments. They immediately fell into deep squats at Mike's
order. 'Caro, are you getting this?'

'Yes, Mike,' Caro sighed, her voice flat.

Behind her, Nettie heard a low grunt and the sudden

slosh and clatter of ice cubes cracking against each other as the antique bath was lifted. In front of her, almost every person in the crowd had their phone out, ready to capture it on film. A few Japanese students squealed. She tensed, bracing herself for the cold.

'Head off, Nets! Head off!' Nettie looked down to see Jules at the back of the crowd, frantically motioning for her to take off the bunny head.

'No!' She shook her head, mortified at the prospect of people seeing her. This was embarrassing enough.

'Yes! *You* need to get wet!'

Nettie sighed crossly but did as she was told. Jules winked up at her, giving a thumbs-up sign with her free hand, but that was all Nettie saw, for in the next moment Trafalgar Square was washed away as gallons of freezing-cold water were upended over her, most of it rushing straight into the suit through the gaping neckline that was left when the head of the costume was removed.

Nettie gasped – and gasped again. She couldn't scream: she couldn't catch her breath to scream. The cold was so shocking, so disorienting, and she didn't even realize she was now on her feet. She could barely see, her hair plastered over her face by the force of the water, and she was only vaguely aware of the crowd's delight as she gasped and jumped on the spot, trying to displace the water that now moated her – with nowhere to escape to – and then the collective intake of breath as she staggered too close to the edge. One of the men pulled her back in time.

Her voice returned. 'Oh my God! Oh my God! Oh my God!' she breathed, unable to stop repeating herself as the mutual shock of fright and cold kicked in. Just to add to this fresh hell, she had almost fallen off the fourth plinth?

'Get it off! Get it off!' she gasped, ice water sloshing around every bit of her body. She was sure she'd be hypothermic within minutes.

'How? How?' the poor strongman asked, panicking at the look in her eyes.

Her voice had fled again, but she proffered her back to him and he easily ripped the long Velcro tape apart, having to jump back himself as the water inside rushed out, splashing the people at the front of the crowd and making them scream with excitement. Nettie stepped out of the unwieldy suit as quickly as she could, her T-shirt and jeans drenched, and her teeth already chattering. She could see Jules at the bottom of the plinth holding up one of the giant White Tiger towels for her – safety! Warmth! – and she scooted down the ladder to a hero's welcome, everyone clapping and cheering.

She felt a hand on her sodden shoulder and she turned gratefully. 'Jules, thank God! Give me that towel!'

But when she turned, it wasn't a friendly face that she saw.

'Do you have the requisite licence for public performance in this space, madam?' the policeman asked, his radio already in his hand.

'What's my dad going to say?'

'He'll laugh.'

'He won't.'

'Babe, you're twenty-six. What's he gonna do? Stop your pocket money?'

'This is serious! I've got a criminal record.'

'No, you haven't. They gave you a caution. Stop being so dramatic,' Jules said without looking up from her phone.

There was a pause. Nettie didn't think she was being dramatic. She'd spent all afternoon in Charing Cross Police Station. 'Well, that's the end of it now. I mean it. I nearly died on the first thing and got arrested on the second. Really, I've done my bit for charity. I'm bowing out while I still can. I don't care if they fire me.'

'Nets, you can't just jib out after the first day. We've promised White Tiger a carefully coordinated twelve-day campaign.'

'*You* promised that. Not me.'

Jules rolled her eyes. 'Look, Daisy and Caro have been working on the marketing already. You can't let them down . . .' Her voice trailed off, her brow furrowed as she continued with her text.

Nettie huffed and looked mournfully out of the window as the bus trundled up Portland Street. She pulled her coat closer to her neck, tightening her scarf, but it was no good – she couldn't stop shivering, and looking out at all the frost-pinched after-work shoppers wasn't helping. She turned back to face in to the rest of the bus again, resting her shoulders against the glass.

'Plus I nearly fell off the plinth. Can you imagine the headlines with that? "Giant Bunny Girl Leaps to Death from Fourth Plinth."'

'Now you're being completely over the top. If you'd fallen, you just would've . . . bounced. Besides, the big fella caught you.'

'Yes! And as for him – can you believe the way those blokes just legged it as soon as the police arrived and left me to get the blame?'

'They did text to apologize. They said they didn't want

to create bad PR for White Tiger. You can't really blame them. They were in all the gear.'

'But *why* did no one get a licence? Surely Daisy would have known we needed one? That's her area. She must have gone to school with someone who slept with the cousin of the housemate of the person in charge of Trafalgar Square licences?'

'With what time, exactly? Flashmob, remember? We're flying by the seat of our pants here. This is barely controlled chaos. It's guerrilla-style. We had to get in, do it and get out.' Jules looked back down at the Twitter page on her phone and gave a low whistle. 'Oooh, and check this out. They're eating it up.'

'Who are?'

'Your public, sweetie.' She passed over her phone. Nettie's Twitter page was almost glowing from the amount of activity on it. Her number of followers was now up to 51,000, and the post that had today's short-film link pasted into it had been retweeted over 9,000 times – and was still rising.

'Do you have any idea how colossal this conversion rate is?' Jules asked, her eyes wide. 'Your fanbase is seriously mobilized. They are *loving* you.'

'Not according to some of these comments,' Nettie said, scrolling down through the comments. '"*Yo ass fat even outta dat soot.*"'

Jules laughed. 'You sound like Mary Poppins.'

'Are they saying I have a fat bum?' She remembered the croissant eaten on the bus this morning. Damn it. Fruit only. Tomorrow, then, she promised herself.

'It's funny *because* you don't. Besides, there's always going to be one or two nutjobs. But most of these are really nice.' She leaned over, resting her chin on Nettie's shoulder, as was her way. 'Look, that one's saying it was a shame your T-shirt wasn't white. Isn't that nice? He appreciated your wardrobe.'

Nettie giggled, joshing her in the ribs with her elbow. 'Stop it.' But she did scroll through the comments with a smile on her face.

All these people had watched her? She couldn't believe it. The numbers were hard to comprehend. It was like . . . it was like walking into Wembley and every person in the place watching her on the big screens. She hadn't even done the Ice Bucket Challenge when it had been the craze of the summer, because no one had thought to nominate her, and now suddenly this YouTube clip had had almost 50,000 views? Most of them thought she was 'cool' and 'badass', and there were a lot of emojis. Her subsequent arrest appeared to have gone down particularly well too – adding to the subversive element, she supposed.

'And is there anything from our special friend?' Jules's chin dug into Nettie's shoulder as she spoke, but neither of them shifted to move.

'Oooh, just give me a week and I'll come back to you on that. I've got twenty thousand messages to get through first.'

'Sarky!' Jules grinned, sitting up at last and taking the phone from her. 'Alternatively, you could just go into his profile and see whether *he*'s tweeted anything today.'

'Oh.'

Jules brought up his profile page and turned the screen to Nettie with a very satisfied smile.

Nettie's eyes widened in disbelief, her hands flying to her mouth as she saw the single tweet he had posted that

day. '*U one crazy chick. #bluebunnygirl #ballzup.*' He had also
retweeted the link to his six million followers.

'He thinks I'm a crazy chick?' she asked hopefully.

'It would seem so,' Jules shrugged, laughing quietly.

'That's amazing, right?'

'Coming from the likes of Jamie Westlake? It's the highest form of flattery, I reckon.'

Nettie turned with a sigh, resting her forehead on the
window. 'He thinks I'm a crazy chick,' she murmured
happily.

'So, about tomorrow . . .'

'Hi, Dad.'

Her father looked up from his spot at the table as he
heard the door close. He was wearing a headtorch and had
that faraway look in his eyes that he always got when
working on one of his special projects. This one was a 1:24
scale model of *HMS Victory* and seemed to Nettie to be like
knitting with matchsticks.

'Hello, Button,' he smiled. 'How was your day?'

She paused momentarily from unwinding her scarf.
How exactly should she tell him that she'd been arrested in
Trafalgar Square, while dressed as a giant blue bunny, for
having a bath of iced water poured over her on the hallowed fourth plinth? Even if it was for a good cause, it was
still ridiculous. And it wasn't like the number of views on
YouTube, or her legion of followers on Twitter, was going
to mean anything to him – not compared with an arrest
sheet. They needed to have the police on their side. She felt
a twist of anxiety in her stomach, knowing she'd let him
down today. 'Oh, you know – dull.'

'Well, only this week and next to go and then you've got

a fortnight's rest. You look like you could do with it. You're white as a sheet.'

'Mm, I'm cold. It's perishing out there,' she said, hanging up her coat, scarf and bobble hat, and walking down the hall to him. She planted a kiss on his cheek. He smelt of toast. 'Wow. That's looking great.'

Her father's brows knitted together. 'Mmm. I don't know whether it's my eyes failing or my hands, but I can't seem to make it work properly. I'm all butterfingers, having to redo everything twice.'

'You're tired too, Dad. You should just . . . you know, rest for a bit. You never stop. I take it you were working in the orchard today?'

'Can't stop, love. Who's going to get those saplings in if I don't? Everyone else is busy with their jobs.'

'As are you,' she said, patting his shoulder and walking towards the fridge. 'Those books don't write themselves, you know.'

'I know, but it's different working for yourself. I can dictate my own hours.'

Nettie glanced back at him. She knew perfectly well what hours those took – he pretended to her that he worked during the day while she was at work, but she heard him tapping away on the keyboard through the night, knowing he was unable to sleep. Those 'power naps' he took in his chair throughout the day were all that passed for his rest, and he kept his days filled up, never allowing himself time to stop and think, to feel, to remember. Instead, he threw himself into community projects that meant endless meetings with councillors and support groups, his days spent canvassing signatures, his evenings taken up with reading reports. He was the person who'd first suggested the idea of a Primrose Hill Christmas Market when Camden Council had turned round and said they didn't have the budget for Christmas lights; it was he who had lobbied for a community orchard to revitalize and regenerate the patch of scrub on St George's Terrace; thanks to him, there were now pretty hanging baskets in Erskine Road; and he had been key in spearheading the campaign to reopen the library and hand over its running to a team of local volunteers when the council had closed it due to cuts. 'Have you eaten?' she asked.

'Just finished. Sardines on toast. I wasn't sure if you were eating out tonight or not.'

She groaned. 'As if I'm going out with Jules again, ever.'

'I've heard that before,' her father chuckled. 'Still cut up about her boyfriend, is she?'

'Well, she'd deny it to the death if you asked her, but I'd say so. I mean, it's been nearly a year now, but she's . . . I don't know, just partying too hard.'

'Grief displacement,' her father said, nodding sombrely as he resumed trying to glue together sticks smaller than nail clippings. 'It's not unusual.'

Nettie glanced back at him, almost bemused by his diagnosis. Could he really not see the parallels? She wondered whether he'd received a text from Gwen too. 'So did you make your word count today?'

'Hmm? Oh, um, no, not quite.'

'But the deadline you set was January, wasn't it?' Her father had always insisted that a deadline – even a self-imposed one – was crucial for condensing and focusing the creative spirit.

'Indeed, but I'll make it up tomorrow. I just had a . . . block, you know. Worked it out now, though.'

'Great,' she murmured sceptically.

'Ah, but one thing I did manage to get done,' he said, pushing his chair away from the table and walking past her to the back door. He opened it and reached for something outside.

Nettie felt herself tense, bracing for what she knew was coming. She had been expecting it any day for the past week. Her father straightened up, bringing inside a small potted spruce, the bonsai of the Christmas-tree world. It was only just over a foot tall, its fronds as wispy as a teenager's stubble.

'Oh, it's looking good,' she said encouragingly as her father carried it in. 'Much healthier looking than last year, anyway.'

'Yes. It's liking this bigger pot,' her father said, pleased. 'Where do you think we should put it? Sitting room?'

She pulled a face. 'Probably on the table again? It's still a bit small, don't you think, for going on the floor?'

'Yes, you're right. It still looks too much like a cat's scratching post, doesn't it?' He laughed lightly, pain in his eyes.

'Maybe next year,' she offered.

'We won't need it next year, Button,' he said stoutly. 'Do you want to put some newspaper under before I set it down? God knows I'll get in trouble if I leave ring marks on the table.'

Nettie ran to the recycling bin and grabbed yesterday's papers, arranging them on the table, then filled a shallow dish with water. Her father set down the miniature tree in the middle of it, and Nettie fetched a small box from the cupboard under the stairs. From it, she pulled out a small red tablecloth and draped it round the base, obscuring the dish and papers; then she took out three baubles – one was a softly felted Christmas fairy dangling from a golden thread, so that from a distance it looked like she was actually flying; the second was a plump gingham goose; the third a tiny china robin with the reddest of red breasts.

'Here, tell me what you think. I bought the new one this morning,' he said, reaching up to the shelf where her mother's favourite potteries were kept (all made by Nettie at school and woe betide anyone who touched them) and handing over a small brown paper bag, the top neatly folded over.

She lifted out an intricately carved wooden snowflake with tiny jingle bells in the centre.

'Do you like it?'

Nettie handled it like it was an injured bird. 'It's beautiful.'

'Yes, I thought so too. Your mother will love it when she gets home.'

Nettie handed it back to him without meeting his eyes and he carefully placed it centre front on the miniature tree. But even on a tree as tiny as theirs, the four baubles did a scant job of decorating it.

'It gets bigger and prettier every year – just like you,' her father said quietly, placing an arm round her shoulder and squeezing it tightly. 'This Christmas is the one, Button, I know it.'

She dropped her shoulder on his head, wishing she could share in his certainty. 'I know, Dad.'

Chapter Seven

'Just think of Jamie!' Jules shouted as another gust of wind reared up from behind her and blew her hair in front of her face.

'That's easy for you to say!' Nettie shouted back, but with a tremor in her voice. She gripped the rope tighter, keeping her eyes dead on Jules's as the expert did the final safety checks.

'Here, here have another tot,' Jules said, running over and handing across the hip flask again. Somehow, she managed to make a fluoro safety vest look like a fashion statement.

'But I've had five already.'

'Yeah, and you still look like you need the bottle. Go on.'

Nettie nodded and took another shot. The liquid amber burned her mouth, her throat, her stomach; but it did blur, slightly, the terror that was darting around her like a firework in a box.

'Are you sure this harness will work?' she asked, turning to the safety instructor again.

'Admittedly it is our biggest size. We usually use this for lifting cows,' he chuckled. 'Luckily you don't weigh the same. It's absolutely fine.'

'You'll be fine, Nets,' Jules echoed, placing her hands on Nettie's shoulders.

Nettie tried to smile back, but she knew she was mad, stark raving mad, to be putting herself through this. She did not like heights. It was her Official Fear. For some, it was spiders or small spaces or the dark or rubber-soled boots. For her, it was standing 308 metres above London with only a rope to keep her alive. The city – her home town – was very, very far below her, cars like scuttling beetles, pedestrians no more than pin-dots from this height. Buildings rippled away into the distance, morphing into an indistinct grey that merged with the far sky. On nearby ledges, charcoal pigeons ruffled their feathers and stared down across their domain.

'So remember, Mike's filming all this. Caro's shooting from the ground looking up.'

'It doesn't make me feel better to know that if I fall, the entire thing will be recorded, Jules.' She pointed a stern paw at her friend. 'And you are *not* to use it if I do.'

'As if!' Jules laughed. 'Anyway, if you did fall, wearing that thing you'll probably bounce.'

Nettie whitened on the spot.

'Hey, hey,' Jules said, paling too and giving her a big hug – well, as big as she could get with Nettie in the bunny suit. 'It was supposed to be a joke. I'm just messing with you. Listen, you'll be fine. Stop looking like that.'

'Like what?'

'Like you're going to burst into tears.'

'But I think I might.' Nettie bit her lip just as the health-and-safety officer came over with the White Tiger media executive, Scott Faulkner, and a photographer from the *Evening Standard*. 'Oh, do you want a . . . ? Yes, of course.'

She quickly pulled the rabbit head on and tried to lock her knees as the lens clicked.

'Right,' said Jonno, the crazy-damn-fool climbing professional who was doing the abseil with her and looked as relaxed as if he was about to drift on a lilo in a pool. 'You set to go?'

She shook her head, but he laughed and patted her shoulder like she was joking. 'That's the spirit. Come on, then. Just remember we're in this together.'

He went and stood by the edge, seemingly unperturbed by the sheer drop a foot to his right. It made a mockery of the steep slope on the ice course in Lausanne last week and Nettie wondered, for the thousandth time, exactly how, in the course of a few days, her life had been usurped by a timetable of daily dares that were damn near killing her with fright. He tugged and pulled at her body harness, which was about to become the only thing separating her life from death, for a final time.

'OK, we're good to go. Now just remember, stepping over is the hardest part. What did I tell you to do?'

'Lean back, feet flat, trust in the equipment,' she replied in a monotone.

'Exactly. Trust in me. Trust in yourself, Nessie. This is going to be fine. You're going to want to do it all again as soon as it's over.'

'I'm really not,' she said quickly, her voice thin with fear that she was placing her life in the hands of a man who couldn't even get her name right.

'That's what they all say. Just trust in me.' His brown eyes were steady upon her and she nodded out of politeness, trying to remind herself this guy was a professional. The White Tiger insurance team had been all over this like a haemorrhagic fever and she must have filled out thirty forms. They wouldn't be letting her do this if it wasn't safe – not because they cared about her, but because her omeletting the pavement in their name really would be bad publicity.

She stepped back so that her heels overlapped the edge of the roof. Half of her was now officially hanging over London, and adrenalin was rushing in torrents through her system, making her limbs tingle, her stomach flip. Everything was suddenly clearer – the white clouds in the grey sky (God, it was such a dreary day; please don't let her die on a dreary day), the still-bright green 'Fire exit' notice by the door, the puffs of smoke coming from some far-off chimney stacks in the Hampstead Heath direction and suggesting a retired gentleman reading his papers in the library of his Victorian house, while she . . .

She tried to focus. Trust in the equipment. Trust in Jonno.

She looked across. He was already dangling back in the harness, his feet propped against the glass wall like he was lying in bed, watching her.

'Ready?' he asked.

Of course she wasn't. It was a ridiculous question. Who was ever ready to step backwards off the Shard, one of the highest tower blocks in London, and pretend to be a *whale* for Chrissakes? And yet her body was disobeying both logic and instinct as her hands – visibly shaking – closed round the rope.

'That's it,' Jonno murmured. 'Now just lean back. That's all it is. Just a lean. The equipment will do the rest for you.'

She couldn't move.

'I know it's hard. This is the ultimate test of mind over matter. Just take your time.'

Take her time? How did eighty years sound?

And yet slowly, in degrees, she realized she was beginning to lean back, her legs bending as she took one foot off the roof and placed it lower, on the wall instead. The paws of the bunny suit weren't grippy, but they were long enough to create some sort of base to push on and she held the pose for a few long seconds, her eyes scrunched shut, her lips unwittingly moving as she willed herself to move the other leg too, her hands registering that the rope was tight, her harness already pulling round her as she leaned into it. Instinct told her everything would free-fall – that the ground would rush up – and she felt her arms and legs go liquid with fear. But everything held. She wasn't falling *yet*.

With her eyes still closed, she moved the other foot in a rush of courage. Perhaps she moved it too quickly, eager to be done with it, for the movement threw her off balance and the other leg slipped off the glass so that she was suddenly dangling above the far-distant street.

She screamed. Jules screamed. Nettie screamed again.

Jonno grinned, reaching over and steadying her as she twirled and spun on the rope, clutching it desperately, her eyes wide open now behind the mask. Oh God, she was going to die. She was going to die on a dreary day dressed as a mutant rabbit. 'No worries, Nessie. That happens to most people. Me too, first time I tried it.'

His voice was so quiet, so calm, that Nettie had to stop screaming to hear him. She had also realized that although she was still dangling, she wasn't actually falling. *Trust in the equipment*. She was shaking from head to toe.

'Ready to put your feet up now? You've done the hardest bit.' Jonno was still holding her rope and she had stopped pivoting.

She nodded frantically. Anything – anything – that meant she was touching the lovely solid glass-and-concrete structure, and not space, was a welcome prospect, even if it was just the soles of her feet.

Sucking in her tummy – thank God for those circuits classes – and bringing up her legs, she planted them one, two hard on the glass. The building didn't move. It would take her weight, it seemed.

'Good girl. Now the rest is easy.'

She watched as he demonstrated the next step, trying very, very hard not to notice how far below him the horizon was.

'Now your turn,' Jonno said, bringing his hands back onto the rope like it was nothing to have only a karabiner stand between your life and your death.

Nettie bit her lip and looked up apprehensively. Jules was standing between the health-and-safety woman and the White Tiger CSR man, her hands raised in a prayer position to her nose and looking even more scared than Nettie. Catching Nettie watching her, she immediately straightened up and gave Nettie a jaunty wink.

For some reason, Jules's nerves made Nettie feel reassured and a sudden rush of whisky-fuelled adrenalin shot through her. Fuck it!

'There you go, Nettie!' Mike said, zooming in on her with his camera as she took her hands off the rope and threw her arms back over into an arch, like a whale breaching the water. Her legs left the smooth safety of the Shard's glass walls and she tipped so far back she could see the pavements, behind and beneath her.

'That's it, Nettie!' Jules hollered.

'And again, please,' she heard Mike call. 'I think I might have missed that go.'

Above her, Nettie could hear Jules letting rip at him, and as she dangled from the rope, upside down, London now her sky and adrenalin and whisky mixing in her bloodstream, there was nothing else for it – she began to laugh.

Their breath hung in the air like steam-train puffs, a white trail that lingered behind them like a floating breadcrumb trail as their feet pounded the frozen ground in unison, hands pulled into loose fists. Em had set a firm pace today, her red ponytail like a warning flag in Nettie's peripheral vision to keep up, and they had done their circuit of Regent's Park in almost record time.

They reached the top of the steps and Nettie jogged on the spot as she 'allowed' Em to go down first (i.e. tried to catch her breath) before following after, her eyes on the black slick of the canal, a murky spine of ice in the water reaching towards the banks.

It was dark on the towpath, even though the street lamps shone, and Nettie felt the familiar frisson of nervousness she always felt when coming to Dan's in the winter months. He was a gentleman, of course, always insisting on walking her all the way home after their many suppers, but she did sometimes wish he would live in a normal house like most normal people. His mother, in Nettie's opinion, had a lot to answer for.

The houseboat – half the length of anything else on the canal and more like a tug than a barge – was called *Puffin*. The crooked stove pipe was already puffing more than they were, the lights glowing orange behind the thin green curtains at the windows. Music – Primal Scream, Nettie guessed – was playing through the speakers loudly enough to make the water round the hull vibrate, and they could tell from the way the dried-up flowerpots had been stacked neatly by the back door that Jules had already arrived.

'Hey!' Em panted, opening the door and peering into the small cabin. Four faces grinned back – Dan, Stevie, Jules and Paddy. The homely aroma of chicken korma from a sachet wafted over them, poppadoms burning in the small oven like black toast. Dan was looking hassled, waving a tea towel round to disperse the smoke, as Stevie and Paddy sat at the table, setting up the cards.

'Oh *grim*,' Jules grimaced as Nettie followed in after her with a stagger, grateful to have stopped running at last, her cheeks pink and large patches of sweat darkening her clothes.

'Oh, you don't mean that!' she retorted, arms outstretched and pretending to give her friend a bear hug.

'Keep away!' Jules laughed, holding up her cigarette as a defensive weapon. 'You could have done us all the courtesy of having a shower before you rocked up here, you know.'

'With what time?' Em asked, immediately beginning her gentle-stretching cool-down routine. She looked annoyingly fresh from the forty-five-minute run, while Nettie, limbs trembling with fatigue, had to sink onto the bench to recover. 'Dan was adamant we had to be here for seven p.m.,' she said from a deep runner's stretch.

'I hardly think twenty minutes would have mattered, here or there,' Jules said. 'Look at you both. You're going to stink.'

'They can have a shower here if they want,' Dan said. 'I've got some clean towels.'

'Clean?' Em scoffed. 'Yeah, right. I've seen your towels, Dan, and I know perfectly well you use them as bedding for the dog.'

As if on cue, Scout jumped onto the bench, standing on Nettie's lap and her tender muscles. 'Ooow!' she winced, trying to manoeuvre the dog into a better position. 'Don't you ever cut his nails, Dan?'

Dan shrugged, handing her a hydrating beer with a wink and a smile, and inadvertently knocking a pile of Doritos to the floor. Scout jumped off Nettie's lap – leaving her wincing all over again – and hoovered them up within seconds.

'Well, so long as I don't have to sit next to you,' Jules said, taking another drag of her cigarette and blowing out the smoke through the corner of her mouth.

'I've got a solution to Jules's problem,' Stevie said with a sly voice. 'We could always make this a game of *strip* poker.'

'Ha! Categorically no!' Jules scoffed.

'Why not, Jules?' Paddy said teasingly. 'You're always cleaning up. What's wrong? Feeling off your game? Not so sure you're going to win tonight?'

Jules stuck her tongue out at him and looked for something to throw, but Nettie knew – as any girl did – that the issue wasn't so much one of skill and bluff as whether or not her friend had shaved/put on decent underwear/juiced this week (delete as appropriate).

'Well, I'm up for it,' Em shrugged, jumping up from a hamstring stretch in which she had almost bent double, and grabbing her beer off the tiny Formica worktop. 'I've had a crap day. I need to blow off some steam.'

'You're telling me,' Nettie grumbled from her now-prone

position on the bench, knowing this was Em's cue for everyone to ask after her job and trying to divert attention away from the subject. Out of the lot of them, Em's was the one that carried true weight and significance. She parried with death every day, after all, and was never shy about recounting stories from her many, many years of further education. Stevie, on the other hand, had only two GCSEs, and Dan was more interested in the latest Arsenal result than his career.

'Bet it doesn't beat my day,' Paddy said, idly shuffling a deck of cards. 'I lost seventy-eight grand in three minutes this afternoon.'

'How many times have I got to tell you, mate? You can't be a broker without knowing how to count,' Stevie quipped. Paddy kicked him in the shin under the table.

'Yeah? Well, I had a water pipe blow in my face earlier,' Dan said, bringing over some more Doritos. 'Freezing, it was. Reckon I'll get hypothermia.'

'Tch. D'you feel another sickie coming on, then, Dan?' Jules teased.

'How about you, Nets?' Stevie asked. 'Any horror stories for you today?'

Nettie pushed herself up to sitting and glanced at Stevie. He grinned as she met his eye, and she knew he knew exactly what she'd been up to today – having raised £17,600 by lunchtime, the clip had been filed and she was trending again – and there was no doubt dangling from the Shard, anything but graceful as she arched back in the bunny suit, was her definition of a horror story.

'Me? No, it was quiet,' she mumbled with a warning look in her eyes, feeling guilty that she still hadn't let Em and Paddy – good friends though they were – into the secret. It wasn't a copyright issue anymore and she knew she could trust them to keep quiet about it if she asked. But something still held her back.

'Well, my day trumps all of yours,' Em said determinedly, going to stand near the pot-bellied stove. If no one would ask, she would just jolly well tell. 'I saved a pregnant woman's life after she'd officially died three times on the table, and then spent the afternoon being hauled in and out of the HR offices because the husband is upset I couldn't slash *didn't* save the baby too, so now he wants to make an official complaint.' Her face was white as she spoke, and for the first time Nettie saw the true cost of her friend's perfectionism. Life and death, every day, every hour, every patient.

Everyone fell silent, the gentle teasing buzz in the overcrowded cabin morphing into subdued sympathy for the unknown woman.

'I mean, the mother was my patient. In a scenario like that, you always prioritize the mother. Always.' She shook her head and took several deep swigs of her beer. Her hand was visibly shaking.

Nettie felt bad that she'd bitterly anticipated Em's news as just showing off. No wonder she had run tonight like she was chasing the wind, no wonder she needed to talk, drink, relax, play.

'Yeah, OK then, you win,' Stevie said finally, breaking the mood. 'Your day officially sucked most. But that doesn't mean you're going to win this game. I hope you're wearing lots of layers.'

Em just shrugged.

'We are *not* playing strip poker,' Nettie said firmly, picking up where Jules had left off.

'Em says we are. She won the Sucky Day Competition and she wants to play,' Stevie countered.

'What's wrong, Nets?' Dan grinned, his feet up on the table as he swigged his beer. 'Can't handle the heat?'

'No! I mean, yes! I mean . . .' she spluttered. 'You know what I mean!'

'You don't have anything we haven't seen before, do you?' He paused, a mock-shock look crossing his face. 'Oh no, wait, I always forget about your third nipple.'

The boat rocked with laughter.

'You are a pig!' Nettie giggled, grabbing a tea towel and throwing it at him, but it unfurled in flight and lilted to the ground like a feather.

Dan laughed harder. 'Tell you what – we'll give you a head start. You can layer up with some of my clothes.'

'I'll look *ridiculous* in your clothes. You're a foot taller than me.'

'Don't worry, it's not like you're going to be in them for long,' he laughed, getting up and disappearing into the private alcove area at the back of the boat.

'I'm not doing it!' she called after him, but he couldn't hear her above the sound of wardrobe doors clattering open and closed, and Primal Scream's banging bass beat.

Chapter Eight

The custard creams were out again, Mike pacing the conference room with a fervour approaching frenzy as he clicked the remote from one chart to the next, all of them showing the dramatic surge in donations and website traffic.

Nettie kept her eyes, as ever, on the rapidly staling biscuits, wishing someone would open the window. The room was airless and stuffy, dark pools of sweat were beginning to stain Mike's cream shirt, and the plastic Christmas tree in the corner was doing nothing to put her in the festive spirit. In fact, even the impressive number at which her fundraising pot now stood – £64,000 and rapidly rising – couldn't lift her mood.

She was having a bad day, even though professionally her career was at an all-time high and personally she was still alive, which was really saying something given that she had survived the risk of hypothermia on Monday, the terror of #whaleing off the Shard yesterday, and the indignity of #planking on top of a red postbox in the middle of Belgrave Square this morning. Ordinarily she would have been able to pull off the pose in a moment, but being dressed in the giant bunny costume had meant she'd had to balance her convex stomach on the postbox's equally convex top. It had been like stacking onions and she had been sure that a concussion, if not an arrest from one of the many foreign embassy guards, was going to be the most likely conclusion of that gag.

'White Tiger are all over this like a rash,' Mike was saying. 'It syncs with their brand image perfectly, and they're already even talking about carrying the Blue Bunny through on their advertising.'

'That makes no sense,' Caro said, twiddling her biro between her fingers. 'We've said this before. Why would a company called White Tiger advertise with a blue bunny?'

'Because the public has clearly *engaged* with the bunny, Caro,' Mike said testily. 'It doesn't have to be literal. And they're the client – let's not forget that. If they're happy, we're happy.'

Nettie wasn't anywhere near as happy as she should have been. While the Internet was hailing Blue Bunny Girl as a new cult trend and she was the new golden girl of the office, there had been no further contact from Jamie Westlake since his donation on Monday – not a smiley face or wink, even; seemingly balancing bunnies on postboxes just weren't funny to him – and she felt disproportionately despondent to have lost the attention of this person she had never met. She was sure Jules was now borderline OCD, checking almost hourly that the number of people Jamie followed remained at eighteen, and Nettie had a dread in the pit of her stomach that to engage him once again, Jules was going to have her do something out there, something crazy, stupid, nuts.

Mike scratched his ear, irritated to have been knocked off his stride. 'Where was I?'

'Advertising,' Daisy said, without looking up from her doodles on the sketchpad.

'Right. Which is incredible news. We are influencing company image, which goes far, far beyond our normal scope and really says something about the success of this campaign.' He pulled both hands into fists and jabbed them in the air. 'So we need to keep it up, people. Donations to the charity – your pot, Nettie – are increasing by a hundred and seventy-four per cent day on day, and we're fully expecting that to triple by the week's end.' He rubbed his hands together, clearly sensing another promotion in the air. 'So where are we with tomorrow's fun and games?'

'I reckon "hashtag unicorning" would be funny,' Daisy said.

'And what's that?' Nettie asked warily but resignedly.

'You just wear a unicorn's head in a random place,' Daisy shrugged.

Nettie sighed. The things that people did for kicks! 'Well, given that I'm already dressed as a bunny, a unicorn's head might possibly be overkill?'

'Oh yeah, good point.'

'What about "hashtag sandbagging"?' Caro offered up.

'Never heard of it.'

'You have to put your arms and feet up on something like, say, a bench and let your middle sag down like a sandbag. Like planking but . . . saggy.'

'I'm not sure I'd be able to keep myself up on anything. That costume's heavy.'

'Right.' Caro slumped in her chair.

'Cat-breading's hilarious, but I don't see how we could make it work for you,' Jules said. 'Your head's too big in the bunny head.'

'What even is that? Did you say "cat-breading"?'

'Yeah. You punch a hole in a slice of bread and then put it round a cat's head like a frame. It is bloody funny.'

'Bloody funny,' Caro echoed with a chuckle, nodding along.

'What a shame it is that my head's too big for that to work,' Nettie said lightly, earning herself a swipe on the arm from Jules.

'How about a photo bomb? That could be good if we get it to coincide with something high profile,' Daisy said, straightening up. 'Are there any big parties, any premieres happening this week?'

'Ooh, that's good, Daisy. I like it,' Mike said.

'Hang on a minute, hang on a minute,' Caro said with quiet excitement as she tapped on her iPad. 'If I'm right, then I think . . .'

Nettie mentally assumed the brace position.

'Yes, bingo! The new Bond's out. It's the world premiere in Leicester Square tomorrow night.'

Everyone's eyes brightened as they swivelled over to Nettie.

'Oh yes,' Jules grinned. 'This is going to be brilliant!'

Getting in wasn't a problem. There wasn't a list in London Daisy couldn't get past, thanks to her five-foot-long legs and an expensive education in Bucks that meant she had a network of influential contacts she leveraged for everything from finding a plumber to borrowing a friend's father's car in the South of France during Cannes week.

In this instance, she had gone to university with the girlfriend of the brother of the girl, Mimsy, who now worked in the marketing division for Eon Productions (the company that made the Bond films), and in return for getting her and the girls in to the premiere, Daisy had promised to get her VIP Veranda tickets for La Folie Douce in Val d'Isère in March. Jules called it 'silver-spoon swapsies'.

They had deliberately arrived early. Not early enough to beat the eight-deep crowd of fans standing behind the barricades who had been camping out since the day before last, but early enough that the paparazzi were still checking their equipment as Nettie, Jules, Daisy and Caro quickly marched down the red carpet and into the foyer of the Odeon cinema, where last-minute tweaks were still being made in readiness for the stars' arrival. It had been agreed – by a vote of their four to his one – that Mike shouldn't attend. His presence, as a lone middle-aged male in a group of young, attractive twenty-something women, they had argued, would only bring attention to them all, and that was the last thing Nettie needed. The bigger her following was becoming, the more she wanted to hide. Accordingly, she was dressed like a shadow in black leggings, a black skinny jumper and ballet pumps, while the rest of the girls were dressed up to the nines. Daisy, who looked like a Bond Girl in a strapless silver lamé dress, had tried cheering her up by saying that she looked like Audrey Hepburn, but Nettie knew Ms Hepburn had never worried about wobbly bits or VPL or blue-tinged feet on a perishing December night.

Inside the cinema, anticipation put a crackle in the air, everyone's eyes fixed to the huge glass doors as the clamour of the crowds grew.

Nettie stood by the far wall with a deepening depression (having been asked on more than one occasion where the toilets were) looking back at the scene outside. An enormous Christmas tree twinkled in the dusk in the middle of the square, outshone by the bright lights of the premiere parties. Teenage girls in furry-lined parkas and beanies were stamping their feet and blowing on their fingers, pressing against the red corded ropes and gathered in small groups, laughing with high-pitched voices and pink cheeks, their excitement visibly growing as the minutes ticked past. The photographers had arranged themselves in an orderly bank just outside the doors, allowing them to get plenty of shots of the stars stopping to chat, sign autographs and take selfies with the fans, before pausing for the clean 'static' shots just in front of them. Someone was hoovering the carpet so that not a footprint or a leaf marred the scarlet perfection.

Nettie couldn't take her eyes off the security teams, who were already in place too, tank-sized chests puffed as they checked their relays. She swallowed nervously. Little did they know what they were going to be contending with tonight. *Her.*

Jules came back with the drinks. 'Here. Down that. You look like you could do with it.'

'What is it?'

'Vodka tonic. We need something fast-acting to get you to loosen up.'

'Right.' Nettie took a large gulp. It burned her throat and made her eyes water. 'Wow, that's strong. Blimey, that actually gave me a flashback to uni!' She wiped her eyes. 'Where are the others?'

'Caro's double-checking the car's parked round the corner. Daisy's at the back door with a face like thunder.

She's having to chat up the porter while she waits for the courier to deliver the suit.'

'Uh-huh.' Nettie couldn't muster any sympathy. It was herself she felt most sorry for tonight. She bit her lip, looking back out into the square again, her eyes on the faces in the crowd. 'Hey, do you think we'll get to see Judi Dench?'

'Hon, we're not going to see anyone. You've got to pick a target, do what you gotta do and get out of there. No time to schmooze or hobnob with the stars tonight, I'm afraid. Besides, her character died in the last one,' Jules added, putting down her sequinned Anya Hindmarch clutch to fiddle with the skirt of her black dress, which was fractionally too tight and looked all the better for it. Jules had an athletic, naturally slim figure but with a hint of ripeness on the breasts, thighs and arms that always managed to make her clothes looks a size too small. Men loved it.

Caro came back to them, her beloved phone clutched to her chest like it was a baby bird. 'Right. The driver's round the corner and good to go. Oh, is that for me?' she asked, picking up Jules's untouched drink and despatching the vodka tonic like it was a shot, smacking her lips together afterwards.

Jules tutted like a weary headmistress and without a word wandered back to the bar to get another drink.

'You look fed up,' Caro said, taking in Nettie's muted mood.

'I feel like Cinders in her "before" outfit,' Nettie grumbled. 'People keep thinking I'm staff. I've been asked where the loos are five times already.'

Caro chuckled. 'Little do they know you're the star of tonight's show.'

Nettie huffed, nervous and wanting it to be over and done with. 'Green really suits you,' she said, envying the sight of Caro in her narrow emerald satin tux and wishing that, just for once, she got to wore something beautiful.

'Huh.' Caro just shrugged and tucked her long, straight hair behind her ears. She never seemed particularly bothered by what she wore, but her skinny frame – which had seen her badly teased at school – looked sensational in clothes and she was able to make an ultra-narrow trouser suit look as relaxed as pyjamas. The trousers stopped an inch above her ankles, but rather than wearing vertiginous heels, she had pulled on a pair of black mannish brogues – 'Perfect for running in,' she'd explained earlier, frantically chewing on her gum, which hadn't done anything to soothe Nettie's nerves.

The foyer was filling up, mainly with the behind-the-scenes people who were the unsung heroes of the project – the lighting director, post-production editors, sound crew and wardrobe team – as well as the producers and executives who made it all happen. There wasn't a single face Nettie recognized and she felt sick at the thought of what she had to do with the ones she would.

'Jules doesn't think we'll get to see Judi Dench. I just love her face. Don't you love her face?'

Caro stopped chewing. 'Huh? She's old.'

Nettie brought her hands up to her face and waggled her fingers. 'Twinkly eyes.'

'What you talking about?' Jules asked, rejoining the conversation, drink clutched firmly in her hand this time.

'Judi Dench,' Caro muttered, scanning the room for celebrities.

KAREN SWAN

'She's got such lovely eyes. I really hope we see her,' Nettie said, wiggling her fingers again.

'I told you, her character died in the last one. She won't be here.'

Nettie felt nerves grip her again, giving her stomach a squeeze that made her close her eyes. She wasn't cut out for this kind of adventure. Jules, Caro, Daisy – they were all, in their different ways, ballsy and gutsy and feisty; they could do this kind of tomfoolery in their sleep. But Nettie? She was a home bird who thought living the good life was a bubble bath and a miniature bottle of fizz sucked through a straw with the latest issue of *Grazia* magazine.

'Well, will we get to see any of the film? We could sneak in afterwards,' she said hopefully.

'Oh really? You think we'll be able to pull that off?' Caro asked sceptically. 'Listen, a clean getaway is all we ask for.' Her phone buzzed in her hand and she looked down at it with a wry smile. 'Oh – it looks like the eagle has landed,' she said. 'Come on. It's this way.'

The girls followed her as she pushed through a door that had a yellow 'Authorized personnel only' sign on it and trooped down a corridor with strip lighting and concrete floors. Nettie began to feel sick.

A glare of light and a sudden drop in temperature indicated a door at the end was open, and they headed straight for it. But as they passed a sign for the ladies', they heard a loud hiss.

'Psst. In here.'

Caro did an about-turn and doubled-back into the toilets, where Daisy was struggling to prop open the fire door with her foot while holding up, behind her, a full-length hanging bag. The zip strained to close in the middle, where it ballooned grotesquely, and a pale blue impression glowed gently through the white plastic.

'Great,' Caro grinned, nodding at the sight of it.

'This thing weighs a *ton*,' Daisy gasped as Caro helped take it.

'I told you! How do you think I feel? I've got to wear the damn thing,' Nettie moaned.

'Did they ask what it was?' Caro asked.

'I said it was a spare ballgown for Helen Mirren.'

The girls burst out laughing.

'What?' Daisy demanded. 'I had to say something.'

'It's a bloody strange ballgown!' Jules laughed. 'Unless the toffee-apple silhouette is where we're all gonna be at next season.'

'Listen, I've just had to chat up a spotty teenage porter with halitosis for forty-five minutes while you've been hob-nobbing in the bar. I'd like to see you think of anything better. What else was I supposed to say?'

'That you got the days wrong and it's a prop for the screening of *Toy Story*?' Jules laughed again.

'Oh, just shut up and help me get this thing in the cubicle,' Daisy muttered. 'If anyone comes in and sees it, we're blown.'

She and Caro carried the hanging bag to the toilet stall, where it promptly jammed in the narrow doorway.

'No, wait, you're . . . Tch, let me,' Caro muttered, pulling it free again and helping Daisy to tug it through the door-way. 'Can one of you push it, please?' she called from the other side of the cubicle.

Nettie walked over and began to push. The suit was engineered with an inner frame and its circumference was several centimetres bigger than the door aperture.

'I don't think it's going to go,' Nettie groaned, pushing as hard as she could, just as it suddenly popped through the doorway and there was a clatter as something – or rather, someone – fell onto the loo.

'Oh my God!' Jules gasped.

'Careful!' Daisy yelled from the other side of the cubicle wall.

Nettie looked back at Jules. 'What's wrong?'

'I've left my bag in the foyer!'

Nettie winced. The bag – albeit bought in the sale – had still cost the same as a washing machine (which Jules had also needed at the time) and many sacrifices were having to be made (the cost of weekly new undies bit into her 'weekend kitty') whilst she tried to save up for one.

'I'm sure it's perfectly safe out there. Why would anyone take it? It's not like the place is packed with destitutes—'

But Jules had already gone, the door slamming on its hinges as her red-soled footsteps skittered along the concrete floor.

'Uh, Houston, we have a problem,' Caro called over the doorway.

Nettie looked back and realized what it was in an instant. Ducking down to see below the stall door, she could see Caro's and Daisy's legs in awkward positions as they tried to manoeuvre round the toilet and the vast, bulbous shape of the bunny suit that had almost filled the tiny space.

'Oh fucking hell! We can't get back out!' Daisy shouted crossly. 'You're going to have to pull it out again!'

Nettie laughed suddenly at the ridiculous conundrum. Why hadn't they thought of that a moment ago? Why were they even doing this? It was the definition of craziness to have blagged their way into this event in the first place, much less to now be wrestling in the loos with a giant, jammed bunny costume. Her nerves quickly latched on to the hilarity of the situation – plus the vodka – and she laughed harder. Maybe, if the suit could stay jammed in there, she wouldn't have to go through with tonight's stunt. They had sailed easily through today's fundraising target of £20,000 so this could be her saving grace.

'Stop bloody laughing and get us out of here!' Daisy shouted again, stamping her new Sandra Choi shoe and accidentally stabbing Caro in the foot.

'Ow!' Caro yelled. 'Fucking hell, Daise! What are you bloody doing?!'

Nettie began to howl. Somewhere along the way they had turned into a *Carry On* film.

'Stop laughing, Nettie! It's not funny!'

'S-sorry,' Nettie cried, wiping her eyes clear but still shaking with laughter as she feebly tried to pinch some of the hanging bag and begin to pull it through. But it was like pulling a button through the eye of a needle and she was still far too amused to be of much practical help.

Behind her, the door swung open again.

'Jules, help me with this,' she giggled, giving another heave and leaning back into a deep squat that she could never manage in her circuits classes.

'Well . . .' a deep voice said behind her. It certainly didn't belong to Jules and she let go of the bag in surprise and fright, falling backwards. But she didn't hit the cold, hard floor. Instead, a pair of arms caught her – just – and lifted her to standing, a waft of whisky and musk wrapping round her like smoke before she could turn.

Behind the cubicle, Daisy and Caro had fallen silent,

their squabble suspended as they held their breaths, wondering who had rumbled them.

Nettie turned, her shoulders by her ears in apprehension as she braced herself for the sight of the security guard about to throw her out. But the khaki eyes looking down at her were glittering with amusement, not suspicion; the narrow suit was no uniform but had a cut that could only have been stitched by Jermyn Street elves; and the face watching her surprise unfold was no stranger's but as familiar to her as her own.

Oh God. Oh God.

'I detect mischief,' the man said with a sudden grin, leaning against the wall, one hand in his trouser pocket.

Nettie shook her head wordlessly. Jamie Westlake was here, in the ladies' loos. He was right here, talking to her, in the ladies' loos.

He raised an eyebrow at her silence. It didn't seem to bother him particularly and she realized he probably got this reaction a lot. His eyes seemed to absorb her without moving, as though he could see all of her – hands, toes, clattering heart – in his direct line of sight.

'No? So what are you doing, then?'

Nettie's mouth opened, but no sound came out and she closed it again.

His eyes lifted off her – her body temperature cooling by five degrees as he did so – and he looked over at the giant blue-tinted plastic bag now firmly wedged in the door. Daisy and Caro had each lifted their feet off the floor and Nettie could only imagine the two of them crouched on the toilet seat, their hands pressed against the walls as they held their breath and waited for – what they must suppose to be – the security guard to leave.

Another laugh suddenly bubbled up inside her at the image, nerves and hysteria one and the same thing now, for the situation – if it had been bizarre before – had now veered into the downright unbelievable. She would remember this moment for the rest of her life. She would dine out on this for weeks. She would tell her grandchildren of the night she gatecrashed a Bond party and—

'What *is* that thing?' He took a step towards the cubicle and she was jolted back to reality.

'It's a dress!' she cried.

Jamie stopped and leaned against the wall again. 'A dress?'

'Mm-hmm,' she nodded furiously.

He arched an eyebrow. 'Bloody odd-shaped dress.'

'Ball dress.' She coughed nervously.

He was quiet for a moment, before turning back to her. 'And this is a ball dress for . . . you?' This time, his eyes travelled over the length of her, tiptoeing round her narrow, black-clad silhouette, the sweep of his gaze over her gentle curves like fingers. It was like being brushed by a feather and she suppressed a shiver.

He saw.

She took a step back, trying to focus. She had to get a grip. There was too much at stake here for her to allow even Jamie Westlake to rumble tonight's skit. 'Helen Mirren.'

'*Dame* Helen Mirren?' Amusement threaded his voice and she wondered if he was buying any of this or just enjoying the charade. His eyes were latched on to hers like they'd been bolted and it syringed the breath out of her so that she could only nod. 'So you're her assistant?'

She swallowed. 'That's right. I have to keep the dress out of sight in case she . . .' Her voice faded as she ran out of lie. 'Um, you know, changes her mind about what to wear.'

The eyebrow went up again. Right one. She made a mental note. For the grandchildren. 'Changes her mind *after* she's walked the red carpet?'

He was tripping her up, knowing far better than she how occasions like this worked. 'Exactly. She likes to change into something, uh . . . more comfortable for the . . . screening.' She kept her eyes off the bulbous silhouette that would span two, if not three chairs in the screening room and make sitting an impossibility.

'I see.' The way he angled his head, the smile on his lips, told her he saw how it was exactly. He was no fool. He straightened up suddenly and made to move towards the cubicle. 'Well, I'd better help you, then. I wouldn't want Dame Helen to be without options tonight.'

'No, it's fine – I've got it,' Nettie said, all but throwing herself in front of the stall, her arms outstretched to block his efforts. 'It has to be, uh . . . confidential.'

He looked down at her, so close now that she could see a few tiny flecks of gold in his irises. How had she never noticed them before? She had gazed at his image on the 'Sidebar of Shame' often enough that she thought she knew every contour of his face, but a flat image conveyed nothing of the aura that came with the 3D model – the stubble coming through that looked like it would be soft against her palm, the ever-ready smile that seemed to start and end in his eyes, the natural forward-push of his lips that she had assumed was a self-aware pout for photographs, the party scent that told her all those mad, bad headlines were probably true.

'Thanks, though, for the offer,' she said, swallowing hard. His eyes were on her mouth. He was actually staring at her mouth.

His eyes rose back to hers and she knew she wasn't imagining what she saw in them. She'd read all the stories about him – she could list, right now, even with her head spinning, five A-list actresses he had had affairs with. He was the bad boy of the music world, bad in any world frankly and far, *far* too dangerous for a girl like her.

'What's your name?'

He wanted to know her name. Jamie Westlake was interested in her, even if it was just for the next ten minutes. Which it would be.

But she didn't have time to reply. The red-soled patter of Jules running back down the corridor made them both look over just as the door was flung open and her friend stood triumphant, holding her clutch bag aloft.

'Oh holy crap!' she cried, recognizing Jamie immediately and falling into the same stunned silence as Nettie had sported not two minutes earlier. Jamie straightened, stepping back from Nettie and the hanging bag, one hand slipping into his trouser pocket as he waited for the intruder to recover. Again, he seemed used to it.

'What the hell's he doing in the ladies'?' Jules asked Nettie, as though it was the fact that he was in the *ladies'* and not that *he*, Jamie Westlake, the most gorgeous man in the world – official – was in the same room as them that was the pertinent point.

'My mistake – I thought it was the gents',' Jamie said with a wink that made Jules's eyes light up. She fiddled with her black dress quickly, all the right bits wobbling, and Nettie's heart sank. See? There it was, the roguish charm, the boyish diffidence that made women the world over just collapse in heaps before him. Jules hadn't even stepped into the room and she was already in full flirt mode.

Jamie turned back to Nettie. 'Well, it was nice meeting you.' His eyes roamed her mouth again. 'I'll be sure to compliment Dame Helen on her dress later.'

'Yes. Fine,' Nettie managed.

He didn't move for several seconds and she willed herself not to swallow, not to betray her nerves. And then he turned and left.

'Have a good night,' he said to Jules as he passed her at the door.

'Oh, I will,' Jules replied in her huskiest voice.

Nettie wanted to hit her, but she didn't move. She waited for the sound of his footsteps to disappear. She needed to be sure he was gone.

Jules didn't.

'Oh. My. God!' Jules scream-whispered, running towards her with her eyes wide with delight and grabbing Nettie's hands. 'What the *hell*?'

'Has he gone?' Daisy asked from behind the cubicle wall, just as Caro groaned and unwound herself from the contorted position she had had to maintain for the past few minutes.

'Jeez, I thought he'd never shut up!' Caro complained. 'Was it that bloody porter flirting? I bet he was looking for you, Daise.'

'The porter?' Jules guffawed as she realized their limited view of the encounter. 'Oh God, don't tell me you missed it!' she laughed, grabbing a handful of the bag and giving it an almighty tug as the others pushed from the far side. The bunny suit came free suddenly and they all stumbled across the room in varying states of excitement and disgruntlement. 'That was only bloody Jamie Westlake.'

Daisy and Caro – who'd almost fallen over each other in a tangle of skinny legs – both froze. 'You what?' Caro asked.

'The bloke just in here was Jamie Westlake.' Jules chewed on her own knuckle.

Both girls looked at Nettie. 'That bloke you were talking to was Jamie Westlake?' Daisy echoed in disbelief. She slapped a hand to her forehead. 'I *knew* I recognized his voice.' Her voice had slipped into the next octave up.

Nettie just shrugged. The momentary high had left her now with a crushing low. Simply being in his orbit had made her feel weightless and sprinkled with fairy dust. She had felt warm and breathless in his gaze, and stepping out of it, even after only three minutes with him, the world felt altered and diminished somehow.

'Well, no wonder you sounded so moronic, then,' Caro said, chewing her gum with the usual speed. 'I did wonder why you could barely string a sentence together.'

'I was shocked!' Nettie protested. 'He was the last person I expected to see in here.'

'Jamie Westlake was three feet away from us and we missed it?' Daisy wailed, off on her own riff of missed opportunity.

'What was he even doing in here?' Jules asked Nettie.

'You heard the man. He thought it was the gents'.'

'Yeah, right. He missed the massive picture of the Victorian lady on the door, did he?'

'Well, I don't know, do I? I was more concerned with trying to stop him seeing the outfit.'

Jules gasped as she looked down at the inflated bag on the floor. 'Did you tell him who you are?'

'No.'

'He asked her name, but she was too star-struck to remember it,' Caro said, rolling her eyes.

'I wasn't! I was just—'

'I don't meant that,' Jules interrupted. 'I meant, did you tell him that you're Blue Bunny Girl?'

'No, of course not!'

It was apparently the wrong thing to have said.

'Why not?' Jules wailed. 'He's following you! You're one of his eighteen. He thinks you're a crazy chick. He thinks you're cute.'

'Not so cute that he recognized me, though, huh?' Nettie said sulkily.

'Oh, get over yourself. You were only visible on the clip for a few seconds.'

Caro wandered over to the bunny costume and unzipped it from the bag. 'Hate to break up the party, girls, but the man's gone, and if he's here, you can be sure all the other A-listers are arriving too. That means we need to get you out on that carpet pronto.'

'Oh God, yeah, I totally forgot,' Jules said, checking the time on her phone. She pulled a face. 'Damn. It's nearly seven thirty. We need to get on with it.'

'I can't believe it,' Daisy whispered to herself, wandering over to the basins and staring at her beautiful reflection in the mirror. So near and yet . . .

Caro held out the bunny suit. 'Daise, go and guard the door. We can't have anyone else barging in. Come on, Nets, hop in.' She winked and gave an enormous grin. 'Ha! Get it?'

Chapter Nine

'So, ladies and gentlemen, this is how we do it,' Jules said with a flourish as she let the newspaper spin into the centre of the French-polished conference table. All eyes came to rest on the photos of the giant blue bunny photo-bombing Daniel Craig and Ralph Fiennes as they had stood, suave in their dinner suits, eyes slightly narrowed to the cameras.

Even Nettie had to smile at the sight of her blue ears protruding behind their heads, her large paws held aloft as she had suddenly popped into view and the cameras had gone wild for it. Craig and Fiennes . . . Mmm, rather less so, but by the time they'd realized what was happening, she was already sprinting down the carpet, dodging security, who were slow off the mark and hadn't anticipated a rogue blue bunny in their security briefings.

Up till then, her notoriety had been an Internet phenomenon, known only to those hipsters and geeks who cared about the tech zeitgeist – Caro was over the moon, for example, that YouTube likes of the clip she had filmed and posted were at 844,000, and crucially, #bluebunnygirl had trended on Twitter for three hours afterwards, delighting Jules. But this was bigger than a Web trend now. It was becoming a cultural tour de force, hitting the mainstream. She had made the local London news at ten o'clock last night and was on the front page of every red-top paper today.

Jeremy Maxwell, the head of CSR at White Tiger and chairing this latest emergency meeting at their plush offices in Mayfair, sat back in his chair. Pleasantries over the Nicaraguan coffee and fresh, warm almond croissants – Mike was making mental notes to upgrade from the biscuit tin the next time they hosted their important guests – had revealed he was tanned and lean from a week's cycling holiday in Croatia, and he exuded the kind of low-key confidence that comes from undisputed power. His company's contract was worth more than £6 million to their little firm; his suit was worth more than their annual stationery budget; his tie cost more than Mike's suit – and as such, Mike was a nervous wreck.

'You've done well. I take my hat off to you all. Especially you, Nettie. What you've been asked to do this last week, it can't have been easy.'

'Thanks,' Nettie smiled, resisting the urge to roll her eyes at his understatement. Easy? She'd like to see *him* whale off the Shard or photo-bomb James Bond. Dressed as a bunny.

There was a small silence and she saw Mike sit forward, leaning his forearms on the table. Everyone sensed the 'but' – it was as present in the room as the Chinese rug and rare orchids.

Jeremy smiled as he looked at him. 'But where's White Tiger in all of this? We're paying you to link us with charitable causes that mesh with the brand, and you're doing a fine job of fundraising and highlighting the works of these charities, a fine job. But I see no mention of White Tiger's involvement in all this.'

'Well, obviously the branding was in place at the Ice Crush clip, and we got the kit on the powerlifters for the Ice Bucket Challenge,' Mike said hurriedly.

'But since then . . . ?' Jeremy gave an exaggerated shrug. 'As much as I want our charitable partners to benefit from their link-up with us, we are not in this merely to provide free marketing for them. That's the quid; where's the quo?'

Mike looked sick and for once Nettie felt sorry for him.

Jules leaned forward. 'You've hit the nail on the head, Jeremy. Absolutely. Where *is* White Tiger? Yes, we've created that most elusive of things – a trend. You can't hold it or touch it or capture it. It's just fleeting, an irrational, collective sense of want or need, and *we've* got it. Right now, in the space of a week, we've snowballed a one-off, freak event into a daily happening that's got people logging on especially to get the latest update. There is nothing hotter or funnier or cooler than "hashtag ballzup" right now.

'But that's only phase one. That was just creating the appetite for this campaign. We had to get that ball rolling first – bringing in the corporate element too early would have scared people off. No one likes to feel they're being bought. The only reason these things mushroom like this is if people feel that they're in on the secret, that *they're* manipulating it – sharing it to their friends, retweeting, liking. It's got to be organic. They want to be the ones in control. Not you, not us.

'Now, we've got the momentum on our side – it's hit the mainstream – but that means the bubble is going to burst at any moment. Timing for what happens next is crucial. The hipsters are going to fall away *unless* we ramp the campaign up again, raise the stakes somehow and keep it fresh. And this is where we need to actively draw in your brand.

The public has already made the connection between the blue bunny and the "ballzup" hashtag, which in turn is connected to Tested. They like it; they share it; they donate to it.

'But in phase two, when the public thinks of the Blue Bunny Girl, we want them to think White Tiger too. She's your product, your do-good mascot. Everyone loves her.' Jules's eyes twinkled. 'And as you can see from these headlines, they want to know more about her.'

'Actually, this is something that's been emerging in our meta-data. They're all beginning to ask the same question now: "Who is the Blue Bunny Girl?"' Scott Faulkner murmured. As White Tiger's UK head of media strategy and Jeremy's deputy, he was fiercer than his boss, the snarling pit bull to Jeremy's sleek Weimaraner.

Jeremy smiled, rubbing his hands together. 'So then we put her out there. Roll her out at the big events. We've got the World Diving Championships in Sydney next month.'

Nettie gripped her own thigh hard. If they thought she was going to dive off a cliff . . .

Caro shook her head. 'No, no, that's too far away, dates-wise. We've got another week left, tops. We need to go out on a high. And anyway, we have to build up her mystique. The last thing we want is to unveil Nettie and have everyone see she's just a normal girl-next-door who still lives with her parents . . .'

Nettie felt her cheeks burn as the suited men's eyes slid over to her quizzically. She looked adult enough in her black trousers and red jumper today.

'Your consumers are thrill-seekers, and right now they're loving the thrill of the chase: what's she going to do next?

Where? Who is she? It's Banksy for . . . not-artists. They're loving that kind of guerrilla element to it.'

'Exactly! We've kept her identity secret till now . . .' Jules paused, 'mainly to stop her getting arrested again, I grant you' – everybody laughed – 'but we should use this as another marketing tool. The public loves a mystery, and it gives the press a game of cat-and-mouse too. Therefore, on no account now should her name get out there.'

Jeremy looked at Scott. 'We'll need to get legal to draw up confidentiality contracts. Anyone who knows her identity needs to sign.'

Scott nodded in agreement.

Caro narrowed her eyes, deep in thought. 'In which case, we'll need to re-edit the clips too. You can see her face for a second or two in the Ice Crush and Ice Bucket shorts. I'll see if I can blur it out.' She made a note on her iPad.

Nettie sat quietly, pleased by this development at least. It suited her very well not to have anyone know who she was. The bigger this thing was becoming, the more she wanted to hide herself away. It didn't feel like it was her out there, doing those things, anyway, and Blue Bunny Girl had an identity that was far removed from hers. Caro was right – it would only be a disappointment for people to see what she was really like; it could even lose her followers, damage the campaign.

'OK. This is all great, but exactly how are you going to make the public link the blue bunny to us?' asked Scott. 'They're logging on to see what she does next; they're donating to the charity as exposure goes up, but where's the benefit to White Tiger? Where's the connection?'

Everyone was quiet. Mike was looking panicked that

what he had assumed was a glory parade had turned into something more worrisome. They needed a *plan.*

Nettie's phone buzzed with an incoming text and she surreptitiously slid it under the desk to read.

She frowned as she saw who it was from.

'Tried to call but keeps going to voicemail. Just checking in. Nothing new to report here. Call me if you need to talk. Gwen.'

'Well, to my mind, she's going to have to go back to what started this off in the first place. She's got to do these pranks at our events,' Jeremy said. 'That way, the branding is there and we're bringing the spotlight onto our community.'

What? White fear prickled through Nettie's veins, emboldening her. She was *not* going down that ice course again. 'No, I'm not a stuntman,' she said quickly. 'What happened was an accident, and not one I wish to repeat – not even to keep my job.'

Jeremy put his hands up in a 'whoa!' gesture and laughed. 'Nettie, Nettie, nobody's going to lose their job. We're in a position of strength here. There's a positive way round this fix. Let's take a moment – we'll think of something.'

But the universe was against her, and time spun slowly out like a thread on a spool. No one had anything to offer. The room fell silent, some people beginning to doodle on their notepads, others chewing on their pens as they stared at the ceiling, and Nettie began chewing her thumbnail, her legs jigging anxiously.

'We'll get a celeb on board,' Daisy said, her eyes brightening with the sudden idea.

'Why? It's hardly subtle, and certainly not cheap,' Scott

said dismissively. 'What would be the point? We've already got a mascot in the bunny.'

'Yes, but you're known for sponsoring big-name athletes and thrill-seeking sports teams – people doing even more extreme things than the bunny – as well as attaching your brand to the wider lifestyle interests of that community: festivals, rallies. So, your person, who encompasses all that, becomes an ambassador for the charity. And you can use someone already under contract to you so you wouldn't need to pay out.'

Jeremy and Scott swapped looks. Everyone's backs straightened.

'And if we have some big, splashy press conference to announce the link-up . . .' Daisy said. 'We'll introduce them with Blue Bunny Girl on the stage so that the connection is subliminally made between them all, creating a trinity of sorts – White Tiger celebrity ambassador, Blue Bunny Girl, Tested.'

'Could we get the celebrity to do some of the crazy stuff with the bunny?' Scott wondered.

'Depends who it is, but in theory, why not?' Daisy shrugged. 'If they're game for a laugh. Fans of the celeb then get exposed to Blue Bunny and vice versa; meanwhile White Tiger reaps the goodwill and, by extension, brand loyalty.'

Scott looked across at Jeremy, nodding. 'I like it. I like it. That could work.'

'I agree.' Jeremy looked thoughtful, pressing his fingers together into the steeple that Mike always copied. 'Who have we got?'

'Where do you start?' Scott asked, blowing out his

KAREN SWAN

cheeks. 'I'll have to get on to the special relations team. It could be anyone from the White Tigers to—'

'But they're in New York. They're your soccer team, right? The ones you sponsor?' Jules cut in. 'We'd need someone who's in London right now if we're going to tie it in to the "hashtag ballzup" campaign. We've got the momentum; we need to stay with it.'

Scott frowned. 'Well, that's going to knock out a lot of them. Most are in the States.'

'Any of the F1 boys?' Jeremy asked.

Scott pulled a face. 'Not sure. Maybe. The next Grand Prix's not till March . . . I could make some calls.'

'They've got to be outspoken and fearless,' Mike said, puffing out his chest and feeling his moment had come to make his mark on proceedings. 'The problem Tested has come up against in the past is that celebs don't want to be associated with something like testicular cancer. It's just not' – he held his fingers in the air and made speech marks – '"sexy". Now, if we were working with one of the breast cancer charities . . .'

Scott frowned. 'Eighty per cent of the athletes we endorse are male, Mike. Testicular cancer concerns them, therefore it concerns us.'

'Exactly. Exactly my point,' Mike said, quickly sliding into a U-turn. 'We've *got* to break this taboo. Men are literally dying because of embarrassment.'

Scott sat back in his chair, regarding Mike warily. 'As I said, I'll have to speak to the special relations team and see who'll best fit. We'll take all these requirements into consideration – London-based, outspoken.'

'Great,' Jules said, pushing back her chair. 'Well, then if

you'll excuse me, I'll start getting the press conference set up. We need to have it sorted for later on today.'

'Today?' Scott laughed.

'This is the Fifth Dare of Christmas in the campaign, Scott,' Jules shrugged. 'Time's not on our side. And if we want to set up a schedule of events for the celeb and Blue Bunny Girl, then we need to crack on. There's only a week left.'

'Yes, right, I see your point.' Scott nodded, his eyes narrowed in confirmation. He gave a more decided nod. 'I'll put a memo out and confirm with you after lunch.'

'Great.'

Ten minutes later they were sitting in the taxi on the way back to the office, Mike pensive and quiet as Daisy rang round the big hotels scouting for a venue and Caro got the latest figures updates from Tested. Jules was already drafting the press release. Nettie was quietly going through the messages on her Twitter account.

Yet again there were more than she could count, more than she could possibly read, and she flicked through them with silent detachment. The more she received, the less she felt they had anything to do with her. They were responding to the Blue Bunny, not her; all the things she was doing wouldn't be half so funny or amusing if it was just her doing them. She would just be any random brown-haired girl planking on a postbox or having a bathful of ice emptied over her, but factor in the giant and very blue bunny costume and the tenor changed completely. It was bizarre, ridiculous, inane. Cool.

She caught sight of a red number one in the top corner of the page, attached to a blue envelope icon.

'What's that?' she asked, showing Jules.

Jules looked up, her gaze distant, her mind still on the draft she was writing. 'Huh? Oh, a direct message.'

'Why's it not with all the others?'

Jules sighed. 'Jeez, you really are a relic. It's a private message that can only be sent if you are following that person and they are following you.'

'Oh. So it's safe for me to click on, then?'

Jules sighed again, visibly weakened by Nettie's technical illiteracy. 'Yes. Your iPad won't explode; the network won't crash; North Korea won't send out a hit squad. It's perfectly safe.'

Nettie shot her friend a sarcastic smile as she clicked on the red number. 'Thanks. I was just *checking*.'

She looked down at the message.

'*Very good. #bond.*'

She blinked, and then blinked again. It was from him, Jamie – a picture of him on stage somewhere, lights everywhere, beside the tweet, that all-important blue tick telling her it was him.

She held her breath and looked around the cab in utter shock, but everyone was busy and preoccupied, and she looked back down at the message again, feeling sick and excited and giddy all at once, as though it was perfectly normal to receive a private message from someone like him on a Friday morning. She remembered the gold flecks in his eyes, the smell of smoke, how his eyes had rested on her mouth . . .

Hesitantly, she replied, '*Thanks.*'

She winced as soon as she pressed 'send'. Oh God. Take it back. Could she take it back? It was so boring. Dull. She was @BlueBunnyGirl, for heaven's sake. She should have said something witty or sarcastic. Or just ignored him. Anything but 'thanks', like a good girl at the table at Sunday lunch.

She sighed and looked out of the window. She was no good at this kind of thing. Jules and Caro and Daisy would all have the sass and fire to reel him in, but she didn't know how to converse with a famous person, how to flirt with a man like him.

She went to close the screen, but to her surprise there was another red number one in the corner.

Already?

She looked around the cab again, wanting to catch Jules's eye, but she was absorbed in her press release, no one paying her the slightest bit of attention and completely oblivious to the fact that a bona fide star was – technologically, at least – in the taxi with them.

She clicked it open.

'You're a lot braver in the suit.'

Nettie frowned. Well, just what did he mean by that? *'Braver than what?'* she typed back, forgetting to try to be cool.

She pressed 'send' again, chewing on her thumbnail anxiously as she waited for the reply. Oh, please let him be online right now. She couldn't bear to wait. What on earth had he meant?

But his reply was almost instant. *'Than in the flesh.'*

She stopped short at the words and their implied meaning, her heart at a gallop as the taxi chuntered down Tottenham Court Road, only a few minutes now from their office in Golden Square, and she prayed for a line of red buses to hold them up, as ever. She wasn't getting out of this taxi until this conversation was fully ended and she knew what he meant – and how. There was no way he could have guessed who she was.

'How would you know?' she replied.

'We've met. Remember?' He was so quick she knew he had to be doing nothing else, right at this very moment – just chatting to her.

A nervous laugh escaped her and she slapped a hand over her mouth, just as the others looked up.

'What?' Daisy asked.

'N-nothing,' Nettie said, shaking her head. 'Just, uh . . . some of these comments on Twitter. Ridiculous.'

Caro rolled her eyes. 'Take them with a pinch of salt. There's some real nutjobs out there.'

'Right, yes, thanks,' Nettie murmured, her eyes falling back down to Jamie's words again. Jamie Westlake's words. To her. Their private conversation.

She was about to reply when she saw there was another message from him. She'd been too slow off the mark.

'Personally would have liked to see more flesh. You're too pretty to be all covered up like that.'

Oh God! He was flirting with her? Now she really didn't know what to say. Her hands hovered above the screen, rigid with nerves.

'You there?' he typed.

'Yes.'

'Say something.'

'You've got me confused with someone else.'

'No.'

'Why are you so sure?'

This time he was the one who hesitated and for a minute she thought he'd broken off, been called away, lost interest.

'The dame wasn't at the prem. I checked.'

He'd made the connection! She ran her hands over her face. How could she have been rumbled already? White Tiger would freak if this leaked now that they wanted to tease the press with it. Jamie had six million followers!

'*You there?*' he typed again.

'*No.*'

'*You never told me your name.*'

'*You never told me yours.*' Oh, eek! She'd fired that off too quickly. It was a ridiculous thing to say. Of course she knew his name. Even if he wasn't one of the most famous men in the Western world, his Twitter account was in his name, unlike hers.

'*LMAO. You going to tell me?*'

'*No.*' Crap. Too hasty again. Why had she said that?

'*Why not?*'

'*Confidentiality contract.*' Yes, better.

'*Snap. I got one of those.*'

'*We're even, then.*' No, no, no. Don't encourage games with him.

'*Let's have dinner.*'

She stared at the words – hard evidence in black-and-white type, proof that Jamie Westlake wanted to eat. With her. Should she photograph them? she wondered. The grand-children would never believe this bit. They'd think she was exaggerating, taking the story too far.

'Nettie, you got any change?'

'What?' She looked up, astonished to find that the cab had stopped outside their office and everyone was getting out. Jules was looking at her in the manner of someone who had just spoken and was awaiting a reply.

'I need a couple of quid and Mike's already scarpered. Bloody typical, and don't we just know he'll question it when I put the expenses claim in?' She leaned against the door.

'Oh yes, right.' Nettie rummaged in her coat pocket before having to give up and look in her bag instead. 'Sorry, sorry, just bear with me . . . I know I've got some somewhere in here.'

By the time she'd scraped enough coins together, Jules in full flow about a proposed change to today's meme in light of the hastily convened press conference, the screen had automatically gone into sleep mode. He was out of sight again. But not out of mind.

Chapter Ten

The Savoy came up trumps, offering one of their conference rooms for strictly two hours between a Christmas lunch that ended at 2 p.m. and a drinks reception that was kicking off at 6 p.m. It was far tighter than they would have liked, they said, but Daisy had done a ski season with the head of front of house and had given her word, pinky-promise, that there would be no sign of the eighty members of the press, photographers or indeed the bunny come 4.30 p.m.

It was hard to believe that at this precise moment in time. Inside the conference room, all was chaos. Jules was micro-managing Mike, who was offloading his stress from Scott as Daisy and Caro raced to get the branding and marketing materials up in time, including blowing up 150 white balloons that had to be arranged in an arch for Nettie and the White Tiger ambassador to stand under.

Nettie herself had been given a rare reprieve from the action – seemingly Jeremy had been alarmed by her readiness to quit and orders had come from on high to Mike to keep her sweet – and was sitting in the lounge beside the vast pagoda that was positioned beneath the glass-domed roof. It looked like a giant green birdcage, more suited to the gardens in *The Sound of Music* than a London hotel, a beautiful curiosity that kept people entranced but aloof. A grand piano was set up in the middle, but Nettie kept wondering if anyone ever went and stood in the pagoda, if anyone had ever dared to sit down and play on the ivories. It seemed such a waste, to her, that something so beautiful and inherently joyful should be just for show.

She sat, still and unnoticed, amid the chatter and bustle of the hotel, the china tea set untouched on the table before her. In the lobby, photographers dashed past in jeans and boots, their black hard cases banging against their knees as they flashed their press passes and raced for the best position to set up. All the tables and chairs around her were taken with couples and small groups talking intently, peals of laughter curling up to the domed roof intermittently as glasses clinked and silver was laid against china – but nothing anyone else had to say could possibly compete with the reruns of the earlier conversation in her head: Jamie Westlake had made contact with her. Direct contact. Private. And she had given him the runaround, racing off like a startled rabbit.

OK, so it meant nothing in real terms. She wasn't a fool; she knew he was only one step away from sexting her. No doubt he did this with fans all the time – it was the digital age, after all. Even groupiedom had changed – a quick, easy, impersonal way to get his kicks before moving on to the next girl. But still, she had it on her page in black and white, something to show her grandchildren fifty years from now: Jamie Westlake had asked her out to dinner.

'Hey, Nets!' The crisp shout jolted her out of her reverie and she caught sight of Em darting through the lobby towards her, one hand raised in a wave, long jean-clad legs flashing like switchblades as she expertly dodged the crowds with an unimpressed expression.

'Jesus, what's going on?' she gasped, kissing Nettie quickly on the cheek and collapsing prettily on the chair. 'It's a bloody bun fight out there.'

'We're hosting a press conference for one of our clients in half an hour,' Nettie said, immediately clicking into gear and pouring some now-lukewarm tea.

Em grimaced as she took a sip. As a stalwart of the graveyard shifts, she liked her tea burning hot, all the better for keeping her awake. 'Sorry. I ordered when I got here,' Nettie said apologetically. 'I wasn't sure if you'd make it.'

'Well, I nearly didn't. A placental abruption almost scuppered my escape,' Em sighed, raking her hands through her ponytailed hair. Even without make-up on, she wiped the floor with the other, made-up women in the room. 'But an offer of afternoon tea, here, after I've worked eleven hours straight? I wasn't giving that up without a fight,' she grinned, squeezing Nettie affectionately on the arm.

'So what did you do? How did you get away, then?'

'Agreed to go for a drink with one of the other registrars if he covered for me.'

'Wow. You must have been thirsty.' Nettie could just imagine her throwing off her white coat and making the dash from Tommy's Hospital to get here when she'd seen the text.

Em smiled, kicking Nettie's foot lightly under the table with her own. 'I wanted to see you, dummy. I haven't seen more than the inside of the hospital for seventy-two hours. I *need* some outside stimulus.' She reached for two of the eclairs on the porcelain plate and wolfed them down with the unselfconsciousness that comes with true hunger.

Nettie supposed her friend had pulled another all-nighter again. No wonder she was as slim as a stem. She, on the other hand, had to almost sit on her hands to suppress the urge to join her in having one; that cream cake would be sitting on her hips in twenty minutes if she indulged.

'So tell me your news,' Em said, her mouth full and a charming dot of cream on the end of her nose. 'Anything. Something to remind me of the world I'm missing out on.'

Nettie hesitated, wondering whether to share her secret. For once, there was so much going on in her life. The campaign had introduced an entirely new dimension – all the crazy stunts, the online following, Jamie's virtual acquaintance . . . Nettie tried to predict how Em would react to the fact that Jamie was not just following her but had DM-ed her too. Delivering babies and saving mothers was important and crucial and noble and everything, but even life-saving doctors had to get their kicks, and this was properly exciting by anyone's standards, most of all hers. After years of stagnation, suddenly her life had become jet-propelled.

Only, she couldn't tell just half the story – the glamorous bit. To explain the campaign, she would have to reveal that she was dressing up as a giant blue bunny for a living, that she'd been spending her days getting arrested, being terrified, generally embarrassing herself . . . There was no way to tell her one part of the equation and not the other. She bit her lip and sat back in the chair, her eyes returning to the pretty, empty pagoda, feeling her excitement fizzle out because the problem they had – the big problem – was that Em still persisted in thinking of her as she was *before*, the girl she'd been when her life had still been a perfect promise and she had potential, not pathos in her destiny. Em couldn't accept that possibilities had closed down for her now, that just coping was the furthest reach of her ambition, and while she was rocketing up the career ladder, Nettie's job was plumbing new depths of the bizarre.

'Not much, really.'

Em didn't blink. 'Any news on the flat hunt?'

'No, not yet. Everything's out of reach. Prices keep rising, so just when I think I've got enough . . .' She shrugged, knowing that Em – whose parents had forked out the deposit for her place in Bloomsbury – was blissfully out of touch with the hardships of getting onto the property ladder.

'Nightmare,' Em tutted, shaking her head sympathetically.

Nettie thought guiltily of the look on Lee's face when she'd told him she wouldn't stretch to that final two and a half thousand. 'What's the latest on that complaint against you?' she asked, changing the subject.

Em rolled her eyes. 'Dropped, thank God. Shock, grief. It makes people crazy.'

Nettie nodded – didn't it just? – and a small, strangely awkward silence bloomed between them. Nettie felt Em's eyes on her and she averted her gaze to the pagoda again.

Em leaned forward in the chair, reaching her hand out to Nettie's knee. 'What is it, Nets?'

'What do you mean?'

'I feel like you're keeping something from me.'

Nettie shook her head. 'No.'

'Yes.' Em cocked her head to the side. 'Have you heard anything from Gwen lately?'

Nettie swallowed. 'Just the usual monthly check-in.'

'Still nothing?'

Nettie shook her head again.

Em leaned forward, her hand reaching for Nettie's. 'Do you feel she's supporting you properly, Nets? Because you know you're entitled to change your liaison officer if you want? If she's not—'

'Really, she's great. There's nothing more she can do than what she's doing.'

Concern furrowed Em's unwrinkled brow. 'It's just that you seem so . . . withdrawn lately. It's like you're here but not here.' Em gave a wan smile at the irony of her words. 'You know I can refer you to some support services? Grief counsellors . . .'

Nettie nodded. 'I know. Thanks. But we're fine, really.'

Em sat back in the chair, man-spreading her legs, fingers interlaced as she looked back at her thoughtfully. 'Just don't push me away, OK? I worry about you.'

Neither one of them noticed Jules approaching, weaving through the chairs with bright eyes. 'Hey!' she said, clasping the back of the empty chair opposite. 'Did someone die?'

Em groaned. 'Seriously?'

Jules just laughed. 'Come on, missus, you're up. We need to get you ready.'

'Ready?' Em enquired.

'Yeah, we've got this press conference in ten minutes. Nettie's co-hosting.'

'*Really?*' Em said, impressed. 'You didn't tell me that.'

'It's no big deal. It's hardly the same as stopping a woman from bleeding to death.'

Both Jules and Em swapped looks.

'Right, well, I guess I'd better get back too,' Em said,

standing up and giving them both hugs. 'You guys around this weekend?'

'Yeah, kicking about. It's the Christmas Market tonight, and we're going to check out the new Bond film tomorrow. Want to join us?'

'Would love to, but I'm on call.' Em shrugged.

Jules pulled a sad face.

They kissed goodbye, both watching as Em darted through the crowds like a kingfisher in the leaves – bright and vital.

'You still haven't told her, then?' Jules asked as Nettie signed for the bill.

'No.'

'Don't you think she'd keep the secret?'

'Of course she would. It's just—'

'Your inferiority complex getting the better of you again,' Jules grinned, shaking her head and slapping Nettie on the back. 'When are you going to realize she's not judging you? She's your friend. She just wants you to be happy.'

'I know.'

'No, you don't.'

Nettie pretended to fuss with her bag as she looked away. Jules, as ever, had hit the nail on the head – being with Em made her feel left behind, reminded her of how far her life had strayed from the path she had intended. Living at home, trapped in a directionless job she'd never wanted in the first place, hanging out only with people she'd known most of her life? She was trapped, stuck, stultified.

They made their way to the small side room where the bunny costume, which had been discreetly delivered earlier in a huge box, was on a hanging rail. Only Mike and the girls were allowed in here, and no one at White Tiger, outside of Jeremy and Scott, knew the identity of the girl in the blue bunny suit.

Nettie looked at the bunny head sitting on the table beside it – the black mesh that covered the eyes but allowed her to see out, vacant and dull, the long ears fallen over the head. How could *that thing* be the source of a popularity boost that now saw her with over 500,000 Twitter followers and 750,000 views on YouTube? It was farcical. Banal.

She climbed into it resignedly. At least she didn't need to do anything other than pose for photos this afternoon. She'd even texted Dan to let him know she could probably meet him earlier at the Christmas Market. Every year it was the same – he never knew what to buy his mum and Nettie factored it in now when thinking about what presents she had to buy.

In the next room, the conference room, the steady hum of conversation vibrated through the walls, interrupting her distracted thoughts. This was a hot ticket, anything to do with the campaign was, and she could physically feel the excitement in the air. It was all because of her – and yet nothing to do with her at the same time. White Tiger had really ratcheted things up today, immediately after this morning's meeting placing a full-page ad in tonight's *Evening Standard*, asking outright, 'Who's the Blue Bunny Girl? And what will she do next? #ballzup #twelvedaresof-christmas #Tested.'

Nettie stood by the door and watched everyone talking intently, heads bobbing, hands gesticulating; loads of them were pointing to and looking at their tablets, smiles on their faces. She knew what they were looking at. The timing wasn't coincidental, the shot having been uploaded exactly ten minutes earlier to show her #moneyfacing. Caro had gone to the bank especially and withdrawn a hundred pounds in every denomination of notes, asking for new ones where possible, including the rare red fifty-pound note, and they'd spent the afternoon folding the notes in half and trying out which illustrated figures could best match to her face.

They'd tried using the lower half of her face with Sir Isaac Newton on the five-pound note, but his wig made it too tricky, and they'd tried Abraham Lincoln on the US bills that Mike had in his wallet from a recent trip to New York. But they'd finally used Her Majesty's image on the twenty, folding it so that just Nettie's eyes were visible. Jules had had to stand at the far end of the office to get enough distance so that Nettie's head was the same size, perspective-wise, as the Queen's on the note. Nettie had been sceptical about the gag at first, but it had looked surprisingly good on the photo, and as Jules kept insisting, it was a tease, that tied in with White Tiger's ad and gave the public a little of what they wanted: a flash of Blue Bunny Girl.

The question was, would anyone recognize her from it? Nettie thought her large, almond-shaped eyes looked too distinctive in the photo. Anyone who knew her was bound to make the connection, she feared, but Jules kept telling her she was being paranoid, a sure sign she was becoming a star.

'OK, they're ready,' Jules said from behind her, and Nettie closed the door on the crowd.

She pulled on the bunny head and struck a pose. 'How do I look?'

'Like a mutant.' Jules held her hand up for a high five. 'Go get 'em.'

*

The journalists clapped as Jeremy introduced her and she ran out to stand with him under the balloon arch.

'Now, as most of you are aware, White Tiger has long fostered a close relationship with our local communities and charities, but Blue Bunny here really is the jewel in our crown. It is down to her fearless – some might say fool-hardy – stunts campaign that she has not only raised £384,000 in a single week, but that doctors and hospitals are already reporting a staggering 690 per cent increase in patients attending male health clinics. How many lives will be saved through early diagnosis and treatment because of this curious bunny?'

Nettie watched the journalists taking this point on board and felt a surge of pride that she was responsible for it. It seemed unreal that her antics and high jinks could have such a palpable effect.

'But we're not going to rest on our laurels. We know there's still further to run with this ball, and I am delighted to announce to you all today that someone with a unique talent, someone who is already an established and cher-ished member of the White Tiger community has volun-teered to sign up to complete this run with us – he's a man who's an icon to many, a man who knows that health comes before wealth. Ladies and gentlemen, I present to you . . . Jamie Westlake.'

Nettie froze as the flashbulbs started going off.

No one could see that she had frozen, of course. The suit was too large around her frame to register small move-ments – or lack thereof – but she alone stood still as Jamie Westlake walked out onto the stage and came to stand with her and Jeremy under the balloons.

He was wearing black jeans and a green-and-black plaid

shirt, and was looking even better than he had last night in the dinner suit.

Last night. There was no way this could be coincidence.

She stared in disbelief. What was going on? Was there any sense of normality left in her life? Even though he'd guessed that the girl with the supposed ballgown was also the girl in the bunny suit, how could he have known about *this*? It was confidential, agreed only this morning. How could he possibly have known White Tiger was looking for a celebrity to spearhead the campaign? White Tiger linked up with athletes, not singers. Didn't they? No, this didn't make sense.

Through the mesh of the eyeholes, she could see Jules, Caro and Daisy all jumping on the spot in delight. Daisy, in particular, looked thrilled that her missed opportunity had come around again.

Nettie looked over at Jamie, her heart beating double time to be in the same room as him once more. He was standing just six feet away, on the other side of Jeremy, holding his hands out and trying to get the journalists to stop asking their different questions all at once.

Jeremy handed the microphone to him.

'Hi, everyone.' His voice was relaxed and slightly gravelly – more gravelly than she had noticed last night and she wondered just how hard he had partied after the screening. 'I just want to say I'm really pleased to be involved with this campaign. I think what they're doing here, with this mad, crazy Bunny Girl is really cool.' A titter of amusement rippled through the audience as he turned slightly towards her. 'She's been putting herself on the line to raise awareness of a cruel disease that is only as successful as it is because people are too bloody embarrassed to speak up.

Well, I'm not embarrassed about it. It's an important message that we need to get out there about men's health and I'll do whatever I can to help break down taboos with this campaign. I'm really proud to be involved with it, so with your help, let's spread the word and make a difference.'

He handed the microphone back to Jeremy.

'Thank you, Jamie. Does anyone have any questions?'

The voices rushed at him in unison again.

'Yes.' Jeremy pointed to a journalist in the third row.

'Is Jamie going to be doing the pranks and stunts with the bunny?'

'Well, Jamie is really the figurehead for the—'

'I might, yeah,' Jamie replied. 'If I can keep up. She's pretty extreme.' He glanced over at her as everyone laughed and Nettie realized she should probably react in some way other than just standing there dumbstruck. She began jogging on the spot, parrying her paws like a boxer.

Nettie could see the girls in the team were still jumping up and down together in a line too, looking ready to scream.

'And who is the Blue Bunny Girl?' a journalist at the front asked.

'I can't answer that, I'm afraid,' Jeremy parried. 'That's part of the fun of the campaign.'

'Is it just one person?'

'Indeed it is. Uh, yes, you in the green top.'

The questions kept coming, but Nettie didn't concentrate. She wanted to get off this stage and out of this stupid costume. It was hot and heavy and ridiculous and undignified, and there was no good reason why it had to continue to be her who wore it.

'. . . if you'd just like to stand here together for the photos.'

She tuned in again. 'Sorry, what?'

'The photos. If you can just stand next to Jamie.'

Nettie walked the few steps forward to where Jamie was waiting for her.

'Hello again,' he said under his breath as the flashbulbs began to pop. She was vaguely aware that his arm was resting round her shoulder, but of course she couldn't feel it.

'Hi,' she said after a moment.

'Surprised?' He was managing to speak without moving his lips, his face turned to the cameras as the flashbulbs popped. He had a way of moving that was elevated, exotic even – like a panther amid gazelles. Everyone seemed skittish and flighty compared to his stealthy self-assuredness.

'Me? No. Why should I be?'

He turned to face her and she could see he was trying to look past the black mesh to see her. She had that advantage, at least, and as the photographers' lights kept flashing, she allowed herself a brief indulgence, her eyes roaming his face with a freedom that would never be possible in his gaze. Was it just her imagination or did he sparkle somehow? He didn't look like anyone she'd ever seen before, as though his very skin was flecked with gold.

Jamie turned to Jeremy after a few moments. 'Right, I think they've probably got what they need, don't you?'

'Absolutely,' Jeremy agreed, turning towards the audience again. 'Thank you very much, ladies and gentlemen. That's all for today.'

A murmur of disappointment crackled in the crowd, but Jamie had already turned away.

'After you,' Jamie said, indicating for Nettie to leave the back of the stage first.

'Thanks,' she said quietly, as Jeremy stepped between them both and walked them towards the small side room she had changed in.

'Uh, you can't come in here, I'm afraid,' Nettie said quickly, as Jamie moved to step into the room behind her.

Jamie looked surprised, Jeremy even more so. 'Nonsense, Nettie,' he laughed. '*Jamie's* allowed to know your identity. He's the public face of the campaign! Come in, come in.'

'Nettie?' Jamie murmured, a small smile on his face as he stared down at her, and she had the sense of being chased, as though him having her name was just the first step in a game.

She slunk into the room to find Mike, Jules, Caro and Daisy lined up like a wedding line (Daisy appeared to have lost a layer of clothing in the time Nettie had been out on stage), idiotic grins on the girls' faces.

'Jamie, come and meet the team – they deal with all our CSR work. You're going to be seeing a lot of each other in the next week,' Jeremy said, handing them each a glass of champagne. 'This is Mike Fortishaw, the team leader.'

Nettie watched as Mike sucked his stomach in for the handshake, gripping harder than was probably necessary.

'Julia Grant's in charge of strategy.'

Jamie looked amused. 'Hmm, I believe we've met before, Julia,' he said, shaking her hand, a wry smile playing on his lips.

'Call me "Jules",' she gushed.

'All right. Jules.'

'And Caroline Broadley, she's our technical specialist,

analysing meta-data and other things I don't really understand.'

'Hi, Caro,' Caro said, looking bored but chewing her
gum at a speed that Nettie knew meant she was anxious.

'Caro,' Jamie repeated.

'And finally Daisy Crompton. Daisy is our projects
liaison officer. It was her idea to bring in a celebrity
ambassador.'

'Well, I'm very glad you had such a fine idea.'

'Daisy's never short of them. Or contacts. Who she
doesn't know isn't worth knowing.'

'I'm amazed we haven't met before, then, Daisy. Or is it
"Daise"?'

'I know, right?' Daisy breathed, holding on to his hand
and covering it with hers.

A man came into the room via the other door, which led
into the lobby. 'Hey.' He had light brown hair, greying
slightly at the temples, and small brown eyes that moved
quickly in staccato bursts, seemingly missing nothing, a
details man.

'Dave,' Jamie smiled, outstretching an arm to bring him
into the group. 'This is my manager, Dave Marshall.'

Dave shook everyone's hands quickly. 'A pleasure . . .
Pleased to meet you . . . Hi . . .' he said with brisk smiles
and handshakes, stopping at Nettie. 'Ah, the legend herself. An honour, miss.' Nettie laughed nervously as he took
her paw and kissed it. Jamie watched with close interest.

'So, that went very well out there,' Dave said, addressing
the group as Jeremy handed him a glass too.

Nettie watched Jamie watching her. She had the safety of
a costume to hide behind; he didn't seem to need it.

'Yeah,' Daisy breathed. 'But how come they got *you*, Jamie? I thought they were going for a sportsman.'

Nettie could have smacked her for flirting with the man, and kissed her for voicing the very question that was driving her to distraction.

Jamie turned his attention to Daisy, and Nettie immediately began scrutinizing his profile instead. It was every bit as magnificent as his face. 'We recorded our first album at the White Tiger studios in London; they were one of the first sponsors to get on board with our first tour. So when Dave heard they were looking for a face for the campaign, he gave me a call. He knew I'd been following it.' He shrugged.

'You're amazing,' Daisy said breathlessly. 'Giving up your time like this.'

'Not really,' he smiled. 'What you're doing's really clever. And I particularly enjoyed yesterday's gag.'

'Yesterday? Oh, you mean the photo-bombing at the Bond film?' Jeremy asked. 'Yes, that did go down well.'

'Not with Daniel.' Jamie laughed. 'I was there. Although actually, I was rather disappointed not to have been caught by the Blue Bunny myself.' He turned back to face her. 'Do you sleep in that thing too?'

Everyone laughed.

'Yes, come on, Nettie,' Jeremy said, realizing she was still in full costume. 'Step out of that terrible costume. You must be sweltering in it.'

'No, not really,' she demurred, holding up a paw.

Jeremy paused, baffled by her insistence on staying bunnied up. 'Well, even so, you can't stay in there all night. I can't pass you a drink, for one thing.'

He laughed, but it was an order rather than a suggestion, and reluctantly Nettie turned and let Jules undo the heavy-duty Velcro across the back of the costume. She stepped out of it, wearing the black leggings and top Jamie had seen her in yesterday. She stood there for a moment, looking ridiculous with the giant bunny head still on over hers and dwarfing her bang-on size-ten frame, before hesitantly taking it off, her long dark hair falling down her back as she blinked in the sudden light. Slowly, she raised her eyes to his.

'Well,' Jamie said softly, smiling with a quiet look of satisfaction as he set eyes upon her flushed face. 'Hello again.'

Chapter Eleven

'In your own time,' Dan moaned as she burst in through the door of the Engineer, waving to Tom behind the counter before squeezing through the chairs to where he was sitting at their usual table. 'You said you were going to be early.'

'I said I *hoped* I was going to be early,' she corrected, kissing him quickly on the cheek and sinking gratefully into her seat. Her heart was galloping like she'd run all the way here. 'I got held up.'

He took in her red cheeks and bright, quick eyes. 'Doing?'

'We were at the Savoy.'

'Ooh, very nice, darling, sweetie,' Dan said, trying to pull off his best fashionista impression, but it wasn't very impressive coming from a Norf Lundun boy. 'Cocktails in the American bar, was it?'

Nettie coughed. That, in fact, had been exactly what Jamie had proposed in the name of 'bonding' – to the team, but with his eyes on her – and she had been more than delighted to make her escape, pleading this prior arrangement and leaving him stranded with Jules and Daisy and Caro. 'It was just work. You? Had a good day?'

He rolled his bright blue eyes, which had a slightly

hangdog look to them today. 'Run off my feet. Apparently there's not a single other person in the country but me who can lag a pipe.'

She grinned. 'Well, don't complain – just think of the money. You'll be able to spoil your mum this year.'

'Yeah.' He looked at her hopefully. 'Had any ideas?'

'Tch, you are a nightmare. Have you really not got a single thought about what she'd like?'

He pulled a face. 'I did think about one of those foot bucket things.'

'Do you mean a foot spa?'

'Yeah, them!'

She sighed. 'You gave her one three years ago.'

'Really?'

Nettie nodded, draining her flat beer and standing up again. 'Come on. Let's have a wander and see if there's anything out there.'

'There never is,' he complained, pulling on his beloved grey Superdry puffa, which she'd bought him last Christmas and which he'd worn to death. 'It's just gingerbread biscuits and them smelly heart pillow things.'

'Lavender sachets.'

'Exactly. We'd be much better off just going straight to Argos.'

'Over. My. Dead. Body,' she said, holding the door open for him. 'See you later, Tom!' she called, waving as she stepped back out into the chilly street.

It was one of her favourite nights of the year – the local Christmas Market had been set up, ready for the switching on of the Christmas-tree lights tonight – and yes, there was a bias towards gingerbreads and lavender sachets, but there were also gorgeous Scandi Christmas decorations made from twigs and bells and brown gingham ribbons, hand-blown tree baubles in the colours of boiled sweets, gourmet sausages being freshly cooked on a metal drum, hand-knitted childrenswear such as strawberry-shaped baby bonnets and 1970s-style dungarees, wooden-toy stalls, French cheeses and eight-foot Christmas trees that fit perfectly in the area's high-ceilinged homes.

It didn't matter about the carefully considered – and budgeted – Christmas list that she'd spent weeks in advance drawing up, trawling through the catalogues as they dropped through the letterbox from October onwards: invariably, year after year, she staggered home from this market with an eclectic, budget-blown hoard of goodies – some of them presents, some of them just treats, like the stollen that wouldn't keep till Christmas Day.

Regent's Park Road was already crowded, the stalls ablaze beneath the brightly illuminated icicles that were strung up above the red-and-white striped awnings. Men ambled slowly down the middle of the street, small children on their shoulders waving sparklers and trying to touch the suspended stars, as their wives tarried by the displays, surreptitiously buying stocking fillers while chatting to neighbours and friends from playgroup.

She caught up with him by a stall that had bags made entirely from Coke-can ring-pulls. He held one up for her approval.

'Dan, your mum's fifty-four, not fourteen. No,' she said, pushing his arm back down and pulling him on.

They began to wander, their breath hanging like snowy plumes in the air before them. It was too cold for snow, the London sky clear and orange-tinted, as ever. A couple of children dodged past them, laughing, their hoods up and faces painted as tigers as they wove through the crowds, their father hurrying after and saying sorry to everyone as he tried to squeeze past.

'Mad, isn't it?' Dan said, standing to the side to let the harried man past. 'The perpetual worry you always see on their faces.'

'Whose?'

'Parents. They look terrified all the time, the lot of them – terrified crossing the road, terrified in the pool, terrified in crowds, terrified at the tops of escalators, terrified around saucepans.' He shook his head. 'Jesus, why would you put yourself through it?'

Nettie laughed, hooking her free arm round his, to keep closer in the crush. 'Well, I guess there must be some upside or no one ever would.'

'Ha, not that I can see – you're broke, exhausted and scared for twenty-five years.' He snorted. 'And given that that pretty much sums up my childhood, it's hardly an enticing prospect for the next twenty-five . . .'

Nettie glanced at him and squeezed his arm tighter. 'You'll feel differently when you meet the right girl.'

'Nope.' He turned his face towards a lingerie stall and promptly turned back again.

'Any word from Stacey?'

She felt Dan flinch and pull away from her slightly, but she kept her grip on him. 'Why would I want to hear from her? She's made her decision.'

'The wrong one, obviously.'

'Listen, I'm not bothered. It wasn't going anywhere anyway.'

'Did you ever tell her how much she meant to you?'

Dan looked down at her like she was mad. 'Why would I do that?'

'Because girls need to be told, Dan. We're not mind-readers. I know you were batty about her, but did she? You need to put yourself out there. If she felt like you were taking her for granted, then maybe it's no surprise that she . . .' Her voice faded away as she saw the expression in his eyes. 'Not that I'm advocating cheating. She never should have done it.'

'Damn straight.' His mouth had set into a thin line and she bit her lip.

They stopped at a stall selling cashmere ponchos. Dan frowned as he picked up one of the edges, baffled by the shapeless, armless triangular shape.

'It goes over your head,' Nettie explained. She pointed to the vendor, who was wearing one, helping another customer.

'Oh right. I couldn't work out—'

'I know.'

'Well, what about one of them? The orange?'

'Yep, it's nice.' She reached for a subtler shade. 'Or your mum would look nice in this caramel one too.'

'Or . . .' He held up another, a bright smile on his mouth, Stacey already forgotten.

She shook her head. 'I think the royal purple might be a bit . . . bold.'

'Yeah, you're right. How much are these, anyway?' he wondered, reaching for one of the tags. 'Bloody hell, how much?!'

'Evening, both,' a male voice said, interrupting them.

Nettie turned to find Lee standing beside them in a green shooting jacket and yellow scarf. 'Oh, hi, Lee,' she said, forcing a smile. She remembered Sunday and felt awkward. 'How are you?'

He threw his hands up in the air. 'It's been flat out this week.'

'Yes,' she nodded, thinking how it was funny everyone always said the same. If they only knew how active *her* week had just been . . .

'Everyone's desperate to exchange and complete by Wednesday so they've got enough time to unpack by Christmas Day.'

'I can imagine.'

'The removals companies are almost at breaking point, all these enormous rugby-playing Aussies and Kiwis and Polish guys on their last legs trying to fit two house moves in a day. It's madness.'

'I bet.'

The estate agent's eyes slid over to Dan. 'How about you, Dan? I hear everyone's been having terrible trouble with their pipes.'

'Vicar,' Dan quipped.

They both laughed.

'I may well be calling you in the new year, actually. Our usual man's been letting us down lately on the rental properties.'

'Who's that, then?'

'Oh, well, I wouldn't want to be indiscreet, but perhaps you might be interested in picking up the contract?'

'Sounds interesting.' Dan nodded. 'How many units you got on your books?'

'A fair few. More than twenty, less than a hundred.' He smiled. 'Put it this way, you wouldn't be short of regular work, that's for sure.'

'Happy days,' Dan said. 'Give me a bell in the new year, then, and we can talk turkey.'

'Righty-ho.' Lee looked back at Nettie. 'Had any second thoughts about the flat at all?'

'Nope,' she said quickly.

'What flat?' Dan asked.

'Oh, no, it's nothing,' Nettie said quickly, wishing Lee hadn't brought it up. 'I just looked at a flat. But it wasn't right.'

'She had first pick and missed out on it by two and a half *thou*.' Lee winced, as though he'd said 'pennies' instead of 'pounds'. 'It had a view of the Hill too.'

Dan looked aghast. 'Two and a half k?'

'She would not budge.' Lee shook his head. 'I tried talking her up. No one else had seen it at that point. It only went to market the next day.' He pulled a face. 'Went to sealed bids yesterday. One eighty-five over asking.'

'Ah well, it just wasn't meant to be,' Nettie said quickly with what she hoped was a philosophical shrug. 'And think of the commission!'

There was a pause and she saw that familiar look of pity climb into his eyes. 'I suppose you're right. These things can't be forced. All in good time, eh?' Lee took an expansive breath. 'Anyway, Mrs Denton isn't going to have a very happy Christmas if I stand here chatting away. A merry Christmas to you both.' He slipped back into the crowd, but Dan didn't notice. He was too busy staring down at Nettie.

'What?' she asked defensively. 'It was out of my budget.'

'By two and a half grand?' Sarcasm tinted the words.

'Two and a half thousand pounds is a lot of money, Dan,

and it was two and a half thousand pounds that I didn't have.'

'Oh, come off it, Nets! *I* could have given you that.'

She swallowed. 'Well, it's the principle of the thing. Grandpa always said, "Never a lender nor a borrower be."'

'Yeah, right,' he scoffed.

'What's that supposed to mean?'

'This isn't about the money and you know it. It's about you refusing to take the next step.'

Nettie stared at him, filling herself up with air as she gawped indignantly, unsure where to start. 'That is not true,' she said finally.

'It bloody well is. You've been talking about moving out for years.'

'And I will. I want to!'

Dan cocked his head to the side. 'Jeez, and you lecture me about putting myself out there? You talk the talk, but you are without doubt the most risk-averse person I know.'

'I am *not*.' Snapshots of the past week rushed through her mind. 'Look what I've been doing this week, for heaven's sake,' she said in a quieter voice.

'That wasn't you.'

Her mouth opened in surprise. 'Yes, it was!'

'No. It was the Blue Bunny Girl. She's not you.'

'Dan, I'm telling you, I—'

'I know it's you in the costume, dummy. But *she's* not *you*. Nets, you're the girl who puts a thermometer in the bath before getting in.'

'How . . . how do you know that?' she blustered.

'Well, what else is it up there for?'

She glared at him. This was the problem with him

treating their house as his own. He thought it entitled him to know every last thing about her.

She turned to stomp off, but he caught her by the shoulders and held her firm. His baggy hangdog eyes were kind and soft upon her. 'All I'm trying to say is that moving out doesn't mean letting go.'

She blinked up at him, her mouth trembling as she resisted the downward pull that would trigger tears. She couldn't bear to break down here, to confirm the suspicions that lurked in everyone's eyes whenever she passed by – but before she had any choice in the matter, he had pulled her into him and wrapped his arms around her so that her face was nestled in his puffa. 'Listen, don't look like that. It'll be all right,' he murmured, the vibrations of his voice ticklish against her ear.

She pulled away and looked up at him. 'Dan, have you or Stevie told anyone else about me being the bunny?'

He frowned, looking confused. 'Don't think so. Why?'

'Because you mustn't. It's really important. White Tiger are making everyone sign confidentiality contracts. Hiding my identity's going to be part of the marketing now.'

'And I bet that suits you down to the ground,' he murmured, watching her closely, tracking the gradual recession of tears from her eyes.

'You've got to tell Stevie. Will you? Because if you—'

'I'll tell him – don't worry. We'll keep your secret.'

'It's really important.'

'Hey – when have I ever done you wrong?'

She smiled, nudging him gently on the arm. 'Thanks, Dan. You're a mate.'

He snorted lightly, his gaze falling back to the poncho in his hands. 'Yeah.'

*

They joined the crowds that had begun to gather round the Christmas tree. More children were sitting atop their fathers' shoulders now, eating hot dogs, and fresh pots of mulled wine were brewing and being dished into cups. Nettie had gone to get a new batch, leaving Dan chatting with some of the regulars from the pub. She wove her way back to them, white plastic cups bending slightly in her grip.

'Here you go,' she said, passing them round to the nearest outstretched hands.

'Where's Jules tonight, then?' asked Jake, a scaffolder she'd gone to school with and the local ladykiller. 'She never misses this. She's always trying to cop off with Jude Law at this do. Reckons it's her best chance, don't she?'

Nettie grinned. 'Oh, I'm sure she'll make it. She got stuck at a work thing earlier.'

'At the *Savoy*,' Dan said, sucking in his cheeks and trying to pull a 'posh' face.

Jake's face brightened. 'Talking of that – did you hear about that thing that went down at the Savoy earlier?'

'Diamond heist?' Dan quipped.

'Nah. They rolled out that blue bunny.'

'Blue what?'

Nettie noticed Stevie give Dan a perplexed look. He glanced at Nettie, but she warned him off with her eyes.

'Oh, mate! Don't tell me you ain't heard about it? It's this crazy chick. She's been doing stunts all over London dressed as this massive blue rabbit,' Jake grinned.

'*Why?*'

Nettie could have kissed Dan. He was the consummate actor.

Jake shrugged. 'Dunno. One of them charity things, I

think, but, mate, mate, it's funny! You should've seen her planking on this postbox the other day. She looked like she was going to face-plant the pavement. Christ only knows how they got her up there. Must've winched her in.'

'No, no!' cried Ray, who – as the local milkman – wasn't usually seen out after 8 p.m. 'It was the thing with her going down that ice course. I nearly pissed myself.'

'Charming,' Nettie muttered.

'Her arms are waving about like she's trying to fly, ears flapping . . .' He laughed again at the memory.

'I can't believe you haven't heard about it. It's gone viral,' Jake said, screwing his face up at the glühwein and reaching for his pint instead. 'Nettie, you've heard about it, right?'

She swallowed. 'Well, vaguely, you know. I haven't actually . . . seen it.'

'You are missing *out*. You've gotta google it. It's well funny.'

Dan shrugged.

'Here it is. This is it,' Ray said, handing over his iPhone. 'That's the best one.'

Nettie saw the YouTube clip with her blue-shaped self paused at the top of the ice wall. Even just the sight of it made her go cold. She looked away as Dan hit 'play' with his thumb and she began to whizz down the ice, her paws like skis and the only things that kept her upright.

Dan chuckled convincingly, playing his part to perfection. Nettie took out her own phone and checked for messages, not trusting herself to be anywhere near as convincing. Anyway, it *was* unlike Jules not to be here. She had presumed the drinks would only take half an hour or so, but it had been a couple of hours now since she'd made her escape. What were they all doing? Had they gone on – to dinner? To a club?

Her stomach lurched at the thought of them all drinking, dancing, having fun, flirting . . . She wished now she hadn't run – not that it had been a conscious decision: the words had been out before she could stop them, her feet through the door in a flash. On the one hand, she wanted to take a flying leap at the man and wrestle him to the floor. On the other, she wanted to sprint in the opposite direction, as far and fast as her legs would carry her. It was disconcerting having someone like Jamie Westlake suddenly step into her life.

She clicked onto Twitter. The 'followers' gauge wasn't moving with the same rapidity, not now she'd moved up into the next level and increments were measured every thousand units, but it was still rising – 503,000 – and the comments, favourites and retweets kept coming, jamming her inbox.

She scanned the crowd, eyes falling on the groups of young women in leggings and DM boots, wrapped in over-sized boyfriend coats and beanies on their heads. She didn't look so different herself, in fact; she'd been born in this tribe.

'Who's doing it tonight, anyway?' Jake asked, craning his neck as a murmur rippled through the crowd, a sign that the authorities were almost ready. 'Not Kate Moss again?'

'No, she did it last year,' Dan replied.

'Shame. Sadie, then?'

'No,' Nettie murmured, standing on tiptoes and trying to get a better view. 'I think I saw pictures of her on some detox camp in Thailand.'

'You been reading that "Sidebar of Shame" again, Nettie?' Stevie laughed. 'Tut, tut, naughty girl.'

She stuck her tongue out at him. 'I reckon it's Gwen Stefani.'

'Nope. They're in Aspen,' Ray said distractedly, his eyes on a blonde in the crowd in a red coat. It was a moment before he realized that everyone was staring at him. 'What? No, no, I didn't read that in— Listen, they cancelled their order till the beginning of January!'

'Yeah, right,' Jake laughed.

'Phew! Am I in time?' an excited voice bubbled up next to them all.

They turned to find Jules standing beside them, rubbing her hands quickly, her eyes as bright as a squirrel's.

Nettie opened her mouth but didn't say anything. Jules just winked at her.

'You haven't missed him, if that's what you're worried about,' Stevie said, passing over his barely touched mulled wine. 'Lover boy's just about to come on, we reckon.'

'Don't I know it,' Jules giggled, nudging Nettie in the ribs. 'My favourite bit.'

'Good of you to join us, m'lady. Nettie's been telling us you've been lording it up at the Savoy today,' Jake called over.

'Yeah, you know how it is,' she shrugged nonchalantly. 'Places to go, people to see.'

A sudden whine through the tannoy made them all wince and turn to the front. The local MP was standing on an apple crate, his arms raised as he appealed for hush.

They duly fell quiet, pinched fingers clasping tepid cups and rosy faces turned towards the tall, dark shadow of the fifteen-foot tree.

'It's wonderful to see so many of you gathered out here tonight,' he began. 'I know the freezing temperatures are making this something of a challenge for the younger members in our audience today, so I'll keep it brief and just say what a pleasure it is to see the community gathered together, once again, for one of the highlights of our year. Thanks to all of you who have supported the Christmas Market by choosing to do your shopping here tonight. Not only are you filling the coffers for the Christmas lights, it's events like this that enable us to keep the high-street brands out and the independents in. We all know this is a special place to live – our island in the middle of the city – and we welcome all the new faces to our streets, along with the old.

'And it is in that spirit that I'm sure you'll join with me in welcoming a new face tonight. His name will be recognizable to very many of you already, and I expect most of you will know his songs by heart, but tonight he's agreed to step in – at the last minute, I might add – as an honoured guest resident, to turn on the lights of our beloved Christmas tree. Ladies and gentlemen, boys and girls, and well-behaved dogs on leads, I give you . . . Jamie Westlake.'

A jubilant cheer rose into the sky as Jamie – dressed now in jeans and a chunky white jumper beneath a grey padded flannel Prada jacket – stepped onto the apple crate, one hand in the air in a wave, his eyes roaming the crowd as that famous grin made the women yelp.

'*What is he doing here?*' Nettie whispered desperately to Jules.

'Helping out.' Jules rubbed her arm. 'We were leaving the hotel and when I told him who was switching on the lights tonight, he told me they've just gone into rehab. Just as well I mentioned it, hey?'

'But . . . he can't be here,' Nettie said desperately, her eyes flitting back up to find him scanning the crowd.

'Why not? It's fucking A that he's here!'

Nettie swallowed. 'People will make the link.'

'Nah, they won't. There's two hundred people out here. Who's going to be looking for it?' She frowned a little. 'What was up with you earlier, anyway? Why'd you go running off like that?'

'I . . . I'd arranged to meet Dan, hadn't I?'

'Seriously? Christmas shopping with Dan?' Jules hissed incredulously. 'Come off it, Nets! I think he'd have understood if you'd told him you were having a drink with you-know-who!' She jerked her head towards the stage.

Nettie turned back to face the front again. Jamie had flicked the switch and the tree shimmered beside him like a woman in couture. The glow of the white lights cast him in high relief, but from the angle and stillness of his body, she could tell that he had found her again.

The pub was rammed. Everyone, it seemed, except the young families had spilled into the Engineer and the crowd was six deep at the bar. The pub windows were already steaming up, and the fire was roaring so hard, it could have powered a steam engine.

'Hurry up! Your beer's going flat,' Stevie said as she rushed over to the table, visibly shivering as the warm air hit her and she shrugged off her coat.

'Gah! It's a scrum out there,' she protested, struggling with her gloves.

'We thought you'd got a better offer and dumped us!' Dan said.

'Better offer? Is there anything that can top being bought a round by you, Stevie boy? It's a rare enough thing,' Nettie teased, dropping onto the seat opposite them with a happy sigh. 'Where's Paddy?' she asked. 'He said he'd be here.'

'Probably in Spearmint Rhino by now. It's his office party tonight,' said Steve.

Nettie rolled her eyes. 'Oh, well. In that case, definitely bottoms up!' she joked, lifting her drink and raising a toast as she soaked in the atmosphere. This evening was the official kick-off for Christmas to her. 'Happy Christmas, everyone.'

The three of them drank deeply, boasting foam moustaches on their upper lips that only she bothered to wipe away. Nettie scanned the crowd, looking – always looking.

'Where's Jules? I thought she was coming with you?' Dan asked.

'Oh, she's—' Nettie faltered. 'She just got chatting to someone. You know what she's like. I was just too cold to stay out there. She'll be along any minute.'

Dan grinned, his eyes behind her on the door. 'When you say chatting to someone, do you actually mean "trying to pull Jamie Westlake"?'

Nettie's expression changed. 'What?'

Dan jerked his head. 'Well, look who's her new best friend.'

Nettie twisted and looked across the room. Jules and Jamie were standing by the gaggle of people bustling in through the door, Jamie slowly unwinding the scarf round his neck, a navy beanie on, his head bowed as he listened to something Jules was saying. She was in full flow, clearly, her dark bobbed hair bouncing around animatedly as she spoke in his ear.

Nettie blinked, transfixed by the sight of him. She didn't think she would ever get used to seeing the flesh-and-blood, live version of him. Even in a room as full as this, he was the most stunning person in it; even in a room so filled with buoyant and excited chatter, his low-key calm was mesmerizing. Cool, not-bothered eyes kept sliding his way, though no one was so gauche as to stare at him outright.

Except her.

She watched as he nodded, Jules turning and making her way over to them – years of experience telling her they'd all be at their usual table under the green globe light. She grinned and gave a massive wink as she saw them staring on her way over, Jamie following behind her and looking somewhat embarrassed. His attempt at passing incognito appeared to have failed.

'Fuck,' Stevie muttered under his breath, both he and Dan straightening up, shoulders back, as the two of them approached.

'Hey,' Jules exhaled happily, as though it was perfectly normal for her to rock up to their local with a megastar in her wake.

'Hi – again,' Nettie said warily as Jamie stood by the table.

'Jamie, this is Dan and Stevie,' Jules said, making the introductions and arching back so they could all shake hands. She placed a hand on Jamie's arm. 'Like I said, they know who Nettie is, so to speak; we can totally trust them. Can't we, boys?'

'Yeah, sure,' Stevie said, pulling his most honest face.

There was a brief pause, the boys seemingly at a loss as to what to say next.

'So, are you going to budge up or what?' Jules asked with a laugh.

'Oh, yeah, sure . . . Sorry,' Stevie said, sliding closer to Dan to make a space. It was too small for another man, so Jules took it.

Nettie was sitting on her own on the bench opposite the boys and she smiled politely as Jamie took the space beside her.

'You did that, uh . . . very well,' she said.

'What? Flicking the switch?' Jamie grinned, as he unzipped his jacket. 'Yeah. Luckily I've been getting lots of practice. I used to have someone turn on my lights for me, but I had to get rid of him. Thought I should learn to do it myself, you know.'

There was a moment's silence before the little group cracked up, Dan and Stevie grateful for the self-deprecation. They weren't the kind of lads to pay homage to starry behaviour.

Jamie kept his eyes on Nettie as she laughed, as though checking he hadn't offended her on his way to relaxing the others.

They looked up as Tom suddenly arrived at the table with a fresh round of beers. 'On the house,' he murmured discreetly.

'Thanks, mate,' Jamie said, 'but there's really no need.'

'It's our pleasure,' Tom said quickly, setting the drinks on the table and disappearing again with the tray.

Stevie groaned. 'Don't tell me – that happens *all* the time to you?'

Jamie shrugged apologetically. 'I know, it's mad.'

'Damn straight it is. It's not like you're ever short for a round, is it?'

'Ignore him – this is his excuse all the time,' Jules sighed with mock-exasperation. 'You always just so happen to be in the loos whenever it's your turn to get a round in, don't you, Stevie?'

'Hey! Some of us aren't lucky enough to have some cushy job where you get overpaid to sit around in a warm office all day, eating biscuits and discussing strategies and targets.'

'Tragic, really – so bitter, so young,' Jules tutted, making them all laugh again.

'So, you a football man?' Dan asked, his eyes steady upon the new guest, one hand resting on the table, fingers ready to drum.

'Yep. I try to keep up with the league when I can, but I travel so much . . .' Jamie shrugged. 'Who's your team?'

'Gooners,' Dan said solemnly. 'You?'

Nettie sensed Jamie's answer would be critical to how well the boys accepted him.

'Same.'

Dan visibly softened. 'Yeah? You ever meet them?'

'Sure. A few of the guys have come backstage after some of my gigs and they've given me an honorary lifetime membership, which is cool. I go to the games whenever I'm back.'

Dan nodded, clearly liking Jamie more by the second, and Nettie had an instinct as to what he was building up towards. She saw the way he inflated his chest slightly, his body preparing to ask the question before the words were out. But he didn't get the chance.

'Oh crap, spare us,' Stevie suddenly muttered. 'Two o'clock.'

Dan crumpled with laughter. 'Seriously, dude, stop saying that. You're not in *Top Gun*.'

But Nettie wasn't laughing. She watched as a well-built man with floppy, dark blond hair and wearing a rugby shirt and pea coat stopped at their table. 'Hey, Nets.'

'Hi, Alex.'

He looked at the others briefly – and unseeingly. Glances were passed between them all, and they grew increasingly more amused as it became apparent that he didn't appear to have clocked who Jamie was. 'Hey, guys.'

'Hey,' Jules, Dan and Stevie chorused, nodding ridiculously and cupping their pints.

Alex looked back at her. 'How are you?'

'Great. Great,' she nodded. 'You?'

'Yeah, great.' There was an awkward silence and Nettie willed him to go, to leave their table and not linger like a bad smell. There was nothing left to be said between them – they had taken three and a half years to say goodbye, but it had been done at last. That was four months ago now and it had been nothing but a relief. 'Good turnout for the lights again.'

'Yes. Brilliant.'

'Your dad will be pleased.'

'He will. He will.' She was aware that she was nodding at a ridiculous rate. She felt like that nodding dog in the car insurance advert, but she already knew that he was about to ask her if there was somewhere they could have a quiet word.

'Although why the hell they got—'

'Alex! Have you met Jamie?' she said quickly, cutting

him off abruptly. She knew perfectly well his views on guitar-led singer-songwriters. He was more of a heavy-metal fiend.

'Hi.' Jamie smiled up at him benignly, offering his hand.

Alex's expression changed, his mouth dropping open as he slowly tried to remember how to shake a hand. 'Hey.'

Another silence ensued, this one stunned.

Nettie was aware of Jules, Dan and Stevie colouring up as they tried to rein in their amusement.

'Right, well . . .' Alex clapped his hands together awkwardly. 'I can, uh . . . see you're all busy, so, uh . . . I'll leave you to it.'

Everyone nodded.

'Bye, then. Good to see you guys . . . Nice to meet you . . . Jamie.'

'Bye, Alex,' Nettie smiled as he scooted off, the crowd swallowing him within moments, Jules, Dan and Stevie bursting into laughter.

'His face . . .' Jules cried, smacking her palm on the table.

'Oh, man, I wished we'd recorded that,' Stevie laughed. 'Talk about willing a sinkhole to open up.'

'He's Nettie's ex,' Jules said, leaning over the table conspiratorially.

'Yeah, I got that,' Jamie smiled.

'They took, like, forever to break up. They were only actually together for about six months before they started with the break-up/make-up routine. On and on it went – he said this; she did that. Honestly . . .' Jules groaned, dropping her head into her hands.

'Yes, *thanks*, Jules,' Nettie said with a withering stare. 'I'm sure Jamie isn't interested in my romantic history.'

'Are you, Jamie?' Jules asked wickedly.

'He's such a tosspot,' Dan muttered with a frown, his eyes still on the spot where Alex had disappeared into the crowd. 'I thought he moved to Camden, anyway?'

Nettie shrugged, cupping a hand round her half-pint. 'Don't know, don't care.'

'He probably thinks *you're* going out together now,' Jules laughed, reaching over and pushing Jamie on the arm.

'What a thought,' Jamie grinned, looking straight at Nettie with glittering eyes.

Nettie tried to smile back, but having Jamie Westlake tease her about the thought of them being together wasn't an easy joke to shrug off.

Dan's attention suddenly switched to what was happening at the table.

'So how did the meeting go?' Nettie asked, aware of how Dan's eyes had narrowed slightly as he sipped his fresh beer and tuned in to the banter. 'Did I miss much?'

'Oh great, yeah. Jamie and Dave have got some really great ideas.'

'It was a shame you weren't there,' Jamie said evenly. 'You are, after all, the person who's got to do everything with me.'

Dan's eyes narrowed further still.

'That's why when Jules said she was hooking up with you here, I thought we should go over the plans. Hope you don't mind?'

'Of course not. What kind of things were you talking about?'

'Tandem parachuting? I thought base-jumping off Nelson's Column might be fun, but apparently you're not good with heights . . .'

It was a moment before Nettie realized he was joking. 'Oh my God! Bastard!' she gasped, smacking him on the arm before she knew what she was doing.

She gasped again, her hands flying to her mouth. He probably had a contract somewhere that meant you couldn't even make eye contact with him and had to curtsey when he passed, and she'd just called him a 'bastard' *and* assaulted him.

Jamie was laughing. 'No? Too much? But I thought you were hard-core?'

'So that's what got your interest in the first place, was it, Jamie?' Jules asked, leaning in interestedly. 'You're an adrenalin junkie?'

Jamie smiled. 'Actually, one of the roadies showed it to me. They were all laughing over it. I expected to see some beefy bloke playing up to the crowds, so when she took off the rabbit head . . .' He turned back to face Nettie. 'You looked so tiny in there. I couldn't believe it, this gorgeous girl looking so stunned. And you hadn't done it on purpose? I couldn't stop thinking about it . . .' He shrugged. 'You must have been so scared.'

Dan replaced his beer on the table with slightly too much force. Nettie was oblivious. He thought she was gorgeous? He hadn't been able to stop thinking about her?

'Only then you went and did the Ice Bucket gag so I figured you couldn't have been that scared.'

'I only did it because *you* donated such a crazy amount of money to make it happen.'

He shrugged, his eyes pinning her in place. 'Good cause. Besides, I couldn't resist seeing you be mental again.'

'Well, sorry to disappoint you, but I'm not mental – I'm officially a chicken. Doing an ice cross course dressed as a

bunny is not my idea of a good time. I can't even ice-skate.'
She shook her head, resting her cheek in her hand. 'It's a
miracle I lived to tell the tale.'

'Seriously? You can't skate?' Jamie seemed astonished.

'No,' she shrugged, before catching sight of his expression. 'Why?' She felt suddenly self-conscious. 'What? Loads
of people can't skate.'

Jamie looked at the others. 'Can you?'

Jules, Dan and Stevie all nodded.

'Not well,' Stevie added.

Jamie looked back at her. 'This is terrible. Everyone
should be able to skate.'

'Should they?' Nettie asked sceptically.

'Of course! Ice skating at Somerset House is one of the
defining moments of a London Christmas.'

'Well, I've never had Christmas anywhere but London
and it's never defined my Christmases,' she said with a
certain defiance.

'Then we must rectify the situation while we still can.'
And he drained his pint in one go, earning himself admiring glances from the boys. He put the glass down and
grabbed his jacket. 'Come on.' He looked at the others. 'You
don't mind, do you?'

Jules, Dan and Stevie gawped back. Dan looked like he
minded very much, heat colouring his cheeks.

'What do you mean? Where are we going?'

'To Somerset House, to teach you to skate.'

'What, *now*? But it's nine o'clock at night!' she spluttered.

'Exactly. It's best at night. The lights are gorgeous.'

'But by the time you get over there . . . even if it is still
open, it'll be fully booked,' Jules said. 'I know. I tried
booking tickets a few weeks ago.'

'Oh, don't worry about that,' Jamie said, rising to standing and holding out a hand for Nettie.

She stared at it in amazement, like Alex had done a few minutes earlier, as though she'd never seen a hand before. 'Well, are they coming?' She indicated to the others.

'They can all skate.' Jamie smiled, calm and clearly in control.

Nettie blinked, her gaze drifting to the others, who were watching the scene with a mix of astonishment, bemusement and envy. Jules's eyes, particularly, were dancing with delight, her mouth open.

'Listen, you don't have to go if you don't want, Nets,' Dan said, breaking the pause. 'Remember we were all going to head back to mine after for another game?'

'Game?' Jamie asked.

'Poker,' Stevie said.

'Strip poker, you mean,' Jules laughed. 'Honestly, you should've seen Nets. She was swaddled in about nine layers of Dan's clothes last time. You must've been boiling.'

'I was,' Nettie giggled. 'But at least it meant I didn't lose!'

'You play strip poker,' Jamie said, almost to himself, watching her closely, laughter in his eyes.

She rolled her eyes. 'Very badly.'

'Excellent.' His smile widened. 'Well, I'm more than happy to play tag if those are your plans.'

There was a horrified silence, and Nettie could guess from the boys' faces that the prospect of stripping down to their boxers in front of Jamie Westlake was as appealing to them as trying on a bikini next to Miranda Kerr would be to the girls.

'Actually, that was just a one-off,' Dan said quickly. 'It

wasn't that good playing like that. Bit gimmicky. It's much better actually focusing on the cards, you know?'

'Eh?' Stevie spluttered, coughing on his beer. 'Listen, you weren't saying that when Em sat on your lap in her undies.'

Jamie looked down at Nettie. 'What do you want to do? I don't want to get in the way of your plans, but I'm pretty busy the next few days; I don't think I'll get any more free time before Christmas, and I wouldn't forgive myself if I just left you *unable to skate*.'

Nettie looked back at Jamie. His gaze was steady and warming. She felt like a flower opening up in a sunspot. Without a word, she raised her hand to his and he pulled her up.

'See you tomorrow, then,' Jules said with unconcealed excitement. 'Have *fun*.' Though she didn't say the words out loud, her tone of voice implied the unspoken 'Don't do anything I wouldn't do.'

Jamie nodded down at them all. 'Good to meet you, guys. See you again soon, I hope.' And putting his hand on the small of her back, he guided her quietly out of the pub, every single set of eyes upon them.

Chapter Twelve

They sped through London like city sprites, his moped weaving easily through the heavy traffic, her grip round him so tight that her arms ached. It had been a shock to see his bike parked outside the pub – she had expected a chauffeured car, or at the very least that he'd hail a cab; she would have been less surprised to find a chopper on the roof than the Vespa, but she understood it now – the full, tinted visors on the helmets were an effective disguise, and as the bright lights gleamed on them, he moved through the city easily, hidden in plain sight.

Her cheek had to rest against his shoulder; there was nowhere else to put it – looking over his shoulder was too scary – and she tried to calm herself as they cut through the dark. If she'd thought sharing a stage or sharing a pint with him was overwhelming, riding pillion on his bike, her arms and legs round him, was almost enough to stop her heart. She could feel his muscles tighten as he angled the bike round cars and corners, the bass of his voice as he muttered at cyclists getting in the way, reckless drivers not seeing or caring that he was there. She couldn't help but smile at the thought of their faces, should any of them be so stupid as to knock him off and see who they'd cut up.

And what was going to happen when they got to where

they were going? Were they really even going to Somerset House? Or had that just been an excuse, a cover story to peel her away from the others and get her alone? Because she had no doubts that he was chasing her. Every look he gave her – since that first moment at the premiere in Leicester Square – confirmed that the heat between them wasn't imagined. He felt it; she felt it. The difference was, he probably did this every night of the week, pursuing every girl who took his fancy – and who would say no to him?

She knew she wouldn't. Couldn't. Her head told her one thing, her body quite another. Her blood felt sparkling, bubbles of excitement fizzing down her limbs, flushing her cheeks, quickening her breath.

She watched as London rolled past them – along Regent's Park and down to Fitzrovia and Soho, over Piccadilly Circus and down the Strand, the distinctive humped arches and pillars of Somerset House cresting before them in under fifteen minutes, Jamie bringing the bike to an easy stop, his feet flat on the ground as he kicked the stand down.

Reluctantly, she loosened her grip and hopped off, handing him the helmet and quickly raking her fingers through her hair before pulling her beanie from her coat pocket and tugging it on, as though trying to hide.

He smiled, somehow sensing her anxieties and taking her by the hand again. 'Are you nervous?'

She nodded.

'You should be.' His eyes danced with amusement as he saw the worry leap in her features again. He laughed, toying with her. 'Relax, I'm joking. I won't let anything happen to you.'

Nettie blinked, still wrong-footed and insecure. Since when had she become someone he protected?

He pulled his beanie down and his scarf up, so that only his eyes and nose could be seen, but even that was enough, and as he led her quickly through the arches towards the rink – a smile on his face and utter certainty in his steps, marching past people before they had a chance to process him – Nettie caught the frowns and puzzled stares on his back, before heads were shaken and the thought tossed away. *No, it couldn't be.*

It was late now, but the rink was still half full. There was no queue at the entrance, thanks to a 'Sold Out' sign propped up in the window of the cash booth, and he walked straight up to the woman at the till. 'I'm sorry, but we haven't booked. Is that a problem?'

It took the girl only a moment to register the VIP standing before her.

'Of course not, Mr Westlake,' she said hurriedly, lifting the barrier for them and picking up the phone on her desk.

'*Un*believable,' Nettie said as they walked towards the desk where the skates were held in racks.

'Hey, there are enough downsides, trust me,' he said, glancing down at her. 'I'd happily give this up to get my privacy back.'

He shook her hand, waggling her arm about. 'Although, if it impresses you that I don't have to pre-book, then maybe it's a sacrifice worth making.'

She laughed, just as they arrived at the desk.

The assistant had clearly been notified of his arrival because she was standing with a manager behind her, ever-ready smiles on their faces, eyes gleaming as though they'd been waiting their entire lives for this moment.

'Mr Westlake, it's a pleasure to have you join us here tonight. What sizes would you like?' the assistant asked.

Jamie gestured to Nettie to answer first.

'Thirty-eight, please,' she mumbled.

'And I'll have a forty-three,' he replied, his eyes on her. 'Stop looking so scared.'

'But I've never done this.' Oh God, what if she fell badly and broke a leg? Or a hip? Fell down and someone sliced over her fingers?

They walked over to the benches and changed their shoes in silence, Nettie tying double knots in the laces.

She stared down at the white boots, the flash of the sharp blade beneath the arch of her feet sliver-thin. She bit her lip, anxiously. This was a really bad idea.

Jamie was standing, waiting for her. 'Ready?'

'As I'll ever be,' she said with a grimace. She pushed herself to standing, walking with a peculiar knock-kneed gait over the rubber mats and reaching for the glass barricades that bordered the ice rink.

It was vast and beautiful, a huge Christmas tree bedecked in white lights at the far end, people sluicing past, the gentle crunch of the ice beneath their blades almost obscured by the music that blew out from the large speakers in every corner.

There weren't many beginners there. No doubt they took the earlier slots, hiding among the toddlers, who didn't have so far to fall. She watched as people glided by in smooth, repetitive laps, arms relaxed and swinging lightly by their sides, the more advanced skaters attempting pirouettes and turns, spraying arcs of ice flakes into the air, laughing when they occasionally got it wrong, slamming into the barricades or sliding into the backs of each other.

Only a couple of people were wobbling around, arms out like scarecrows, legs as stiff as forks. She saw one girl at the far end, almost bent double as she gripped a plastic penguin that appeared to be the skating equivalent of a buoyancy device.

Nettie looked around desperately, knowing salvation when she saw it and finding a rack of plastic penguins lined up by the gate.

'Oh, I'll get one of those!' she said brightly, heading towards it.

But Jamie shook his head, his khaki eyes shimmering with amusement. 'No need. I'll be your penguin.'

She laughed. 'You'll be my penguin?' It sounded so funny, ridiculous. It *was* ridiculous. But he was still standing by the gate, an arm outstretched to her.

Her laughter died in her throat. He could have been standing at the edge of the cliff, enticing her to jump, and she'd still take his hand. She stepped towards him and onto the ice, her fingers gripping the sleeves of his jacket in panic as she felt the perilous smoothness beneath her feet. The last time she'd felt this sensation, she'd been whizzing down it on a seventy-degree slope dressed as a bunny, and she suddenly wished she was in the costume again now. It had protected her then and she felt exposed and vulnerable without it now.

'I've got you,' he said quietly, his body relaxed and stable as she tried to settle to the feeling, trying not to wince as the other skaters flashed past, making her feel giddy in their backdraughts. 'Ignore them. They'll go round us. Just take a deep breath and look at me.'

She did as he told her to, trying to calm her breathing, but looking into his eyes had a stimulating, not sedative effect on her and she felt her pulse rocket again.

'It's OK. It's just you and me.'

Strangely, it was. The world fell away like shards of glass in a broken window, revealing nothing but black space beyond so that just the two of them were left, the night air cool on their skin and the earth slipping slowly under their feet. Being on the ice, being in his arms was like being weightless, living in a world with no gravity – she didn't know how to push against anything; she couldn't start or stop; she could only slide, spin, drift, fall, float . . .

The first time she realized they were moving was when he began to turn, leaning in slightly to change their direction. Her grip tightened again, panic like a bullet, but he didn't flinch, didn't even blink and she felt her muscles soften, letting him lead.

She even smiled, nervous little laughs escaping from her like whinnies as she began to adjust to the sensation, trusting in him.

'You're so good,' she gasped, wondering how he could do this backwards.

He shrugged. 'I learned as a kid. It helps.'

'Where did you grow up?' she asked, feeling shy, wondering if she was allowed to ask, to know. Or was that prying? Did he have to keep his life a secret from people like her? Normal people?

'Kent. My parents still live there.'

'Oh.' She blanched as a girl did a fancy jump as she passed them, landing on one foot, her other leg outstretched. 'Do you . . . do you get to see them much?'

'Not as much as I'd like, but then, it's been hard recently with the tour. They flew out for some of the Oz shows, though.' He shifted position slightly so that his hands were underneath her elbows. 'How about you? Where did you grow up?'

'Primrose Hill.'

'Really?' He seemed impressed. 'So you're not part of the fashionable influx, then?'

'No. I've lived there all my life.'

His eyes danced. 'What do they call locals from there? "Primrosers"?' His look became devilish. 'Surely not "prim roses"?'

She laughed at the pun, wishing she could smack his shoulder, but she didn't dare move her hands off his arms. 'No!'

'Very glad to hear it,' he murmured, making her laugh more.

The ornate embellishments of the neoclassical building slipped past in her peripheral vision, the white lights twinkling as though the stars had dipped down from the sky just for them, and she felt like Cinderella at the ball, dancing with the prince. Her eyes brightened with amusement as she remembered Jules's excitement on the park bench only the weekend before, telling her she would have this, her Cinderella moment.

The colour in his eyes deepened as he watched her smile and laugh and panic and gasp and smile again. 'And have you got any brothers or sisters?'

She swallowed. She had always hated that question. 'No. You?'

It was his turn to pause. The silence dragged on so long she again wondered whether maybe she wasn't allowed to know personal details about him. Maybe this wasn't a two-way street. Perhaps, as a celebrity, he had to keep those details hidden from people like her: fans, the public.

'Two little sisters,' he said finally. 'One's a teacher; the other's a quantity surveyor.'

She laughed. 'Imagine how much more interesting it is for them when they get asked the same question. "Oh yes, my sister's a surveyor, and my brother's a global super-star."'

Jamie smiled, but his eyes darted away, as though embarrassed and she felt like she'd trodden on a landmine, made a wrong move that had blown them into the sky.

She swallowed, hearing the slice of ice from his skates. Her legs weren't moving at all. She was simply gliding along after him, being pulled like a cart.

There was another flash of colour and energy beside them and Nettie gasped, almost losing her balance, as a girl – the same one as before – leaped and pirouetted on her way past them. Nettie stared after her, wondering whether her timing was coincidental or deliberate. Had she recognized Jamie? Was she trying to impress him? Get his attention?

She felt Jamie's grip tighten on her arms, a silent pulse of communication, and she looked back at him, his gaze a steady horizon she could cling to.

'So, what about Dan?' he asked.

'Dan? What about him?'

'You're obviously close.'

'Yeah,' she smiled, groaning gently. 'I guess you'd say he's the nearest thing I've got to a brother.'

He paused. 'Actually, I wouldn't say that at all.'

She frowned. 'Huh?'

'Well, he clearly doesn't see you as his little sister.'

Her lips parted as she got his meaning. 'No, it's not like that.'

His eyes scanned her. 'For you, maybe.'

'You've got a suspicious mind. We're just friends.'

'So nothing's ever happened between you?'

She laughed. 'Why? Are you jealous?'

'Has it?'

'Not really, no.'

He arched an eyebrow, effortlessly turning her as they approached the end of the rink. She realized she'd forgotten they were moving. 'That isn't a "no".'

'It was ages ago.'

'When?'

'I was fifteen, something like that. It was nothing. Just a kiss.'

Someone else skated past them close by, too close for her liking, and she saw Jamie's eyes dart after the man, then the rest of the rink. He looked back at her. 'Then maybe you should let him know that. Put him out of his misery.'

She laughed, but it wasn't happily. 'I don't *need* to. He doesn't think of me like that. We're just friends. He's like family.'

He sliced to a stop suddenly, but her skates didn't work like his; she couldn't work them at all and she slid straight into him, his chest a wall that she wanted to press into.

'Oh!' she gasped, not sure how to step back and away. She could only extricate herself from him if he stepped back, but he wasn't moving, and his arms had closed behind her, penning her in.

She looked up at him.

'So then, it's not like this?' His voice was quiet, a new tone of intensity in it that she hadn't heard before. This wasn't a tease or a joke; his light flirtatiousness of just a moment before had suddenly gone.

She swallowed, feeling the heat turn up. Because what was *this*? Was it the same for him as it was for her?

She shook her head in reply, not sure if her voice had fled too.

His eyes lifted from hers, the corners of his mouth turning up by a degree as he tucked a stray tendril of hair back from her face. 'Good.'

Thank God he was holding her up. She'd never be able to stand on her own, even if she wasn't on the ice. She could feel the press of his chest against hers, the weight of his eyes on her mouth, she knew what was coming next and her eyes closed in readiness. It was as inevitable as her next breath, the moment they'd been barrelling towards since he'd burst in on her yesterday. He had tracked her down, found her, chased her, brought her here and there was no turning off this road for either of them. Not yet.

Not . . .

She frowned as he stepped back. Opened her eyes.

Not now?

'We should go.'

She blinked, feeling the world reassert its might, colour and noise intruding as he led her back to the gate. Her blades sank into the safety of the deep rubber mats and she watched as he walked to the bench and untied his laces, shame spreading like a bloom across her cheeks. What had happened? Had she . . . misread the signs? How could she have got it so wrong?

She looked around and caught the stares of every person on the ice, all of them watching. They all knew; they'd all seen. Tears bit as she saw their smirks, the heady exhilaration that had come from relinquishing control on the ice receding like a storm tide, gravity suddenly a crushing force on her chest as she plummeted back to earth with a thud.

Chapter Thirteen

'Jules, you know that time I told you I was terrified of heights?' Nettie called over her shoulder, although she didn't need to shout too hard: the wind was doing a great job of carrying her voice.

'Yeah!'

'Do you remember it?'

'Yeah! Remember it well, actually! You were frozen on the spot when we were doing that team-bonding course in the treetops.'

'Exactly.'

'What about it?'

'Well, which bit of it did you think I was making up?'

Jules's laugh carried over Nettie's shoulder and out into space. Which wasn't that far, given they were now almost at the top of the O2 and officially fifty-two metres above London's pavements.

Nettie kept her eyes on the guide in front. They were all harnessed to the frame that ran alongside the walkway going over the top of the arena, and for the moment they were all dressed in matching blue suits. For the moment.

'This is *nothing* compared to what you did on Tuesday,' Jules called, just as the thirty-degree gradient flattened out and they arrived on the viewing platform.

'Maybe let's not revisit that particular memory just now, OK?' Nettie asked, taking in the view and trying to feel the beauty, not the terror.

It was just after dawn and the sky was still warming up, tints of colour bleeding through the pale atmosphere and staining it peach. Below them, London looked blackened and bony, showing her there was nowhere to hide – there were no feathery treetops to shelter the birds, no flowerbeds to soften and brighten the streets. Instead, bare leaf canopies fanned against the horizon like hard corals; puddles were iced over on the flat roofs of tower blocks, the Thames sluggish and sandy on its run out to sea, the hesitant sun admiring its reflection in Canary Wharf's tinted glass windows.

She should still have been in bed, trying to catch up on some of the sleep she hadn't caught last night, but there had been no option about the timing of this adventure. The tours were booked out for months in advance and it was only yesterday's starry publicity that had seen the management agree to a before-hours private tour that would tie them in to the Sixth Dare of Christmas. Only Mike was a no-show, proclaiming his Saturday mornings with his family as sacrosanct, which Jules translated as meaning he'd already paid his green fees.

'Well done, everyone,' the guide said, as they all tried to catch their breath. 'Now, I know we ran through the drill on the ground, but I can't stress enough how vital it is that you keep the harness attached to you at all times. If you were to unclip and slip, well . . . you'd come off a lot worse than James Bond did.'

'Got it,' Jules nodded firmly, like she was the one who was about to disrobe.

They turned at the sound of the puffing, just as two more members of staff – the poor juniors lumbered with carrying the suit up here – arrived. At least she could get the rabbit suit on over the climbing suit.

'There's quite a strong wind today,' the guide said, as another strong gust circled them. 'So keep low.'

'That's easier said than done when you've got the waist circumference of a ferry. If I get down, I'm not sure I'll get back up again,' Nettie quipped.

'That's why you've got me, babe,' Jules said, unzipping the plastic hanging bag and pulling out the suit. 'Shall we?'

Nettie sighed. 'So, owling.'

'You just crouch down on your haunches like this and hang your arms down like wings. You're meant to look like an owl roosting,' Caro said. And then seeing Nettie's expression, she added, 'It really is very funny when you see it. People have done this in the maddest places.'

'I'm surprised you didn't want to photograph me on the top of Nelson's Column,' Nettie said, stepping into the suit, her feet sliding into the paws like they were outsized slippers.

'Actually, that was a location we discussed,' Daisy said, looking long and lean in her suit.

'Oh my God! I was *joking*!' Nettie gasped, momentarily taking her hands off the handrail and almost giving the guide a heart attack. 'It's fine, it's fine,' she muttered. 'I'm still attached.'

'But then Jamie came up with this yesterday afternoon. It is far more original, you've got to admit.' She simpered slightly. 'He's got some great ideas.'

Nettie swallowed at the sound of his name, still feeling sick, still confused by what had happened between them last night. After the humiliation of their non-kiss – a moment that she had so clearly anticipated – she had insisted on catching a cab back home. She hadn't been able to meet his eyes, rushing off before he could start up with the excuses.

'You mean *Jamie* came up with this?'

'Yeah, he's playing here tonight and he said he'd done this tour the other day. That's the thing – he's been everywhere, seen everything. He can think of these things. He's just been exposed to so much more life than us. Living on the road does that to you.'

'Huh, never would've guessed,' Jules said with a roll of her eyes, but her gaze coming straight back to Nettie. It was obvious she wanted every last detail of what had happened between them last night, but what was Nettie supposed to say? That she'd puckered up and he'd backed off? Her cheeks stung just from the memory of it. How was she supposed to face him again?

'And since when did a singer start dictating our campaign policy?' she asked tartly.

Everyone looked at her in surprise.

'Well, he's the charity ambassador now,' Caro said as if it was obvious.

'But he has no experience of running something like this. He's just a celebrity, a famous face. What we're doing is serious. We're dealing with big budgets from a multinational company, making a difference on the front line of cancer.'

Still there was silence.

And then, like skittles hit by a ball, they all fell about laughing.

'That's brilliant! You sounded just like Mike!' Daisy cried.

'You sounded so *serious* and you're standing there in that stupid costume!' Caro screeched.

'Good one, Nets!' Jules giggled.

Nettie balled her hands – or rather, paws – trying to keep her temper. It was fine for them. They were just the support team; they weren't having to sacrifice their dignity or pride, day after day. They just had to book the trips and hold the cameras. They didn't have to face him like she did.

She reached out for the bunny head and pulled it on over her own roughly. There was no point in arguing – it was just better to be done with it – and without another word, she assumed the position and made like an owl.

'You've made us breakfast?' Daisy cooed, touching Jamie's arm. 'You really have thought of everything.'

Nettie and Jules swapped looks. Their teammate somehow managed to make it sound like the two of them were alone in a hotel room, rather than the vast black, domed arena of the O2. Nettie eyed the impressive spread of croissants and pastries, fruit and yoghurts with no appetite.

'Well, I can't say I made it myself,' Jamie said, catching sight of Caro sticking her gum in a yellow paper napkin and surreptitiously grabbing a handful of grapes.

They had been welcomed back to earth by a black-and-plaid-clad assistant who'd been waiting for them, giving them passes to enter the arena and join the main man himself.

All around them, roadies were hauling massive black boxes onto and under the stage on wheeled tracks, miles of cables criss-crossing the stage like it was the National Grid.

A vast screen was being manoeuvred into position on the far right of the stage.

Nettie hung back in the shadows. The arena seemed big enough when it was filled with 20,000 people, but less than 100? It felt as dark and large as the moon.

'So did you get the shot?' Jamie asked, folding the newspaper he was reading and directing the question entirely to her as she and the team emerged onto the stage, where he was sitting on a chair. He stood up, jamming his hands into his jeans pockets, his smile relaxed and betraying no sign of the awkwardness she carried from last night.

'Yes.'

'Is it up yet?'

'You'll have to ask Caro,' she shrugged, keeping her eyes away from him. 'She deals with that side of things.'

'I'm gonna wait a couple of hours,' Caro said, her cheeks as full as a hamster's. 'Most of our followers will still be in bed, and we need to get the donations rolling in first.'

Jamie took a few steps towards Nettie. 'Well, can I see the picture? Promise I won't share it.'

'Daisy's got it,' she said quickly, pointing to her team-mate behind him while changing direction herself, pretending to be interested in the rigging high, high above them.

He watched her for a moment before turning and walking over to Daisy, who took her time in scrolling through all seven photos that she'd taken on the top.

'So, do you get, like, nervous before coming out on a stage like this?' Jules asked, looking between Nettie and Jamie with a suspicious expression.

Jamie straightened up, but his eyes were following

Nettie again as she trailed a hand over a Marshall amp that was almost as big as her. 'Yes, of course.'

'Don't you ever worry you'll forget the words?'

'All the time.' He looked back at Jules. 'But once you're out there, the adrenalin takes hold and you're just . . . in the moment. It becomes instinct.'

Behind his right shoulder, Daisy looked like she was going to faint. 'And you're a man who follows his instincts, right?' she practically mewed.

'Yeah.'

'So when are the rest of the band arriving?' Caro asked, still eating grapes at a rapid pace.

'After lunch. We don't usually have such an early call.'

'So you're just here because . . . ?' Daisy asked, with hope in her eyes.

'The campaign. I just thought that I may as well get here early and see how you were all getting on.'

'So sweet,' Daisy whispered.

'That's really considerate of you, Jamie,' Jules said, her eyes still sliding between Nettie and Jamie, while Nettie stayed silent.

A stocky man in an AC/DC T-shirt came over. 'They're ready to do that tour now, if you want, Jay.'

Jamie looked up. 'Great. Would you like to see backstage? Ron's got it set up for you.'

'Would we?' Daisy echoed, clapping her hands and jumping to her feet.

'Cool,' Caro muttered, making her way over to Ron too.

'Does this mean we'll get to see your rider?' Jules asked with a flirty tone.

'What's that?' Daisy asked, worried she was missing out.

'Their list of demands – you know, white peaches in

their Bellinis, virgin handmaidens to peel and hand-feed them their grapes,' she laughed, giving a cheeky wink.

'Actually, it's usually just a tube of Pringles and a bottle of Jack.'

'Yeah, yeah, yeah, tell it to the judge,' Jules said over her shoulder, still laughing.

Nettie moved to follow after her, but Jamie caught her by the wrist.

'Hey, just a sec,' he said, his gold-flecked eyes focusing on her and her alone in the huge black hall. All around them, people were bustling about, hauling and heaving, calling and cursing, but none seemed to notice the two of them.

'But . . .' Nettie looked over to find the girls were already out of sight.

'Not so fast. You ran away from me twice last night.' He walked her a few steps towards the stage and, placing her with her back to it, released her wrist. 'I get the distinct impression you're avoiding me.'

She crossed her arms over her chest defensively. 'Funny. I have the distinct impression you're following me.'

He studied her for a moment. 'Well, maybe I am.'

She tipped her head to the side fractionally, her arms folded over her chest like she was cold, keeping him away. What did he want? Rejecting her last night, chasing her again now? 'Why?'

'Why not? You're a beautiful girl. You must get loads of men chasing after you.'

The world seemed to spin faster. He thought she was beautiful? She swallowed. 'Not famous ones.'

'Does it make a difference?'

She gave a dry laugh, remembering how everyone had

stared last night, witnesses to her humiliation. 'I think it must do, yeah.'

He was quiet for a moment and the amusement faded from his eyes. 'Actually, you're right. It does, sometimes. I tell myself I live pretty normally, but . . .' He exhaled. 'There are times it gets in the way. Like last night.' His eyes skipped over her face like a laser, contracting the world, the dome down to just a black sheet billowing around them, like lovers in a bed.

'Hey, you took me for a skating lesson,' she said quickly, trying to keep the conversation general, not wanting to revisit the humiliation. 'It was great. Thanks very much.'

He watched her, undeterred. 'You know what I mean.'

'Do I?' She hoped she wasn't blushing, knew that she was.

'I just didn't want an audience. For *once*.' She heard the note of exasperation in his voice, wanted to laugh out loud at the irony of where they were standing, right now – one of the biggest stadiums in Europe. 'Nettie, look – we scarcely know each other. And I know it's weird for you – there's a lot of strange shit that comes with knowing me, but . . . I like you. You're funny and cute and pretty weird yourself. I'd like to get to know you better, but it has to be in private.'

Shock made her laugh. 'God, you move fast!' she exclaimed, holding her arms tighter to her body.

'I didn't mean . . .' His voice trailed off as he watched her, an unreadable expression in his eyes. 'Look, time's a luxury I don't have. I'm moving around constantly. I've had to learn to read people quickly. Sort the good from the bad, if you like.' His hand touched her arm. 'And that's harder than you'd think. This industry attracts . . . Well, it doesn't tend to bring out the best in people. It's a mad job.'

'Not as mad as mine,' she muttered, looking out into the rows and rows of empty seats that extended into the blackness, out of sight. There were more seats than she could count and she didn't need to ask if every one of them would be filled tonight – the concert had sold out in an hour when tickets had been released; she knew because she and Jules had been two of the many trying to get through online. She tried to imagine the thousands of people who'd be here in just a few hours, screaming his name, lifting the lid off the place so that London rocked to his beat.

And right now he was standing here, with her.

He smiled, as if detecting a chink of light. 'That's true. Your job is bloody odd.'

'It's not usually. Everything's just . . . off-kilter at the moment.'

'But you must be enjoying it? Everyone's mad for you.' His fingers brushed hers. 'Including me.' He was staring at her, a smile on his lips, his fingers resting lightly on top of hers, and for a split second she remembered the fantasy of what this would be like to have Jamie Westlake touching her and looking into her eyes. But it paled beside the reality. Her imagination wasn't wild enough to have conceived the emotions he aroused in her. Every nerve ending was vibrating, her body shot through with adrenalin.

'Do *you* love it?'

'I love this,' he said, motioning to the arena around them. 'Playing live's what it's all about for me, but I'd gladly turn my back on the rest of it.'

'The paparazzi, you mean?'

'Them and the industry politics too – image, branding,

all that crap. Sometimes it seems so difficult just to get to play the songs I want to play.'

'But you're a massive star. Surely you get to control what you do and don't do.'

'You'd think. But I've been around a while now. The powers-that-be want me to bring in a younger fanbase. Collaborate with the right producers and DJs, even if it's not where I want to be.'

She hesitated. 'I heard you're doing a duet with Coco Miller.'

He glanced at her. 'Did you? And who did you hear that from, then?' His gaze was unnerving.

She tucked her hair behind her ear, embarrassed that he'd caught her out, reading gossip about him, rumour, innuendo. 'Well, actually, I didn't . . . didn't actually *hear* it. I r-read it somewhere.'

'You should believe very little of what you read about me,' he said, turning to face her again, a reluctant smile breaking through on his mouth. 'Although that bit is actually true.'

'So you are singing with her?'

'It's a shit song and Coco's . . .' He sighed, stopping short, and Nettie bitterly wished he'd not been so discreet. 'Well, Dave represents her and he's trying to break her over here. He said if I do this with her, get her some headlines over here, he'll give me carte blanche on the next song.' He shrugged. 'That's what I mean when I say don't trust what you read; it's all just a game. You'll only see what they want you to see.'

'What's the name of the one you want?'

'What, song or girl?'

'S-song,' she stammered, taken aback by the question, again feeling like he'd tripped her up.

His eyes were roaming her again. 'It's called "Night Ships".'

She blinked at him. 'Are you going to sing it tonight?'

He shook his head. 'It's not finished.' He locked her gaze with his. 'But I'll play it for you when it is, if you like.'

Her mouth parted. If she liked? If she *liked*? She stared back at him; he didn't seem to understand the impact of his words. He said such normal things, clearly oblivious to the stark fact that nothing about him was normal. She didn't feel normal around him. The oxygen felt thin and too pure; she wanted to gasp for air, to hold on to the walls for balance.

'Will you come tonight?'

The question startled her almost as much as the touch of his hand on her arm. She went to shake her head, but he beat her to it.

'If you come, I'll say something about the campaign.' A smile started in his eyes.

She arched an eyebrow, a smile escaping her. 'That's blackmail.'

'Not at all,' he demurred. 'You're simply . . . incentivizing me.'

His hand slid down her arm, finding her hand and squeezing it lightly. She looked away, feeling overwhelmed. 'Say you'll come.' His eyes had found her and wouldn't put her down.

She swallowed, remembering last night's pain as she'd sat in the taxi home, creeping into the house and diving under the duvet, knowing sleep wouldn't come. It had hurt far more than it should have done; she barely knew him, and what was ever going to come of it anyway? She had way more to lose than he did. 'I can't.'

'You'll be perfectly safe; we won't be alone. It'll be you, me and nineteen thousand, nine hundred and ninety-eight other people.'

She laughed even as she shook her head. 'Sorry, but I've got plans.'

'Cancel them, then.' His expression changed. 'This is work. We've got work to do.'

'Oh.' She felt foolish again. She'd thought . . . 'You mean you want me to wear the costume and do an appearance or something too?'

He winked, laughing lightly at his trick. 'No. I want *you* to be there. I'm just messing with you.'

She rolled her eyes and groaned.

'Hey, where were *you*?' Daisy demanded, coming back onto the stage and stopping dead at the sight of them talking, side by side. Daisy's eyes dropped to Jamie's hand, covering Nettie's. She quickly withdrew it and straightened up.

'Y-you went off too quickly. I got lost,' Nettie said as Caro and Jules reappeared too. Their happy-go-lucky expressions all changed when they saw Nettie had been left behind with the star. 'Was it good?'

Daisy didn't reply. Betrayal swam in her eyes like a shark.

Caro shrugged. 'Dressing room was boring. You need to have higher standards. J-Lo demands all white. Or is it Mariah Carey?' She stopped chewing to concentrate. 'Anyway, whatever, that sofa in there is rank.'

'Duly noted,' Jamie quipped. 'Did you see the rider, Jules?'

'I certainly did.' Her eyes were again sliding between him and Nettie. 'I agree with Caro. You can hardly call a bottle of whisky, Sky Sports and *Top Gear* magazine living the dream.'

'Well, what would you suggest?' he asked, jumping athletically onto the stage. Nettie tried not to stare.

'Well, if it was *me*, I'd have baskets of kittens and men in loincloths to give me a massage,' Jules cackled.

'Niche,' Jamie said slowly. 'What about you, Caro?'

Caro considered. 'Sour Skittles, a gaming chair and Xbox, and the whole place black with just lava lamps.'

'Huh.' He turned. 'Nettie?'

'I don't know. I didn't see it, remember?'

'Yes, but if you could demand anything back there, what would it be? What would make you relax?'

A double bed ran through her mind as he locked her gaze again. Was this . . . was this normal? Did every girl feel like this in his presence? Yes, probably. More than likely, she told herself as he walked towards her again. 'A bath and a good book and a glass of champagne,' she said quickly, opting for the safety of a stereotype to hide behind.

'A bath in the dressing room?' He had his back to the others now and a glint glimmered in his eye that made her blush again, shocked to see what was running so clearly through his mind. She felt her body respond in an instant, a heat running through her limbs and pooling in her belly.

'You asked.'

Jamie's name was shouted suddenly and he turned, shielding his eyes against a bright light coming from the far end of the arena. He gave a thumbs-up. 'Damn. I've got to go. *Sound checks.*'

'Bummer,' Caro said, quickly reaching for two Danishes

and putting one in her jacket pocket. The girl was permanently famished.

'Any of you free to come tonight?' He deliberately, it seemed, didn't look at Nettie, and she felt her stomach plunge at his question. She had thought he had been asking only her. She stared at the ground, not sure which way was up with him. Would he have asked them all if she'd said yes, or had it been his intention to invite the entire team along?

Jules's eyes widened. 'You mean backstage passes?'

'Of course.'

'I am *so* in,' she said, rubbing her hands together in excitement and prompting a stern look from Nettie. They were supposed to be seeing the Bond film tonight.

'I've got a dinner!' Daisy wailed, her hands clutching her hair. 'I've got nearly all the food. Ten people coming over. I couldn't cancel on them.' She looked at Jamie. 'Could I? Maybe I could. Do you think I should?'

'You shouldn't,' he said firmly. 'That's too many people, and no one likes a flake. How about you, Caro?'

'It sounds great, but I've got tickets for Cirque de Soleil tonight. There's a group of us going.' She gave a shrug.

'Never mind.' He turned to Nettie. 'Nettie?'

She blinked. Was she going mad? They'd already had this conversation.

'I've already got plans,' she said, looking pointedly at Jules. 'We made plans, remember? We're supposed to be going out together.'

Jules laughed. 'Give me a break! If you think I'm missing watching this man in action to watch James Bond save the world, think again!' Then Jules saw Nettie's expression. 'But we can always see it tomorrow, if you like.'

'I might join you, in which case. I haven't seen it yet either,' Jamie said casually, as though it was perfectly normal for one of the biggest rock stars in the world to announce he'd accompany them to the cinema.

'*You've* already seen it. You were at the premiere!' Jules pointed out with a laugh.

'I know, but I was distracted that night. I couldn't keep my mind on the film.' Every sentence was coded; every look was loaded.

'Will we get to meet the rest of the band too?' Jules asked, shooting strange looks over at Nettie.

He looked back at her. 'Of course. Anyone you want to.'

Jules raised a prayer to the skies. 'I love my job. I bloody love my job.'

'Great,' Jamie smiled as Ron reappeared. 'We've arranged some cars to take you on to wherever you need to go.'

Daisy's eyes widened happily. A chauffeur? 'Well, actually, I need to go to Selfridges food hall.' She looked across at Jamie. 'They do the *best* truffle oil there, and I believe in spoiling my friends.'

Jamie nodded. 'Great.'

'I'm going to Selfridges too, then,' Jules beamed. 'Methinks tonight warrants something new. Nets? Coming?'

'No, I need to get back.'

Jules gave an irritable groan.

'Caro?' Jamie asked quickly.

'Thanks, but I brought my bike,' Caro shrugged.

'Great, so then two cars, Ron – Oxford Street and Primrose Hill.'

Ron nodded, waving an arm out to indicate for the women to follow him.

'So I'll see you later,' Jamie said as Jules and Nettie

walked past him. 'I'll be on at nine. *Don't* be late.' His eyes were on Nettie, but she wouldn't look at him. She didn't dare.

'It's a date, handsome,' Jules said with a jaunty wink, making him chuckle.

'It certainly is,' Jamie replied, still pointedly staring at Nettie until she was forced to look up and stare back. She lasted three seconds.

'What?' Jules laughed as Nettie jabbed her in the waist with her elbow. 'Where's your sense of fun?' she asked, hooking her arm through Nettie's as they walked off the stage and into the warren of corridors out the back.

The waiting cars gleamed in the morning sun – waxed coats and tinted windows setting them apart from the dusty and dented hatchbacks parked at odd angles in the loading area as the crew buzzed about busily, their day already in top gear.

'Sure you won't come with?' Jules asked as Daisy slid into the car ahead of her.

'No, thanks,' Nettie said quickly.

'You're absolutely sure?' Jules tried again, pulling a sad face.

'Totally. It was an early call this morning. I'm tired, that's all.'

'Well, if you had a *late night* . . .' Jules cackled with a wink-wink tone.

'Later, Jules!' Nettie said, cutting her off and quickly sliding into the comforting cocoon of her own car, the cream leather upholstery butter-soft around her. There was a TV screen set into the back of the driver's headrest, and a tray of snacks – salted endamame, olives, vegetable crisps, Maltesers – on the armrest beside her. She looked at the bottle of Dom Pérignon already set in an ice bucket by her knee and wondered what the driver would think if she actually started quaffing that at nine in the morning.

The car moved so smoothly and quietly it was a moment before she realized they had even set off, sweeping noiselessly through the acres of currently empty car parks.

She popped a Malteser in her mouth – she knew chocolate for breakfast was hardly the way to start the day, but it wasn't as bad as drinking the champagne – and anyway, her heart had already been working harder this morning than a marathon runner's.

She didn't know this area of London well. Diametrically opposite to her quarter, she seldom had cause to come over here and she stared blankly into the rows of Victorian cottages and block council estates, a succession of graffiti tags making it clear this was someone else's patch.

Her hand found the TV remote and she switched on the screen. Predictably, it was already tuned to MTV and she jumped as the full power of Beyoncé's vocals flew at her, her finger desperately jabbing at the volume button to turn it down. She found mute first, grateful for the sudden silence and content to simply watch Beyoncé's powerful dance moves as she helped herself to more Maltesers.

Another Beyoncé song came on, then another and she realized she was watching a greatest-hits compilation. Idly, she switched the channel. Beyoncé was OK, but she'd never really been her thing. She found BBC News Channel and settled in to get the headlines.

Her hand reached for the Maltesers again, only to hit porcelain and she realized she had unwittingly eaten the lot of them. OK, there had probably only been ten in there, maybe fifteen – well, twenty, max – and she glanced at the driver in the rear-view mirror, embarrassed, but his gaze was dead ahead. This was what came of skipping meals, she could just hear her mother saying in her head, and she wished she'd had some of the fruit laid out at the O2. But who was she kidding? There was no way she could eat when Jamie was sparring and dancing around her, playing games, tying her up in knots so that her head was spinning and she was left breathless.

She wondered if any of his songs were playing on the music stations and she began channel-hopping again, craving a glimpse of him, an opportunity to blatantly stare at him and not have to cope with him staring back. Everything was just happening so fast. This time last week, she'd only just woken up to the mind-blowing revelation that he'd started following her on Twitter – that he actually knew she existed. Fast-forward seven days and he was smack-bang *in* her life – working with her, chasing her, flirting with her. *'I'd like to get to know you better, but it has to be in private.'* Did he do this with every girl who caught his eye? Were they as rattled as her? Because she wasn't sure her nerves could take it; it was like having a heat-seeking missile trained on her.

She flicked through some more channels, stopping as she found Coco Miller on VH1. Her hair was longer, and tousled in this video – her breakthrough hit in the States. She looked more all-American here, styled in denim cut-offs and a white T-shirt knotted in front, sitting in a pick-up truck with a guy in a baseball cap and a sneer. Nettie watched with growing despair as they parked in a corn-field and the camera cut to Coco dancing on the bonnet, her hair falling through her upstretched arms, face tilted to the moon. She looked ravishing; what man wouldn't find her alluring?

Did Jamie? Nettie thought back to the photos Jules had shown her of Coco and him coming out of the nightclub, hands tightly gripped, private smiles on their faces. *'You'll only ever see what they want you to see.'* Had those pictures been staged, or was that just wishful thinking on her part? He didn't know that she'd seen those photos.

She sighed, growing depressed, as the camera panned out on Coco twisted in white bed sheets, Marilyn-style. They probably *had* hooked up at one time or another. They looked like they should. They fit somehow, the two of them burning more brightly than those around them.

To her surprise, the car door opened suddenly and the driver was unexpectedly in her frame of vision. She was startled, mainly because she hadn't noticed the car had stopped moving.

'Oh . . .' she said, switching off the TV and reaching for her coat, sliding out. She hadn't even straightened up before she realized the problem. 'Oh, no, I'm sorry. It's meant to be Primrose Hill, not' – she looked around – 'Notting Hill.'

But the driver gestured towards the four-storey white Georgian terrace in front of her. 'Mr Westlake's orders, miss,' he said, closing the car door behind her and walking round to the driver's side, just as she saw a figure come to the window on the first floor. And her stomach tightened again.

Chapter Fourteen

The first thing she saw was the chandelier – it hung like a small planet in the hallway above a black-and-white marble floor, the staircase's metal balustrades swooping to an elegant curve on the bottom step. Jamie himself looked incongruent standing amid it all in his jeans, boots and a faded T-shirt.

'I hope you don't mind,' he said wryly, stepping back to allow her past, as she stopped dead on the top step. 'I'd prefer not to let anyone see me here,' he added after a moment, and she suddenly realized he was referring to fans, stalkers and the like. She walked into the house, warily, and he closed the door behind her.

'I thought you had sound checks,' she said, staring back at him. Where were they? And why had he brought her here? He'd seen her just half an hour ago.

'Actually, the band's not needed till four today.'

'But you said—'

'I got someone to say that when the others came back from the tour,' he replied. A flicker of amusement danced in his eyes. 'Yes, I was trying to get rid of them.'

Her stomach fluttered. He'd set all this up? 'Why?'

'They're great, but I meant what I said earlier – I want to get to know you better. We're going to be working very

219

closely together this week. We need to be able to trust one another.' His eyes flitted over her lightly and she felt that familiar rush again that came whenever she stood in his gaze. 'Don't you think?'

She blinked, aware of a small blush of pleasure creeping up her cheeks. She couldn't quite hold back a smile. 'But why bring me here? You were just talking to me at the arena.'

'No, I was stopping you from bolting again,' he asserted. 'And after last night, I wanted to be sure.'

A frown wrinkled her brow. 'Sure of what?'

'That you were as gutted as I was.' His eyes fell to her mouth, her skin alive suddenly to the temperature of the air around them as she saw the look in his eyes. 'There's always so many damned people about. Here it's . . . nice and private.' He took a step towards her and she felt the moment that had eluded them last night flutter down again like a butterfly caught in a net. Her heart rate rocketed in an instant.

'It is *nice*,' she said in a half-whisper, a smile placing an ironically understated stress on 'nice'.

'You like it?' he asked, his eyes dancing too now, only a half-step left between them.

Her peripheral vision took in the vast, white, luxe space. She was sure the cubic volume of her own house – which wasn't remotely small; in fact, it had often felt rattlingly big when she was growing up – could fit into the ground floor alone. 'Well, I like that it's private,' she said, feeling good sense and hesitation desert her. She would deal with tomorrow tomorrow. There was nothing beyond this moment, this man.

Except—

Except for *that* man. She noticed him suddenly and jumped, a small gasp escaping her at the sight of him – tall and heavily built, Thai, she reckoned, standing immobile at the far end of the corridor with his hands crossed in front of him.

Jamie looked behind him; his body relaxed.

'Everything's secure, sir,' the man said.

'Thanks, Pho,' Jamie said, but his eyes were back on her. 'Nettie, this is Pho, my security adviser.'

'Oh.' She swallowed and looked back at Pho. 'Pleased to meet you.'

'Ma'am,' Pho nodded, before turning and slipping away as silently as he'd come. She realized she'd seen him before – hanging around at the door at the pub last night, conspicuous in his suit, and again at Somerset House, something in his posture drawing her eye among the crowds.

She looked back at Jamie, to find him watching her. 'You OK?'

'Of course,' she nodded, a little too quickly.

They paused a beat, but the intimacy of the previous moment had gone again and she wanted to cry. Would he ever kiss her?

'Come on, I'll give you the tour,' Jamie said, putting his hand on the small of her back and leading her deeper into the house. He showed her the basement 'leisure complex' – subterranean pool, cinema room, sound studio – and the kitchen, a rich melange of walnut units and a cubist island cut from a single block of swirling chocolate and caramel-hued granite. He showed her upstairs, where they wandered from bedroom to bedroom – all of them white and high-ceilinged, with dark parquet floors and *verre églomisé* mirrors set into panelling in the walls, light flooding in through the full-height French doors and Juliet balconies, where bathrooms were clad in veined marble and appled limestone, with glass walls separating the baths from the rain showers, and walk-in wardrobes that were bigger than her kitchen.

The bones of the house were a dazzling display of good taste, reflecting proportion, light and stealth-wealth textures, but it was becoming less and less clear why he'd brought her here. There wasn't a rug on a floor, a print on a wall. Not a table, chair or bed. The place was completely empty.

'So what do you think?' he asked her as they came back into the kitchen again. She looked around. There was nothing to sit at, nothing to sit on. If she'd assumed him bringing her here was a prelude to a seduction, she'd been wrong again.

She gave a weak smile. 'It's amazing.' He inclined his head a little and she sensed she'd said the wrong thing. 'What?' she asked.

'You hate it.'

She folded with a nervous laugh. 'How could anyone hate *this*?'

'Well, you don't *like* it.'

'No, it's not that. It's just, well . . . empty.' She shrugged, looking around again, her eyes following the intricate grain of the chocolate granite island unit. How the devil had they got it in here? Surely they must have taken off the roof and craned it in? 'Is it yours, or are you looking to buy it?'

'I've just bought it.'

'Oh, right.' She couldn't even begin to guess at what this must have cost.

'On the advice of my financial advisers. They think it's a gold-clad investment.'

'Uh-huh,' she murmured, looking at the Molteni oven. 'Well, I'm sure it must be, yes.'

'But . . .'

She looked back at him to find him staring at her intently. 'Huh?'

'But . . . ? Go on. Say it.'

'There's nothing to say. It's wonderful. Amazing . . . Although you must have a *lot* of stuff to fill this,' she murmured, her eyes falling to the skirting boards, which came almost to her knees.

When he didn't reply, she met his eye again. One eyebrow was cocked. He was waiting.

'Fine,' she sighed, throwing her hands up in the air. 'It's just a bit *grand*. I mean, is this . . . is this really how you want to live?'

He stared at her, his eyes narrowing slightly and she knew she'd said the wrong thing. 'So you think it's like a mausoleum.'

'No! But you're . . . young. I would just have expected that you'd want something . . . fresher.' She couldn't read his expression and she felt her panic rise, defiantly sticking a hand on her hip. 'Anyway, what does it matter what I think?' She wondered whether he'd value her opinion if he knew she was still living in her childhood home.

There was a pause before the index finger of his right hand found hers on the worktop and tapped on it lightly. 'I keep asking myself the same question, but it does,' he said quietly. 'Besides, I'm pleased you've been honest. I thought the same.'

She looked at him in surprise. 'You did?'

He nodded. 'And you've just confirmed for me that I should sell it.'

Oh. Nettie kept her mouth shut this time. This house would be in the tens-of-millions price bracket. She didn't feel qualified to offer formal opinions on the topic. She didn't want him making decisions of that magnitude on her say-so.

'Have you got another place in London?' she asked as he walked towards the vast glass wall at the back and slid it open, leading her out to the garden. They stepped into a clipped oasis, evergreen box balls and bay trees planted in neat rows round small lawns. She followed after as he led her down the narrow garden. A fat-breasted robin, its feathers ruffled, hopped on the ground beneath a rosebush.

'No. This is the first place I've bought. I was never sure where I wanted to set down roots, and with travelling about so much, there wasn't really much point. But I don't think I can do another year living in hotels. This area seemed as good a place as any,' he said, turning and placing a hand to her elbow. 'Here, be careful – it looks a little icy.'

She trod carefully, aware of his touch through her coat. 'You'd be better off in Primrose Hill. No one would bother you there.'

He pulled a face. 'It didn't seem like that in the pub last night.'

'That was because you'd just switched on the lights! They'd ignore you within a week.'

'Being ignored? Huh, sounds surprisingly good,' he grinned, as they approached a screen of mature yews. She had assumed they were at the bottom boundary of the garden, but to her surprise, she saw a discreet opening had been cut between two of them. He indicated for her to lead the way and she stepped through gingerly, a gasp escaping her as she took in the unexpected sight. Ahead was an enclosed seating area, two outdoor charcoal-grey rattan sofas and a vast daybed arranged round an open fireplace that had been built into a standalone brick wall. The fire was roaring, grey smoke twisting out of the short chimney into the grey-blue sky, red-hot embers spitting out occasionally where they twisted and hissed into oblivion on the cold Yorkstone slabs.

'Take a pew,' Jamie smiled, motioning for her to move from her frozen position on the spot.

'I can't believe you've got a fireplace in the garden,' she murmured in amazement, walking slowly towards the nearest sofa. She didn't dare go *near* the daybed, could barely even look at it, in fact.

'Does it change your opinion of the house?'

'It could do, actually,' she laughed, sitting down primly in the corner as he wandered over to a table that had been laid out with plates covered with silvered domes. 'God, an outdoor *fireplace*. I love it.'

'I'll keep it, then,' he said. 'Hot chocolate?'

'Ooh, lovely,' she sighed. 'You know they've forecast snow this afternoon?'

'Have they? We'd better keep you warm, then.' Her eyes met his at the loaded comment, but he just grinned. 'Take your shoes off and put the blanket round you.'

'This one?' she asked, trying not to purr as she draped the orange and camel H-embossed cashmere blanket around her. 'OhmiGod, that's so nice,' she whispered in amazement again, as she snuggled into the warmth.

Jamie grinned. 'Good. Now try this. It's from Switzerland.'

He handed her a steaming mug and came to sit with her a moment later, a cup in his own hands and setting down a plate of . . . She looked at him in astonishment before a laugh escaped her.

There was no way that could be coincidence.

He shrugged. 'Yesterday at the Savoy – after you left – we somehow got on to talking about our ultimate breakfasts. Caro said full English, Jules said continental, Daisy said Buck's Fizz and strawberries, and Jules answered for you.' He looked very pleased with himself as she bit into the thick white bloomer bread. 'Toasted banana sandwiches and hot chocolate.'

He chuckled as she took another sip of the drink. 'I really can't believe that's your all-time favourite breakfast.'

'What's wrong with it?' she grinned back. 'My mum always made it for me when I was little.'

'And are you still little?' he teased.

'Well, what's yours, then?'

'A bacon butty sets me up pretty well. I'm, you know, pretty normal.' He laughed again as she took another bite of the sandwich, eyes closed with pleasure.

She put a hand over her mouth as she answered back flippantly, 'Listen, there's *nothing* normal about you – that much I do know.'

He pretended to look offended. 'And how am I not normal?'

The spectre of last night's missed kiss drifted between them both again – the growing crowd recognizing him, becoming excited by him, the very molecules in the night air beginning to jangle and jostle because he was in it. His

226

knees were angled towards her on the sofa, his head resting on his hand; he couldn't see the way the firelight made his skin glow. He couldn't see what she could see – that even if he wasn't one of the most famous men on the planet, he could still never be ordinary.

She blinked, knowing she couldn't say that. 'Well, you have a fireplace in your garden, for a start.'

He shrugged. 'That's just a designer's whimsical idea. Nothing to do with me.'

'You have hot chocolate and banana sandwiches left here, steaming hot, by invisible garden pixies.'

He grinned. 'You just have to believe.'

'I doubt you've even once cooked a meal, cleaned your house, washed or even bought your own clothes in the past . . . hmm, five years?'

He inhaled sharply, as though wounded by the observation.

'You probably fly by private jet.'

He didn't reply.

'And you only date supermodels.'

His mouth opened to protest, but she held up a finger. 'It's well documented in every single magazine and newspaper, so don't try to deny it. Your private life is a matter of national interest.' She was on a roll now. 'Plus you've bought a house with a *panic room* in it.' She gestured back towards the immaculate townhouse, only the roof visible from this secluded spot. 'And you have a bodyguard.' She paused. 'Apart from that, you're right – bacon butties for breakfast? You're completely normal. A man of the people.'

He nodded in silence, his eyes steady upon her. 'I guess when you put it like that,' he said finally, but his tone was flat and she sensed her joke had been too sharply edged, drawing blood. 'Hardly an attractive proposition, huh?'

She gripped her fingers tighter round the cooling mug, suppressing the sudden urge to tell him why all of that, *all* of it, seemed normal in comparison to the freak event that defined her life. But she had already gone far enough, souring the mood and undoing all the magic he'd conjured for them in this wonderful, intimate space. She sighed – would she ever get it right around him? She was as jumpy as a cricket in his company, her emotions too big and wild to contain in his presence, excitement and desire and fear and happiness and trepidation conflagrating in a combustible mix.

'Although you were wrong about one thing.'

'I was?' She cocked an eyebrow.

'I buy my own clothes.'

She reached out and patted his shoulder, resisting the urge to caress his cut deltoids. 'Well done,' she teased, grateful for the reprieve. 'What, exactly? Your socks?'

'T-shirts, actually. I'm particular about fit and feel. Selfridges are the only UK stockists of the brand I like.'

'Ah, that's a shame. Daisy and Jules are there right now – they could have picked some up for you.' Her eyes twinkled mischievously; he was so easy to tease.

'Or we could go.'

'Us?'

'Why not? I could do with some new ones for tonight.'

Ones? 'Oh, don't tell me – you wear something once and then throw it away?'

His eyes glittered. 'Actually, no, but it gets hot under the lights. I need several for each show.'

'Uh-huh,' she smiled. 'Listen, tell it to the judge. If you think this is persuading me you're Mr Normal, it's not.'

'Why not?' He shifted position slightly and she could feel the heat from his legs radiating towards her.

'Because you're going to Selfridges to buy T-shirts, for a start. Normal people go to Gap or M&S or Topman.'

'Fine. We'll go to Topman.'

'But what about the inferior fit and feel?' She laughed, enjoying herself enormously. 'And anyway, you'd have your bodyguard in tow.' She pulled a face. 'Not cool. They should probably close the store for you.'

Jamie was quiet for a moment, his eyes scanning her face before he reached for her mug, taking it from her with a solemn expression. 'Up.'

'Huh?'

He caught her by the wrist and pulled her to standing. He stared down at her, oblivious to the fact that his proximity to her whipped the air from her body. 'We're going shopping. For T-shirts. In Topman. With no bodyguard.'

The laughter in her eyes died. 'Is that wise?'

'Probably not,' he murmured. 'But it is normal.'

Ten minutes later they were on the bike, weaving through the chaotic city traffic, which was almost prescriptive for the last Saturday before Christmas. Buses, cabs and cars jostled irritably for space on the overcrowded roads, Park Lane almost at a standstill as they zipped speedily past them all, the late-morning sun reflecting off their visored helmets.

Her cheek resting lightly on his back, her hands clasped as loosely as she dared round his waist, she looked at

London's festive guise with rare detachment. Usually she was on those pavements, standing at the bus stops texting or dodging the rain as she darted in and out of the shops with her shopping list in her pocket. She rarely looked at the decorative window displays, hardly noticed the lights strung overhead; those weren't the things her eyes noticed or looked for.

But now, as a passenger on a bike, with her arms round a man who unseated her world, she was standing at the periphery of her own life like a watch eagle and she saw the festivity in the air, felt the party spirit. Her city – usually so defined by its greenness – was now white and red, silver and gold, the shuffling bustle of the crowds counterpoised by elegant mannequins striking *Vogue*-ish poses, snowy wonderlands set behind glass windows as yet contradicted by the bare hardness of the streets.

Roadworks were causing the traffic to snake up through Bayswater, so Jamie nipped through the park instead. He turned right at the Dorchester, and drove expertly up the narrow back streets that cut out the unnecessary crawl along Oxford Street, emerging again several minutes later onto New Bond Street. As they stopped at the lights, his foot on the ground, he didn't turn his head once towards the luxury boutiques that lined the road on either side, even though he could go into any of them and buy anything. He kept his gaze dead ahead and she smiled to think how normal – no, scruffy, poor, out of place – they both looked to the well-heeled shoppers on the Mayfair streets. 'You sure you don't want to go to Selfridges?' she called. 'There's still time.'

'You're funny,' he quipped as the lights turned green and he pulled quickly away, turning towards the Topshop flagship store on the corner of Oxford and Regent Streets. He parked quickly on a back street, but even though it was quieter there, Nettie noticed he didn't remove his helmet until the last minute, quickly pulling his beanie out of his coat pocket and covering his hair, before putting on a pair of sunglasses too.

'No.' She shook her head, reaching up and taking them off him again, folding them closed. 'They draw attention to you. No one wears sunglasses in a shop in December.'

He watched her and she saw the tension around his eyes showing he was, quite literally, exposed now. No disguise. No bodyguard. She remembered Pho's expression when Jamie had insisted he didn't escort them on this expedition, the way the security adviser's eyes had slid disapprovingly in her direction for a fraction of a second. She hesitated, feeling her sense of fun begin to dissipate. 'Although . . . now you look just like you.' She bit her lip. 'Maybe a cap would have been better.'

'Harder to get in my pocket, though.'

'Yeah . . . Maybe keep the helmet on?'

He laughed suddenly, grabbing her hand and she gasped involuntarily at his touch. He really did need to give her written notice if he intended to get within a half-metre of her – her nervous system couldn't cope. 'Fuck it. It'll be fine. Let's just go in, buy a T-shirt, be normal.'

'We can do that,' she grinned.

'You do realize *you* couldn't do this if you were in your costume.'

'No!' she scoffed.

He raised a knowing eyebrow. 'Trust me, you'd be mobbed.' And with a squeeze of her hand, he broke into a fast walk, leading her down Upper Regent Street for fifty yards – his head bent as low as possible, her jogging to keep pace beside him, before they took a sharp left into the store. But he didn't slow down there. If anything, it was busier in the shop than outside, and he rode the escalator with his head still down, face to the wall. Nettie tried to look casual, unnerved by his jumpiness.

They got to the menswear level and Jamie raised his head just enough to scan the shop floor for T-shirts. 'Great. Over here,' he said under his breath, grabbing her hand again and pulling her behind him like a kite as he wove through the rails with the same agility as he'd used on the bike. 'What do you think?' he asked, holding up a white T-shirt, screen-printed with a kitten in sunglasses.

Nettie stared at him. 'Really?'

He pulled a face, grabbing the next T-shirt along – a Rudolph motif with actual jingle bells sewn onto the antlers.

'Oh my God! Tell me you're joking,' she laughed.

'I'll get one if you will. We could both wear them on Christmas Day.'

'Uh-huh. Sure thing,' she said sarcastically.

'I'll Facetime you to make sure you're keeping to your end of the bargain,' he said, his eyes capturing hers and holding her for a moment.

'What . . . what are you doing for Christmas, anyway?' she asked casually, one hand nervously flicking the shirts beside her.

He put down the T-shirts and wandered over to the next rail. 'I'm going away. Staying at a friend's place.' His voice was quiet, his eyes – like hers – always flicking around the room, scanning the crowds. 'I haven't had a holiday in eighteen months, so . . .' he sighed. 'Just this week to get through and then I've got three weeks to myself.'

'Oh. That's nice.'

'You?'

'At home. We always spend Christmas at home.'

He looked back at her. 'In Primrose Hill?'

'Yep.'

'I bet that was great for you growing up, wasn't it? Knowing that all the presents under the tree were yours?'

'Something like that,' she lied.

'I had the opposite. My little brother was a nightmare for finding the presents and opening them all. Our poor mum could never outfox him with hiding places.'

Nettie frowned. 'Brother? But I thought you said you had two sisters?'

There was a pause.

'I do.' He swallowed. 'Ed died six years ago.'

The way he said the words, so quickly, answering a question before it was even asked . . . she knew from experience it meant the pain was still raw. She wanted to ask him what had happened but didn't dare.

'Oh my God. I'm so sorry,' she whispered, mortified.

'Don't be. It's not your fault,' he said, a smile on his lips that didn't quite reach his eyes. 'And it was a while ago, so . . .'

Six years didn't seem like a while ago to her. He moved over to the next rail and she followed after, sheepishly. 'Well, will your family be with you for Christmas?'

He glanced at her and she sensed rebuke in the movement, as though she'd gone too far, crossed a line. What was it he had said about them trusting each other? 'No. Milly's teaching in Tokyo for a year, and Kate's spending it with her new in-laws – she got married in the spring. And my folks are on a cruise. I had thought I was going to be abroad anyway, and by the time my schedule became clearer, they'd already booked this trip. It doesn't matter, anyway. Christmas is for kids. It isn't the same when you're grown up, is it? You don't care about stuff in the same way. I'm more excited about the prospect of just having some time off.'

'So who are you going to be with, then? You're not going to be on your own, surely?'

'Not the whole time. Some friends will be joining me later.' He caught sight of her expression. 'What? Trust me, solitude is a luxury for me. No one telling me where to be or what to do.'

'Right,' she said sadly. She couldn't imagine not spending Christmas with her family.

They had been wandering aimlessly through the rails for a few minutes now, too much chatting, not enough T-shirt-hunting.

'Oh wait, I've got it – this is the one,' he said, his signature laid-back smile on his face once more as he held up a T-shirt with a grizzly bear snarling on the front. 'Think the crowd will go wild for it?'

'I think they'll go wild regardless of what you wear,' she replied.

He glanced at her again, his khaki eyes flipping her stomach over like it was a pancake. 'Well, then, this one maybe?' He stepped closer and held up a black T-shirt that had 'Now or never' emblazoned across the front. He dropped his voice. 'It's a pretty damn good motto to live by, in my opinion.'

She looked up at him, her heart rate accelerating. 'But

will you cope with the fit and feel?' she asked teasingly, just as a distinctive sound made them both startle. A teenage girl in high-waisted jeans and a parka was standing ten feet away, her phone up to her face as she clicked and clicked again, the shutter opening and closing with the speed of a professional paparazzo's.

'Jamie! Can I have a selfie?' the girl asked confidently and with absolutely no sense of intruding.

Jamie instinctively turned away, dropping his head down, getting his glasses out of his back pocket.

'Sorry, do you mind?' Nettie said tartly, the words out before she could stop them. 'This is a private trip.'

'Yeah, but a selfie's only gonna take, like, a second.'

'Yeah,' someone else said too, and Nettie turned to find another couple of girls also standing there, phones at the ready.

Nettie twisted to find Jamie, his back to them all, head down as low as he could get. Nettie felt her anger flare.

'Sorry, but like I said, this is private. Jamie's not working right now.'

'Yeah, but Jamie's never off duty for his fans, are you, Jay?' one of the girls called, pushing past the rails to get closer.

Nettie stood in her way.

'What are you, his assistant or something?'

'Something,' Nettie replied crisply, rising herself to her full height, but although she was ten years older than this girl, she was several inches shorter, and the girl was already trying to get past her.

'Oh, go on. Just one, Jamie.'

'We need to go,' Jamie said to her quietly, his hand on her wrist suddenly as she felt him begin to tug her away.

But in coming over to her, he was within touching distance of the girls and their camera phones were up suddenly, documenting every microsecond, their excitement and agitation growing by the moment to have him so close.

Nettie saw people beginning to turn and point – 'Hey, isn't that . . . ?' – the clamour growing as Jamie's name rippled over the clothes and down the escalators, the number of onlookers beginning to swell as word spread like wildfire.

Jamie pulled her along behind him, but it was difficult to navigate with no clear routes past the clothes, and people were coming and standing at almost every point, blocking the way past. There was growing commotion now, voices rising, girls beginning to rush and push, as she and Jamie turned back, again and again, running out of directions to turn to. They were fast becoming hemmed in.

Suddenly, now, Nettie understood the look Pho had given her.

'The escalators are this way,' she said, pointing to the opposite direction to the one he was heading towards.

'No, too dangerous,' he said firmly, the tension she had glimpsed earlier setting his entire face now in a concrete mask – all life and colour gone. Nettie immediately saw his point. There could be a serious accident if overexcited teenage girls on their way up passed him going down.

'This way, the changing rooms,' he said quickly, turning on his heel just as a horde of girls spilled from the lifts on the far side, screaming his name. Nettie froze. She'd never seen anything like it. She couldn't believe how quickly everything had deteriorated. One minute they'd been joking about, the next they were looking for cover from two hundred hysterical strangers all wanting to touch him, be with him, have their photo taken with him.

What had she done? Goading him about having security, teasing him about being too precious to come out and buy a simple T-shirt. But it hadn't been a pose; this was his reality. He wasn't free to move about like a normal person. This was the price he paid for the jet-set lifestyle she had only ever read about in magazines, and it wasn't a joke. This wasn't funny.

'Nettie!'

She turned back at his shout, but he was across the shop floor now – unaware that she hadn't been behind him – an advancing crowd flooding between them and cutting them off from one another like an incoming tide. She couldn't barge past these people, who were already shoving each other, and there was no question of him walking into the middle of them. A few more minutes of this and there was going to be a riot.

'Just go! Get out of here!' she shouted over, waving her arms in the air to force him back.

'No!'

'Yes, I'm fine!' she shouted. 'Just go!'

For a moment he stared at her across the crowd, desperation in his eyes that this had happened – that they'd been separated, that he'd been noticed, that he'd so hopelessly failed at being normal – but then a security guard appeared and dragged him away and he was gone, blocked from her sight, and she stood alone and still in the store, just another girl, just another fan.

Chapter Fifteen

'Hey.'

Nettie looked up from her cross-legged position on the floor to find Dan leaning on his elbows across the counter and grinning down at her. 'Hey.'

'I thought you might be here.'

'And here I am . . .' she smiled, watching as several snowflakes fell from his hair towards her. 'Oh! It's started snowing, then?' The weather had been forecast to close in this afternoon, but she hadn't really believed it would after seeing the clear skies at sunrise.

'No. I just need to wash my hair,' he said, keeping a straight face until she'd grimaced. She shook her head despairingly and carried on unpacking the books from the box and scanning the ISBN codes.

He watched her for a moment. 'So what you doing?'

She arched an eyebrow. 'Registering the new titles.'

'Need a hand?'

She groaned as she glanced back up at him. 'Just tell me what it is, Dan. What do you want?'

'Nothing.'

'Have you changed your mind on the poncho?'

'No.'

'So then, what? You can't expect me to believe that

you've just wandered into the library and offered to help out of the goodness of your heart? I don't think so.'

'No, I was just wondering what you were up to, is all. You'd already gone out by the time I moseyed over this morning, which is *not* like you, as we well know.'

'Thank you.'

'Your dad said you must have had plans; I didn't like to point out to him the possibility that you might have got lucky and not come home last night.'

'It wouldn't matter if you did. I'm twenty-six,' she replied tartly.

'I know, but we all know you pulling an all-nighter is up there with solar eclipses.' He registered her expression. 'Sorry.'

She sighed but offered no explanation, instead continuing to scan the books, the pile beside her growing taller and taller.

Dan watched for a moment, before curiosity got the better of his pride. 'So which was it, then? Out early, or out all night?'

'Oh, Dan! You are so nosy!' she said exasperatedly, unwrapping her legs and standing up.

He shrugged, but his big blue eyes wouldn't shift off her, trying to read her.

'Look, I was *working*, all right?' she said, rolling her eyes.

'By seven o'clock on a Saturday morning?' He made a buzzer sound, the kind they used on game shows when a contestant's answer was wrong. 'Nope, not buying it. Try again.'

Nettie sighed, knowing exactly what he was thinking – that she'd spent the night with Jamie. She felt her heart constrict again at the memory of last night's mistake, this morning's disaster. She glanced at Dan – what he suspected was so far from the truth, and she wasn't sure she had the energy to explain to him that while he'd been eating his cornflakes, she had been owling as a mutant bunny on top of the O2; that while he and her father had been discussing bikes over their customary Saturday-morning elevenses, she had been in the middle of a stampede on Oxford Street.

'Believe what you like. That's the truth.'

Dan cocked an eyebrow and she looked left and right to make sure nobody was standing in earshot. 'You can see for yourself – Caro should have uploaded it by now . . . Besides, I'm surprised you're not working today. You said you were flat out.'

'Boy's gotta rest,' he shrugged, flashing her one of his best lazy-boy smiles.

'Hmm. Excuse me,' she said primly, raising the hatch and pushing past him with the armful of new books. They had often argued over his lackadaisical work ethic and she knew she wasn't the only one in the wrong job. Born to a single, working mother, his early years had been spare and hard, a ragamuffin childhood spent in holed jeans and too-small shoes. But his mother was a beautiful woman who knew how to work her wiles, and as she exchanged husbands for alimonies, their circumstances had changed quite drastically. She had even sent him to a private school for a while – two terms, apparently – but Dan had had none of it, being disruptive in class, teaching all the kids swear words and bunking off lessons until eventually he achieved his objective and was 'asked to leave'. Nettie often joked that he was the only plumber in London who knew Latin accusatives, but there was nothing funny about it; turning his back on his mother's lavishness and embracing the life he felt he was 'born to' was the only way he knew to reject her and the choices she'd made. It was no coincidence that while his mother lived in a £2-million villa in Highgate, he chose to live in a pint-sized houseboat, and he no sooner wanted to be a plumber than Nettie did, but it disappointed his mother's social ambitions, which was precisely the point.

Dan walked after her, ignoring her disapproval. 'So when are you finishing here, then?'

'Why?' she asked, stacking them on the 'new releases' shelf.

'I just thought we could go for a walk or something. I feel like I've hardly seen you this week.'

'You saw me last night, you fool,' she scoffed, before her eyes widened with sudden realization. He took a step back as she whirled round.

'What?' He held his hands up like she was pointing a gun at him.

'Has Dad sent you over here?'

'No!'

'He has. He has, hasn't he?'

'No, I'm telling you.'

She hugged the books to her chest. 'It's because of the tree, isn't it?'

'No.'

'I know it is. Just say it.'

Dan exhaled, knowing his cover was blown. 'Fine. He just wants to be sure you're all right. When he found you were gone so early this morning . . .' He shrugged.

She resumed stacking the shelf. 'I am fine, I promise. I really was working.'

241

He watched as she walked back to the front desk, ducking under the hatch.

'Is that all it is? I mean, I know your job's off-the-scale mental at the moment but you seem . . . distracted. Stevie thinks so too. Everyone's worried this is too much on top of—'

'Dan, please,' she pleaded. 'Let it go. I've told you I'm fine.'

He held his hands up. 'All right, all right. You can't say I didn't try.' He kicked the base of the desk lightly with his feet. 'So when are you knocking off here? I can meet you for a pint if you like?'

'Not for another hour or so.'

He gurned, before dropping his forehead on the counter. 'Can't you skive off a bit earlier?'

She looked up at him from beneath raised eyebrows. 'You know I can't. It's four-hour shifts, and the next volunteer is . . .' Nettie scanned the rota. 'Oh, it's Mary. She definitely won't get here early.'

'Fine,' Dan said, smacking the desk lightly with his palm. 'Well, then I shall wait for you.'

'You really don't have to.'

'I know.' He winked as she pulled a sheaf of papers out of a drawer and, ducking back under the hatch, walked over to the community noticeboard by the front doors. Unlocking the glass cover with a key in her pocket, she began taking down the old, expired notices and replacing them with the new ones – mother and baby groups, Pilates classes, guided walks, missing persons flyers, film night, book clubs . . .

'We could make an evening of it if you want?' he asked, watching the way she fastidiously checked the leaflets were level and smoothed them of wrinkles before placing a drawing pin in each corner. 'Got any plans?'

She stalled, thinking of the vast arena that was already gearing up for tonight's performance – last-minute touches being finalized as the light and sound systems were rigged up, the carpets vacuumed, the bins emptied, the staff clocking on and manning the exits, girls up and down the country already on trains, tickets clutched in their hands, make-up freshly applied . . . She thought of Jamie running through the set on that big stage, or maybe sitting on the so-called 'rank' sofa with his tube of Pringles and car magazine. Had she intruded on his thoughts all afternoon, the way he'd intruded on hers? Blink too long and she saw the image of him now scorched on her retina. She'd had to turn the radio off to silence the DJ talking up tonight, playing his songs . . .

Jamie had DM-ed her several times to check she'd got out OK, little understanding that no one had had any interest in her the second she was no longer with him, but her replies had been muted. What had happened this morning had left her rattled. No, more than that, scared. How could he live like that, only safe with a bodyguard in tow, only safe for as long as he wasn't recognized? And she knew he must never get to go unrecognized; his looks made people stare before they even clocked who he was.

'Nets?'

'Huh?' She realized Dan had asked her something again. 'If you've got plans, it's cool.'

'No, no,' she said quickly. 'I mean, Jules and I were going to see the new Bond tonight, but I don't think, now . . .' Her voice trailed off at the thought of seeing Jamie again, tonight, those things he'd said. She felt at war with herself, her nerves shredded. It would be so easy to go along with it all, allowing herself to be swept up in the glamour and excitement of a fantasy coming true, but hadn't this morning showed her that real life would always intrude? She couldn't pretend this was normal, and after this morning, neither could he.

She inhaled sharply, her mind made up. 'Sounds good.'

He relaxed into a smile. 'OK to hang at your place? I'm out of coal, so it's a bit chilly . . .'

She rolled her eyes. 'It's fine. Dad's engrossed in *HMS Victory* anyway. I don't think he's ever going to leave the kitchen again.' She locked the glass door and pocketed the small key. Dan was standing still, watching her. 'You OK?'

He blinked. 'Yeah. Yeah. I'll see you over there, then,' he said, pulling the hood up on his puffa and walking backwards towards the door. 'Toffee vodka, right?'

'I would kill you,' she laughed.

'Don't I know it,' he grinned, turning on his heel and ducking his head low as he stepped out into the snow.

The flame flickered weakly in the black arched Victorian fireplace. Theirs was one of the only houses in the square to boast a 'real' fire, but the wood her father had last picked up at the service station wasn't aged and it hissed and spat sparks out onto the orange Boucherouite rug.

Dan had 'baggsed' the sofa and was stretched lengthways across the orange velvet chesterfield, his feet dangling over the end and a bowl of crisps resting on his stomach. A fresh pint was positioned in perfect reach of his hand on the floor.

Nettie was huddled in her mother's favourite chair, hugging a cross-stitched cushion that read, 'Fall down seven times. Get up eight.' Her face was pointed in the direction of the telly, but she had yet to notice that Dan had surreptitiously switched it over to the football highlights, his eyes sliding over to her every so often, grateful and incredulous that she hadn't realized. She was still distracted by Jamie's last message – the one she hadn't responded to, checking that she was still coming tonight.

'Hungry yet?' Dan asked, trying to get her attention.

'Hmm? Oh, no . . . Unless you are. I can eat if you want to.'

Dan frowned. 'I've never known you so unbothered by your stomach before. You're not on another of those bloody diets, are you?'

'No.' She realized she had forgotten her fruit-only resolutions earlier in the week, although the combination of terror and lust had seemingly revved up her metabolism, as her jeans felt looser than usual.

The doorbell rang and she waited a moment for her father's voice to ring out, saying he'd get it. But all was silent from the kitchen and she got up with a puff.

'Probably Jules,' Dan murmured as she slipped into the hall.

'Yep,' Nettie said, recognizing the slight silhouette through the frosted glass.

'Hey!' Jules said in greeting as she opened the door. 'You need to get a wreath put up on that d—' Her eyes fell to Nettie's 'Saturday night in' attire – Jack Wills tracky bums, fleecy striped socks and one of her dad's old jumpers. 'Seriously? That's what you're going in?'

Nettie closed the door to a sliver, frantically shushing her and trying to keep Jules's voice from carrying throughout the house. 'I'm not going, I told you.'

Jules barked a sharp laugh. 'Ha! Right, pull the other one.' She was looking sensational in second-skin over-dyed black jeans, thigh boots and a coral-pink leather biker jacket. Her smoky eye make-up alone must have taken half an hour.

'I mean it, Jules.' Nettie's voice was a whisper. 'Dan's here and we're just going to have a chilled one.'

'But . . .' Jules was gobsmacked. 'We had plans.'

'Yes. To go to the cinema. I never said I wanted to go to that concert.'

'You didn't have to say it!' Jules almost shrieked. 'You were as manic as me trying to buy the freaking tickets six months ago. It went without saying . . . I thought you were joking!'

'Sssh!' Nettie hissed desperately, putting the door on the latch and closing it behind her as she came to stand on the step. 'I just don't want to, OK? Please don't make a big deal about it.'

There was a long silence as Jules stared at her in angry disbelief as it dawned that Nettie wasn't joking. 'Look, what the hell happened with you two last night? You're being dodgy as hell. One minute you won't even look at him, the next you're huddled in a corner, whispering on your own together, and now you're being weird *again*.'

'Look, I know what I'm doing. It's for the best, Jules.'

'Aye, aye,' Dan's voice piped up, the door opening wide behind her, 'what's going on here, then?'

'Nettie's bailing on me, that's what!' Jules fumed back.

Nettie looked between her two friends pleadingly. 'Dan and I have got plans, Jules.'

'*We* had plans!'

'Different plans. And they changed, so . . .'

'Oh, right. So I'm just expected to go on my own, am I? Rock up to the VIP area like Billy No Mates?'

'Go where?' Dan asked, baffled.

'Jamie's playing at the O2 tonight and he asked us to go, that's what! Only, Nets is trying to make out she's got to honour a commitment to watch telly with you instead.'

Dan looked back at Nettie with unusual scrutiny. 'Why didn't you say?'

'Because I just don't want to go, all right?' She looked back at Jules. 'And I'm sure they'll all be really welcoming and friendly. It's not like you can talk at these things anyway.'

Jules glared at her. 'I would *never* do this to you. I'd never drop you in it, even if I was in your shoes.'

'I'm sorry, Jules. I just . . . can't.'

'That's it, is it? You can't?'

'Hang on, is this about last night? Did something happen?' Dan asked, straightening up so that he towered over her in the doorway. 'Did he try it on with you? Did he try and make you do something you—'

'No! It was nothing like that. Really. I . . .' Nettie shrugged hopelessly, looking back at Jules. 'I'll make it up to you, I promise.'

'No, you won't. Everything's run on your terms. Your story's so much worse than everyone else's; no one else's problems can possibly compete. We just have to get on with it, while you . . . you get the special treatment.'

'Jules—' Nettie said, her cheeks stinging like every word was a slap.

'Forget it,' Jules said, turning on her heel and storming back down the path, almost going flying on an icy patch.

The snow wasn't settling, but the temperatures were plummeting again.

'Jules!' she called, making to run after her; but she stopped abruptly in her tracks as a uniformed driver suddenly jumped out of a glistening Mercedes that was parked on the street and helped Jules to the car. Nettie's mouth dropped as he opened the gleaming back door and Jules climbed in, disappearing behind the blacked-out windows. She'd hired a limo?

Nettie shivered as she looked onto the reflected vision of her house, wishing she could see her friend through the windows. It was a moment before she realized the driver was walking up the path towards her.

'Hello?' she said questioningly.

'Good evening. Are you Dan Parker?'

Dan nodded back stiffly, reaching suspiciously for the package the driver held out to him. The driver looked across at Nettie. 'And, Miss Watson, I was instructed to give you this in the event that you didn't accompany Miss Grant.' He held out a white envelope.

'What's that?' she asked.

The driver didn't reply – he probably thought she didn't need him to tell her it was a white envelope – and she took it from him, opening it with fumbling hands.

'Prefer mine,' Dan mumbled, only just suppressing a grin as he tore open his package. Nettie was aware of the way he sucked in his breath as the silky red football shirt fell free of the tissue paper, black scrawled signatures – some personalized to Dan himself – all over the front.

'You've got to be kidding me . . .' he said under his breath, holding it up to the street light. But Nettie wasn't concentrating. It wasn't joy she was feeling at the sight of her gift, a handwritten note. It was a threat of sorts, really, and the shock made her laugh out loud.

'*If you don't show, nor will I.*'

She looked back at the driver. 'This is a joke, right?'

The driver didn't respond. Nothing about him suggested 'jokey'.

'He surely doesn't mean . . .' she faltered.

The driver's expression was impossible to read – had he read the contents of this? – but a tiny shrug of his hands indicated he knew nothing beyond these orders.

She read the words again and again, vaguely aware of Dan reading over her shoulder. He couldn't mean he wouldn't go on stage tonight. Could he? He wouldn't let down all those people . . . There was no way he could mean that, and yet . . . what other translation could there be? They hadn't made any plans for the campaign next week. They hadn't made plans for anything beyond tonight.

She looked back at the driver, too stunned to move.

Behind him, the rear window of the car slid down and Jules's furious face peered out. 'What's going on?'

The driver arched an eyebrow. 'I'll wait, shall I?'

They were quiet in the car. Jules still wouldn't look at her, and the bottle of champagne was untouched in the ice bucket between them.

'Look, I'm sorry, OK?' Nettie tried again, placing a hand lightly on Jules's arm, but she snatched it away. 'You were right. I know I've been selfish and . . . self-absorbed.'

Jules stuck her nose in the air.

'You've had a lot going on too, I know that. Mike totally should have given you that promotion in the summer: you deserved it. We all know he's so threatened by you he's terrified of giving you extra power. He knows you're the real leader of this team, not him.'

'Damn straight.'

'And I know it's been really hard living without a washing machine.'

'You've got no freaking idea,' Jules muttered.

Nettie lowered her voice, knowing she was stepping onto thin ice. 'And I also know you're still cut up about he-who-must-not-be-named, even though you'll deny it to the death.'

'Oh no. I am *over* him. He was a lying, cheating *git*,' Jules said fiercely, whipping round so quickly her own hair hit her in the face.

'I agree,' Nettie said quickly. 'I never liked him.'

'Thought he was God's gift just because he had that sexy grin—'

'Ugh!' Nettie pulled a face.

'And looked fit in the buff.' Jules stopped talking abruptly, her eyes misting over. Nettie reached for her arm again, the gesture breaking her trance. 'I was glad to see the back of him.'

'Totally,' Nettie nodded firmly. 'He's nowhere near good enough for you. He was punching way above his weight scoring with a girl like you, and one day, one day he'll realize it.'

'And it'll be too late.' Jules's eyes were shining.

'Yeah.' Nettie squeezed her hand.

'Way too fucking late,' Jules murmured, dropping her gaze.

'If he could only see you tonight, he'd die of regret on the spot.'

Jules gasped. 'Instagram me,' she said, contorting herself into a seductive pose. 'And make sure you get as much of all this in as poss. It's got to be clear we're in a limo.'

'Of course,' Nettie said, twisting in her seat as Jules quickly uncorked the champagne and filled a glass to hold. She flashed a truly dazzling smile. 'Which filter?'

'Hefe. I always look good in that.'

Nettie smiled, relieved she'd been forgiven. 'Done.'

She passed the phone back to Jules and looked out through the dark windows. The O2 was just ahead of them, billowing against the horizon, and they had been crawling along in heavy traffic for several minutes now. They stopped at some sort of security checkpoint and she saw the driver flash a pass, upon which a barrier was raised and they pulled into an adjoining lane, clear of traffic.

Ahead, blue lasers swung and flashed in the sky like samurai swords. This was the only place to be in London tonight, and they were VIP all the way.

Jules giggled with excitement and held up her glass as they sped up again. 'Bottoms up, then.'

The same thing happened twice more – the driver flashing a pass to various security guards – and Nettie only just had enough time to drain her drink as they drew up to a large loading area round the back that was cordoned off and heavily guarded.

'Here we go,' Jules squealed as the door was opened and she stepped out, straight into a wave of noise. 'Whoa!' she cried, putting her hands to her ears.

'Wow!' Nettie echoed, doing the same.

Ron was waiting by the door, seemingly for them. Nettie smiled her thanks to the driver, wondering whether to tip him, wondering whether he'd radioed ahead.

'Don't worry – we've got some noise-cancelling head-phones you can use if you want,' Ron said as they ran up to the door, eager to get out of the cold. Nettie wasn't in the best-considered outfit, given the very limited time frame she'd had to get ready, and she felt underdressed compared to Jules, in her boyfriend jeans, strappy heels, acid-peach T-shirt and khaki jacket.

'Are you *kidding*?' Jules laughed, hooking her arm through Nettie's and dragging her onwards as he quickly turned and led them both through a long, concreted corridor. He walked quickly, the girls almost having to break into a trot to keep up.

To their left, behind the makeshift wall, was the stage and Nettie could feel the vibrations from the amps pulsing through her feet and making her bones hum as the music boomed. High-pitched screams came in a constant pulse, the sound like a force field that instinctively made her want to step away and take cover.

She checked the time on her watch as she heard singing. Ten minutes past nine and he was on already. She felt a pinch in her stomach and a stain creep across her cheeks. Of course he was! How stupid she'd been to think he'd keep all those people waiting just for her – and she'd betrayed her egoism by falling for the bluff. She'd come, he would know now, in the very hope that he'd been telling the truth, flattering her . . .

'Yeah!' Jules yelled, beginning to dance as they walked.

Nettie smiled back as Jules grabbed her arm excitedly, but she couldn't let herself go in the same way. She felt breathless and overwhelmed by the scale of everything – the noise, the size, the energy that was electrifying the air.

She could feel it crackling around her. It was the flip side, the good version to what had happened earlier. And this was just his *job*. He'd been right earlier when he'd said his job was odd. What was wearing a fancy-dress costume for a couple of weeks compared to this?

She wondered where Ron was taking them. Down to the mosh pit? Into the wings? The anticipation of seeing Jamie again made her heart try to compete with the bass beat and she forgot all about the look on Dan's face when she'd turned to him at the door.

They climbed a few steps and turned into another corridor, which had a run of doors on both sides, huge black-and-white posters of Jamie slapped up along the walls, lest anyone should forget who was playing here tonight. She dared herself to look into his khaki eyes as they walked, a kind of endurance test. Maybe if she could practise holding that gaze before she had to do the real thing . . . ?

Ron had stopped outside a door and popped his head in. 'Sorted.'

'Oh *cool*!' Jules said, walking straight in, with the familiarity of someone who'd been here many times before, rather than just the once. She must have said something inside, for Ron nodded and Nettie stepped out of the way to let him pass, watching as he ran off in the direction from which they had just come and talking into a walkie-talkie.

When she turned back, Jamie was in the doorway, watching her, wearing the faded black jeans he'd been in yesterday and an indigo T-shirt, the fit and feel of which looked indecently good.

'You're not on?' she asked, after what seemed like an age.

'I said I wouldn't, didn't I?'

She gave a nervous laugh. 'Yes, but . . . I didn't think you actually meant it.'

'Didn't you?' His eyes were steady upon her, unrelenting. 'And yet here you are.'

She looked away. 'I wasn't sure if it was' – she swallowed – 'a joke, some sort of game.'

'I never say what I don't mean.' He seemed amused. 'So now *I'm* late because *you're* late.' He walked out into the corridor towards her with a slow tut. 'You've made all those people wait . . . Can you hear them?'

She should have done. They were right behind the wall, but as he stopped in front of her, all she could hear was the rush of blood in her ears.

His hands brushed down her arms, leaving a ripple of goosebumps in their wake. 'I'm sorry about earlier. I felt like such a shit for leaving you there.'

'What are you talking about? It would have been dangerous if you'd stayed. The second you went, I was fine. I just felt so bad for making you go out without Pho.'

'He was pretty mad with me when I got back.' His eyes danced. 'I guess he's never tried to impress a beautiful girl before.'

She didn't know what to say to that and her eyes fell to his chest. 'Nice T-shirt.'

'Thanks.'

'Selfridges?'

He shrugged, a low laugh escaping him. 'What can I say? They deliver.'

She laughed too. 'Good. I'm glad.'

'*I'm* glad that you're here,' he replied quietly. He still hadn't shaved and his stubble was now a light beard. It brought out the colour in his eyes and framed his mouth. He took her hand and wagged her arm lightly. 'Although it's just as well I resorted to blackmail. I didn't think you'd behave.' His eyes fell to her lips as they parted into a shocked 'o'. Yet again, silence bloomed between them. Words couldn't say what eyes could. 'Come on, then. We'd better give them what they want.'

He put his hand in the small of her back and walked her down the corridor to where Ron was now standing by a door, a guitar in his hands.

'Ready?' Ron asked, handing it over, and Jamie slung the strap over his neck, the instrument moulding into his body as familiarly as a child, the way she wanted to.

'I am now,' he said, glancing at her as he adjusted the strap. 'Don't. Leave.'

She shook her head, overwhelmed. Overpowered. Her head had no chance against her heart.

Ron opened the door and the wall of sound fell upon them, Jamie's name amplified into a war cry that sounded to the heavens. He took a deep breath, a grin growing on his face as he took one last look at her, and then he disappeared through the doorway, the roars and cheers exploding in on themselves a moment later, like fireworks that kept repeating to something ever more beautiful, as the light found him and all those eyes came to rest upon him and him alone.

'Come on, you can watch from over here,' Ron said, leading the girls through the doorway and up another set of steps. Everything was draped in black cloth, the noise like a heat, a cloud she had to push through.

She started as something touched her shoulder, turning

KAREN SWAN

to find Jules standing behind her with an expression of envy, excitement and concern marbled on her face.

'Oh my God! Like, get a room!'

But Nettie clutched her by the arm. 'Jules, you've got to promise me you won't tell him.'

Jules looked taken aback. 'But—'

'Promise me! I'll never speak to you again if you tell him.'

Jules looked shaken by the wildness in her eyes, the ring of truth in her words. 'Of course I wouldn't,' she said.

'You have to say it.'

Jules blinked, the excitement and envy disappearing from her face now so that all that was left was the concern. 'I promise, Nets. He'll never hear it from me.'

Chapter Sixteen

The after-party at Bodo's Schloss was everything Jules had ever dreamed and she was in her element, dancing on a table with another girl and impressing the band's bass guitarist with her air guitar. Many eyes were upon her and Nettie felt grateful, for once, that she was too far out of reach for Jules to drag her up there too, which was the usual way of things.

Instead, Nettie was sitting in the middle of a semi-circular booth, with Dave, Dave's wife, Minnie, and Jamie himself. Nettie had Minnie to her left and Jamie to her right, and so far was doing an admirable job of appearing nonplussed to be sitting with the star of the show. His left arm was slung out along the booth behind her, his left thigh so close she could feel the heat from it, but he had yet to graze a single finger along her neck or touch his leg against hers – and the wait was killing her.

Because Jules had been right earlier. They had a chemistry together that was impossible to ignore. She'd known it the moment she'd laid eyes on him at the cinema on Thursday night – had it really been only forty-eight hours since then? – and she knew just what they were spinning towards. It was as predictable as the rising of the sun, and for all her futile efforts to keep him out of her life, it was already too late: he was in, straight into the smack, bang centre of her world and she wouldn't sleep now till she knew the feel of him; she wouldn't eat till she knew the taste of him; she was addicted even before their first high.

People kept coming over to their table to congratulate Jamie, slapping him hard on the shoulders and fist-bumping him in the case of the men, the women bending down to kiss his cheeks, flashing plenty of cleavage and lingering looks.

Nettie didn't know how to react to them. Jamie seemed as friendly to one as to the other, showing no particular favouritism or interest, but neither did he reassure her with a squeeze of her hand or something that told her – and all those other girls – that he was with her tonight. Nettie kept scanning the crowd for sign of Coco Miller. She'd thought she'd overheard someone saying she was here. Or was that just paranoia?

'So how did you and Jamie meet, Nettie?' Minnie asked her, recrossing her legs and seeming genuinely interested as she sipped through the straw of the famous ski-boot cocktail.

'Uh, through work.'

'You're a singer too?'

'Oh!' She laughed quietly at the idea. 'No. Nothing so exciting, I'm afraid. I work for an agency that handles the CSR of big companies – corporate social responsibility,' she added, knowing from experience that that would be the next question. 'We connect big corporations with charities or community projects and create campaigns that help raise public awareness and funds for them.'

'Oh, so you're like a charity fundraiser, then?' Minnie said brightly, holding out the boot for Nettie.

'Basically, yes,' Nettie smiled, finding her straw and drinking too. Her head was spinning, her entire body fizzing and she'd barely drunk a drop yet.

'Oh, I get it! You're involved with that thing Jamie's doing with the bunny?' Minnie said excitedly.

'That's right.'

'Oh my God – have you met the Blue Bunny Girl? She's amazing!'

'Thanks,' she laughed, before adding quickly, 'I'll tell her you said that.'

'Do you know her?'

Nettie nodded, drinking a bit more.

'What's she like?'

'Um, normal, I guess.'

'Oh, I bet she isn't,' Minnie squealed. 'She's so hard-core. I'd be terrified if I ever met her. Jamie's obsessed, isn't he?' she said, directing the question to her husband.

'Yeah, I reckon so,' Dave laughed, shooting Nettie a knowing wink.

Nettie blushed. Really? Did he really mean it? Jamie, obsessed with *her*?

'It's so amazing you got him,' Minnie continued. 'I mean, he never says yes to that kind of thing, does he, Dave?'

'Actually, it was all his idea,' Dave said. '*I* was the one trying to talk him out of it. He's in the middle of a world tour. We're doing the States in the new year – thirty dates there, then down to Brazil and Argentina.' Dave shook his head. 'And with the single out next week, he should be trying to find time in his diary, not filling it up even more.' He gave a big shrug. 'But he's a stubborn bugger. There's no talking him out of anything he wants to do.'

He drained a shot just as the crowd on the dance floor before them parted and a waiter came through, carrying an open nebuchadnezzar of champagne topped with a sparkling, hissing and crackling light fountain. A cheer went up as it was set down on the table in front of Jamie and he looked across at her, as if assessing her reaction. Compared to the frenzied revellers cheering and dancing and drinking around them, he seemed curiously calm – the eye at the centre of the storm, inured to the fact that all of this was for him, because of him, that everyone wanted to be with him, one way or another.

Maybe he'd burned off his energy earlier. Images of him on stage flashed back to her – the way he'd run across it for two hours, jumping on and off the massive speakers and jamming with his band, making jokes with the crowd, his laugh sexy and low as he chatted, strumming chords all the while as hundreds upon hundreds of girls reached forward, their arms outstretched, phones recording him. Every time he'd come off stage, he'd come off on her side, speaking to her quickly – was she enjoying it? Was she OK? Was there anything she needed? – as the sweat rolled down him from the heat of the lights, his eyes fixed upon her as he rehydrated. Only once had he exited on the other side of the stage, when he'd changed his T-shirt, but she had still been able to see him and the tight roll of muscles beneath his tanned skin as he pulled an identical T-shirt over his head.

'Just another quiet Saturday night, huh?' she quipped, a tremor in her voice.

'Exactly.' His eyes held hers and the noise around them tuned out. It was like stepping into a soundproofed studio, their togetherness filling the space, their silence louder than any amp.

Was she imagining this? Was her mind playing tricks? Was all this hyper-inflated to her because of who he was? Had his fame distorted things? Was she acting on a lust that had been fostered when he was nothing more than a face on a wall, a voice in her ear? Not a real person but an idea, a fantasy?

But no, it couldn't be – she was only here now because *he'd* chased *her*, brought her back here with his own driver, made threats to stand up all of London if she didn't show . . .

The light fountain burned itself out and the waiter pulled it from the bottle's neck, struggling to tip the heavy bottle to pour it into their glasses. Champagne splashed everywhere, making Nettie shriek as cold droplets made contact with her bare skin. Jamie laughed, jumping up from the booth suddenly and grabbing the bottle himself, his thumb positioned over the neck as he began shaking it up and down.

Dave was on his feet in an instant, clearly knowing what was coming, but Nettie and Minnie weren't so fast and in the next moment cool crystal champagne was sprayed through the air and all over them. The room erupted as Jamie turned in circles, the bottle emptying fast, but not fast enough.

The girls screamed with delight, but there was no way out of the booth for either of them with Dave at one end and Jamie at the other. Minnie – more seasoned in these matters – climbed up onto the table, holding her hand out to help Nettie do the same, but Jamie, spotting their escape attempt, stood on the spot and directed the spray at them both, making them dance as the champagne rained down.

Nettie had never laughed or shrieked so hard, her heels drumming on the table as she was steadily soaked.

'Oh my God! Make him stop!' she squealed to Minnie, who had her hands and face in the air, mouth open and trying to drink the fizzy stuff like a toddler catching snowflakes on her tongue.

Finally, eventually, the steady stream dwindled to a trickle and she pushed her wet hair out of her eyes to find Jamie standing still, watching her, his shoulders shaking as champagne dripped off her nose and eyelashes.

He held a hand out to get her down from the table and she jumped, straight into his arms.

'I can't believe you just did that!' she gasped, pushing her hair back again.

'Enlightened self-interest,' he grinned.

'Huh?'

'Well, now we need to get you out of those wet clothes,' he murmured, a low flame flickering in his eyes.

'Yo! Jay!'

A microphone was suddenly thrust between them. Gus, the band's bass guitarist and seeming target of Jules's affections, was standing beside them, a guitar hanging from his neck and a bottle of tequila in his hand. 'Seems like a fine time to debut the new tune. You up?'

Jamie's shoulders sagged ever so slightly, a tiny movement only she caught, and she understood what it meant – he'd done his job for tonight. But he took the microphone without breaking eye contact with her. 'Three minutes, thirty-eight seconds,' he said, gently grazing a finger down her cheek. 'That's all this will take.'

She nodded, too overwhelmed to reply as Jamie's eyes fell to her mouth for a moment, before he turned and headed into the crowd. Seconds later she heard the guitars start up and then there he was, standing on one of the speakers, looking straight at her, singing every word straight to her.

She stood as still as a heron in the water, dripping wet and transfixed as the minutes counted down: one, two, three . . .

The seconds . . . fifty-three, fifty-four . . .

And then he was back in front of her – warm and tall, smiling and intent, oblivious to the way everyone rotated round him like he was the sun to their stars, the dance floor beginning to heave again now that he was standing on it. The crowd swallowed them up, holding them in a loose embrace.

'You're late,' she managed.

'A capella version,' he tutted, shaking his head slightly. 'Gus can't resist going long on the solo.'

'Ah.'

The room contracted down to just the two of them again and they both knew this was it.

'Let's get out of here,' he murmured, his eyes on her mouth.

'OK,' she breathed.

He inhaled sharply and grabbed her hand.

'Jay?' Dave asked, looking on in surprise as they dashed past him.

'Speak to you tomorrow, Dave,' Jay said firmly.

'Bye, nice meeting y—' she began to say to Minnie, but Jamie was too quick for her to finish, pulling her along after him as he ducked everyone's stares and led her to a side door the staff had been using. They darted through it into a narrow passage, Jamie's grip firm and sure around her hand as she half ran after him, towards a fire door that led outside. They burst out into the night. It was sleeting, the snow orange as it dashed past the street lamps like arrows.

'Where's the driver?' Jamie asked the security guard, who immediately stamped out his cigarette in surprise.

'Round the front, Mr Westlake. We thought you'd be leaving by the front as usual.'

'Get him here, now. I don't want anyone seeing us.'

'Yes, sir.'

He turned back to Nettie. She had her arms wrapped tightly around her torso, her wet clothes clinging to her and leaving her shivering in the cold. 'I've left my jacket on the seat,' she said. 'I should probably go and—'

'Min'll take it for you.'

'Oh. OK.' The way he said it – so sure – she couldn't help but wonder whether Minnie had done this for his other girls, swept off their feet so quickly they too had left their coats.

Another bolt of panic hit her, an adrenalin shot to the heart, as he shrugged off his jacket and put it round her shoulders, his touch like electric shocks. What was she doing? There could be no good outcome from this. She was flying too close to the sun here, dazzled and disoriented. His world was too bright, too big for her, and the flames that had been growing between them would be mere embers by morning.

'Come back inside. You can't stand out here in wet clothes,' he said, opening the door and leading her back into the corridor again. The door closed with a thunk and they stared at each other in the dim light. Alone at last.

Those 20,000 people gone.

The VIPs in the next room gone.

Jules, Dave, everyone gone.

And then the barriers, the reservations, all the reasons why this was not a good idea – they were gone too as he rushed at her, cupping her face in his hands and kissing her with a passion that stripped the world down to just the two of them.

When they finally pulled apart, she wasn't even sure if she was still standing. Gravity had lost its pull. He looked down at her. 'Drive a guy crazy, why don't you?' he murmured, a small smile creeping into his eyes as he put his hands on her hips and pushed her gently against the wall. He kissed her again, his hands closing round her neck, his fingers reaching through her hair, tugging it back gently so that she was held in place, looking up at him. 'Your place or mine?'

The question was like a nail hitting a pipe and laughter burst out of her. If he only knew what 'her place' translated into in reality – in his head, he probably imagined a flat in the inner suburbs, maybe a flatmate and an overused microwave, an Ikea bed and Habitat sheets. If he only knew what her life was like in reality.

'Your house is completely empty.' She smiled, amused that he needed reminding of this.

'Yes, I'm staying in a hotel.'

'Oh. Which?'

'The Ritz.'

She suppressed another bubble of laughter. Of course he was. 'I guess yours, then,' she whispered, marvelling that he – the man who had held London in his palm tonight – should be choosing her.

The door opened and the guard peered in, looking only vaguely surprised at the sight of the two of them pressed against the wall. 'Your car, Mr Westlake.'

Jamie took her hand and kissed it. 'Let's go, then.'

She swept an arm over the sheet. It looked like cotton, felt like silk. She tried her leg. Then the other. 'Amazing,' she murmured.

Beside her, Jamie gave a tiny groan in his sleep. He was lying on his stomach, his right cheek pressed against the back of his hand and his mouth parted slightly. Her eyes ran over him, every detail a story she wanted to hear: the cut of his shoulders – did he lift weights? The small whitened scar on his lower back – a teenage fight, or a childhood accident? The tan – a holiday with another lover?

A siren outside made him stir again. She turned her head towards the window, her eyes falling to the heavy cream silk curtains, the elaborate drape of the pelmet too fussy and feminine for a man like him. She eyed his T-shirt still on the floor where she'd pulled it off and her stomach tightened as she remembered how he'd thrown her down on the bed a second later. She took in the plentiful, Versailles-styled flower arrangements that adorned every flat surface, the giant curved TV opposite the bed, the Chippendale-style furniture.

The gulf between them was everywhere she looked, not only in the obvious indicators of wealth and privilege but also the everyday items: his phone on the table beside him a new-generation model that, as far as she was aware, hadn't been officially launched yet, the Amex Black credit card beside it, even his T-shirt, which looked like standard cotton but felt cloud-soft to the touch, much like these sheets.

She sighed and performed a few small 'sheet angels', luxuriating in their silkiness against her skin. Her grand-children would never believe this, but then this bit she would be keeping for herself. She wasn't going to tell anyone – not Jules, not Dan . . . It was her memory, perfect and pure in its secrecy, her go-to pocket of happiness for when the clouds gathered, as they inevitably would, already were – even now. This was hers. Her moment. Her happiness. No one could take it from her.

'*What* are you doing?' he mumbled in a quiet voice, startling her so that she jumped and recoiled into a ball, clutching the sheet against her chest.

'Oh my God, you frightened me,' she gasped.

'You're frightening me,' he quipped, pushing his chest off the bed and resting his head in his hand to watch her.

'I was just admiring the sheets,' she said after a moment, embarrassed to have been caught out and feeling the heat rise in her cheeks.

'Funny. I was just admiring you in the sheets.'

She smiled, relaxing. 'Yeah?'

He grinned, leaning over her. 'Yeah.'

His body was warm with sleep, the tension that had vibrated in it last night as he came down from the show now soft and heavy. She kissed him slowly, savouring these bonus moments, knowing the clock was ticking, aware she couldn't outstay her welcome.

'Are you tired?' she asked, her voice lilting like a feather in the sequestered room.

'No.' As if to prove it, his hand began to wander and she

sighed. Imagine a world where she could stay here with him, where getting out of bed to answer the door to the butler was the worst thing that could happen. (They had put in a middle-of-the-night order for smoky-bacon crisps, smoked salmon sandwiches and champagne, and his knock on the door had felt like a violent intrusion into their bubble.)

'I meant from the show,' she giggled as he nuzzled her neck, burrowing into the nook like a baby animal. 'You didn't stop.'

He pulled back and gazed down at her, propped on his elbows. 'I am, yeah. It's pretty draining.' He pulled the sheet down to her hips and began walking his fingers up her navel. 'We'll have to stay in bed *all* day so I can recover.'

She laughed again, feeling ticklish and a little shy in the morning-after light. 'Ha! You can, maybe.'

He arched an eyebrow. 'I hope you're not trying to suggest you're getting up anytime soon.'

'Well, it sounds like you need your rest.'

'I think you'll find I can't rest *without* you. I've barely slept since Thursday, trying to figure out ways to track you down and get you alone.'

'Oh . . .' she murmured, losing herself in his gaze and feeling her heartbeat skip to a new rhythm.

'Besides, you couldn't leave even if you wanted too. I've got guards on the door,' he said, lowering his head to her breast.

She laughed, as he tickled her with his breath. 'Pho's there to keep people out, not in.'

'Not today.'

She arched an eyebrow. 'Well, too bad, mister. I've got plans.'

'Like you had plans last night, you mean?' he teased.

'No. This one *can't* be broken.'

He shook his head disbelievingly. 'Don't try telling me you've got to work. It's Sunday, and Caro already told me you shot today's meme on Friday. Even Blue Bunnies need a day off.'

'Urgh,' she groaned, remembering the indignity of batmanning in Hyde Park, her long paws hooked onto one of the pull-up fitness bars, her ears dangling down to the ground. 'I should be so lucky.'

He sat up slightly and propped his head in his hands as he looked down at her. 'Well, what are you *supposedly* doing if not working?' A shiver rippled over her bare skin as the cooler air crept beneath the duvet and she watched him watch the goosebumps ripple across her, his finger smoothing them down again.

'Just stuff,' she smiled teasingly as she looked up at him, raking her fingers through his hair.

'Tell me.'

'Nope.'

'I said, tell me.' His fingers tickled her waist, making her squeal.

'Nope.' She laughed, wriggling madly but refusing to give in.

He stared down at her and she could see he couldn't read whether or not this was a flirtatious ruse. 'You don't have plans at all. You're lying.'

'No, I'm not.'

His eyes met hers, khaki and gold, hypnotic, mesmerizing, confused. 'Cancel them then.'

'Nope.'

There was a silence, and the smile faded from her lips as

she realized that somehow, somewhere – without meaning to – the joke had stopped. She looked away, feeling reality begin to inch over her skin with sharp fingernails.

She wanted to stay in this fantasy, hide away in this hotel suite with him. She didn't want to move from his bed or leave this room. But those were impossible dreams, and as the laughter dimmed in her eyes, her rejection came across not as coquettish or hard-to-get, but bald and absolute.

He pulled his hand away. 'I don't understand.'

Panic and desolation scurried through her. Of course he didn't. How could he? She rolled away from him quickly and got out of bed, her eyes scanning for her clothes, which had been left strewn across the room, creating a chronology of last night's events. 'I do have to go. I'm sorry.'

'But, Nets . . .' He sat up in bed, bewilderment all over his features as he watched her step into her jeans and hook up her bra. She couldn't look at him as she slid her T-shirt over her head. She couldn't bear to see the look on his face. 'I thought we could spend the day together.'

He made it sound so simple, such a straightforward request, and she felt the panic rear up in her. He was beginning to probe now, detect the flaw, his antenna up that something about her wasn't quite right. She searched desperately for her shoes, finding one covered under a towel which had been abandoned, damp, on the floor on their way back from their midnight shower. 'I can't.'

'Why not?' He watched her buckle it up. 'You don't have a boyfriend, do you?' he asked, a worried laugh in his voice. 'That Alex bloke? Jules said it was on and off—'

'No!' she cried. She glanced at him as she retrieved her

other shoe from under the bed. 'Of course not. There's no one else.'

'So then . . . ?'

She fastened the sandal, catching sight of her knickers across the floor and running over to stuff them into her pocket. She looked back at him finally, feeling her heart plunge to her feet as their eyes met again. 'It's not you. Really.' She gestured hopelessly to the grand suite, the luxurious retreat where they'd so hedonistically given in to each other for a few short, magical hours. 'You're . . .' She stared at him, seeing in his khaki eyes the growing confusion, hurt, anger. How could she put into words what he was? Intoxicating, exciting, magnetizing. How could she explain that he made her feel hopeful when all she ever felt around anyone else was hopeless? How could she explain that that was precisely the problem? For as long as her life didn't change, neither could she. To all intents and purposes, she was stuck. 'You're incredible. This has been amazing. I'll never forget it.' Her voice clotted and she looked away. She had to get out of here before the tears fell and he saw how messed up she really was.

'*Forget it?* Jesus, Nets, this is ridiculous – what the hell are you running out for?' He jumped out of the bed, grabbing his boxers and stepping into them. 'Look, just hold on a minute. Slow down.'

'I'm really sorry,' she said, dashing from the room, the door slamming hard behind her.

She ran down the corridor, jabbing hard on the lift button. It came almost immediately and she stepped in just as she heard the suite door open and he called her name. But she didn't turn round. She knew better than anyone that there was no point in looking back.

Chapter Seventeen

It was getting dark when she put her key in the lock. The sun had given up, making way for the moon, though it was barely mid-afternoon.

She dropped her keys on the table in the hall, able to see her father in the kitchen, still at work on the model ship. Had he been there all night? All weekend? Had he been waiting up for her?

'Hello,' he said in a tone that she recognized – relief obscured by jollity – dropping his tweezers onto the table as she walked into the kitchen.

'Hi, Dad.' She kept her voice light, her expression blank as she came over to him and gave him a brief hug. 'You're still working on that?'

'You know what they say about idle hands.'

'Soft skin?' she quipped, wandering over to the fridge and peering in. It was more a force of habit than of need, but she wanted to avoid his enquiring gaze. No doubt he was registering she was still in last night's clothes.

'I thought we'd have lamb casserole tonight.'

'Great.' She reached for a can of Coke and closed the door again. 'Want some?'

'No, thank you.'

She grabbed a glass from the cupboard and poured with

her back to him, knowing he was staring. She felt oversized and over-strong, as though she could crush the glass in her bare hands, rip the door from its hinges. Everything in her felt too big – her loss, her pain, her heart . . .

'You just missed Jules.'

'Oh really?'

'She said you were supposed to be seeing the new Bond film together.'

She took a deep gulp of the Coke. 'Oh, that,' Nettie shrugged, patting the back of her hand to her mouth for a moment, stemming the emotions, before turning to face him. 'It was just a loose arrangement. We can go one day after work this week.' Her eyes fell to the bare little Christmas tree on the table as she sipped her drink. She looked away again quickly.

'Everything OK?'

'Of course.'

'You seem on edge, love.'

'I'm fine,' she said brusquely, her thumb tapping quickly against the counter. 'So did Dan stay last night?'

'No. He left shortly after you.'

'Yeah. He probably went to meet Stevie in the pub.'

Her father glanced at her, as though debating whether to reply, before picking up the tweezers and resuming his painstaking work. 'I must say I was surprised when Jules came by here,' he said with deliberate levity. 'I thought you were with her.'

'We don't live in each other's pockets,' she snapped, flinching as she saw her father startle from her tone, his hands slipping. 'I see her all week at work, remember?' she added more softly. She bit her lip and closed her eyes momentarily, remembering Jules with the guitarist last night and all her phone calls she'd rejected today, knowing all too well the post-mortem her friend wanted to conduct on last night's events. But how could she face her – her best friend – when she couldn't even face herself for what she'd done today?

There was a pause. 'So what have you been up to, then?' her father asked again.

'Nothing.'

There was another pause, but her father didn't stop working this time. 'And by "nothing" I take it you mean walking?'

Nettie looked away with an irritated sigh, staring out into the garden, but the world had turned to shadows and her own brittle reflection was all that she could see.

Her father's chin pushed into the air a little, even as he tried to tie a ratline to the rigging. 'I thought you said you'd stopped. You agreed you weren't going to do that anymore. It's too upsetting for you.'

For her, or for him? 'It was only today,' she lied. 'I just felt like it.'

Another pause. 'So where did you go?'

'Queen's Park.'

He nodded. 'Nothing, I suppose?'

'Dad, do you think I'd keep it a secret if there was something to tell?' she demanded, feeling something in her snap and replacing her glass on the wooden counter so hard he winced. 'Of course there's nothing to tell. There never is! This is it! It is only ever going to be this! Why can't you wake up to that? Why do you spend all your time pretending that everything is perfectly normal when it's *not*? It's the very opposite of normal.'

'Button—'

'And stop calling me that! Why do you keep calling me that? Like I'm some little girl when I'm not! I am twenty-six years old, not six. It's my life.' She stabbed her chest hard with her thumb. 'It should be my life by now!'

Her father blinked at her, the tweezers falling from his hands again. 'I'm sorry, love. I didn't—'

'No! You didn't!' she cried, her hand just catching the glass on the edge of the worktop and sending it crashing to the floor. Coke splattered all up the white units, flecking her mother's cream handbag and the backs of the chairs, and seeping into the cracks in the floorboards. She stared down in disbelief at the tiny smithereens that were all that was left of her parents' wedding crystal, her arms out-stretched, her face contorted in a silent spasm. She balled her fists, fury at the sheer bloody cosmic injustice of it all overtaking her, and she let out a strangled scream that sounded like an animal in a trap – injured, terrified, impris-oned – her life not her own anymore, as she walked and waited and hinged her happiness upon texts that told her nothing. Nothing had changed. Nothing ever would.

Her father ran over to her, his arms closing round her rigid body as she cried angry tears that made her eyes sting and her cheeks burn; she couldn't pull her hands out of the fists; she couldn't relax her core. It was too much.

'Look, come and sit down, love. You're worn out. Let me make you a cup of tea and we can talk. You know there's nothing a good cup of tea can't remedy.'

Nettie shut her eyes, trying to block out his words. She thought she might scream if she heard that refrain again. Tea was *not* the bloody answer. It would *not* make this OK.

The abrupt ring of the doorbell made them both flinch, breaking apart to stare back at the door. A single figure

KAREN SWAN

stood silhouetted in the frost glass. '*Fucking* neighbours,' she hissed angrily, fiercely wiping her eyes dry with the heels of her palms and making to stride down the hall. If they dared to ask her to keep the noise down . . .

'Nets, I'll go,' her father said firmly, the rims of his own eyes reddened as he waited for her to calm down.

The tension in her slackened at the sight of his trembling self-control and she nodded, feeling ashamed as she watched him walk to the door, dignity in every step. Unlike her, he had never faltered, never crumbled once in these four years. He spoke to the neighbours in the gardens and around the square with a calm affability that she had never been able to replicate. When they asked how she was doing, she thought they were prying; when they didn't, she thought they were indifferent. But he projected a quiet constancy all the time, even when it was just the two of them. She hadn't once seen him cry or rage or stare mute at a wall looking for answers. He just kept on keeping busy, keeping calm, staying friendly. The same as he ever was, as though it had never even happened.

How could he do it, day after day, year after year? If she didn't remember his face so clearly, that day when he'd walked in and found her sitting with the police in the kitchen, she might have thought he didn't feel as much as her, that his love wasn't quite as strong as hers. But she did remember that look; in fact, she would never forget it. It had been the proof she'd dreaded, that their lives had changed forever.

He opened the door. 'Hello, Gwen.' His tone betrayed his surprise.

Nettie tensed as she saw Gwen's russet curls and rosy cheeks. She was wrapped in a red wool coat and tartan

276

scarf, her hands still gloved as she came to stand in the hall.

Nettie walked to greet her, her heart in her mouth, but before she could ask the question that began every single one of their conversations, Gwen turned to her with a smile. 'So, are you ready?'

Gwen paid for the cab as Nettie and her father stared up at the fine steeple that dominated the angular church of St Martin-in-the-Fields, as though trying to outreach the famous column in the centre of Trafalgar Square.

'You OK?' she asked her father, noticing him fiddle with his tie again. He was looking uncomfortably smart in his grey suit and trench coat, which didn't quite fit anymore. He rarely wore a suit these days and it sat upon him like a bad disguise today. All his anima and ebullience were gone and he looked diminished, aged and anxious on the church steps.

'This is a waste of time,' she said in a low voice, not wanting to be overheard as they watched the cabby hand Gwen her change and receipt.

Her father placed a hand on her shoulder, his voice equally quiet. 'Gwen's been telling us about this every year. She obviously thinks it will help.'

'I don't see how. It's just going to be depressing to be surrounded by all these other people who are . . .' her voice shook, 'just like us.'

'No, not depressing. Reassuring. She wants us to see we're not alone.'

She looked at him. They both knew that after the initial wave of condolences, they had been alone – left to get on with it, pick up the pieces and patch their lives together again. Yes, Gwen kept in monthly contact. Yes, people asked how they were getting on, but they both felt obliged to show a smiling face, not to appear to be defeated by their very public tragedy. It was the question in everyone's eyes whenever she walked down the street or popped into the newsagent's or helped out at the library; even at the Engineer it was the backstory that defined her. *Why?* they wanted to ask her. And she could never answer. It was what she wanted to know herself.

'Let's just give it a go,' he said quietly. 'We'll sit at the back and if . . . if it just feels wrong, we can leave without anyone noticing. OK?'

She sighed, her eyes scanning the square. She looked over towards the fourth plinth – empty today, as it was supposed to be, and she tried to envisage herself, her own ghost, scrambling up the ladder in the bunny suit, ready for a soaking, Mike parading around with his sash and megaphone, rounding up the tourists and students. To think that it had been only six days ago, to think it was one of the crazy ways she had come to be propelled into Jamie's orbit . . .

Her chest tightened and she inhaled sharply.

Gwen joined them on the steps, a kind smile on her face. 'Shall we go and get a seat?'

'We'd like to sit at the back, if that's OK,' Nettie said quickly as her father protectively looped an arm through hers.

'Of course. Although we'll need to go in now, then. Everyone wants to sit at the back on their first visit.'

They walked tentatively up the steps. Small groups of people were milling about, no one quite sure whether to make eye contact, and Nettie and her father kept their own eyes down as they passed.

They stepped into the cool shadow of the nave, stopping at the sight of the filled oak pews, bent heads – hatted, bald, ponytailed, coiffed, bobbed – rippling in lines towards the front. There were so many . . .

They stood in silence, staring – aghast and reassured all at once by the sight of so much loss. If there was a loss for every two people here . . . Her eyes filled with tears.

'Come,' Gwen whispered, guiding her and her father to the back row.

They waited in silence for those on the steps to make the same pilgrimage, for the doors to close and the organ to start. Nettie listened with her breath held as the vicar spoke about hope and the light, of eternal promises that would one day be kept; she sang the carols she'd known since childhood, her eyes taking in not the gilded, panelled ceiling or the gallery, the chandeliers or the beautiful ivory walls but the backs in the crowd, wondering if their pain matched hers, if their story could possibly be as terrible as her own. Were they really like her – normal on the outside, broken on the inside?

Her father was silent beside her. He didn't sing the carols; he didn't bend his head during the prayers; he didn't hear the eloquent and empathetic speech from the guest speaker, a former newsreader who had once been the voice of the nation, had maybe even read some of their tragedies from his autocue. Her father sat with his hands clasped loosely on his thighs, his eyes fixed on the east window, a modernist installation that – Nettie recalled from the headlines at the time – had been commissioned to replace the original stained-glass window shattered by bombs during the Second World War. It was ostensibly a striking metalwork lattice, with a crucifix form created by narrow placement of the frets, a simple circle – or hole – in the centre allowing the light to rush through like a flood of water. His eyes didn't move from it once, caught – it seemed – in meditation.

People were coming to the lectern, standing in a quiet, patient line, some of them reading short prepared speeches about who they had lost and when, others speaking off the cuff, from the heart, their words spontaneous and raw.

After the ninth, Nettie closed her eyes, wishing she could close her ears too. She didn't want to hear these variations on her own theme. Gwen had been wrong. It didn't make her feel better to hear other people's pain; it only swelled hers. What world was this where so much loss could be borne? How had any of them ever come to be in this position? What had they done to deserve it? She shifted position, restless and agitated, feeling like a bird in a cage.

Her father's hand found hers and she looked at him, her eyes shining, her lips rolled tight. He nodded. 'We'll go in the next song,' he said under his breath, squeezing her fingers.

They both looked over at Gwen, who simply nodded in understanding.

Nettie tried tuning out again as the people continued to talk, trying to exorcise their ghosts, but the details filtered through – a son, drugs; a sister, mental illness; a husband, money troubles . . . Common, everyday troubles that millions of people suffered – and endured. Why hadn't their loved ones managed it too?

She swallowed a hiccup. Her body was still jangling from the outburst in the kitchen, her nervous system flayed from the emotional assault; she saw Jamie's reproachful face with every blink, and she pressed the beads of her spine hard against the unyielding pew. How much longer?

She looked to the front again. The last person was standing at the lectern now, a woman in her fifties with thin blonde bobbed hair and glasses, wearing a navy overcoat with a silk scarf. Her voice was timid and tremulous as she read from a sheet of lined A4 paper, all her longing and devastation captured and pressed into that page like a dried flower. Nettie held her breath as she listened to this last story – a horror story told by a neat middle-aged woman, of drug offences and prostitution arrests, the words tripping off her tongue, sleek from practice. How had this tale become *her* narrative? The woman looked like she should run a book club, listen religiously to *Woman's Hour* every morning while she did her ironing or took tea and a biscuit.

She watched as the woman walked back to her seat, head bowed, the man she sat down beside putting his arm round her shoulder and whispering something in her ear.

Nettie didn't notice the cello had started up. Not immediately.

It was only the shuffle of the choir rising to stand that made her look front again. To her surprise, it wasn't the choristers, who had made the procession past earlier in their red-and-white cassocks, hymn books opened in their palms, but instead an ensemble cast wearing black trousers and red T-shirts with the charity's logo across the front in yellow.

The cello's song rose and swelled like steam. The cellist was out of her line of sight, but the notes from the honeyed strings filled the arched space like sunlight and Nettie felt the fibres in her muscles tighten and quiver, as though they were being pulled up on pulleys.

'Come on, then,' her father whispered, patting her hand, as eager as she to escape, and sliding along the pew, keeping low and trying to remain unnoticed.

The choir began to sing.

'In my dreams, I see your face, walk with you, hold you safe . . .'

Transfixed, she reached for her father's sleeve without looking, holding him in place, as the words fell like rain. *'I'm so empty and silent without you . . .'*

Most of the singers were women, but not all, their arms hanging empty and still at their sides, eyes on the conductor as they sang in precise synchronicity. Nettie straightened, trying to get a better look as the purity of sound swirled around her like a wistful wind. They didn't look remarkable, these people; she was quite sure that to hear them sing individually, they would probably be nothing special, but together they were more than the sum of their parts, their voices gathering her up and folding around her. She felt held.

Her father felt it too, relaxing back into the bench again, his hand falling warm and heavy over hers. They sat like that together, at the back of the church, unseen and unknown as the song put exquisite voice to the loss that both filled them up and hollowed them out. It was the first time . . . the first time since *that day* that she didn't feel alone.

And when the voices hushed, when the singularity of their collective loss and pain began to fade to an echo, her father stood up. And after four years of denial and pretence and soldiering on, he finally began to speak.

Chapter Eighteen

Daisy was loitering by the lifts and filing her nails when the doors opened and Nettie stepped out into the office the next morning. She immediately noticed someone had put up a blue LED-lit Christmas tree in the corner by the loos and strung it with silver tinsel; a couple of empty red foil boxes sat at the foot of the tree like they'd been kicked there by the cleaner and all festive feeling deserted her at the sight of it.

So this is Christmas, she thought wryly.

'Hi, Daise,' she mumbled, walking past with a wan smile as she shook snowflakes from her hair. It had begun snowing again overnight but still wasn't settling in the city – although the Home Counties had had up to four inches, much to the dismay of London's children, who wanted to build their first snowmen of the season. 'How was your dinner party?'

'Just tell me. You may as well spit it out,' Daisy said, hurrying after her as Nettie unbuttoned her coat and hung it on the coat rack, her hair already picking up static from the carpet.

'Tell you what?'

'About Saturday! The concert!'

'Oh.' Nettie hesitated, unwanted memories, images and

sensations flashing unbidden through her mind again. 'It was fine.'

'*Fine?*'

'Great. It was great. He was—'

'Amazing, right?' Daisy perched one small buttock on her desk, her long legs wrapped round each other in a gangly spiral.

Nettie nodded and tried to smile as she slipped into her seat and booted up the computer. She could feel last night's sense of communion beginning to desert her. She didn't want to think about him.

'That's it? That's all you're giving me?' Daisy demanded, arms outstretched.

Nettie racked her brain, trying not accidentally to spill any details about how Jamie had kissed her with his hands around her cheeks, or the groove along his stomach, or how he'd made her laugh with butterfly kisses on her inner thigh – all the usual thoughts that were occupying her every waking and sleeping moment. She held a finger in the air, pleased as she thought of something. 'We went to the after-party at Bodo's Schloss. I drank a cocktail from a ski boot.'

'Who was there?' Daisy's eyes were on stalks, her palms flat on the table.

Damn, she'd barely noticed. She'd had eyes only for him. 'Um, Tinie Tempah—'

She was saved by the sudden heavy thud of Jules's bag being swung onto the desk – although judging by the look in Jules's eyes, maybe 'saved' wasn't quite the word.

'Morning,' Daisy said tartly, taking in Jules's office warrior pose – her hands on her hips and eyes trained on Nettie like sniper rifles. 'What's up with y—'

'Give us a minute, would you, Daise?' Jules ordered, without looking at her.

Nettie swallowed as Daisy – for once – did as she was told first time, shooting Nettie an 'oh crap' look as she left.

Behind her, Nettie could hear the sound of the kettle boiling, a small clatter of cups being brought down from the cupboard, the sucker of the fridge door being opened. Daisy's face appeared sporadically around the yucca plant.

'I could be dead.' Jules's words were hard and metallic, glinting and cold.

Nettie opened her mouth to respond, but Jules was too quick, too angry for her to compete.

'For all you know, I've been raped and murdered and dumped in a landfill in Solihull.'

Nettie's mouth opened again. Solihull? 'Jules, I'm sorry. You looked like you were having a great time. I didn't think—'

'No. You didn't. Because not only did you not know if *I* was OK, none of us knew if *you* were OK either. Did you ever stop to think about that? No one knew where you were.' Jules flicked her eyes up to check no one was standing too close. She leaned forward, her voice so low it was more of a rumble. 'I rang him, you know. Gus gave me his number. He didn't know where you were either.'

Nettie felt her cheeks stain at the rebuke, at the thought of them all discussing her. 'I am not a child. I don't have to account for my whereabouts to anyone.'

'You just ran out, he said.'

She swallowed, humiliation like a rain that poured upon her. 'Yesterday was just a bad day, OK?'

Jules shook her head. 'No, it's not OK. You would think that you, of all people, would understand—'

'Don't!' Nettie was astonished to realize she was on her feet again, her finger jabbed towards Jules in warning, her own eyes blazing. 'Don't you dare!'

'Ladies.' They turned to find Mike standing by the desk, watching them both with concern. 'Everything OK?'

Jules straightened up, tugging down irritably on the hem of her top. 'Fine, Mike,' she said through gritted teeth, shooting another fierce look towards Nettie and making it perfectly apparent that it wasn't fine at all.

'Nettie?' Mike asked, plainly able to see her rapid breathing and flushed cheeks.

She blinked and looked across at him. 'Fine,' she replied too after a moment.

'Good,' he said with evident scepticism. 'Well, let's get the meeting underway, then, shall we? Caro's bringing the teas.'

Both women looked down at their desks in silence, shuffling papers aggressively and slamming drawers as they hunted for pens.

In the conference room, Nettie sat down in her usual seat, watching in disbelief as Jules pointedly walked to the other side of the table and sat with Daisy and Caro.

Both Daisy and Caro swapped looks.

Nettie sighed and placed her attention on Mike. Fine, let Jules be petty, then, she thought, sticking her nose in the air. If she wanted to involve the entire office in her tantrum, that was her business.

Mike looked out upon the unorthodox seating arrangement with a furrowed brow. 'Right,' he said slowly, twiddling his pen between his fingers. 'Caro, if you could brief us on the latest figures, please.'

Caro opened her laptop. 'Twitter – five hundred and

fifty-eight thousand followers now – there was a spike after the batmanning, not so much with the owling that we posted the day before. The public is clearly liking the direct connection between Bunny and Jamie, the alliance seems to be going over well, so I think we should home in on that for the remainder of the campaign.'

'Good, we'll feed that back to White Tiger,' Mike said, making a brief note. 'What else?'

'YouTube is at one point three million views now, if you combine the clips of the ice course, Ice Bucket Challenge and Shard all together, although Ice Crush is still the leader individually. Obviously that's generating some serious income now, but as I think I've said before, it would be good if we could get more film footage up, and not focus quite so much on stills for the last few days. It gives the followers something to really keep sharing and coming back to. A photo is more disposable, more forgettable.'

'Nice point. Duly noted,' Mike said, again scribbling notes. 'So the pot now stands at . . . ?'

Caro smiled and shook her head. 'Donations to Tested via Nettie's link now total £633,792.'

Mike whistled, dropping his pen to clap Nettie. Caro and Daisy joined in too and Nettie quickly clapped them back. 'Team effort, everyone.'

'Damned right – it was my idea,' Jules muttered, her hands pointedly flat on the table. 'All you are is the model.'

Nettie blinked at her, hurt by the viciousness in her tone.

'Right, well, moving on,' Mike said quickly. 'I've had a call from Jamie Westlake's manager this morning.'

Nettie's head jerked up. Dave?

'Yeah, where are they? At the meeting in the bar on

Friday, they said they'd be here,' Daisy said with evident disappointment. Nettie realized she was wearing lipstick.

'Well, he's emailed to say they can't make the meeting.'

Nettie froze. He was supposed to be here? 'Is this because of that melee in Topshop at the weekend?' Caro asked.

'What melee?' Mike asked sharply.

'You must have heard about it, Mike – it was all over the Interweb. Jamie sauntered into Topman on Oxford Street and there was practically a riot.' She shrugged. 'Maybe nothing to do with it. Just saying.'

Nettie thought she was going to be sick.

'Well, his no-show today doesn't change the plans we've already got in place to coincide with the launch of his new single this Friday,' Mike continued. 'You may recall we were discussing ways we could tie in with the publicity for that, join forces if you will – obviously getting the bunny in the music video is one way of increasing exposure.'

'Yes, but not necessarily donations. I still like the idea of a song vote,' Jules said. 'It's dynamic, interactive, and Jamie seemed well up for it.'

'Yes, the problem with that idea, Jules, as Dave clearly pointed out at the time, is that these decisions about what song's going to be released from the album and when are made by the record company well in advance.'

'I get that, but it's not like there'd be any chance of our song beating his anyway. It'd just be a stunt to get the public involved.'

'Sorry, can we rewind a bit, please?' Nettie cut in. Exactly how much had she missed at the bar in the hotel? She had assumed they'd all just been flirting with the star, not actually working. 'What's this?'

Jules didn't reply, prompting Mike to sigh impatiently, and Caro explained on her behalf.

'Jamie had an idea for a song vote, a bit like a "battle of the bands" skit, although given that none of us can play any instruments, we can hardly perform . . .' She shrugged. 'So he said we could do it with a choice of songs instead, getting people to vote for which song he should release as his next single. The public get to choose by donating to either the one that we, or rather you, would endorse, or the real one which he'd endorse. We'd split into teams – "hashtag teamjamie" and "hashtag teambunny" – get everyone to vote, and whichever song raises most money, he'll release. He was well up for it.'

Nettie blinked. 'And what would our song be called?'

Daisy frowned. '"Ships In the Night", was it?'

"Night Ships." The song he'd told her he wanted to release all along. No wonder he was behind the idea. A sick feeling swilled in the pit of her stomach as a thought came to her – what if all this, *them*, was just a marketing ploy to boost his sales? They were assuming this campaign was benefiting from the link-up with him, but was he riding on *her* coat-tails? Had he really been chasing after her, or her profile? Hadn't he told her that his label wanted a younger fanbase?

'Well, Dave made his feelings on the matter very clear,' Mike said.

'So did Jamie. And he's the star,' Jules snapped testily. 'Anyway, we all know there's no way his song wouldn't win. It's got Coco Miller in it, and who can resist her?'

Nettie flinched at the barb. She couldn't believe Jules could be so mean – or angry.

'Not necessarily. Jamie doesn't *want* to release the duet

with Coco,' Nettie said archly. 'He wants to release "Night Ships".' She paused. 'What if he's using the campaign for his own ends?'

'So what if he is?' Jules batted back. 'Even better – that makes it a win-win.' The more he does to promote our profile, the better. She looked back at Mike. 'Look, there's no doubt this stunt would get a huge reaction and we can still feature in the video with him, just for our song.'

'It's not about who wins or which song he releases,' Daisy said, bringing her support to the debate. 'There's no doubt it would get a huge reaction. *Any* new Jamie Westlake single is a big deal. He's got massive reach and we could really build it up over the course of the week, bringing it to a climax on Friday, the last day of the campaign. Just think how much money we could raise! The promotional opportunities on this would be enormous, even outside of the Net – radio airplay, maybe some TV coverage . . .'

Mike sank back in his chair, outnumbered. 'We would need to convince the record company there's absolutely no chance of the wrong song being voted in . . .' He slapped a hand across his forehead suddenly. 'No, wait. It won't work, and I'll tell you why – the wheels are already in motion. Dave told me they've got the Jingle Bell Ball at the O2 tomorrow night. Jamie's performing the new single with that American girl.' He glanced at Nettie. 'You need to go to that, by the way. Dave thought it would be an ideal location for whatever meme you had planned. Guaranteed blanket media coverage. Target audience.'

Nettie opened her mouth to protest – she had been hoping to see Dan tomorrow night; he and Stevie were always in the pub for the quiz and she wanted to make it up to him for running out on Saturday night – but Jules beat her to it.

'No biggie,' Jules said, nonplussed and refusing to give up. 'Jamie and Coco could do their duet tomorrow night, as planned. Then he could debut "Night Ships" on Wednesday.'

'*Where*, Jules?' Mike demanded, growing exasperated. 'Where can they do that with such short notice? This is what I mean. These things are decided and booked months in advance.'

She shrugged. 'We'll think of something; Daisy will know someone who can help out. We haven't done too badly so far, have we? Besides, we'll need that extra day to rehearse. It will give us time to get straight with it and record the video.' She shrugged. 'It really is very simple.'

Mike sighed, not so sure that it was, but worn down. 'Fine, I'll try sounding it out to Dave again.'

Jules gave a victorious smile as she twiddled with her pen, and Nettie felt a twinge of anxiety to see her friend's talent and ambition so clearly laid out like this. As the mastermind of this campaign, she could walk into any job she wanted tomorrow.

'In the meantime, regardless of whether the song vote comes off, we need to plan a gag to do onstage at the ball tomorrow when Jamie's singing. We can start tweeting about it today and create extra hype for his performance tomorrow tonight. The ball is being televised live and is so high profile that I think we can put a real premium on minimum donations. I'm thinking fifty thousand?'

Nettie's phone buzzed with a new text and she picked it up. It was from Gwen.

'*Urgent. Call me.*'

She stiffened as suddenly as if her bones had been shot through with steel rods. Jules noticed, a quizzical look coming into her darkened eyes before she quickly and pointedly looked away again.

'I have to take this,' Nettie said hoarsely, pushing her chair out and standing up.

'I don't think so, Nettie,' Mike said sarcastically. 'This is important.'

'So's this.'

'Sit down. You can sort out your social life later.'

She should have been angered by his facetious comment. As it was, she hadn't heard it. Her eyes were glued to the words on her screen and she hurried from the room in silence.

'Nettie!' Mike shouted as she ran through the office to the fire escape and stood on the back stairs, the dial tone ringing in her ear as she gazed out into the alley behind them. It was a depressing sight. The London stock bricks, which would once have been a honeyed yellow, were now blackened with grime, and black bin bags bulged out of wheelie bins, large cardboard boxes stacked against the wall and sodden from the sleet and snow.

The line connected and she straightened up abruptly. 'Gwen, hi. It's Nettie.'

'Hi, Nettie. You got my message?'

'Yes,' Nettie nodded, trying to read Gwen's tone. It was placid, as ever. Gwen wasn't given to extremes of emotions. Nettie supposed that was what made her so good at her job, given that ninety-eight per cent of the time she was having to mete out bad news. 'What is it? Just tell me.'

There was a brief pause as Gwen took a deep breath. 'We've found her, Nettie. We've found your mother.'

Chapter Nineteen

Nettie felt her legs buckle and she sank to the step, her face in her hand. 'How? When?' Her voice was a whisper.

'This morning. She walked into one of our outreach centres.'

Just like that? She just walked into a centre, walked back into their lives? The nightmare was at an end? Nettie curled up, her body folded tight, one hand over her face as she tried to brace against the onslaught of emotions that always had to be so tightly packed away. But there was no holding them back now. It was over. She could relax, just let it all go. She felt the ice that floated like flotsam in her veins begin to warm and thaw. Colours could regain their vividness, music its lyricism—

'Nettie? Are you there?'

'Yes,' she said, her voice split. She raised her head again, staring at a hairline crack in the plaster on the wall opposite as she took a few deep breaths and tried to calm her mind. She had to be practical. Think.

She blinked. 'Which one?'

'I'm sorry?'

'Which centre did she go to?'

'Shirland Road. Listen, there's—'

'W-where's that? I don't know it.' Panic shot through her

limbs. She had covered most of London in the past four years. She should know it.

'Maida Vale.'

Nettie sat straight. Maida Vale? She could be there in ten minutes if she caught a cab from here. 'OK. I'm on my way.'

'No, Nettie – wait.' Gwen's voice was jolted out of moderation.

'What?'

'She isn't there now.'

Nettie felt the thaw halt, nature hold its breath. A false spring? 'But . . . what do you mean? You just said—'

'She's gone again.'

Nettie blinked, white noise buzzing in her head. No. 'Gone how?'

'She didn't want to stay.'

'I don't understand.'

'She just wanted to let you know she's all right.'

'But—'

'She says she's not ready to come back yet.' Gwen's voice tiptoed down the line. 'I'm sorry, Nettie. I know this is upsetting to hear.'

Upsetting? Breaking a heel on her favourite pair of shoes was upsetting. Scratching the car was upsetting. This . . . this was . . . desolation. It was like living with no skin, a glass heart that couldn't beat. This was surviving, not living. There was more life in her shadow.

'But if she made contact, if she was the one coming to you, then . . .'

'It means that she's closer to coming home, yes. But not yet. She needs more time.'

'More time? She's had four years!' she shouted, her hand

gripping the phone so hard her knuckles glowed white. She pulled herself to standing, her hands clutching the sill.

'I know.' Gwen's voice was soothing, understanding. How many times had she heard this very story? How often had she relayed this message to other families? 'And you've done so well, Nettie. You've been so strong. I know this isn't the news you wanted to hear, but it's not unusual in disappearances of this length of time. Return is very, very difficult and is rarely accomplished in a single visit. But hopefully, hopefully this is the start of the road back.'

'You don't know that.'

'No. There are no guarantees.' Her voice softened further, as though her words themselves were abrasive. 'We've always had to face the possibility that she won't ever come back.'

Nettie gripped her face, her fingers pressing on her temples so that she saw black spots behind her eyelids. The buzzing in her head was getting louder, a pressure building in her brain. No. No. 'No.'

'Net—'

The phone fell from her hand, Gwen's voice like the distant whine of a mosquito as she looked out onto the bleak landscape – the littered, puddled alley and, above it, moss-infested Victorian rooftops, cracked panes of glass in the sash windows. Her eyes fell to a bottle of gin, half gloved in a brown paper bag by the back corner of one of the bins. The place was neglected and decaying, almost Dickensian in its squalor. For the people living on these streets – the homeless, the forgotten, the missing, her mother – not much had changed.

She had to find her.

*

Nettie walked for hours, oblivious to the cold pavements transmitting their chill up through her thin leather soles and making her bones ache. The snow was beginning to settle at last – seeping into the suede of her boots and staining them – but that only made her search all the more determined. If her mother was out here, she couldn't just be left on the streets. Not in these temperatures. Not now she had a location.

She had gone straight to the outreach centre on Shirland Road. Gwen had rung ahead, somehow guessing at Nettie's plan and authorizing the duty staff to speak to her and transmit whatever information they could. It meant she knew now that her mother's hair was grey – the auburn highlights long since grown out – and short, properly short, which was going to be disconcerting as Nettie had never seen her mother with anything shorter than shoulder-length hair before.

She'd been wearing dark grey trousers of a track-pant style with a bright pink trim down the sides, trainers and a black fleece. Nettie couldn't imagine that either: her mother had always worn dresses and skirts and colour. She *loved* colour – their house was yellow, for Chrissakes! Their garden a riot! And when Nettie had been a child, she'd always stood at the school gates in bright florals, swirling skirts and floaty boho dresses with crochet tops. She wore stacked bangles and hooped earrings and wedged sandals that she could run really fast in. She couldn't imagine her mother in trainers and black and grey.

This was another reason why Nettie had to find her *now*. Take her home *today*. Why did no one else understand the urgency that tomorrow, in all likelihood, her mother would change clothes and these crucial extra identifying characteristics would be halved? Tomorrow she'd just be looking for a grey-haired, short-cropped woman, a stranger.

She searched with frantic eyes, her hands pushing back hedges and bushes, her panic growing as she wandered down narrow side streets and emerged on grand avenues with vast iced Regency villas that held no interest for her – those streets were too clean, too tidy, their outdoor lights too bright, their parked cars too shiny. An aimless drifter would immediately attract attention. Her mother wouldn't go there.

She tried to keep to the shaded nooks and dark warrens, the rougher areas, but it was harder than it looked. Google Maps didn't come with a socio-economic listing and she felt like a stranger in her own city, even though she was only two miles along the Prince Albert Road, which ran home. Here, in Maida Vale, everything felt sprawling and Big City, effortlessly leaching into Paddington, Warwick Avenue and St John's Wood without definition or intention. Primrose Hill wasn't like that: it wasn't a district; it was a village, bounded on all sides by the canal, railway and Regent's Park, and she had grown up within its delineated confines with a distinct sense of seclusion in the centre of the capital city. She had felt safe, locked in by its boundaries, but what if – she realized now, for the first time – what if it had made those on the outside feel locked out?

Had her mother tried to return before? Had she seen her own image on the 'missing' posters on the trees and lamp posts, outside the library and community centre and churches, and known there was no way to come back *quietly*?

Nettie called her name as she checked the garages, inside wheelie bins, behind sheds. She checked in the greasy spoons and coffee shops, stopping only briefly for lunch – a warming bowl of *moules* eaten standing up in the window of Café Rouge, her eyes checking every single person who walked by – before resuming her search again. She walked past the cricket ground and tennis courts, past the restaurants and bars, past the church halls and estate agents' offices. She did Little Venice twice – once on each side of the canal – staring nosily into the brightly painted houseboats that had geraniums and poinsettias stacked on the decks, firewood and watering cans, bikes and gas canisters chained to the roofs.

She felt the canal was her best hope. It seemed the place most like home – the Romany colours of the houseboats not so different from their own yellow house, and certainly standing in contrast to the muted etchings of the Farrow & Ball-painted villas, their vibrant and profuse potted flowers jungle-wild in comparison to the clipped and snipped window boxes and front gardens ten feet above on the streets. She was sure her mother would be drawn to these colours, the sounds of music drifting through the windows.

She walked slowly along the slippy towpath as cyclists glided past her, standing on their pedals and correcting their handlebars, dodging pedestrians walking carefully with arms linked or being pulled along by tiny, sniffing dogs. Joggers padded past with soft-footed strides, hats and gloves on, headphone wires dangling down their tops and their breath coming in white puffs. They all had somewhere to be, these people – all had somewhere to go – and she watched them with envious eyes. That was one of the things that had surprised her most when her mother had first gone and she had first started to search – how hard it was just to wander. When you have no money to go to the shops or the cinema or the garden centre or bingo hall, the day contracts down to finding the next bench to sit on, the next bin to raid, the next roof to shelter beneath. At least, that was how Nettie imagined it to be. She had spent so many hours, days, weeks, months, years trying to get inside her mother's head, to try to understand *why*, to try to decipher *where* . . .

But the day wasn't open-ended like hope. Light faded and the sleet turned to snow as the nip in the air began to bite again. She also had an open blister on her left heel. She stopped against a lamp post, taking a minute's rest as she wondered where to go next. A white van sped past, wipers on max and its fog lights dazzling her, making her wet eyes shine.

She turned on the spot, unsure of where she was now. She'd lost track of where she'd searched and where she hadn't; she didn't recognize this street, but perhaps she had come into it earlier at another junction? Or maybe not. Had she . . . had she passed that letterbox before?

One tear fell as her panic rose again and she pressed her hand to her nose to try to stem her breath, to calm down, but time was passing and the trail was cooling. Her mother had been here, in this very vicinity, six hours earlier. She may even have passed this lamp post, that house, those cars . . . But the weather was getting worse, as forecast. She would be driven to find shelter, if not now, then soon, within the hour. No one could stay out in these conditions without suffering from exposure. She would be hidden for another day.

Some people were walking down the street, their heads up, arms swinging as they headed back to warm homes and the families and sanctuaries they took for granted. She stepped closer to the lamp post, out of their way, dropping her head down as they passed. Their eyes slid only very fractionally her way, not slowing down or curious about the girl in the thin coat and wrong shoes, crying in the lamplight.

Except one. She saw the shoes stop – brown leather lace-ups with sturdy rubber soles, ideal for walking in, and non-slip too. Ecco, if she remembered rightly.

She looked up with a hiccup to find her father's arms already outstretched. His beard was as white as Father Christmas's as it caught the snowflakes, his pinched cheeks and dull eyes the signal that he too had taken the call and been out all afternoon, searching.

She walked into his hug, all the fight going out of her as he stroked her wet hair.

'Come on, Button. Let's go home.'

Jules was sitting on the doorstep when they turned into the square, the giant bunny head on the ground beside her.

Nettie deflated at the sight of her, coming to a stop on the pavement outside the house, pulling her hands out of her pockets and only vaguely aware of her phone dropping to the frozen ground. 'Not now, Jules,' she said quietly, with a shake of her head, too tired to fight.

But there wasn't war in Jules's eyes. Wordlessly, she got up and wrapped her arms around Nettie's neck, the snow sifting over them like statues. 'I'm sorry,' she mumbled. 'I'm so sorry.'

Nettie's father patted Jules's shoulder lightly as he passed. 'I'll get supper on,' he said, putting his key in the lock.

The women pulled apart, Nettie struggling to meet her friend's eyes as Jules handed back the phone she had dropped. The screen had cracked. She clicked it on and stared at the screensaver photo, a picture of her and her mother – cheeks pressed together, eyes bright – that had been taken at a friend's barbecue, just months before her mother had walked through the door for the last time. The crack split not just the screen, but the photo too, running between them like a seismic fault line and telling a truth she didn't want to face up to.

Jules put a hand on her arm and Nettie looked up at her. How did she tell her – anyone – about this latest development, this horrid twist: that her mother was alive, but her rejection remained absolute? Was that *better* than not knowing if she was alive or dead? Whether she was in this country or abroad? What did it say about her that her mother, even after all this time, still couldn't walk through that door, that she wasn't enough to return home to? Nettie felt ashamed, inadequate, lacking and insufficient because her mother's problems were bigger than her love.

Jules missed nothing. She saw the evasion in her best friend's face, the fresh devastation. 'Come on, let's go in – it's bloody freezing out here,' she said, taking Nettie by the arm and, picking up the rabbit head, leading her into the house. She saw Nettie flinch at the sight of it as she shut the door. The house felt chilly, and only the lights in the kitchen were on as her father saw to supper. 'Oh no, don't worry about this,' Jules said, patting the rabbit head fondly. 'I did it today. I've just come straight over from doing the skit, that's all.'

'W-what did you do?' Nettie asked tonelessly, leaning into the cast-iron radiator and trying to absorb all the heat.

She felt frozen to the bone, her body composed of fifty-five per cent ice, not water.

Jules brought up an image on her own phone. 'Look, there it is.'

Nettie smiled at the image of the twisted bunny body (a T-shirt straining over its rotund torso) lying on a skate ramp under a graffitied arch, its head seemingly separated from the torso and placed a metre away. 'Horse-manning?'

'That's my girl,' Jules said, like a proud mother.

Nettie's gaze fell to the figure standing behind the bunny – it was Jamie, an axe slung casually over his shoulder. His eyes were dark and hard; he looked menacing. She felt her breath catch, her heart snag at the sight of him. 'Why's *he* in it? He's not been in any of the others.'

Jules looked at her. 'No, but it sets up the battle. Look at his T-shirt.'

She looked more closely. Jamie was wearing a black T-shirt which read, '*#teamjamie*'. And when she looked more carefully at the bunny's T-shirt, she saw it read, '*#teambunny*'.

'Mike's promised to sell Dave his soul if the wrong song wins, so it's on. Bit of a shame really that there's no way we can rig the vote,' Jules said craftily. Nettie managed a weak smile. 'Anyway, we're going large on it for the rest of the week. Everyone went nuts. We got twenty-six thousand retweets in ninety minutes and hit the fifty grand mark just after lunch.'

Nettie blinked, knowing she should feel excited, knowing she should care. But she couldn't feel anything.

'Yeah, we went to the South Bank to do it,' Jules continued. 'The skaters were cool.'

Nettie nodded. 'I bet.'

'Yeah,' Jules said, but her tone was subdued again and they stood for a moment in silence. She looked at Nettie, still pale, still swaddled in her thin coat and wet shoes. 'Aren't you going to take those things off? You're soaked.'

'I know. I . . .' Nettie stared down at her ruined boots. 'I think I need to have a bath. I can't seem to warm up.'

'You're, like, almost blue. How long have you been out there for, anyway?'

Nettie shrugged.

'Are you *kidding*? Since the meeting? Nets, you'll get hypothermia!'

'I'm fine. I just had to . . . look.' The suppressed tears made her voice wobble like a slackline and Jules rushed to her again.

'What is it, Nets? What's happened? Tell me.'

She shook her head, letting her hair fall forward, one hand pinching the bridge of her nose. 'It's nothing.'

'It's not nothing. *You* wouldn't ever walk out of a meeting and disappear for the day like that without good reason. Something's happened.' She ducked down, trying to peer up at Nettie's hidden face. 'If you don't tell me, I'll just ask your dad – you know I will.'

Nettie gripped the radiator as she leaned against it, inhaling deeply. 'Mum walked into an outreach centre in Maida Vale today.'

Jules gasped, gripping Nettie's arm in excitement, slapping her other hand over her mouth. 'Oh my God!' she cried after a moment. 'That's amazing!' She saw Nettie's face. 'No? Not amazing?' She frowned. 'How is that not amazing?'

Nettie rolled her lips and swallowed. 'Because she's still missing.'

There was a long silence. 'I don't understand,' Jules said, tense.

'She wanted us to know that she's all right. That was all.'

Jules shook her head, like the words were a fly in her ear, something to be shaken out and swatted away. 'You mean . . . they didn't hold on to her?'

Nettie looked away.

'But why didn't they grab her? Or . . . or sit on her, I don't know! Whatever the fuck it takes?'

Nettie closed her eyes, remembering the words Gwen had repeated to her over and over in those first, bewildering weeks, four years ago. 'Because as a sane and functioning adult, she is legally entitled to disappear.'

Jules stared at her, her dark eyes blazing with fury. 'Bullshit!' she exploded. 'That is an utter crock of shit. After . . . after everything you've been through in the last four years? What about what *you're* entitled to?'

Nettie put a hand on her arm, a plea for silence. As much as she appreciated Jules's fierce loyalty, it was too much on top of her own emotions right now. She needed to be alone, somewhere she could hide away until she'd pushed, squeezed and jammed her emotions back into a box and could feel less. 'I'm going to run a bath.'

Jules watched her climb the stairs, feeling helpless, regretting her outburst. 'Is there anything I can do? I'll do it quietly, I promise.'

Nettie shook her head but managed a smile. 'I'll see you tomorrow, OK?'

'Sure,' Jules mumbled, listening to the stairs creak, the sound of a door being opened. She sighed, before picking up the rabbit head again by one of the ears. She glanced into the kitchen, ready to shout her goodbyes to Nettie's father, but he was standing by the sink and staring out into the flecked sky. He looked held together by cloth and wishes, his shoulders an inch closer to his ears than they should have been. Upstairs, the sound of water began to whistle through the pipes.

Jules dropped her gaze to the floor. There was no answer to this, no Band-Aid to make it better. Slowly, she walked to the front door and closed it behind her with a click.

Chapter Twenty

'I thought I'd find you here,' she said, crouching down by the figure doing rapid press-ups on the hand bars.

Dan lifted his head fractionally but didn't slow down. 'Yeah?'

Nettie heard the coolness in his voice and congratulated herself on the fantastic job she was doing of pushing away everyone closest to her. 'Yeah. You must be mad doing this in the snow,' she said, resting her chin in her gloved hands. Across the grass, she could see Scout sniffing in the undergrowth, his short tail wagging excitedly at something.

'Means I've got the place to myself,' he said, panting slightly.

She looked around the outdoor workout area at the pull-up bars, parallel bars, push-up bars . . . There was a bar for every type of torture, as far as she could see. And no one using them.

They were at the bottom of the hill, beside the children's playground, but everyone else was on the grass, desperately trying to roll meagre balls into snowmen, even though it was the 'wrong sort' of snow and their efforts collapsed into powdery heaps.

'Ha. Well, then maybe I should have a go. See if I can grow me some muscles.'

Dan snorted in reply. Even though there were no rules, as such, it was usually only men who used this facility, although there was never any shortage of women running up and down the paths.

'What? You don't think I can?' she asked, flexing a bicep that was well hidden under her Sweaty Betty layers.

'By all means, knock yourself out,' he said, springing himself up and back from the push-up bars and gesturing for her to have a go.

'All righty,' she said, rubbing her hands together before assuming the same position and trying to push up. She managed eight.

Dan tutted, moving over to the parallels. They came to his hip height and Nettie watched as he stood between them and jumped up, one hand on each bar, his ankles crossed and legs bent. He began dipping quickly, working out his triceps, working off his irritation.

There was room for two, she figured, coming and standing in front of him, between the bars also. 'Hmm. Doesn't look so bad,' she said, watching him bob up and down. She put her hands on the bars and jumped up, locking her elbows. And promptly froze.

She could dangle but not move. Or move but fall. Those seemed to be the options her body was presenting her with.

Dan looked annoyed by her hovering in front of him as he continued to dip, although she figured she had his attention here.

'So, listen, about the other night.' She wrinkled her nose, bit her lip. 'I'm really sorry.'

He snorted again, looking down at the ground.

'Really I am, Dan. I know I left you in the lurch.'

'Whatever.'

'Not "whatever". It was a crummy thing to do.'

'It's no biggie to me. If you didn't want to chill, you could've just said.'

'But that's the thing! I did want to hang out with you!' she said, her arms beginning to shake. She shifted her hand slightly. 'Jules and I had made arrangements to see the new Bond, but then she bailed to go . . . go to the concert and I thought that meant I was free. I had no idea she was going to turn up and expect me to go with her.'

'No idea?' Dan panted, but his voice was still incredulous as he continued dipping at the same rate as when he'd started. Nettie was beginning to think he was bionic. That or he was more exceptionally pissed off than she'd appreciated. 'She's got backstage passes for Jamie Westlake and you're telling me it was a *surprise* she turned up on the doorstep? After he whisked you off on a just-for-two VIP trip the night before?'

'It wasn't like that. It was a work thing. She'd agreed to go to it, not me.'

'So then why did you go?'

Nettie blinked. She shifted her hands on the bars – they were freezing, even through her gloves. 'You saw the note.'

He laughed. 'Don't tell me you *believed* it? Jesus, Nettie! Can you be that naive? It was a line. A cheesy pick-up line.'

'No. He—' She stopped. What good would it be to tell him that it had been true? Jamie had been waiting for her, true to his word. Dan wouldn't want to hear that either. She realized now that Jamie had been right in his observations – this wasn't protection she was seeing, the surrogate big brother looking out for her; it was jealousy, plain and simple.

He finished his reps and jumped off, turning away as he clapped his hands together and swung his arms out, back and forth like a boxer.

Nettie jumped down after him, grateful to be able to release her arms again, and watched as he went over to the pull-up bar, not sure what to say. How had she never seen it before? She'd been so sure he'd seen their awkward, clumsy teenage kisses in the same way as her; it had never occurred to her that maybe he'd been waiting for . . . For what? The stars to align? Their chemistry to mutate as their lives progressed?

He would deny it all, of that much she was certain. He jumped, his arms up and gripping the overhead bar, his palms facing inwards. He began to lift, his energy levels seeming to increase rather than falter, a sure sign he was angry.

He did thirty pull-ups, then dropped down again, looking irritated to find her still standing there. 'What are you doing here, Nets? What do you want?' he snapped.

'I'm sorry, that's all. I didn't mean to hurt you.'

He looked baffled by the sentiment. 'You didn't,' he said, his usually soft, dopey face almost a sneer. 'You couldn't.' His words were like punches, deliberately hard, knocking the wind from her, but she had heard this tone in his voice before, usually when his mother announced her latest divorce.

She stared at a blade of grass peeking through the snow. 'Why aren't you at work, anyway?'

'Oh, uh . . . they've given me the afternoon off because I'm out tonight.' That wasn't quite true. Mike – no doubt at Jules's bullying behest – had given her a 'duvet day', but she didn't want to tell Dan about Gwen's call when he was mad at her like this. He was entitled to be angry about her treatment of him, and telling him the latest twist in their family drama would oblige him to forgive her.

'Let me guess – Jamie again?' Dan shook his head in disbelief, his hands planted on his hips as she bit her lip. 'So what's it now, then? You're going backstage at the . . . I dunno . . . the *Oscars*?'

'The Jingle Bell Ball.'

He groaned.

'It's a link-up with White Tiger, Dan. They're our biggest client. I don't have a choice.'

'Right. Right, yeah. White Tiger.' He sighed, raking a hand through his hair and shaking his head. Jamie's name hovered, unspoken, in the air between them. 'Whatever. It's none of my business. I don't care.'

Nettie stared at him. It didn't seem like that. 'Look, I'll make it up to you, I promise. The campaign's only running for another few days and then he'll be gone and life will be back to normal again.'

He snorted. 'I actually think you believe that.'

'Dan—'

'Wake up! Do you really think someone like him blows into your life and out again, and everything just stays the same? I mean, you know he's seeing other girls, right? I take it you saw the pictures of him and that blonde singer coming out of Mahiki last night? He's a player, Nettie. He plays by different rules.'

She felt winded. What photos? 'D'you mean Coco?'

'I dunno what the hell her name is,' he scowled.

'You don't understand. It isn't what it looks like. They share a manager. They've got a song coming out and he's just helping her get some press.' But even as the words left her mouth, she heard how feeble they sounded, a pathetic excuse.

Dan laughed, but his eyes were bleak. 'Yeah, right, sure he is. That's exactly what it looked like.' He shook his head as she stared back at him, feeling a rising sense of panic; she had never felt so estranged, so far away from her oldest, dearest friend. How had things become so messy, so quickly? How could almost a lifetime of friendship unravel in the space of days? Only a few days ago they'd been laughing in the market, shopping for his mother just like they always did, meeting up with friends and bagging their usual table in the pub, Scout sitting on her feet and hovering up the crisp crumbs.

She blinked. 'Dan, we are still . . . friends, aren't we?'

It seemed an age before he answered. 'Whatever that means,' he muttered. 'I'll see you around,' he said, pulling up the hood on his sweatshirt and jogging away.

'I can't believe we're back here again,' Jules said as the taxi was waved past the security barrier and they diverted into the VIP lane that took them round the back of the arena. 'Three times in a week. We're getting to be pros.'

'I know,' Nettie murmured, feeling sick at the sight of the giant arena. It was too soon for her to come back to the scene of the crime. She didn't want to see him again. It was too much. She closed her eyes, trying to visualize a rowing boat drifting on a still, misted lake – happy place, happy place – but all she saw was an edit of Saturday night's highlights: his driver taking her to him; the way he'd waited for her to show; the way his eyes had held hers every time he came off stage for a water break; the sense of inevitability between them.

But then the way it had ended between them had been inevitable too.

Dan's words echoed in her head and she knew he was right – even if he wasn't right about Coco (and she hoped to God he wasn't: the bed sheets were still warm), he had blown into her life and would blow out again soon enough. Nothing would ever be the same.

She turned to look at Jules, who was reapplying her lip gloss. 'You should do tonight.'

'What?'

'On stage. I want you to do it.'

'Nettie, no, I can't.'

'Yes, you can! You did it yesterday. There is absolutely no good reason why it has to be me in the suit.'

'I'm afraid there is. Dave is insisting upon it.'

'Dave?'

'His manager.'

'Yes, yes, I know who he is. But why is he insisting on it? What does it matter?'

Jules shrugged. 'Only thing I can think is that Jamie's insisting on it.'

Nettie shook her head. 'Nuh. Uh-uh.'

Jules shrugged again. 'He wanted to know where you were yesterday.'

There was a silence as questions immediately began ringing out like church bells in Nettie's head. 'Well, w-what did you say?' she asked, growing pale, shifting forward in her seat anxiously.

'I told him you had the day off.'

'And he bought that?'

'Seemed to. He was in a foul mood, though.'

'Oh.' She sat back in her seat again.

Jules sighed. 'Please will you just tell me what happened with you two? You obviously left the club together.'

She looked out of the window and sighed, knowing she couldn't keep it a secret forever. Jules had been there. She turned back. 'Yes.'

'And . . . ?' Jules prompted.

Nettie bit her lip, gave a small shrug. 'We went back to his hotel.'

Jules closed her eyes and held her hands up in a 'stop' gesture. She took a deep breath before opening her eyes again. 'I am calm. Pray continue.'

'Well . . . what else is there to say?'

Jules pinned her with a look. 'Obviously I don't want details. That would be indelicate. And I am a lady . . .'

Nettie felt a smile twitch her lips at her friend's high drama, and she allowed herself to relive the good bit just for a moment. It was like peering into a box.

'Just tell me it was amazing.'

Nettie blinked. 'Of course.'

Jules waggled her head excitedly and gave a small scream. 'Oh my God! I knew it!'

Nettie couldn't help but smile. Jules's was the right response to her crazy, mad situation. 'And did you cop off with the guitarist?'

'Gus? Yeah. I think musicians might be the way to go.' Jules gave a smile that bordered on . . . shyness. Nettie looked at her in surprise.

'Have you seen him since?' she asked.

'Might've done.'

'*When?*'

Jules tried to look lackadaisical – and failed. 'Last night,' she squealed, holding her hands up for Nettie to clasp. 'He came over.'

'Gus Chambers was in your flat, last night?'

'I know! It's insane. They'd been in the studio all evening, laying down the new track. He came over after.'

'Wow!' Nettie uttered, stunned. 'I'm . . . I'm so surprised. You never said.'

'I was going to tell you last night, but . . .' Her happy-go-lucky expression faded. 'It wasn't the time, obviously.'

Nettie nodded, feeling bad that her news had over-written Jules's, once again.

'Anyway, I'm keeping dead quiet about it at work. God, can you imagine' – she rolled her eyes – 'can you imagine if Caro or Daisy found out about it? And I don't even want to know what Daisy would do to *you*, dark horse,' Jules teased, pushing lightly on her thigh.

Nettie shook her head. 'No. I only saw him the once. It's not the same.'

'But don't you *want* to see him again? I don't get it. How did you leave it with him?'

Nettie looked out of the window again, wishing her reflection wasn't so clearly written there, the humiliation still box-fresh. 'Badly. I left him standing in the corridor in his boxers. I just left him there.'

Jules looked horrified, her fairy-tale fantasy shattered on the ground. 'Oh shit.'

'I know.'

'But why?'

'I just . . .' She sighed, staring into the palms of her hands. How could she articulate it? 'I panicked. I mean, he was talking about us spending the whole day together and it was making me feel . . .' She looked back at her friend. 'It

314

was making me *feel* ... I had to get out of there, you know?'

'Not really,' Jules said softly, rubbing her arm. 'But yeah.'

The cab was pulling up to the stage door they had entered through on Saturday, although Ron wasn't here to greet them now.

A sudden thought struck Nettie. 'Jules, you haven't told Gus, have you, about me, I mean? If he was to tell Jamie—'

'Hey. I've already told you. My lips are sealed. It's your story to tell and no one else's,' Jules said, handing the driver a twenty-pound note and asking for a receipt.

Nettie felt a pinprick of relief. She couldn't bear the thought of Jamie knowing the truth about her life.

'Although, for what it's worth, what happened is hardly a reflection on *you*. I mean, he wouldn't think worse of you because your mum—'

She was stopped by Nettie's expression.

'Well, anyway, you know my thoughts on the matter,' she mumbled, rubbing Nettie's arm lightly.

They stepped out into the snow. Thanks to a driving wind, the snow seemed to be falling horizontally – as though gravity had loosened its grip; certainly Nettie felt rudderless herself as she watched the flakes spin and drift, bouncing on air pockets. Jules struggled to get the rabbit's body past the cab door.

'Earth to Nets!' Jules called, holding out one of the bags for Nettie to take.

They staggered up to the door together, heads down in the wind as though pushed back by the sound. A man with a clipboard and headphones was standing there, swaddled in a puffa, looking at them suspiciously as the bulbous rabbit costume glowed blue in the hanging bags.

He pushed the headphones back to free one of his ears and be able to hear them. 'Jules Grant and Nettie Watson, White Tiger,' Jules said. 'We're with Jamie Westlake.'

The man reluctantly scanned his list, appearing disappointed to find their names. 'What's in the bags?' he asked, leaning forward to peer in.

'That's confidential, I'm afraid.'

'I need to see inside the bag, Miss.'

'No can do. It's for Jamie Westlake's stage act later,' Jules said with her best 'sorry-not-sorry' smile.

'I can't let you in without checking the bags. You could be anyone rocking up here with . . . well, whatever that is in there.'

'Fine, then, so long as you call Jamie and get *his* permission to look. I've got a number in my phone,' Jules said, struggling to pull her phone from her jeans back pocket.

The guard carried on looking suspicious, intrigued by the unusual packages. 'Oh, fine. Go through,' the man muttered, losing interest and waving them past.

They walked along the corridor they had travelled down on Saturday, turning left up the short flight of stairs and into the whitewashed corridor where Jamie's photos had, until so recently, been plastered like wallpaper. Only a few remained now, images of tonight's other artists flanking him.

A lot of them were boy bands, pretty, post-pubescent groups aimed at the teen market, their arms wrapped round each other and pork-pie hats on their heads as they dipped towards the camera. Coco Miller – the golden girl, the latest pop princess, Jamie's most recent conquest? – dazzled in her poster, an image taken from her new album showing her running from the camera, her long hair streaked across her face, her mouth open, eyes glinting.

But Nettie couldn't take her eyes off Jamie's image. He was a man, not a boy, a musician, not a showman, and the very sight of him sent shockwaves through her. She was dreading seeing him again. She'd been so overtaken by events with her mother that she had managed to keep him to the periphery of her thoughts in the past twenty-four hours, but she was back on his turf now and memories, sensations, scents tossed about wildly in her mind. There was no escaping him here.

'Don't look so worried,' Jules said, barging her affectionately as they walked towards the dressing room they remembered from Saturday, constantly dodging people with familiar faces. 'Hey, wasn't that Calvin Harris?'

'Was it?' Nettie thought her voice sounded odd.

Jules looked at her. 'Listen, he'll be cool. He was fine yesterday. There was no rancour or spitting whenever your name came up,' she teased.

'Really?' Nettie asked, her arms aching from trying to keep the unwieldy costume from dragging on the floor. She hoisted it up over her shoulder.

'Really.'

They stopped outside the closed dressing-room door, Jules's hand already raised in the air to knock, when Nettie caught sight of the name in a tab to the side. 'Wait! This isn't Jamie's,' Nettie said, holding her friend's arm still as she looked around them.

'Bollocks. I just thought he'd have the same one.'

'Mmm,' Nettie said, wondering who was on stage right now. The noise level was thunderous and everything was shaking – the floor, the ceiling, the walls, her heart.

'Well, he can't be far, right?' Jules asked, turning to continue down the hall.

Nettie trudged after her, reading the names on the sides of the doors as they tried to get out of the way of a woman – a backing dancer? Nettie wondered – running past in five-inch heels, shorts and a sequinned bra.

'Jules, I think we'd better ask someone,' she said as they got to the end of the corridor. 'They could be God knows where and this costume is too heavy to be double-backing on ourselves.'

'Hang on a minute, hang on a minute,' Jules said with a grin, pulling her phone out from her back pocket. 'I'll text Gus. Mr Lover Lover,' she murmured.

Nettie leaned against the wall with her eyes closed, her palms flat to it and feeling the vibrations that came from 20,000 girls screaming all at once, a 1,000-watt amp and a drum kit. She tuned it all out, rehearsing what she would say to Jamie when she saw him: *Nice jeans . . . Have you seen the weather? . . . Good luck out there . . . It's not you, it's me . . .*

'Bingo. He's sending someone to collect us.' Jules pocketed her phone again. 'I wonder if it'll be Ron.'

'Hmm?' Nettie was distracted. She wanted to get that first look over and done with, behind her. Because then they could just move on with the new status quo between them.

A door at the far end opened and she jumped as a sudden peal of laughter curled into the corridor before it was slammed shut again.

'So, you remember what you're doing out there?'

Nettie turned back to face her, trying to focus. She still had a job to do. 'Yep. Harlem shake.'

'And you watched the clips for those links I sent through?'

She nodded. 'Jamie plays the first bit solo, and then when the drum comes in, that's when I . . . shake?'

'Exactly.' Jules patted her on the shoulder with a grin. 'It's just as well you're disguised up there.'

'You're telling me.'

'I wouldn't want to do that in front of all those people.'

Nettie tried not to think about it. She just wanted to go and do it; do it and go. Jules, she knew, was desperate to stay for the after-party and meet all the other stars, but Nettie knew there was no such obligation for her to stay tonight.

Besides, her father was doing his lasagne. That alone was worth staying in for.

The sound of running feet made them both turn to see Gus approaching at some speed.

'Hey!' he laughed, scooping Jules into his arms as he passed and kissing her.

'Hey,' she giggled, tipping her chin down coquettishly. 'I was expecting a minion to rescue me.'

He pulled a sad face. 'Will I do?'

'If you must,' she joked, elongating the word and rolling her eyes. They kissed again and Nettie turned away, embarrassed.

Gus looked up as though only just realizing Nettie was standing there. 'Sorry, hi. We haven't formally met. Gus.'

She raised a hand shyly. What had Jamie told him about her? That she was a freak? A psycho? 'Hi. Nettie.'

Gus looked down at the bulging bags by their feet. 'This is it, then, is it?' he asked, picking them up effortlessly.

'Certainly is,' Jules said, following after as he began to

lead them back down the corridor from which they had come.

'I can't wait for this. It's going to be so mad. The band's really psyched. Have you heard them through there?' He jerked his thumb towards the arena on their right. 'We thought it was loud on Saturday for us. That's nothing compared to what One Direction gets. I swear to God it's almost frightening. You just think, if they were all to stampede . . .' He shook his head, chatting easily.

He pointed to a room just ahead that they had already passed by. 'Home sweet home.'

'Well, no wonder we couldn't find you!' Jules said, indicating the empty tab beside the door.

Gus grinned. 'Jamie prefers it like that. Stops the groupies hunting him down.' He shrugged, seemingly baffled.

They walked in, Gus putting the bags in a cupboard on the left wall. There were three other people in the room. Dave and Jimmy, the drummer, were playing *FIFA* on an Xbox.

'Hey!' they both said in unison, taking a hand each off their remotes to wave from across the room.

'How are you?' Dave asked her, just as Jimmy scored a goal and pulled his T-shirt over his head in celebration. 'Agh! Bastard!'

Jamie was sitting on the arm of a black leather sofa, his guitar on his knee as he tightened some strings. He had looked up as they walked in, his hand falling from the strings at the sight of her.

She swallowed, feeling her cheeks burn, her throat close. The same question – the one he'd been asking her when she'd run out through the door on Sunday morning – was still in his eyes.

'Hi.' Her voice was tiny, audible only by microphone, visible only by microscope.

He nodded his head in silent greeting, barely a greeting, as he looked away quickly.

All her rehearsed speech flew out of the window and she felt the atmosphere in the room thicken like cream on the heat, cocked eyebrows saying what mouths wouldn't. She felt like her lungs were being squeezed at the bottom, as though she could only scoop cups of air, and she stood helpless in the room, not sure what to do. Even Jules seemed paralysed by the frosty reception.

'Drink?' Gus asked, coming to Nettie's rescue this time and holding up a whisky bottle.

'Um . . .'

'Yes, go on. It won't kill you,' he said, pouring a fingerful into a tumbler and handing it to her with a friendly wink.

'Babe?' Gus asked Jules, handing one to her too and earning himself a round of cocked eyebrows from the band.

Nettie despatched the drink quickly. It made her throat burn, but that only matched the flames in her cheeks. Jamie hated her – he had managed to convey that with one look and no words; frankly she could do with some fire in her belly.

'Here, take a seat,' Gus said, wiping a heap of jackets off another sofa with a sweep of his arm.

'Thanks,' Nettie mumbled, sitting in the corner, her arms and legs pressed together, trying not to take up any space, trying to become invisible.

Gus pulled Jules down onto his lap and began nuzzling her neck. Nettie pretended to be interested in the *FIFA* game on the giant screen.

A door on the far wall opened and a dazzling girl stood

in the doorway of a bathroom. She was wearing a pair of gold silk shorts and a red scooped vest, some long gold necklaces that swung by her navel and wedge trainers. Her skin was so taut and smooth, Nettie thought she could write a letter on it, the year-round tan suggesting either an LA zip code or jet-set diary. She was more dazzling than even her photographs had suggested, Nettie thought, depressed.

'Who're they?' Coco Miller asked, clocking Jules and Nettie immediately, her catlike eyes narrowing.

There was a brief pause as each of the men waited for someone else to volunteer the girls' identities. They all knew the girls had overstepped their roles from the professional into the personal.

Finally Dave spoke up. 'Coco, this is Jules and Nettie from White Tiger. You remember how we said about the charity link-up?' His tone of voice was cajoling, slightly weary.

'Oh, that's *you*, is it? You look so . . . normal,' Coco said her, plumped upper lip curling slightly as she abruptly turned away. 'Listen, Dave, there's absolutely no way their song's going to win, right? I'm really not happy about all of this, you know. *I* never signed up to it. I just wanted to record with Jay.'

'I know, and trust me, there's not even a chance of your song not coming out,' Dave said soothingly. 'It's just a publicity stunt for the charity. The single's coming out on Friday, as agreed. Nothing has changed. It's a guaranteed number one.'

Coco stretched. 'Good,' she murmured silkily, walking over to where Jamie was sitting. She ruffled his hair as she passed, lying out along the sofa so that her legs stretched towards him like a horizon.

Nettie felt sick as Dan's words – a not-so-friendly warning – became a taunt. She hadn't been able to resist looking the photos up online when she'd got home and they were worse, far worse than she'd expected. No wonder Dan had looked at her with such pity. Jamie had been grinning, his arm round Coco's shoulder as she whispered something in his ear, the two of them looking like lovebirds. Lovers.

Jamie resumed strumming a few chords, his head bent down, humming so softly Nettie could barely hear him.

She kept her eyes on the patch of floor immediately in front of her, worried he would sense her stare, worried he'd somehow tune in to the thoughts flashing through her mind – her lips on his neck, his lips on her breast, his laugh in her ear . . .

There was a brisk rap at the door, a sudden crackle of static. 'Ten-minute call,' a voice said from the hallway.

'But we're only seventy-six minutes into the second half,' Dave complained, motioning to the screen.

'I'd get out while your dignity's still intact, mate. You're already losing. I'll have given you a proper kicking by full time,' Jimmy laughed.

'Oi!' Dave protested, but throwing his remote down on the sofa and getting up. It was time to work, not play, and the diffident atmosphere in the room changed with his movements. 'Right, everyone happy?'

Nettie looked away. The question wasn't being directed at her, but it stung anyway. She was the very definition of *not happy*.

'So, to run through: we start with "Crystal Dawn". Jimmy, remember we've cut the solo to eighteen bars on this to get the set done on time. They're threatening to pull the plugs if anyone runs over.'

Jimmy gave a salute in understanding as he too got up and opened a water bottle, drinking several large gulps. Nettie watched as he began cutting the top off the bottle with a pair of scissors – emptying the contents over himself after the big drum solos was his party piece.

'And, Gus, if you blow this amp too, I'll fucking kill you,' Dave continued.

Gus saluted as well.

'Jay, Nettie'll come on after "Rocks and Bones" when you start your spiel, OK? Remember the hashtags. *Don't* forget the hashtags: the sponsors want those mentioned. Then we go into the cover of Harlem shake, blah, blah, blah.' He looked over at Coco. 'And you, Ms Miller, we're keeping the best for last, so just be your usual gorgeous self. Trust me, you're going to love the response you get. Those kids out there are getting the world exclusive on your new duet, and this stunt has got them going wild, so we want to give them a bit of banter between you two, OK? Wait for Jay to introduce you once Nettie's off. I've got them to autocue your words for you.'

'Don't need it,' Coco said with a knowing smile, pointing one toe to nudge Jamie's leg. 'I can wax lyrical about this man.' She extended her leg as she said this, her pointed foot now almost touching his crotch.

Everyone laughed except two, Jamie's eyes flickering towards Nettie for the briefest moment, before looking down again quickly. He looked angry.

Jules got off Gus's lap and Nettie stood up, smoothing her jeans. She had to get changed. She had to get away from here.

'I need to check my strings. See you after?' Gus said to Jules, kissing her on the lips.

'You'd better,' she murmured, her face splitting into an enormous smile as he gave her a wink, before trooping out through the door with Dave, Jimmy and Coco, their voices echoing loudly down the hall.

Jamie turned to place the guitar he'd been tuning back on a stand in the corner as Jules went to the wardrobe and grabbed the bunny costume. She turned to Nettie and silently mouthed, 'Talk to him,' before disappearing into the bathroom, ostensibly to hang it up.

Jamie turned back, seeming as surprised as she was to find they were suddenly alone together.

They looked at each other in silence across the room, the memory of him standing in the corridor in his boxers, calling after her, still an echo in both their minds. A moment passed between them, the electric charge that always came when their eyes locked – a blue flicker across the room, but before she could even open her mouth, he looked away again, the ball of his jaw pulsing with checked anger. 'See you out there,' he said to the floor, moving towards the door, brushing past her.

'Wait!' The word was out before she could stop it, a ball of fire shot from the cannon into the night.

He stopped dead, his neck bent as he stared down at her, and she swallowed to see the coldness in his eyes. The intimacy of only three nights ago was as distant, now, as a star and it seemed almost impossible to recall how easy she had felt in his company – lingering glances, private smiles, a magnetism between them that had seemingly propelled them from the virtual reality of the Twittersphere into the flesh, blood and beating hearts of one another's orbits. She had felt thrown towards him by the gods, able – somehow – to forget that he was one of them. But not now.

'I-I wanted to say I'm sorry. For the other night. I-I mean, morning,' she corrected herself, cheeks burning. 'I know it was unforgive—'

She saw his eyes fall to her hand and she flinched to realize that she was holding his wrist. She dropped it with a start, sensing she had crossed an unspoken boundary. He was standing so close she could feel the heat – the anger – radiating from him in waves, but a cold, galactic sea was freezing the air in the small space between them.

'Don't stress,' he said with a dry laugh that held no humour in its walls, and deep inside herself, she felt her heart, paper-thin and fragile, collapse in a heap of ashes. 'Nothing I haven't seen before.' He looked back at her with . . . She frowned to see it . . . Was that superiority in his eyes? Where last week there had been amusement and gentle teasing, flirtation and curiosity, a meeting of equals, now there was a gulf between them, the one she'd expected to find from the start: he had drawn a line – he was the star, she a nobody, just a stupid girl in a stupid bunny outfit who had to go out there and do a stupid dance in front of all those stupid—

'Shit! I forgot my—' Coco panted, stopping dead in the doorway.

The intrusion broke the deadlock of his cold stare and Nettie gasped like she was breaking the surface of the ocean, gulping for air. She looked over at the beautiful singer, who was watching them with disbelief, guessing, somehow knowing . . .

Nettie stepped back, out of his orbit, her back slamming

into the wardrobe door so that she took a half-step forwards again – startled as a rabbit. Ironically.

'I've got to get ready,' she said in a broken voice, unable to meet either of their eyes and breaking into a run past them both, bolting the bathroom door behind her.

She leaned against the door, her breath coming in hiccups as she struggled to keep down the emotions that kept trying to rise in her. Hot, tight tears budded at her eyes.

'Jay, what the f—!' Coco's hissed whisper was clear through the door.

'Coco, don't. Just don't.' Jamie's voice was low, barely audible.

Not wanting to, but not able not to, Nettie shifted her position to bring her ear to the door. Quite literally, her ears were burning.

'You slept with her? *Her?* That little mouse?'

'Just leave it. It was a mistake.'

'The freak bunny girl? What were you *thinking*?'

Nettie heard him sigh. 'Clearly I wasn't . . .'

'What are you doing?' Jules whispered behind her, but Nettie held a shaking hand up to silence her.

'. . . just a groupie. It was a one-time thing.'

The word was like a punch, throwing her across the room.

'Nets, what the hell?' Jules cried, running over to her, seeing the hot tears begin to splash.

Nettie couldn't reply. The words kept going round and round in her mind, her body like a cauldron – her blood hot and swirling, getting hotter, making her dizzy, making her sweat . . .

'What just happened? Did you talk to him?' Jules asked,

snapping her fingers in front of Nettie's gaze, trying to get her attention.

But Nettie was lost. Groupie? He couldn't say those things! They weren't true; they weren't fair. She couldn't believe he was capable of such cruelty. That look he'd given her, that name . . . Did he really think those things about her? Was that what he was going round saying about her? To Dave, and Gus, and Jimmy? What about to White Tiger? To Jeremy and Scott? Would it get back to them? He couldn't get away with this.

'Speak to me, Nettie, for Chrissakes.'

And then it came to her. The perfect reply. Nettie looked at her, a sudden calm settling upon her like a cooling mist and making her friend frown at the abrupt change. 'Jules, I need to get dressed.'

Gus had been right. The noise level at this ball made Saturday night's gig seem like a few friends playing the village hall. The average age of the audience was lower by about ten years and that meant, in Jules's opinion, a difference of three octaves and ten decibels.

Nettie stood in the wings where she had stood only a few nights before in very different circumstances. But she had been lost back then – falling. Now she jumped on the spot, dressed in the costume once more and getting the adrenalin pumping. The noise of the crowd was lifting her and she couldn't wait to get out there and do this. Finish it.

Jamie had finished the third song, his guitar resting now on one of the amps as he took the mic from its stand and began to talk, milking the crowd with his charm and humour, working them en masse, the way he'd worked – duped – her.

'Nettie, could you please just tell me everything's OK? I'm worried. You don't seem yourself,' Jules shouted.

'Don't worry. This is going to be great. It'll be the biggest hit yet,' she shouted back, trying to be heard through the costume and over the music. 'Caro's going to freak!'

And then suddenly she heard her name. Blue Bunny Girl, being repeated over and over, in a chant, getting louder and louder. She stopped jumping. They were all calling for her?

'Shit!' Jules laughed. 'You'd better get out there!'

They high-fived, Jules pushing Nettie onto the stage.

The arena erupted as she ran out, the lights finding her as she ran from one side of the stage to the other, whipping the crowd to ever higher frenzies, her arms up, ears flapping, before coming to a stop in the centre of the stage and standing with her legs wide, paws raised in the air, soaking it all in.

Her heart was pounding in her chest, louder even than the music. The rush being out here, all these people . . . Suddenly she understood it; she got why musicians and actors loved to perform.

Jamie had picked up his guitar again and was walking towards her slowly, his eyes on her as he strummed, unable to see her face or the expression in her eyes, but ever the professional, he was doing a fine job of hiding his contempt. She stood there, swaying languidly, watching him all the while – hating him, hating that she still felt a pull to him even as she hated him.

And then Gus dropped the bass beat, Jimmy hit the drums, and as the lights began to strobe, she went for it, writhing and jumping and convulsing like a mad thing, not caring, hearing the laughs, the screams of delight. She was free in here; it didn't matter. No one knew who she was or what she wasn't.

Jamie was laughing too. She could see his shoulders shaking as he played and she shook it all out, burned it all off, and everything that had gone wrong between them – the confusions and misunderstandings, unspoken explanations and soured passions – melted away so that it was just them, in this moment, on stage in front of all these people.

But four minutes was all she got of that freedom. Four minutes and it was all over and she was left remembering what he'd said as she lay on her back, panting on the stage of the O2 arena, with 20,000 people shouting her name.

Jamie offered a hand and she let him pull her up, her flinch not visible beneath the costume as he put his arm round her shoulder, flashbulbs going off as their partnership was cemented. The crowd was going wild and she wriggled out from under his arm, running from one end of the stage to the other.

Jamie walked over to the microphone and picked it up from the stand again.

'I guess you're all pretty fond of my new friend, huh?' he asked the crowd.

Cue frenzy. Nettie punched the air delightedly and did a little jig.

'Yeah, me too.'

She ran to Gus and hugged him. The crowd whooped. She ran round to the back of the stage and hugged Jimmy. The crowd roared.

As she went to leave him, she picked up Jimmy's water bottle, the one he kept beside his drums, ready for his pièce de résistance in the next song. Fanning herself with one of her paws, she ran to the front of the stage again. She could see Coco standing in the wing, waiting to come on for her duet, her arms crossed and a scowl on her face.

Jamie was watching on, bemused – but also now confused. She was supposed to have left the stage after the shake. 'London, give it up for my good friend Blue Bunny Girl!' Jamie shouted into the mic as she came to stand in front of him, waving to the crowd with her left hand.

As the crowd gave her another roar of appreciation, she mimed surprise, flinging both arms up like a gun was being pointed at her, the water in the bottle flying backwards in a perfect arc. It landed on Jamie in an almost solid heap, the noise from the crowd cutting out like the National Grid had been unplugged.

But only for a second.

In the next instant, they lifted the roof, cheering and screaming and whooping, whistling and clapping as Nettie pulled a pose and bounded happily off the stage to where Jules was standing, open-mouthed.

'Oh my God!' she hollered. 'Nettie, what did you *do*?'

'You should know, Jules. It's your favourite – "hashtag Blakeing",' Nettie laughed, disappearing into the shadows with a victor's strut.

Chapter Twenty-One

'Right, well, today's off,' Mike said in his tetchiest voice, walking into the conference room. Caro hastily took her feet off the table.

'Off? What do you mean, off?' Daisy asked, watching as he irritably threw his paperwork down on the desk.

'Jamie's refusing to show. Says he wants no further involvement after last night's humiliation.'

'Oh, come on!' Nettie said, swinging defiantly in her chair, her hands on the armrests. She still felt high from last night's win. Groupie? Ha! 'How was it humiliation? It's one of the memes.'

'Which he knew nothing about! It would have been a courtesy if you could have kept him – no, *all* of us, in fact – informed!'

Nettie tutted. 'He needs to grow a sense of humour,' she muttered.

'He was wearing a mic pack, Nettie! It blew an entire circuit when the water hit him.'

Nettie tried to look serious, but the laughter wanted to burst out of her like, well, water from a dam. The thought of blowing the electrics at the O2 was too much.

Another memory of working the crowd last night rippled through her and she smiled to herself.

'It's not funny!' Mike said, seeing the way her eyes danced.

There was a pause.

'It kind of was,' Daisy said, clearly also trying to swallow down her laughter.

'Yeah, and the Interweb's gone fricking mad for it,' Caro added, nodding vigorously and chewing her gum in tempo.

'Language, please, Caro,' Mike sighed. 'We're not on the streets in here.'

'Do you want to hear the stats?' she asked, one eyebrow cocked.

Mike, resting his weary head in one hand, gestured for her to continue.

'Twitter retweets for last night: three point two *million* . . .'

Every single one of them gasped, Mike sitting as upright as if he'd been pulled up on strings.

'Twitter likes: also three point two million. Total Twitter followers: three point four million. YouTube views for this link' – at this point, she took a breath – 'five point seven *million.*'

Mike closed his eyes and pulled a fist, whispering, '*Yesss,*' under his breath.

'And total donations to Tested as of nine o'clock this morning: one . . .' She dared to breathe again, making them all groan.

'Spit it out!' Daisy harried her. But Caro just smiled.

'One million, three hundred and seventy-four thousand, eight hundred and twenty-two pounds *and*' – she held a finger in the air – 'thirteen pence.'

'Oh my God! We broke a million?' Daisy yelled.

'And then some!' Jules hollered, jumping to her feet,

along with Caro and Daisy, and running round the room
and waving her arms in the air. Even Mike was joining in
the group hugs. They were making so much noise, Nettie
noticed the people in the events management agency
across the road staring in at them.

Jules dragged her to standing, throwing her arms round
her neck. 'You do my head in! Do you know that?'

'I told you it'd be the biggest one yet,' Nettie yelled as
Jules clasped her arms and they skipped round in a circle.

'We freaking rule!' Caro yelled.

'Let's get drunk!' Daisy cried, punching the air delightedly. 'I know someone at the—'

'Ladies, ladies.' Mike came swiftly to his senses. 'While I
applaud the sentiment, it is only ten a.m. and I'm afraid we
still have work to do.' He sat down in his seat again and
waited for the girls to do the same.

The excitement fizzled out of them like air from a punc-
tured ball as they dropped back into their seats, chewing
on the ends of biros and drumming their nails as they took
in Mike's subdued demeanour.

'The fact remains that we now have a problem. As successful and funny as last night's skit was, we're screwed
without Jamie. We were doing well before him, but it's the
two of you *combined* that's given this campaign a whole
new platform. You're a dream together, a marketing power
couple.'

'You're the new Beckhams,' Jules teased, giving her a
wink.

'It's gone global, Nettie,' Mike said sternly, trying to
establish a sensible tone. 'Or at least it *had*. The song vote
had the potential to break us out to yet another level.
Internet traffic was our highest yet yesterday. "Hashtag

team-jamie" and "hashtag teambunny" were the top trends on Twitter, and actually, after the prank last night, you're in the lead, Nettie, for the song.'

'But no one's even heard it yet!' she half laughed. This was crazy.

He shrugged. 'It doesn't seem to matter. They just love you.'

'It'll change by Friday, don't worry,' Caro said assuredly, knowing that would be Mike's next concern. He had promised the record company #teambunny wouldn't win.

'That's if we still have a vote by then. Obviously without Jamie, there's no contest. We need to get him back in the game. We have to change his mind.'

His eyes had settled upon Nettie, his fingers pointed together in a steeple.

'Uh . . . why are you saying that just to me?' Nettie asked him nervously.

'Because you did this to him. It's because of you he bailed. You're the one who's going to have to try to build a bridge and repair the relationship.'

Nettie spluttered, sitting up adroitly. 'Y-you mean, you want me to *apologize* to him?'

'You were the one who went off plan and covered him in water in front of all those people. It's not going to mean anything coming from me.'

'No.' She shook her head firmly and crossed her arms above her chest. 'I won't do it.'

'Nettie, you have to. There are three days left of the campaign. You've raised almost one and a half million pounds for the charity.' He leaned in, gathering her gaze with a conspiratorial glint. 'Don't you want to get to two?'

She blinked. Over her dead body was she apologizing to

that man. After what he'd said about her? Uh-uh. No way. Not happening. 'No. I'm good, thanks. Very happy with that number. It's a good, solid number, one and a half mill.'

Mike smacked the desk with his palm and pushed himself back in his seat, staring up at the ceiling for strength.

'Nets,' a softer voice tried.

Nettie looked across at Daisy, who was leaning on the table, a compassionate look on her face.

'Look, I know you and Jamie don't really . . .' She rolled her hands in the air in front of her, searching for the right words. 'You don't really hit it off. You're not each other's cup of tea, and that's fine . . .'

Under the table, Jules's foot gave her ankle a swift kick.

'But couldn't you put your personal differences aside – for the good of the campaign?'

Nettie stared at her in dismay. They had no idea of the gravity of what they were asking her to do. She looked over to Jules for support – she'd have an alternative idea, a better idea; she always did.

'I hate to say it, but they're right.' Jules shrugged.

'Jules!' Nettie cried.

'Listen, you know I'd disagree with them if I possibly could, but the finish line is in sight, Nets. It's only for a few more days. And then you don't ever have to see him again – if you don't want to.'

'Ha! See him again?' Daisy trilled. 'We should be so lucky. By the time we clock off on Friday, he's going to be on a private jet to the Caribbean.'

Nettie felt a jolt of ice arrow through her veins. It was true. If he wasn't gone from her life already, he most certainly would be then. 'How do you know that?'

Daisy stared back at Nettie, pleased to have Jamie's ball

in her court for once. Nettie tried not to be riled. She probably knew the sister of his travel agent's dog-walker. Or
something. Daisy planted her hands firmly on the desk.
'Look, we have got three days left to spend with one of the
hottest men on the planet. Don't blow it for the rest of us.'

Nettie swallowed, squeezing her eyes shut and letting a
woolly silence blanket them. There was no way to get out
of this. Without a rock solid explanation as to why she had
every reason to consider herself the injured party, she was
cornered. And no way, *no way*, was she telling them what
she'd done – going back to his hotel, running out the next
day, how Jamie had called her a 'groupie' to Coco Miller.

'Fine,' she said finally, through gritted teeth.

'Yes!' Caro and Daisy high-fived each other, Mike punching the air again in a short victory jab like Andy Murray.

'You're doing the right thing,' Mike said, the colour
returning to his cheeks.

Nettie watched, feeling an impression of an idea beginning to gather in her mind. 'But it's not going to be an
outright apology,' she said quickly, making them all halt
their celebrations again.

'Huh?' Daisy asked.

'What?' Caro mumbled.

'Well, this is the digital age, right – or so you all keep
telling me. I say we use the momentum we've got with all
the views and retweets and whatnot, and put a bit of
pressure on him to relent, rather than me just apologizing
to him. I mean, he's being a pretty sore loser. Everyone else
thinks the gag is great.'

'Well, they would! But we don't want to do anything
that's going to embarrass him further, Nettie,' Mike said
gravely.

'Of course not. But we can play this a bit more cleverly than a simple "sorry", can't we? I mean, let's work the crowds. If they like it so much, let's get them involved. Let's get *them* to convince *him* to forgive *me*.'

'So you mean peer pressure, but on a global scale?' Jules asked with a laugh. She gave Mike a wink. 'There's no stopping her now.'

'You know, I actually like that idea,' Caro said, chewing at speed and nodding intently. 'It's always better to keep the conversation flowing, and they're already really mobilized – we can see that from the conversion stats, and with last night's clip still trending, we should take advantage of the discussions happening out there. Everyone's already intrigued by the link-up. He's sexy; she's funny. He's famous; she's cool. Plus there's a real groundswell out there about wanting to know who you are, Nets. It's on loads of chat forums and fan pages. We could feed that into it – maybe tease that we'll do a big reveal on Friday too.'

'No! I don't want to be revealed,' Nettie said quickly.

'Why not?'

'Because it's too big now. I don't want . . . I don't . . .' Her voice trailed off.

'That's totally fine, Mike, isn't it?' Jules asked rhetorically. 'Isn't it?'

'Uh, yes . . . yes, fine,' Mike said reluctantly.

Caro exhaled, bored. 'Whatevs. But if they think you two have had a tiff, so much the better. Any publicity is good publicity.'

Mike rolled his eyes. 'Why a straightforward "sorry" won't suffice I don't know. It'd be a lot faster.'

Daisy's phone rang. Her eyebrows furrowed as she clocked the number on the caller display. 'Hello?'

Everyone looked up in surprise. No one ever took phone calls mid-meeting. Mike looked outraged, but Daisy simply put her finger to her lips to silence him.

They all fell quiet, watching as she uh-huhed into the phone, her eyes sliding over to Nettie. She gave her a wink, their rivalry over Jamie a moment ago already forgotten.

'Who was that?' Mike demanded the moment she put down the phone.

'*The One Show.*' Daisy looked at Nettie, a grin growing on her face. 'They want you and Jamie for a fifteen-minute segment tonight, and he's to perform one of the songs.'

'Oh. My. God!' Jules cried, clapping her hands together.

'But that's so soon!' Nettie gasped.

'We've got to get you to the studios for six o'clock,' Daisy said, opening her iPad and bringing up a train time-table. 'Which is easier said than done, given that they're recording the Christmas specials in Salford this week.'

'Well, how long will it take to get up there?'

'About two hours, I reckon . . .'

Caro looked out of the window at the heavily falling snow. 'That's if the trains are even running.'

'Oh crap, that's all we need,' Daisy muttered, remembering too late the difficult travelling conditions.

'Ladies, langu—' Mike started to protest, but no one was interested.

'Have they spoken to Jamie's camp yet? What if he says no?' Jules asked.

'Of course he won't! He's about to release the Christmas single. He wouldn't do that,' Daisy said with certainty, just as her phone rang again. Her eyes fell to the caller ID. 'Oh *shit!*'

Mike groaned again. They all watched anxiously as she

took the call. '. . . See what I can do. I'll come back to you in the hour.' She dropped the phone on the desk again. 'So he did do that,' she shrugged. 'He's not going.'

'The bastard!' Nettie gasped, shocked by the extent of his reaction. 'What about the charity? He's going to deprive them of a prime-time slot on TV just because his precious pride's been hurt?'

'You have *really* pissed him off,' Caro chuckled wickedly.

'It's fine. We can sort this,' Daisy said confidently. 'We're going to sort this. Worst comes to worst, I'll call my ex. He's a producer on BBC Two. He knows people.'

Caro dropped her head to the table and began banging it against the top. Daisy watched on in bafflement.

'Look, Nettie's on to something with this peer-pressure thing,' Jules said, appealing for calm. 'If he's not going to do the honourable thing, then we're just going to have to play dirty and force his hand. But how?'

The room fell silent as everyone thought, brows creased as they doodled, twirled biros, chewed pencils, spun on the chairs . . .

'We could photograph Nettie holding a sign saying, "*Sorry*"?' Caro piped up after a while. 'Or . . . or a load of messages in a short film – you know, like in *Love Actually*?'

'I loved that film,' Daisy sighed.

'Yeah,' Jules nodded. 'That could work.'

'No, it doesn't. It still means *me* saying sorry when *he's* the one with no sense of humour,' Nettie protested.

Everyone rolled their eyes.

'Could you not just—' Mike pleaded.

'No!'

There was an irritated silence.

'Well, then we have to get the public behind *you*,' Daisy

said. 'Yeah, they need to feel sympathy for you because you've been dumped, basically. We need for them to see you as the victim here. He doesn't want you anymore.'

Nettie willed her to stop speaking, for the sounds to stop coming from her mouth now. They were too close to the truth.

'Doesn't want you . . .' Mike murmured. 'Hey, what's that song . . . ? You know . . .' He began humming, clicking his fingers and doing just enough of a shoulder-wiggle to alarm the lot of them. 'Oh, who was it? Who sang it? You know . . .' The answer came to him in a flash. 'Human League!'

'Who?' Caro asked, her upper lip curled in a sneer.

He closed his eyes and began singing again. '"*Don't you want me, baby?*"'

'Oh yes!' Jules said, her eyes wide with excitement and joining in. '"*You know I can't believe it when you say that you won't see me,*"' she sang. 'The lyrics are perfect!'

'What, so we'll get Nettie . . . singing it?' Daisy asked doubtfully.

'No! She can mime it – we'll do a spoof video for it. Have her looking sad by a window, her ears all droopy, a picture of Jamie in a frame on her lap . . .'

Caro sat back in her chair and grinned. 'That'd be so funny.'

'It could say he has to forgive her if we get to £100k. I mean, he can hardly very well *not*, can he? And we can get people to retweet if they agree he should take her back, getting it trending again. He can't ignore that. We could do with another hashtag too,' Daisy said. 'Something like "hashtag lovebunny" or "hashtag secondchance".'

'It'd have to double as today's upload,' Jules said, rubbing her temples and looking stressed. 'There's not time for two skits. We'll barely get this done as it is.' She looked around the table. 'Are we in?'

'We're in,' Mike said, giving the table one of his customary slaps as he rose to standing. 'Let's do it.'

'Great. Let's go.'

'Another cupcake?' Jules asked. 'My treat.'

Nettie looked up at her from under her lashes. She could scarcely bring herself to tear her attention away from the screen. She shook her head fractionally.

Jules sighed and got up, ordering a fresh round of tea and returning with a carrot cake, two saucers and a knife a few minutes later.

'What? You're looking thin. You've been doing too much walking lately. You'll start slipping down the pavement cracks if I don't keep an eye on you.' She cut the cake in half and slid one piece, on a saucer, towards Nettie.

'I don't understand why he isn't responding,' Nettie said, oblivious to the temptation under her nose. 'I mean, it's at nearly half a million retweets already, and eighty-six grand. That's a *lot* of people calling for his forgiveness. How stubborn can one man be?'

'Very, apparently. Anyway, they'll be responding all right – in a soundproofed room somewhere off the M4. Dave will be doing his nut over this.'

Nettie's eyes flicked up. 'Why Dave?' She stiffened in suspicion. 'Have you been communicating with Gus?'

'No!' Jules protested, spraying crumbs over the table. 'But it's obvious, isn't it? Jamie's had a fit of pique and very visibly let down a small charity that needs his patronage and which he was waxing lyrical about last week. What a flake! The press'll destroy him. This is a PR dis-as-ter.' She winked. 'They'll be having crisis talks right now, I promise you. He is having a *shit* day.'

'I hope you're right. We're stuffed if something doesn't happen soon. I've got to be on that train in an hour if I'm going to get up to the studios in time.

'It'll be fine,' Jules said dismissively. 'Dave's a business-man. He won't let Jamie damage his brand like this. Jay's just throwing his toys out of the pram, but he'll come round.'

'Don't call him that.'

'Who? What? What'd I say?'

'Jamie. You called him Jay, like you're in his posse.'

'Entourage.'

'Exactly. And you're not. I don't care if you're shagging his guitarist. You're my friend, not his.'

Jules cocked an eyebrow. 'Has it come to this? Oh my Gawd.' She rolled her eyes. 'Just chill, babe. It'll all come good.'

Nettie looked around the cafe, their usual haunt when it was too early to go to the pub. The neon-pink 'Primrose Bakery' sign in the window cast a fondant glow onto the pistachio walls, the elaborately iced confections in the dis-play cabinet as intricate and highly coloured as jewels. A mother and her tweenage daughter were sitting at the next table, comparing their manicures. Nettie looked away quickly, trying to pretend to herself that she hadn't noticed them, that she didn't remember that bond.

She examined her own nails. Last night had been a mis-take, she saw that now. She'd had enough time to calm down, watched the clips at least twenty times herself, a sick feeling steadily growing in the pit of her stomach as she saw the look of betrayal in his eyes as she ran off stage, victorious and so pleased with herself.

She had gone too far – justified or not – and jeopardized the final days of what had been a phenomenally successful campaign. She should have just said sorry. She'd never see him after this Friday anyway. How bad would it have been to just DM him an apology? She would still get the last laugh. People were going to be laughing and sharing the clip for a long time to come. In fact, he may never live this down. Every interview he ever gave – well, if he ever gave one – every article written about him would feature her trick and his incensed, selfish response. She would haunt him for the rest of his career, although that was scant recompense compared to what she was facing – having Jamie Westlake as the One Who Got Away was a far worse fate.

An idea came to Nettie suddenly. 'Text Gus.'

'What? Why? You told me *not* to.'

'I know. Tell him I'm going to go on the show anyway to talk about the campaign and that if they ask me about why he isn't there, I'll obviously have to tell the truth that he's being a bad sport. I'll say how devastated everyone is by his abandonment of the campaign. Use that word. Abandonment.'

Jules's shoulders slumped slightly. 'Nets, I don't want me and Gus to get drawn into—'

'Could you just do it? Please? What choice do we have? He's obviously not going to be bullied by the entire Western world.'

Reluctantly, Jules fired off a text. 'And make it look like you're warning him, like you're on their side,' Nettie said, biting a nail as she watched Jules's fingers fly over the screen. 'Did you use the word—'

'Yes, yes.' Jules pressed 'send' and replaced the phone on the table, casting Nettie an unhappy look.

Nettie gave her a 'what?' look back, the two of them sitting in antsier silence as the minutes ticked past.

Jules had begun picking the cake apart crumb by crumb when her phone rang suddenly.

Jules looked at it in surprise, before slowly bringing it to her ear. 'Yes?' she said in a sing-song, telephonist's voice. Her expression changed. 'Oh, hi, Jay . . . Of course.' She held the phone out to Nets. 'It's for you.'

Nettie took a deep breath, giving a thumbs-up sign as she took the phone. 'Hello?' she asked innocently.

'If you think I'm letting you sit on that sofa and destroy my reputation for a second time, you can think again.'

Jamie's voice was a low rumble, like a faraway explosion finally reaching her and splitting open the earth at her feet. She felt her heart fall to her gut at the sound of his anger, his contempt for her wringing the breath from her lungs.

She squeezed her eyes shut. How could they have gone from lovers to enemies in the space of a couple of days? She forced herself to rally, not to be cowed.

'I take it that means you'll be there, then,' she said in a voice that quivered only a little.

'You're damn right it does.'

'Well, that's great. I know Tested will be very relieved.'

There was a pause down the line. 'Fuck you, Nettie.'

He hung up, leaving her reeling as she dropped the phone down from her ear.

Jules reached over the table in concern. 'Christ, what happened? What did he say? You look like he just hit you.'

Nettie swallowed, managed a smile. 'It's fine. He'll be there.'

'Really? You look terrible.'

Nettie blinked, forcing herself to stand and pick up the packed bags by her feet. 'I'm fine.'

'But—'

'No buts. There's no time for chatting, Jules,' she said, taking a shaky breath. 'I've got a train to catch.'

Chapter Twenty-Two

They had taken a punt on the pressure campaign working and couriered the unwieldy bunny suit ahead of her journey. It was far too bulky and conspicuous for her to travel with and was already hanging up in her dressing room when she arrived.

The room itself wasn't vast – not like Jamie's at the O2 – but it was freshly painted with a desk and sofa, and, to her astonishment, a bottle of champagne, a fruit bowl, a basket of muffins, a bouquet of white roses and a handwritten note of welcome from the head of guest relations. She only had half an hour till she was supposed to be on – it wasn't like she needed hair or make-up – and she wondered when she was supposed to eat and drink it all.

'Gosh, is all this for . . . me?' she asked, sure she must have been shown to the wrong room.

'Of course. We're so excited to have you on the show,' Debbie, the press officer, said as she rearranged the roses. 'Alex and Matt can't wait to talk to you about the campaign. It's just incredible what you've done. Do you know one of our researchers said you'd achieved more in terms of fundraising and raising the profile of male cancers in this last fortnight than has been achieved in the previous thirty years?'

Nettie was stunned. 'Really?'

'Yep,' Debbie nodded. 'In fact, we're running it as the lead lifestyle story on *Breakfast* next week. The number of men – particularly younger men – booking to go to their GPs for tests has increased by eight hundred and forty-four per cent.'

'That's amazing,' she said, feeling humbled and ashamed that while she'd been bemoaning wearing the suit and trying to wheedle her way out of the skits at every opportunity, the campaign had been making a real and tangible change to men's health. What had started as a desperate blag to keep her job after a drunken prank, a pathetic attempt to keep the attention of a rich and famous man, had snowballed somewhere along the line into a health marketing campaign that was actually working! Of course, Jules's scheme to get her married to Jamie Westlake and have his babies hadn't quite gone to plan, but . . . She bit her lip. 'Is Jamie here yet?'

'No. We're expecting him in seventeen minutes.'

'Seventeen minutes?' Nettie's eyes widened and not just because the number was so precise. 'But isn't that cutting it fine? We're on in just over twenty, aren't we?'

'Don't worry. His helicopter pilot's already radioed ahead so we know they're on schedule. Jamie's performed on the show before, so he knows the drill. He'll go straight to make-up and see you in the green room.'

Nettie swallowed. 'Oh. OK, then.' If Debbie wasn't worried, why should she be?

'So I hope everything you'll need is here,' Debbie said, her eyes skimming over the VIP welcome and making a final check that everything was as it should be. 'Daisy was adamant that we need to keep your identity a secret, and only myself and the presenters know your name, but if you can change into the suit first, before coming to the green room, OK? That way, no one will be able to put two and two together.'

'Sure.'

'And . . . well, I don't know what you usually wear under the costume, but a word of warning – it is very hot under the lights. That jumper, for example, would be a mistake.'

Nettie looked down at her chunky marled sweater. There was significantly more snow in the North West than there had been in London and she'd dressed for the weather for once. 'Oh right, thanks.'

'Is there anything else you need?'

'No, I think I'm fine, thanks. This is . . . amazing.'

'Any problems, I'll be in the green room. It's just straight down this hall, to the right. There's a sign on the door – you can't miss it.'

'Great, thanks.'

Debbie turned to leave, hesitating as she got to the door. 'Would you mind if I ask you something?'

Nettie looked up. 'Not at all.'

'I, uh . . . I don't usually do this. You can imagine, everybody who's anybody comes here sooner or later, but . . . well, would you mind signing your autograph? It's for my son. He's twelve and officially your biggest fan.'

Nettie stared back in astonishment. Someone wanted *her* autograph? 'O-of course,' she said, gathering herself and patting her coat pockets for a pen. 'I'd be delighted.'

Debbie gave a relieved smile, her hands folding over her heart. 'Oh, that's so kind of you. Strictly speaking, we shouldn't ask. It's not forbidden as such, but you could say it's an unspoken rule not to do it, but I don't think my son would speak to me ever again if I didn't ask you.'

Nettie smiled, dazed that this was happening. 'Um, is it OK to do it on this jotter here?'

'Great. His name's JoJo.'

'"*Dear JoJo . . .*"' Nettie murmured, her tongue poking between her teeth slightly as she concentrated. She stopped. 'Oh God, I nearly signed it, "*From Nettie*"!' she laughed, correcting herself in time and signing, '*Blue Bunny Girl*'.

Debbie took the autograph with a delighted smile. 'Thank you so much. I will officially be crowned Top Mum tonight.'

'Great title to have,' Nettie grinned, nodding as Debbie closed the door softly behind her.

Nettie stood alone in the dressing room, the pen still in her hand and taking in the glistening fruit and scented flowers, the stuffed sofa and chilled champagne. So this was a taste of it – life on the other side, how the stars lived, a glimpse into the luxuries and privileges that came with fame. Being treated as someone special, being pampered.

Of course, her experience within it was faceless. Three point eight million people now followed her Twitter feed every day, but no one knew her name or what she looked like. They didn't know where she'd gone to school or the regrettable men in her past. They certainly didn't know about her deepest shame, a missing mother who chose not to come back.

Copies of the day's newspapers were fanned out on the desk and she picked up the one on top, flicking the pages listlessly, depressed by all the paparazzi shots of people whose names she knew but didn't know why, climbing out of taxis or posing at drinks parties. Why did they chase fame, these people? What was it they hoped it would give them? She couldn't think of anything worse than losing her privacy, of living in the glare of a spotlight.

She stopped at a page – a double-page spread – that seemed to glitter with gold dust. It was a round-up of the Jingle Bell Ball, a montage of all the night's stars variously commanding the crowd with arms in the air and white-toothed smiles. She was there too, of course. It surprised her, though it shouldn't have – she, or rather the Blue Bunny, had been one of the stars of the night, but she'd never thought about it beyond revenge; the team hadn't thought about it beyond Web reach.

Somehow, seeing the image of her and Gus hugging on stage, part of that world, brought what she was doing into three dimensions. It was easy for her to hide herself in that suit; it was so huge it physically removed her from each situation, but as she looked at Jamie's face as the water hit him – her paws in the air in a 'what?' position, the crowd open-mouthed – she saw that for him, it wasn't some sur-real joke that had accidentally tapped a public nerve and grown into a monster. This was his career, his reputation, his life. And she'd made it the butt of her joke.

No wonder he hated her.

In the bottom corner, she saw a small photo taken at the after-party. Jamie was sitting on a sofa, Coco to his right, her legs draped over his lap again, both of them looking to the camera with slitted, suspicious eyes, as though they'd been caught in the act of doing something illicit.

Had they? She blanched at the sight of them together, feeling like her heart was being pinched. What was the truth about the two of them? Jamie hadn't, in their brief time together, mentioned Coco's name to her – he certainly hadn't acted as though he was with anyone else on Saturday night, but Coco had seemed jealous when she'd guessed he had slept with her.

Nettie looked away, remembering what they'd called her: *That little mouse . . . freak bunny girl . . . a groupie.* It was none of her business anyway, not her concern. Tossing the newspaper onto the sofa, taking a breath, she walked over to the costume, innocuous on the peg in its hanging bag. Who would have thought one big bunny could have caused so much trouble?

With a sigh, she brought it down and began to get undressed.

She walked into the green room several minutes later. Debbie was there, standing by a table and talking on her phone. She hung up when she heard the door close, her face brightening into an excited smile as she saw Nettie, or, rather, Blue Bunny Girl standing there.

'Oh, it really is you!' she exclaimed, rushing over.

'It's me,' Nettie said, throwing her arms out a little, feeling silly again.

'Would asking for a selfie be too much?'

'Not at all.'

Debbie clicked. 'If I tweet this now, saying you're on in two, we should see a sudden *surge* in the viewing figures.'

'Two minutes?' Nettie echoed, looking around the empty room. 'But where's Jamie?'

'Oh, he's in make-up. Don't worry – they've got a live link to me. I was speaking to them just then; he's coming down in a moment.'

'Wow. That's close,' Nettie said quietly, wondering

whether this tight schedule was in fact a way to avoid seeing her till the last moment.

'Oh, we've had worse than that before, believe me,' Debbie laughed. 'Honestly, why we all want to do live TV is beyond me. We're living on our nerves most of the time, but I guess we must like the rush.' She shook her head.

The door opened again and they turned as one to find Jamie standing in the doorway. It was as though a god had walked in: the actual composition of the air seemed to change and Nettie sensed Debbie shift.

Nettie offered a little prayer, yet again, in gratitude that she was wearing a giant bunny head that hid her face and allowed her to stare at him, unabashed and unregulated, immediately followed by her usual curse that she was wearing this damned giant bunny costume in front of one of the sexiest men in the world.

She watched in silence as he came over, wearing jeans and a khaki shirt that colour-matched his eyes, his attention resolutely not on her.

Nettie felt a stab of apprehension as she remembered the anger in his voice on the phone. What was he going to do? Sabotage her back on live TV?

'Hey, Debbie,' he said, greeting her with a kiss on both cheeks. 'Good to see you again.'

'A pleasure to see you, Mr Westlake. Is everything OK for you?'

'Absolutely,' he nodded, looking over at Nettie. He stepped forward, trying to peer past the black mesh that covered the bunny's eye sockets and which allowed her to see out but no one to see in. His face was just inches from the rabbit head and her eyes roamed him like a foreign land, taking in the slightly forward thrust of his jaw, the hard glint in his eyes.

'That you in there, Nettie?' he asked.

'Who else?' Her voice in reply was surprisingly flinty.

He straightened up, nodding slightly, no trace of a smile on his lips. 'Who else indeed.' His hands were in his jeans pockets.

Debbie looked between them both, hesitation on her features – had she been expecting hugs and kisses? 'I must say, everyone's so delighted you've agreed to the interview as well this time.'

'Yes, well, I'm intending to let Nettie do most of the talking.'

Debbie gave a nervous laugh, before her expression changed suddenly as she remembered something. 'Oh God! Where's my brain? We must get you rigged up to the mics.' She jogged over to the nearest table and picked up two small, black square packs with wires hanging from them. She handed one to Jamie, who instantly, expertly, slotted the clip of the pack into the back of the waistband of his jeans, stringing the wire up under his shirt and clipping the mic to the front.

Debbie handed the same to Nettie, realizing their conundrum in the very same moment. 'Oh!'

'Uh . . .' Nettie looked down at herself. There was nothing to clip the pack on to, on the outside of the costume.

'Have you got a waistband inside the suit that you can clip it on to?' she asked.

'Uh, well, just my . . .' Nettie lowered her voice, not wanting Jamie to overhear. 'You said it would be hot, so I . . . you know, took off my jeans,' she whispered. 'Will it be too heavy for my . . . pants?'

Debbie looked panicked. 'Oh golly. I'm not sure.'

'I haven't had to wear one of those things before.'

Jamie was watching with dark interest. 'What's wrong?'

'Nothing,' Debbie said brightly, before lowering her voice to Nettie. 'We'll just have to hope for the best and pray it doesn't slide south. How do you get this thing on?'

'Oh, there's a Velcro tape along the back,' Nettie said, turning round so that Debbie could undo it.

A sudden sound in Debbie's ear made her stop. She pressed her fingers up to the earpiece. 'What? Speak up – I can't hear you . . . Well, what's he doing over *there*?' She rolled her eyes. 'You've got to be kidding me. I can't deal with this now . . . No, I'm rigging the mics for the next—'

'Let me,' Jamie said, calmly stepping forward and taking the mic pack from her hand. 'I've put on enough of these things to do it in my sleep.'

Debbie hesitated. 'Well . . . if you're sure,' she said, looking at Nettie.

'Really, there's no time,' Jamie said. 'Go do what you need to do.'

'Thank you. I'll be straight back,' she replied, hurrying off.

The door hadn't even closed behind her when Jamie ripped the Velcro apart, making Nettie jump as her bare back was suddenly exposed.

She stood very still, mortified that this was happening. Why – *why* had she listened to Debbie? If she'd just kept her mouth shut, Nettie would still be wearing her jeans and jumper, happily bundled up, instead of standing here now in a bra and G-string under the bunny costume.

'Oh,' he said after a moment. 'There's not very much for this to . . . uh . . . clip on to.'

'Well, it's going to have to do,' she muttered, flinching as his cold fingers brushed against her warm skin and clipped the pack on to the waistband of her knickers.

She felt the waistband sag beneath the weight and she groaned. Thank God he couldn't see her face right now.

'Here, you need to pull the wire through to the front and up so that it comes out at the neck,' he said, pushing his hand round her waist to her tummy, the wire pinched between his fingers.

She held up one bulky paw. There was no way it would grip the tiny mic, even if she was able to stuff the large furred arm down the front of the suit – which she wasn't. 'How? How am I supposed to do that?' she asked, feeling increasingly desperate.

'Jesus, Nettie,' he muttered.

'It's not *my* fault!'

There was a brief silence and then . . .

'Well, just lean forward a bit.'

She obeyed, biting her lip as she felt him trying to trail the wire up her torso with his left hand, while reaching for it from the top with his right. He couldn't help but brush her skin as he leaned and reached over her. She couldn't help but jump at his touch. He kept pausing as though expecting her to scream for help, or at least slap him.

'It's fine. Just . . . just get on with it,' she muttered, hoping he couldn't see the goosebumps. She closed her eyes shut, '*Groupie, groupie, groupie* . . .' running on a ticker tape behind her eyelids.

His right hand found the mic and he visibly relaxed as he drew it out through the top and clipped it on to the collar of the suit. 'There.'

He stepped back and swallowed – 'Oh wait' – before

356

remembering to retape the Velcro at the back, protecting her modesty again.

'Thank you,' she said to the floor.

A man came to the door and peered in. He was wearing headphones. 'Ready?'

Jamie nodded, but his eyes were still on her.

'You're on. Follow me, please.'

They crossed the room, Jamie holding the door open for her, which – to her utter indignity – she could scarcely squeeze through; she heard him give a quiet snort behind her.

Ahead, the lights of the set blazed, the glass backdrop that overlooked the pedestrianized square outside like an inky mirror. She could see Alex and Matt on the sofa, already doing their intro, playing a series of shots of Jamie in concert, followed by clips showing the highlights of the campaign.

The man in the headphones laughed silently as he led them across the studio floor and gestured for them to sit on the sofas. The presenters greeted them with cheery hand-shakes, just as the clips finished on her throwing the water over Jamie just last night at the ball. 'I loved that one,' the man in the headphones whispered, doing a final double-check of their mics. 'Best one yet.'

Beside her Jamie stiffened, but he didn't say a word. He couldn't; the cameras were rolling again and Nettie heard their names being introduced to the audiences both in the studio and at home. ·

Jamie waved as the wolf whistles and cheers greeted them. Nettie worried she was going to fall off her seat – it wasn't easy sitting in the costume, and the framed bulbous torso rested on her lap uncomfortably.

She tossed one of her ears back as she looked around, amazed to see some #bluebunnygirl signs being held up in the audience. She waved shyly. She had assumed everyone was cheering for Jamie.

'Welcome, guys,' Matt said. 'We're so pleased to have you on the show. And we're actually going to get to talk to you tonight, as well as watch you perform, Jamie!' Matt laughed. 'Our researchers have been going into overdrive.'

Jamie laughed too. 'Well, this is an important issue. I thought I might have something worth saying, for once.'

The presenters smiled, charmed by his un-rockstar modesty.

'Absolutely. I know this is an issue very close to your heart –' Alex smiled kindly.

Nettie felt Jamie stiffen beside her.

'Because, of course, you lost your own brother to the disease several years ago now.'

There was a short silence as Jamie struggled to find his voice. Nettie was stunned. They had gone straight to the kill?

'. . . That's right.' Jamie hadn't shifted position. He was looking laid-back, a smile upon his face, but up close, as she was, she could see it stopped before it reached his eyes, could tell he felt ambushed, that this was precisely the reason he never gave interviews. She felt sick. It was because of her that he was even sitting here. She had, after all, effectively blackmailed him to turn up.

Nettie felt her blood run cold as the words settled. His brother had died from testicular cancer? It all made perfect sense – his interest in the campaign was suddenly explained. It was nothing to do with her at all – he hadn't followed her or donated because she was frightened or small or cute, but simply because she had accidentally put a spotlight on, as Mike would say, an unsexy disease. Had he been using her all this time? What was she to him? Just collateral? A decoy to boost his sales? A distraction for the record company so that he could release the song he wanted? A marketing tool to raise money against the disease that had killed his brother?

'I suppose that's why you agreed to become involved in the campaign?' Alex added.

He nodded. And then added after a moment, 'And because they offered me a pet bunny,' he grinned, changing the course of the conversation and suddenly throwing an arm around Nettie and pulling her towards him matily. She knew he was only able to do that because he wasn't actually touching *her*. 'She's mad, right?'

'That's for sure,' Alex smiled. 'Nettie, how does it feel in there?' Alex asked her. 'It must be awkward moving around in it?'

'It is really unwieldy, yeah,' Nettie replied. 'Now I know how pregnant women must feel – I keep getting stuck in doors, behind chairs; I can't see my feet – and these ones are pretty big!' she laughed, leaning back slightly to lift her paws.

'But it's amazing what you've achieved in it,' Alex continued. 'Did you ever think it would be such a phenomenon?'

'Oh God, no!' Nettie guffawed. 'It started out as an accident that was then posted . . . accidentally. But once we saw the impact it had had on people, we knew we had to try to keep the ball rolling. It's an important message we're trying to get out there.'

'It certainly is,' Matt said. 'And, Jamie, I gather you were an early fan of the campaign, even before you were asked to become involved?'

'That's right.'

'How did Blue Bunny first come to your attention?'

'Oh, uh . . .' Jamie thought back, sitting with his arms stretched out on the back of the sofa. 'Well, we were doing a gig in Rome and hanging around backstage, waiting to go on. Gus, our bass guitarist, is a bit of a snow-sports nut and he was checking out the Ice Crush event on YouTube when he saw the link and showed it to us.'

'And what . . . you thought, that looks completely insane. I'm up for joining in on that?' Alex laughed.

He grinned. 'No. I just thought she looked cute.'

'Who, Bunny or . . . the girl inside?' Alex teased.

'Oh no, no. I meant Bunny,' Jamie corrected quickly.

Matt looked across at her. 'Because, of course, that's the big thing about this, isn't it? Everyone wants to know who you are.'

Nettie nodded. 'They do seem to be *quite* curious.'

Everyone laughed, even Jamie, the consummate professional.

'Why *have* you kept your identity a secret?' Alex asked.

Nettie paused. 'Well, to be honest, I guess I was just embarrassed at first to be, you know, wearing this costume. It felt a bit ridiculous. But then, as the campaign took off and they started asking me to do madder and madder things, it sort of made me feel braver, somehow, being incognito. It's easier to throw off your inhibitions when you're not being you.'

'So you're not a daredevil in your own life, then?' Matt asked.

'No, not at all.' She shook her head, one ear falling over

her eye again. She pushed it back. 'I can't even . . .' She stalled as she realized what she was about to say. 'I can't even ice-skate and yet I ended up doing the Ice Crush course in this costume,' she said slowly.

They laughed again, Jamie very still beside her.

'And will we ever get to know who you really are? Because, I mean, your achievements, what you've accomplished for the charity, Tested, are really quite remarkable. You must want some sort of recognition, surely?'

'No. It's not about me. I'm just glad I haven't been dressed up like this for no good reason! That would be pretty depressing.'

'Well, what about you, Jamie? You know the girl inside the costume now. What can you tell us about her? Any teasers for our audience, because I can tell you, we've had a huge response since they heard you were both coming on the show.'

'Um, well, she's a brunette.' Jamie looked at her. 'I can say that, right?'

Nettie shrugged. 'It doesn't narrow it down too much,' she quipped.

He laughed, looking back to the hosts.

'Anything else?' Matt asked, as Jamie stayed quiet.

There was another pause. 'She's from North London. Has an ex-boyfriend who's still in love with her. Very private. Likes smoky-bacon crisps.' He shrugged.

'I've got it!' Matt cried, pointing at them with a laugh. 'I know exactly who you are!'

They all laughed again. There was so much obligatory laughing to do under these spotlights.

Nettie felt a trickle of sweat run down her spine.

'Of course, there was a big hoo-ha earlier today about

whether this wonderful partnership – which was only announced a few days ago – was in tatters already,' Alex said, leading in to the next discussion.

Nettie froze inside her suit, but Jamie just cocked his head to the side questioningly, his smile never slipping.

'Twitter's been in uproar all day, imploring you to give Nettie a' – she made speech marks in the air with her fingers – '"hashtag secondchance".'

'Has it?' he asked.

'Haven't you *seen* it?' Matt asked, leaning forward.

Jamie shook his head. 'I don't know what you're talking about.'

'Blue Bunny's made a video spoofing the Human League song "Don't You Want Me?"'

'Oh, is that about *me*?' Jamie asked, turning to face Nettie without actually looking at her. 'I vaguely heard about it.'

'Well, she's holding a framed picture of you in it,' Matt laughed.

'Sorry – we've been in the studio, getting the two tracks finalized for the vote on Friday,' Jamie shrugged. 'And we're in post-production for the video with Coco. It's been kind of mad recently.'

'Yes, of course, there's been a *lot* of coverage of you and the American singer Coco Miller recently.'

'That's right. We're doing a duet together.'

Alex smiled. 'And can I ask, are you . . . a duo outside of the studio too?'

'You can certainly ask,' Jamie quipped, before lulling into silence – a silence that stretched as the question everyone wanted an answer to (Nettie included) hung in the air. He shifted position on the sofa. 'Well, look, I won't deny it's been a *productive* collaboration,' he said finally. 'We're happy. We've been having a lot of fun together.'

'Fun?' Matt grinned.

'Yes.'

Both the presenters sat back with delighted expressions, Matt rubbing his hands together excitedly at the scoop. Nettie didn't move a muscle. Not one. She sat as frozen as a lump of ice on the sofa, profoundly grateful for the giant costume that was shielding her from the scrutiny of millions of viewers right now, hiding the tears that had begun snaking down her face as he sat beside her and broke her heart in front of the nation.

'Well, she's a beautiful girl,' Alex smiled.

'Yes, she is – inside and out,' Jamie agreed.

'And I guess it must help that she's already in the business too. She understands the lifestyle,' Matt prompted.

'Yes, that's a big thing. It's a pretty crazy lifestyle.'

'That's putting it lightly. There was that incident only this weekend, wasn't there, when you got caught in a store and some fans were injured on the escalators?'

Jamie nodded. 'Sadly, yes.'

'Can you tell us what happened exactly?'

Jamie inhaled deeply and Nettie could tell he was uncomfortable to be discussing this. 'I'm not really sure. It was just a freak thing. I'd popped in to get a few things and got separated from my security team. Some people recognized me and it got crazy pretty quickly.'

'But there's a point in the footage when you actually seem to be trying to push your way *back through* the crowds. That's the definition of madness isn't it? Who were you trying to get to?'

'Oh.' Jamie laughed awkwardly. 'One of my assistants

got separated from us, and it was the first time she'd ever encountered anything like that. It can be pretty scary.'

'I bet,' Alex empathized. 'Is she OK?'

Jamie's mouth set into a flat line. 'Yes. She's learned very fast. She's already playing the industry better than me.'

Still Nettie didn't move.

'Well, that's good to hear,' Alex said. 'How about you?' she asked, turning to Nettie again. 'I imagine it's been a baptism of fire, finding yourself spearheading the highest-profile charity campaign of the year?'

'You could say that.'

'Have you enjoyed it, though?'

'Absolutely. We're having a ball. I'm going to be sorry when the campaign's finished.'

'Which of course will be in just two days,' Alex said, pulling a sad face.

'I know, such a shame,' she said, shaking her head.

'Will you be sorry to hang up the suit? You're almost as famous as Jamie now.'

'No, I'm not,' Nettie laughed.

'Almost four million Twitter followers would beg to differ,' Matt smiled.

'But it's not about me. It's all an illusion. The crazy things they're seeing on the films have nothing to do with who I am. There'll be a new fad ten minutes from now, anyway. That's the nature of the beast.'

Matt nodded. 'Well, we'll certainly all miss your double act. Can you give us an indication of what we can expect for the final two days? Anticipation is high.'

Nettie shrugged. 'I'm not sure exactly. It'll be based around the song vote obviously. Have you heard?' she asked, looking over at Jamie.

He shrugged back. 'I just do what I'm told.'

'So you're not involved in the actual strategy of the campaign?' Alex asked her.

'Not hugely. They don't tend to tell me what I'm going to be doing until the last minute. I think they're worried I'll freak out and run away. Put it this way, if I'd known when I woke up last Tuesday morning that I was going to be dangling off the Shard . . .'

Everyone laughed.

'There's a rumour that maybe you're going to reveal your identity on the final day,' Matt said, leadingly.

She shrugged. 'I don't think so.'

Matt laughed. 'She's not giving anything away, ladies and gentlemen,' he said to camera. 'We're just going to have to wait and see.' He clasped his hands together. 'Well, thank you both *so* much for coming in and speaking to us tonight. Jamie, I know you're going to set up over there and sing for us in a few minutes. Tonight, you're singing the second of the two songs that people are voting for as your Christmas single – is that right?'

'Yes. This one's called "Night Ships".'

'And this is the first time you've performed it, I gather?'

'That's right. This is the Team Bunny single.'

'Well, we can't wait to hear it. It's a great honour having you here and we wish you all the best for the final days of the Ballz-Up campaign on behalf of Tested. Jamie Westlake and Blue Bunny Girl, everybody!'

A round of applause started up. Nettie made to stand, but Jamie discreetly put a hand on her leg to stop her. 'Not yet,' he said without moving his lips.

It was another minute before they could move, the

cameras cutting to a prepared scene from a new Oscar-tipped film and after shaking their hosts' hands heartily, they walked back into the shadows.

'Your brother—' she began.

But Jamie didn't reply. The cameras had stopped rolling; the pretending was over. He walked away from her, towards the empty stage that was waiting for him, signing a few autographs on his way. Doing his job. Nothing more.

Chapter Twenty-Three

'How are you getting back?' Debbie asked as they all travelled down in the lift together.

'Train,' Nettie said, shifting her weight and keeping her gaze down, away from Jamie.

'It's a great service, isn't it?' Debbie asked. 'So fast. Sometimes I pop down to London just to do a day's shopping.'

Nettie smiled and nodded.

The door opened and they walked across the lobby to the front desk. A tall, bushy Christmas tree was standing resplendent in the centre, twinkling and glittering in its gold-baubled glory and reminding Nettie, yet again, that there were only three days left to Christmas. She leaned against the desk, staring back at it but seeing, in her mind's eye, her own version in Primrose Hill – the wispy sapling on the kitchen table, scarcely dressed, with just one decoration for each year her mother had been missing. It hadn't felt right, somehow, to celebrate Christmas without her, but they hadn't been able to ignore it either – something in them struggled to keep life as normal as possible, and the tiny potted spruce had been their compromise: a diminished Christmas for their diminished lives. Her father hoped to plant the tree in the orchard one day, when – if –

her mother came back, as a testament to these years of waiting.

'Could you call Mr Westlake's car to the front and order a cab to the station, please, Amy?' Debbie said to the receptionist.

The receptionist frowned, trying not to gawp at Jamie, who had dipped his head, his collar of his jacket pulled high. Nettie realized he was trying not to be recognized, again his default position whenever he was in public. It seemed wearing. Exhausting.

She glanced around the atrium – he wasn't succeeding very well. Glances were already skating their way, people picking up somehow on his presence.

At least she didn't have that problem.

'Um, I'm afraid the station's closed, Mrs Laing.'

'What? Why?'

'There's been a landslip outside Nuneaton. There won't be any trains running before the morning.'

What? Nettie closed her eyes, exhausted and worn out.

'Ah.' Debbie inhaled deeply – weary after a long day too – before turning and looking at Nettie. 'I'm so sorry about this.'

'Hey, it's not your fault,' she said, mustering a smile.

'We will of course put you up in a hotel for the night.'

'Oh no, really, that's not necessary. I'll sort something out myself,' Nettie said hurriedly.

'No, no, you shouldn't have to go to that bother when we can sort it for you really very easily. We have accounts with several of the main hotels in the city.' She looked back at Amy again. 'Amy, could you arrange a room, please, for Miss Watson for the night?'

'She can come back with me.'

It wasn't the most gracious offer in the world. Jamie's voice was brusque, his shoulders giving an 'or not' shrug as they all turned to him. 'If she wants to get back to London tonight.'

She? The cat's mother? Nettie stared at him, feeling her anger rise again, like sap in a tree. Could he not show her any respect?

She felt something in her sag as she remembered precisely why not, what she was to him.

'No, it's fine, thanks,' she replied stiffly. 'I'll get the train in the morning.'

'But I've got a perfectly serviceable helicopter.'

'I'm in no ru—'

'Oh, for Christ's sake!' he snapped. 'Now you're just cutting your nose off to spite your face. Do you want to get home or not? Stop being so bloody stubborn.'

'Me being stubborn?' she gasped. 'Who's the person who ignored half a million people earlier today just to indulge his tantrum?'

'It was not a tantrum. You made an idiot out of me up there.'

'That's because you are!' The words were out before she could stop them.

She watched as he opened his mouth, ready to continue the fight, but he caught on something, seeming to become aware suddenly of Debbie's and Amy's aghast expressions. He closed it again, drawing himself up. 'Fine. Have it your way.'

Nettie bit her lip, willing herself not to cry. Her emotions felt scratch-ready; one touch and they'd fall out of her. She turned back to Amy, her cheeks flushed, her breathing fast as she tried to calm herself, placing her fingertips on the edge of the desk. 'Sorry,' she said to the women, in a voice so faint it was barely a whisper. 'We're very tired.'

Amy seemed not able to reply – perhaps she couldn't believe that Nettie, this unremarkable *nobody*, had called Jamie Westlake an idiot.

'Amy, get that room sorted for Miss Watson, please, pronto,' Debbie said, her voice a whip. 'It's been a long day.'

'Yes, Mrs Laing,' Amy nodded. A light flashed on her phone and she picked it up wordlessly. 'Thank you.' She replaced the phone again. 'Mr Westlake, your driver's here.'

'Thank you, Amy.' He nodded to Debbie. 'Debbie, see you soon, I trust.'

'Always a pleasure, Mr Westlake,' she smiled, shaking his hand.

His eyes flittered towards Nettie, not quite finding her, words written on his face but blocked in his throat. He turned and walked away through the glass doors, his boots heavy on the marble floor, his head dipped down as much from the avoidance of scrutiny as the low temperatures.

'Right,' Debbie smiled, seeming to breathe more easily now that the star had gone. 'Let's get this room sorted out for you.'

'Thank you,' Nettie murmured, grateful that it was over. Devastated that it was clearly over.

'Chalcot Square, please,' she said to the cabby, stepping in and rubbing her hands as she sat down. It had stopped snowing, down here at least, but the temperatures were bitter and her cheeks were slapped red from just a few minutes' queuing at the taxi rank.

The cabby turned off his light and pulled into the traffic, turning right onto Marylebone High Street and past the froth of customers spilling in and out of the shops. Nettie frowned as he drove past Lisson Grove, the turn-off for Primrose Hill.

'Hey, you should have turned down there,' she said, leaning forward on the bench seat.

The cabby slid the glass partition open. 'Roadworks, love. They're laying them fibre-optic-cable whatnots. It's a nightmare. I'm gonna take the Edgware Road and cut through St John's Wood.'

Nettie sighed and sat back again. She didn't suppose an extra couple of minutes were going to make much difference now, anyway. The morning was all but gone and she needed to change before going into the office.

She began texting Jules. *'Back! Finally!'*

Jules's reply was almost as fast as if she'd been in the cab with her. *'TGFT! Thought the polar bears had got you. You were amazeballs last nite.'*

'Thanks.'

'How was he with you?'

'Fine,' she typed, before then adding, *'Not chatty.'*

'No screaming-diva hissy fit?'

'No. V. professional.'

'Shame!'

Nettie sighed. She could well imagine the wink that accompanied the comment in person. *'Will be in office in an hour. Got to change first.'*

'Don't bother. Mike out for the afternoon trying to buy his wife's pressie. Get to Westfield for 5 p.m.'

Nettie frowned. *'Shepherd's Bush? What we doing there?'*

'Call me when you get to landline and I'll explain.'

'OK x.'

Nettie slipped her phone back in her pocket and looked out of the window. They were chugging along the Harrow Road, below the flyover, which was already congested as the great Christmas exodus to the Home Counties began. The driver turned into Warwick Avenue – Maida Vale territory – and she stared flatly out at the streets she had marched along with frantic haste only a few days ago.

Everything looked different since then. The snow that had started that afternoon had settled like a puffy duvet over the garden walls and ball-shaped bay trees, bringing the hard edges of the urban landscape out of focus. It was bigger, softer, quieter now. Snowmen had been built in some of the front gardens, and she could see crystal-thin slabs of ice had formed at the edges of the canal, the chimneys from the houseboats puffing like steam-engine funnels as their inhabitants tried to keep off the damp chill from the water. The pavements and middles of the roads were almost bare, the snow worn away by heavy traffic as workers trudged to their offices for the last full working day before the festive break, but footprints could clearly be seen in the lower-density areas – between parked cars and round tree trunks, going up to sheds and down side streets – and she knew she could have followed these footprints on the lesser-worn paths to the shadier, quieter fringes if she'd just thought a bit smarter and come back.

The cab came to a stop, the driver tutting loudly and pulling Nettie's attention away from the hidey-holes. There was a flashing amber light ahead, a man standing in a helmet and high-vis jacket holding a red 'stop' sign. Cars on the other side of the sign sluiced past, the sound of their wheels in the slush a wet hiss.

Nettie looked back out of the window. They were on a wide street, brick villas with white-rimmed windows flanking the road on both sides. Between two such houses directly opposite was a vaulted Edwardian glass roof, which straddled an open area that spanned maybe ten feet. She cocked her head to the side, intrigued.

'Do you know what that is?' she asked the driver.

He turned with his eyebrows already raised, ducking low in his seat to see what she was pointing at.

'Oh, that's Clifton Nurseries. Oldest garden centre in London, that is.' He glanced back at her. 'Got a nice cafe in it, but it's well expensive.'

Nettie looked back at it. 'But *where* is it? It's so narrow.'

'Opens up round the back. Gorgeous in the summer, I've got to admit.'

Nettie stared at it. She had walked down this street on Monday after her mother had turned up in Maida Vale, she was sure of it. She remembered the road sign – Clifton Villas – but not this. Had she walked past on the wrong side of the street, missing the narrow entrance to a supposed Elysium? Or had she run down it in haste, dismissing it as too big and grand and well lit for those trying to hide?

The driver took his foot off the brake, the engine beginning to growl again as the clutch bit.

'Actually, I think I'll get out here,' she said quickly, reaching for her purse in her bag.

'But I thought you said . . .' But he didn't bother finishing the complaint, merely sighing wearily and hauling the cab out of the line of traffic as he tutted.

'Thanks,' she said, handing over a ten-pound note for a six-pound fare. 'Keep the change,' she said, hoping to appease him.

'Right, ta, love,' he nodded, immediately appeased. 'And merry Christmas to you.'

She walked towards the narrow opening and stood beneath the glass porch. It was like standing in the nave of a glass cathedral, snow-capped box trees in every shape – balls, twists, pyramids – lining the walkway, their dense canopies twinkling with white pin-lights.

She walked slowly along it, resisting the urge to bury her fingers in the soft snow, her mouth parting in wonder as it opened out into a dense grove that spanned what must have once been three gardens. Leaves of every hue tickled the air; church candles flickered in glass lanterns; stone statues nestled between screens trained with winter ivy; Christmas trees shimmered with baubles; greenhouses glowed like orbs.

It was like stepping through the wardrobe into Narnia, an enchanted oasis hidden in the centre of the city – its living, breathing heart. She saw bent and twisted olive trees, freshly imported plum-coloured acers that shimmied their leaves like grass skirts in the arctic breeze, tight-budded roses and feathery lavenders. Even at this, the barest, boniest time of the year, when nature slept in the parks and gardens, this space brimmed with life and growth and beauty. How many people walked past without ever knowing it was here?

She stopped and picked up a twiggy door wreath. It was decorated with cinnamon sticks and pine cones, a more bohemian, craftsy alternative to the blue firs and crimson berries she saw everywhere else. It would suit their idiosyncratic house, and as Jules had said, theirs was the only house on the square that didn't have one. But she put it down again, unable to give herself up to the lure of a little retail therapy, a last festive splurge.

She walked past the greenhouse, her eyes tracing the naked wisteria branches that spanned the ceiling like veins. Ahead was a large conservatory, more of a palm house, really. Giant snowflakes were dusted onto the glass panes, twinkling box spirals positioned outside the door. It glowed with amber firelight even at this midpoint of the day, and she walked in, appreciating at once the radiant heat from a wood-burning stove in the corner, the hallowed alto of carols coming from a distant speaker. A whitewashed counter was laden with cloched cakes and pastries, the day's specials were written in sloping script on a blackboard behind, and mismatched tables and iron trellised garden chairs were scattered in clusters across a black-and-white tessellated floor.

Nettie rubbed her hands as she looked about, breathing into her cupped palms as she felt herself begin to warm. There were various couples and small groups at the tables, a low hum of chatter as steam from coffees twisted and cakes crumbled beneath the flash of forks.

She walked over to the counter and ordered a version of the same – coffee-and-walnut cake with a white Americano. The cabby had been right – she almost winced as she handed over another ten-pound note – but she walked to a table in the far corner, nearest the stove, and shrugged off her coat with relief.

She had to bring her father here, she thought, as she pressed the edge of the fork into the sponge. One of the young ash trees in the community orchard had been damaged in the storm winds they'd had a few weeks back, and although their budget probably wouldn't stretch to buying a replacement from here, the sheer variety of stocks made it worth coming over for an inspirational look-see, if nothing else.

She cupped a hand round her drink, staring into space and wondering if they were open on Boxing Day. The pain of enduring Christmas Day could usually be smudged by fretting over the turkey, and her and her father distracting themselves with presents or 'checking in' for the Queen's Speech, but Boxing Day was an enforced lull that was harder to escape.

She watched the girl working behind the counter as she carefully sliced a new cake; she stared at the tiled floor that seemed to move in her peripheral vision; she eavesdropped on the couple of girls at the next table who were deploring a new boss.

The door opened and her gaze swung slowly over as one of the gardeners walked in backwards, pulling a wheeled trolley with white-blossomed camellia stacked on its deck.

'Just on the shelf there, thanks,' she heard the girl behind the counter say, pointing to a bare timbered shelf on the left-hand wall.

Nettie sighed, knowing she had to move sooner or later. She couldn't sit here all day, tempting though it was. She reached down for her bag and pulled out her purse to leave a tip. She found a two-pound coin and set it on the saucer, reaching for her coat and shrugging it on again.

She stood, her fingers fumbling with the buttons, which had always been fractionally too large for the buttonholes.

'Thanks,' she said, raising her hand automatically as she walked across the floor. 'Lovely cake.'

The girl behind the counter nodded and smiled. 'Thank you. Come again.'

Nettie opened the door and walked out into the icy blasts again, shuddering as the chill breeze wrapped round her neck like a scarf. She would have to get another cab again now, and that could take a while in a residential area like this, particularly on the day before Christmas Eve.

'Oh!' She turned back, remembering to ask about their Christmas opening hours. The glass door had closed behind her already, but a sheet was neatly taped to it, listing the revised times to those already etched into the glass.

She read it, disappointed to see that they were closed for the entire Christmas week and not open again until 2 January. She bit her lip, knowing she'd have to think of something else to keep her father's spirits up.

She went to turn, but—

Her subconscious registered the anomaly, of something animate that had become too still. Frozen. The hairs on her neck were bristling and she had a sense of being watched, of eyes like weights upon her. Slowly she raised her gaze, but something in her already knew what she was going to see, her instincts racing ahead of time itself to get there first like a precocious child.

The world warped. Time became pliant as rubber, slowing and stretching within her breath as she registered the face on the other side of the glass. On the cusp of silence, she heard the alto of an angel and knew her prayer had been answered.

Chapter Twenty-Four

'Come on, come on, it can't be that bloody hard,' Daisy hissed as she struggled to get her legs in the suit, barely enough room in the changing cubicle for the long paws to fit.

'I'm doing my best,' she hissed back. 'What's happening out there?'

Daisy didn't reply for a moment.

'I can see the police. There's about eight of them.'

'Does it look dodgy?'

Another pause. 'Well, there's a few people looking.'

'They're probably worried there's a terrorism threat or something.'

'Yeah, maybe,' Daisy whispered. She turned back to the cubicle, sticking her head round the curtain. 'They're not stopping, though.'

'Do up the back,' she said, turning so that she was facing the mirror. 'God, this is so weird,' she grinned, patting the blue bunny's swollen tummy; she hadn't yet put on the head. 'My head looks like it's shrunk.'

Daisy laughed as she patted the Velcro strip closed. 'It so does.'

The sudden metallic whine of a microphone made them

both wince. 'Well, that'll make them stop and stare,' Daisy groaned.

She felt a sudden flash of adrenalin. 'But everyone's in place, yes?'

'Yep. Jamie's being hidden in Gucci.'

'Huh,' she muttered. 'And I get H&M. Typical . . . How about—' But she was interrupted by a guitar chord starting up on the concourse, the electric sound like a pulse, a single shockwave that made everyone stop and turn. 'Who's that?'

There was another chord – long and echoey, reaching to the furthest reaches of the mall; then he segued into the intro for "Crystal Dawn", one of Jamie's biggest hits.

'Gus,' Daisy murmured, placing herself flatter against the curtain as a couple of girls rushed past, curious to see what was happening.

'Can I look?'

'Nope, definitely not.'

She sighed in protest, wishing she could take a peek, but she had pulled the rabbit head on now and Daisy was right – they couldn't afford for anyone to see her before the pertinent moment.

The drums started up. They had been cleverly hidden under a sheet, and the guy selling calendars and annuals had been only too pleased to set up his screens around them.

'What's happening now?' she hissed.

Daisy stuck her head back round the curtain. 'Definitely a bit of a crowd forming.'

'Not too much, I hope?'

'Don't worry – the police seem to have set up some sort of cordon round the performance area.'

And then suddenly Jamie's caramel voice filled the halls – deep and languid, the signature trace of huskiness in his voice that made women everywhere weaken sounding even richer live, his guitar adding in with the others as the sound was steadily built up in layers to full ripeness.

The cheers and screams began as people realized what was happening.

'You'd better go. Get in position,' she hissed to Daisy.

'All right. See you out there. Remember, second song when it goes into the chorus—'

'Yes, yes. Now go.'

She stayed behind the curtain, too nervous to stick her head out and risk a glimpse of the excitement out there. She couldn't chance being seen.

Alone again, the day's events gripped her with icy fingers. Her emotions felt like walls she kept walking into – huge, immovable slabs of fear and panic. She shook her head, trying to chase them away, at least for the next few minutes. But it was the thought of what was coming after that was making her scared, the next steps . . .

She peeped out. Word had spread and the crowd was growing quickly, the audience singing in time with Jamie. She felt the hairs prickle on the back of her neck at the sound – the band was slick and well rehearsed, experienced and vastly overqualified to be playing in a shopping mall. They were world class.

The first song was over all too quickly and she took a deep breath, trying to remember everything they'd been going over this afternoon. It had been frantic, the atmosphere tense as they tried to cram everything in to the little time they had. It was all very well Caro saying they should go for film clips and not photos, but it took up so much more time, especially when Jamie was being so evasive – Dave had been fielding his calls all day, saying first he was in the studio, then at a boxing lesson, then having lunch with an old friend, and the upshot was that they hadn't rehearsed together, which may be fine for the seasoned performer, but it wasn't great for the little CSR team trying to wing it.

She stuck her head round the curtain again. This was it. Not a customer was in the shop – everyone was gathered on the concourse directly outside (it was why they had chosen to change in the cubicles of this store, of course) – and even the staff were standing in their own shop windows, their noses pressed to the glass. She crossed the floor quickly and stood behind a pillar by the door. Not a soul noticed her, not even the few reporters who'd been lucky enough to receive a phone call from Dave twenty minutes ago, giving them the exclusive.

Jamie was singing the first verse of 'Night Ships,' his lips close to the mic stand, his hands effortlessly strumming the guitar and his eyes closed. He was dressed down as usual in dark grey jeans and a navy jumper, a crescent of white T-shirt just visible at the neck, but it wouldn't have mattered what he wore; he still stood out from everyone else – his skin had a lustre to it that came from sleeping in good beds and taking frequent breaks in good climates; his body was fit and sculpted from working one on one with professional trainers. The equation was clear – living the best meant you got to look the best.

She heard the cue to get into position – the break in Jimmy's rhythm – and she stepped out from her hiding place and ran into the back of the crowd, ducking low and wriggling through the bodies, people too absorbed in Jamie to take any notice of her until she suddenly emerged out at the front and ran into the space that had been created for her by the police cordon, just in front of the band. She struck her first pose just as the guys launched into the chorus, and she began the routine she had been trying to choreograph and master herself all afternoon.

A cheer erupted as the crowd realized what was happening again. All around them, dotted among the strangers, was the rest of the team, even Mike, throwing their shapes in their set positions before slowly making their way towards her, the crowd automatically stepping back to allow them past.

They came together as an ensemble, dipping, spinning and bobbing in unison, the crowd beginning to clap along now, all the cameras coming out and filming them as people realized they were part of today's skit – a flashmob – and wanting to record it, to say, 'I was there.'

Amazingly, she remembered every step, even though it had been a *huge* oversight to rehearse without wearing the costume. Moving around in it was so much harder than it looked. It was so heavy for one thing – it must have weighed at least ten kilos – and it was hard to jump around and move nimbly when the ears kept falling in front of her eyes. But she did it.

And it was over too soon, far too soon. The song finished on a roar, Jamie's arm rotated high in the air as he swung out his guitar with the other, Gus and Jimmy beaming back at the crowd with self-satisfied grins. Everyone was calling for more, an encore, but their job here was done. The police had limited the publicity exercise to two songs only, citing safety concerns if the crowd grew – which it surely would as the minutes ticked past and the word spread. People would be dashing over here, even now, and the police were already struggling to keep people back.

'Thanks very much, everybody,' Jamie said into the microphone, eliciting more screams. 'Happy Christmas!'

He turned and headed to where Dave was standing at the back of the performance area. Security had cleared an exit route through to the fire escape and they had an unimpeded path out. She had already been briefed by Dave to follow after the band and leave with them; unlike the rest of the team, she couldn't afford to be 'seen' afterwards.

She ran after the guys, but the long paws of the suit made it awkward and she fell behind them slightly. She tried to pin her ears back, but they kept falling forwards again.

'Come on, fat bum!' Jimmy laughed, glancing behind and finding her trailing. 'They'll catch you otherwise.'

'I'm coming!' she called, panting as she turned into a fire escape, remembering to thank the security guard holding it open for her. They were in a narrow stairwell of concrete stairs, the treads less than a third of the length of her paws. 'Oh crap!' she yelled as she caught sight of them and started trying to climb them sideways.

'Helicopter's waiting!' Dave hollered from two levels above. 'Hurry up.'

She swore viciously, doing her best, but she'd like to see anyone else go faster, frankly. She established a strange step-hop pattern, almost crying with relief as she got to the top and saw the door onto the roof.

The men were all waiting for her. 'You ever been in one of these before?' Dave asked her.

She shook her head, her long ears hitting Gus in the face.

'You gotta run and get low, OK? God only knows how buoyant you must be in that thing. We don't want you taking off too.'

Everyone laughed except Jamie. He was staring out through the small, round window in the door, looking at the helicopter, his hands jammed in his pockets.

'Ready?'

She nodded and gave a thumbs-up sign, just as a door to their right burst open and a man in a beanie and turquoise down-padded North Face jacket ran into the small area.

'Miss Watson, have you any response to the allegations made about your mother?'

What? She whipped her head round, recoiling from the man as he thrust a digital recorder towards her face. What allegations?

'What the fuck?' Dave spat. 'Oi! Get out of here! You're not supposed to be up here! This is strictly off limits!'

But the man never took his stare off her, his eyes trying to see beyond the black mesh that kept her a secret. 'Just a comment, Miss Watson. Why do you think she left? Do you know where she is? Do you even know if she's alive? Has there been any contact at all?'

She was up against the wall, unable to breathe, to process, to comprehend what he was saying. How could this be happening? How could he possibly know?

No. No.

She had to get out of here. She had to warn—

The man flew backwards suddenly, his feet leaving the ground by a two-foot clearance as he slammed hard against the door he had just come through. Jamie was leaning over him, his arm drawn back, his hand in a fist, his mouth in a snarl so that the reporter cowered on the floor.

Dave grabbed Jamie roughly by the arm, forcibly dragging him away from the reporter. 'Get in the chopper, Jay!' he was shouting, trying to get Jamie to look at him, but Jamie wouldn't take his eyes off the intruder, his chest heaving as he readied for the fight. 'Get in the fucking chopper, Jay. *Now!*' Dave shouted again. 'I'll deal with this scumbag, all right?'

Jamie turned, as though hearing him for the first time. His arm dropped.

'Come on, mate, let's get out of here,' Gus said, patting him on the shoulder and forcing him to turn away.

Jamie looked at her, his attention on her now. 'Get in the helicopter, Nettie.'

She obeyed without question as he opened the door, daylight dazzling them all momentarily before she dipped low and began her lolloping run towards the helicopter landed on the roof.

The rotors were spinning so fast, but still not as fast as her heart. This was a nightmare, the worst possible thing that could have happened, the very thing – the only thing – that had necessitated the need for her anonymity.

Jamie got in the helicopter first, extending an arm and – with a helpful push on her enormous backside from the rest of the band – pulling her in awkwardly after him. She perched on the edge of the seat as Jimmy and Gus followed.

'I'm afraid that's the downside of fame,' Jimmy said sympathetically as he pulled on his safety belt. 'You know you've made it when you get doorstepped like that.'

'What was he even on about, anyway?' Gus asked, sitting opposite her.

She stared at him, too stunned to speak.

KAREN SWAN

She felt something on her knee and looked left. Jamie was leaning towards her. 'You OK?'

She blinked, but he couldn't see that.

They saw Dave run out from the building, ducking low beneath the rotors, something in his hands. 'Here you go,' he said. 'That's what this is all about apparently. *Evening Standard* have got the scoop, but they're all running it tomorrow.'

'What is it?' Gus asked, reading the newspaper that Dave passed in to them.

'Look, I'm gonna stay back here and sort things out.' Dave looked at Jamie. 'I think you've broken his jaw, Jay.'

Jamie tutted and looked away, his own jaw firmly set. She noticed he was rubbing his knuckles.

'Go back to the hotel and I'll catch up with you in a bit, all right?'

Jimmy gave him a fist bump and Dave stepped back, sliding the door shut, then ducking low and running out of the draught again, back towards the building.

The pilot was doing his final checks now.

'Jesus Christ, Nettie – your mum just upped and left?' Gus spluttered as he read the article. Her eyes stopped at the headline: 'Tragic Family Secret of Charity Star.'

All the guys looked at her in amazement and pity, Jamie rubbing his face in his hands.

Slowly she reached up and lifted off the bunny head. Her curly, dark hair swung free, settling at her jaw.

'*Jules?*' Gus cried.

'But where's Nettie?' Jamie demanded, sitting back like he'd been slammed there.

Jules looked back at him, looking every bit as stunned. 'I don't know.'

'What do you mean, you don't know?'

'She's not answering her calls. I spoke to her at lunch when she got off the train and since then . . . we've not been able to get hold of her all afternoon.' She bit her lip as shock and panic and worry combined. 'I don't know what to do, Jamie. It's not like her to go AWOL like this. I think she's missing.'

Chapter Twenty-Five

The pot-bellied stove glowed orange, the cracking of the coals in its belly like a siren call, keeping her eyes fixed on the flames. Potato soup bubbled on the hob, the golden scent of the bread rolls in the oven beginning to permeate the small cabin.

It was perfectly still beneath them today, the water dark and viscous beneath an ice-glazed veneer, and even the moorhens and ducks weren't venturing in, roosting instead in their twig- and feather-filled nests on the banks.

Dan came and sat beside her again on the small L-shaped bench. The brown floral covers were worn and bald in places, her hands motionless on Scout's wiry coat as he slept in a curl on her lap. 'Warmer yet?'

Her eyes slid over to him and she tried a smile, but the right muscles wouldn't work. Nothing would behave as it ought. Not her body, not her instincts. She was at odds with nature today, at odds with herself.

His hand covered hers lightly. 'Are you going to tell me what happened?'

She looked at him, willing him to read her mind, to understand what she'd done and not make her have to say the words out loud and give voice to her monstrosity. But he couldn't. Though he knew her better than almost anyone else, he would never be able to guess or predict or understand what she had done.

He squeezed her hand again. 'Nets?'

'I found her.'

The light that darted through his eyes was like a comet, the spark in his muscles making his hand flinch, an automatic impulse as his brain processed the apparent contradiction: good news – and yet she was here.

'I found her and I ran.'

She watched the shadow in his eyes now, chasing after the light and extinguishing it.

'Why?'

The question was seemingly simple, but there was no answer. Not that she knew of. 'I don't know.'

She remembered again the vision of her mother standing on the other side of the glass – haunted eyes in a thin face, hair that had been hacked with scissors, and the colour of squab, unisex clothes that came from a charity bin. Her mother – and yet not.

Not the mother she remembered laughing at the square's annual barbecue, tongs in hand and a frilly apron on, not the mother who had sat her on her knee and read her the entire collection of *Mallory Towers* with a different voice for every character, not the mother who made Christmas puddings for the church fair every Christmas, not the mother whose hair smelt of meadows.

She had expected change, deterioration even, but four years of missingness had corroded more than a daily routine and the woman who'd blinked back at her had been a stranger.

She squeezed her eyes shut, a gasp escaping as a realization hit her. 'What am I going to tell Dad?' She looked at him. 'How do I tell him that I turned my back and left her there?'

'He'll understand.'

But she shook her head. He wouldn't.

Dan was quiet for a bit. 'Have you told Gwen?'

'No.'

'Why not?'

She shrugged. 'I feel too . . . ashamed. I've spent all these months and years telling her how much I want my mum back and the second my wish is granted, I *reject* her.' A spasm of pain crossed her face at the brutality of the word.

'I bet she'd say this is quite normal.'

She shook her head again. 'It's normal for the missing person to take several attempts to return. It is not normal for their family to slam the door in their face.'

'That isn't what you did. You were just shocked, that's all; it gave you a fright. These things don't go like they do in the movies, you know.'

'Don't they?' she asked with a flat tone. She stared at the sprig pattern on the sofa, plucking absently at the loose fibres on one of the holes. 'No. She's gone for good now. I bet she's left the area already.'

'You don't know that.'

'I do. We've always been able to read each other. She was going to do it, you know? Come back. I could see it in her eyes.' She gave a bitter laugh. 'She was probably gearing up for some dramatic entrance on Christmas Day or some-thing.' She stared into the flames, lost in the memory. 'She held her arm up to me, like she wanted me to take her hand.' She shook her head again, blinking back to the present.

'I really think you should speak to your dad and Gwen.'

'I can't. He'll never—'

'You can, Nets. He'll understand. He's angry too.'

She looked at him in surprise. 'We're . . . we're not *angry*.'

'Nettie, how could you not be? Everything you've been through – all that worry and shock, the searches, walking every weekend, waiting every night, not knowing if she's alive or dead, safe, nearby, abroad. You haven't had any-thing concrete to hold on to. Sometimes I think it would have been easier on you to just know she was dead . . . You've put your life on hold while trying to keep it together. Anger is frankly your basic right. You'd be a psycho *not* to feel it.'

She shook her head, rebutting his words. 'No, it's my fault. I'm the one who keeps on making everything harder than it needs to be, refusing to accept the plain fact that she's gone. That part of my life is over, and yet – ' Her voice broke – 'I just can't let go of the dream of how things should be; the family I ought to have had.'

'And what would that have been?'

'A mum who'd never left, a dad who wasn't frightened to feel. A – ' She hesitated. 'A brother.'

His eyes met hers with a start. It was the only time either one of them had ever put a label on the bond that had been forged over years of casual Saturday drop-ins, evenings at the pub and poker nights on the barge. She knew now he had hoped for possibly more, but even without Jamie coming into her life, that moment between them in their teens had flickered and died on its own. It wasn't what they were to each other, and she sensed that deep down, he knew it too.

'I'm not going to lose you too, am I?' she asked quietly.

His jaw was jutting, his blue eyes burning with rare

intensity, but he dredged up a smile that made her muscles ease. 'As if,' he scoffed. 'We need each other whether we like it or not. You and me, we're like mathing pepper pots. I'm the guy with too many dads; you're the girl with no mum.'

Nettie couldn't help but smile at his bald, unsentimental logic.

A bubble of boiling liquid spat from the pan suddenly, leaving a grey smatter on the ceiling. 'Oh shit, the soup,' he remembered, getting up from the bench and running over to the kitchenette, jumping and cursing as droplets of the boiled soup landed on his wrists.

She watched as he shoved his hands into the oven gloves and slid out the tray of rolls, but she felt so far away from the warm little cabin on the iced water, she didn't particularly register the invasion of 'Drinking From the Bottle', Dan's ringtone, coming from the worktop.

Dan glanced at the phone, the pan in his hand as he poured the soup into bowls. He looked up at her. 'It's Jules.'

She snapped into focus. 'I'm not here.'

'But—'

'I can't speak to her right now. She's just going to freak at me for not going to work and I can't deal with that right now. Please, Dan.'

She looked at him with desperate eyes and he nodded. 'Sure.' He picked up the phone. 'Hey, Jules . . . No, I haven't seen her . . . What's up?'

Nettie looked away as he listened, though his gaze remained upon her. She looked into the gardens of the house on the opposite bank, her eyes on the black woven daybed – no cushions at this time of year – on the first-floor veranda. She tried to imagine who got to lounge on it, stepping through the grand French windows and out on the deck, maybe holding a morning cup of tea or an early evening drink, enjoying the peaceful rhythms of the canal and being a part of a life that didn't have a horror at its core. Downstairs, she could see lilies in the window, shadows flickering on the wall as the inhabitants moved about in the evening light, confident that their only onlookers were the pigeons in the bare trees.

She hadn't heard him hang up. She was surprised to find him still looking at her. Surprised by the expression on his face.

'Dan? What is it?'

He came and sat beside her again, the steaming soup and risen rolls forgotten on the counter. He looked at the floor, unsure how to say what had to be said. 'The press have found out who you are,' he said quietly.

'What?' she murmured, recoiling fractionally.

'They know you're the Blue Bunny Girl.'

He looked anxious, but she didn't notice. She had retreated into her mind again. How had they found out? She had been so careful – keeping a low profile any time she was in danger of being photographed, not travelling with the costume . . . It came to her almost immediately, the one slip-up, as though it had been hovering on the fringe of her consciousness, just waiting to step into the sun.

'Nettie, how does it feel in there?' She hadn't noticed at the time, too busy trying to settle her nerves and keep up with the game that Jamie was playing for the public, but Alex had said her name on live television. Live television! And once they had that, all any enterprising reporter would have to do was grease the palm of a security guard at any of the high-profile events she had appeared at and needed

to sign in for – someone like the nosy guy on the door at the O2, for instance; Jules had given their full names.

She sighed. 'I don't care. I've got bigger things to worry about. Tomorrow's the last day of the campaign anyway. It's hardly the end of the world.' She looked across at him, wondering why he was looking at her like that. 'What?'

'Nets . . .' Dan's voice was urgent; he looked like he was going to be sick. She realized he had visibly paled. 'That's not all. There's something else you have to know.'

She stared at him, instinctively knowing what was coming.

'They know about your mum.'

He picked up on the fourth ring. 'Hello?'

'Dad? It's me.' She couldn't control the tremor in her voice or the slide up to the next octave.

'Button, what's wrong? Where are you? Jules has rung twice looking for you.'

She covered her mouth with her hand, not sure she could go through with this.

Dan put a hand on her shoulder and squeezed it, giving her an encouraging look as she faltered.

'Nets? Are you there?' he asked into the silence.

'Y-yes. I'm sorry. I—'

'Darling, what's happened?'

'There's something I have to tell you and it's, uh . . . it's going to be hard for you to hear.'

There was a pause and she wondered whether he was sitting down. 'OK, then.'

'I've been involved in this thing for work for the past few weeks. It's stupid, really. You may have heard of it – the Blue Bunny Girl campaign.'

'Yes. There was an article on her in the *Telegraph* yesterday.'

'Was there?' she asked in surprise.

'Yes, she's raised nearly two million pounds for charity.'

Nettie swallowed. It was that much now?

'I'll keep it for you to read,' her father continued. 'It's quite extraordinary, it really is, but nobody knows who she is.'

Nettie took a deep breath. 'Well I do. She's . . . uh . . . me.'

There was a long silence. '*You?*'

'Mm-hmm,' she nodded, dreading the next bit, already knowing that the pride would be building, the elation . . .

'My girl is the Blue Bunny Girl?' he asked, his voice choked. 'You've raised all that money?'

'Yes, but, Dad, that's not why I'm phoning,' she said hurriedly. She had to contain this before his happiness set in. It would make the rest of it so much harder to bear. 'The thing is, it was meant to be a secret. I didn't want anyone finding out who I was – for obvious reasons.'

He got the point immediately, just as she had. 'But they have,' he said for her.

The sob burst out before she could stop it. 'I'm so sorry, Daddy! If I'd ever known for a minute it would become as big as it has, I never would have done it. It all just started by accident, but then, when it started to grow, I thought it would be OK as long as no one knew who I was. We've gone to such lengths to keep it a secret, but someone slipped up yesterday. They said my name on TV and now the papers are . . .' She squeezed her eyes shut, her hand clapped over them. 'They know about Mum.'

'Oh, Button.' Her father's voice was thin to the point of

translucence, like it had been planed away, peeling back in curls.

'I'm so sorry. I never should have done it. I never should have risked putting you in this position.'

There was another silence and she wondered if he was crying. 'No! I'm proud of you for what you've done, Nets. All those people you've helped.'

'But—'

'No buts. What you've done is important. It's bigger than us.'

'But the papers, Dad. You know what they're like.'

'Yes. I know what they're like. We'll be their latest sob story.' His voice was flat; he sounded so tired. 'And we'll just have to weather it. They'll move on to something else in a few days.'

They both fell quiet, already imagining the mawkish headlines.

She heard something in the background. It sounded like the doorbell. 'Just a sec—' he began.

'No! Don't answer it!' she cried, stopping him in his tracks. 'It'll probably be reporters, Dad. They'll want an interview or quote or something. They'll take your picture.'

'Oh.' Her father sounded taken aback. She could hear the sound of his footsteps on the wooden floor. 'Oh Lord,' he muttered after a moment. 'You're right. There's a crowd of them out there already.'

'Where are you?'

'In the bedroom. They haven't seen me.'

'Dad, it'll be fine. Just don't answer the door. And when we've hung up, take the phone off the hook, OK? I'll be right over.'

'No, I don't want you trying to get past them, love. They're . . . It's not right. You don't need this.'

'Dad, I'm not going to leave you alone in the house with a pack of journalists on the doorstep!'

'Sweetheart, I will be fine. I'll upend a bucket of cold water on anyone who tries standing on our doorstep.'

She laughed faintly. He would too.

'What about you?' Concern threaded his voice. 'Where can you stay tonight? I don't want you coming back here to this.'

Her eyes roamed the tiny houseboat. It was cosy but too small. The sofa she was sitting on opened out to make a double bed for Dan, but there was nowhere else for her to stay, except beside him, and there was no question of that. 'Don't worry about me. I'm a big girl. I'll sort something out.'

They were quiet for a moment. She felt suffused with guilt – not just to have put him in this position, effectively under house arrest until the media lost interest, but also with the events of this afternoon. She had shunned her own mother, the woman who was his wife, his life partner. He had been alone long enough already and now she had sealed his fate.

But she shook her head, letting the silence blanket this latest secret. Some things had to be said face to face; it would have to wait for another day.

'I'm really sorry, Dad.'

'I'm not,' he replied firmly. 'I couldn't be prouder of what you've achieved. This is just a storm in a teacup.'

'Ha! You think?' she sniffed.

'I know. Now go and ring Jules and drink some toffee vodka or something.'

She groaned. That was what had kicked off this whole sorry, mad, wild adventure in the first place. 'I'll ring you tomorrow, Dad.'

'Night, sweetheart. Don't let the paparazzi bite.'

Chapter Twenty-Six

She walked again. But it was different this time. Her eyes weren't casting into every crevice, following sounds or chasing shadows. She wasn't fidgety and alert, every fibre in her muscles ratcheted to full tension, ready to tear. Instead, her feet dragged, her head lolled, her face obscured by the deep hood of her coat. Occasionally she stopped and looked for a road sign, something to tell her where she was – not that it mattered anyway. It wasn't 'where' that mattered; it was 'who', and she didn't have the answers to that anymore. She didn't recognize the daughter who turned her back on her mother and left her father exposed to public scrutiny, who neglected her friends for the good of a corporate secret, who fell for a star but treated him like dirt.

She was adrift, caught between worlds, and as she walked through the quiet, frosted streets, it was with the intention of getting lost. She wanted to hide, not seek this time, be the little girl who got to curl up in a cupboard and hear everyone calling *her* name; she wanted to be sought, for once. She was so tired of being the one to count to ten and go to find. She just wanted it all to *stop*.

Her feet moved, though she gave no conscious commands. She didn't know what time it was, only that the

Royal Parks were locked, forcing her to walk the perimeters and stay in the light, moving from one amber street-lamp pool to the next when all she wanted was the shadows.

No car had passed her for fifteen minutes by the time she got back to the black gates of Primrose Hill. It was the witching hour, the very dead of night, although shadows fell long and thin along the pavements from the full moon.

She stood by the railings, one hand clasped round the cold steel and staring up at the Hill's small white summit. The yellow house was a four-minute walk away behind her; the journalists would be sure to have gone for the night – they couldn't stay out all night in the snow, surely – and she could slip in unnoticed, dive under her duvet and sleep for a year. Instead, she scaled the railings with the ease and experience of someone who'd been doing it all her life – she had been nine when she'd first jumped the gates and it was second nature now. She didn't want comfort, or oblivion; she didn't want to feel slaked. She just wanted, for once, to *feel*.

She broke into a sprint up the path, fists pumping, her body fierce and light – the soup at Dan's had gone untouched, the two of them too distracted to eat – surprised by how shaky her legs felt as she got to the benches at the top. She walked round the mount with her hands on her hips, like a marathon runner in recovery, London slumbering like a black dragon before her.

At her feet was the Blake quote, '*I have conversed with the spiritual sun. I saw him on Primrose Hill.*' She didn't need to read it; she knew it by heart. How many days had she spent on this spot, waiting for her own epiphany? A miracle that would never come.

She sank down onto her bench, the one with her mother's name on it, the one that her father had sold their car for, in order to afford – a public love token intended, if ever her mother saw it, to propel her home to them. But if her father had been standing in her place at the nursery today, would he have done the same and turned his back? Would he have recognized her as his wife? She had been so much changed. Nettie realized it wasn't just her mother she had been missing; it was the idea of her too – but she didn't correspond to that now. The person staring back at her through the glass had been no one's mother, no one's wife, no one's daughter. Her mother hadn't just removed herself from their lives; she had removed *from* herself what she was in their lives. Their connection had snapped, a thread that been pulled too taut and sprung back into itself.

Her phone in her pocket buzzed suddenly, making her jump.

'*And the view's so nice.*' She stared at it in alarm. What? Who? The number was unrecognized in her contacts list.

She knew the line well enough: it had been written on the path for years, till the rain had eventually washed it away. But why would someone send her that at this time of night? And why would they send it unless they knew she was here?

The hairs rose on the back of her neck. Someone was watching her.

She looked out into the shadows, her body tight and coiled, ready to run, her lungs full, ready to scream.

'Blur, in case you didn't know. Though I'm guessing you probably did.' His voice was gentle, wary of frightening her. She stared at him in disbelief, too many questions rushing forwards at once as he stood just off the summit on the path, his hands jammed in his pockets, his shoulders hunched around his ears in the plunging temperatures.

Convinced she wasn't going to scream bloody murder, he walked up to the bench. 'May I?'

She scooted over slightly, even though there was enough room for eight people on there. 'Why are you here, Jamie?'

'I was worried about you. We all were. Jules has been frantic.'

She swallowed and looked away, the humiliation sweeping over her like a million pinpricks. He already knew, then. It was official – her shame was public and tomorrow the rest of the city would wake to find her in the headlines again. 'Jules knows I'm fine. I got Dan to tell her.' Her voice was as stiff as if it had been whipped.

He smiled. 'It's not the same as seeing you, though.' He stared at her profile, noticing the dampness on her lashes, the jut of her lip. 'Nothing is.'

She glanced at him, immediately wishing she hadn't. She turned away again, back to London. 'How did you find me?' Her voice was small and sullen.

'Jules told me about your walks. Every Sunday, no matter what, she said.' His tone invited an answer to the implicit question, but she remained silent. 'I thought you might be on one today, so I've been driving around on my Vespa.' His gaze was fixed on her profile. 'I caught up with you at Baker Street.'

She looked at him again. Baker Street? But that was several miles away. He'd followed her all that time? 'You didn't think to offer me a lift?' she asked archly, no trace of a smile on her lips.

'You looked like you needed to walk. I just hung back.'

'Why? You'd found me. I was safe. Why not just go home?'

'I wanted to be sure you stayed safe.' His expression darkened. 'And thank God I did, frankly. I'm mad as hell with you – you must be crazy coming into a park on your own like this after dark.'

She gave a shallow sigh, the sound clipped and irritable. 'I don't care. I don't care what happens anymore,' she said dismissively. She was all out of manners, all out of cute. She was done. Spent. 'Nothing I do makes any difference anyway.'

He stared at her. 'You don't mean that. You've just raised a small fortune in under—'

'That wasn't me. It was a freak thing that took on a life of its own. I had very little say in any of it.'

There was a small silence. She watched a faraway plane flash in the jet sky.

'Well, you turned up, didn't you?'

She raised an eyebrow, the expression in her eyes bleak. 'Before you attribute any nobility to my actions – if that's even possible in that bloody costume – I thought I was going to get fired. You, on the other hand, did it all for your brother,' she added pointedly.

But he was undeterred. Seemingly tonight was all about her. 'So? You still put yourself on the line. You've risked injury, embarrassment, humiliation . . . the very real threat of falling in love with me.'

'Ha!' The laugh was a curt dismissal. She didn't have the appetite for jokes tonight.

'You are a cruel mistress, you know that?' He rested his arm on the back of the bench, propping his head in his hand, his eyes on her as he shook his head. 'Besides, I knew what I was getting myself into. The second I clapped eyes on you, I knew I'd risk pretty much anything to get you.'

'Well you must be regretting it now,' she muttered after a pause, her chin down, eyes on her feet as she scuffed them lightly in the snow.

'No.'

She gave him a sideways look. 'No? Not even after Watergate?'

He laughed at her pun. 'I figured you were pissed off about the photos of me and Coco – which was the point. The record label's been trying to encourage a thing with me and Coco for months. I played along for once.'

'And how. They couldn't believe their luck when you said what you said on *The One Show*,' she said bitterly.

'Because you were driving me nuts, Nettie!' he said passionately. 'Don't you get it? Nothing's ever happened with her. I just wanted to make you jealous. I wanted to see if you even gave a damn.' He gave a short laugh. 'Be careful what you wish for, right?'

'Oh.' Her heart missed a beat. 'Well actually, it wasn't the photos. Well, not *only*, the photos. I was pissed off that you called me a groupie.'

He pulled a face. He looked upset. 'You heard that?'

She looked away, giving a careless shrug even though her heart was pounding again.

'Look, I was trying to get Coco off the scent. She knew I was getting involved with someone and I didn't want her knowing it was you. Discretion isn't her strength.' He shifted position slightly, turning to face her. She remained silent. 'Anyway, how could I be sure you weren't one? After you ran out, I didn't know what to think. I was half expecting a selfie you'd taken in the bathroom to pop up on Instagram.' He saw her expression. 'What? You think it'd be the first time it's happened? You gave me nothing else to go on.'

She looked away but he reached over and hooked her chin with his finger, forcing her to look at him. 'Listen, I've been in this industry a long time now. I got my first record deal at seventeen. Every week a different country, a different hotel—'

'A different girl?' she asked tartly.

'Yeah. And it gets old.' His eyes fell to her mouth, making her breath quicken, but his hand dropped down and he pulled back slightly.

She saw him notice the brass plaque between them. She watched him read it. *'For Sian Watson, who loved to sit here. Much missed.'*

She looked away before he could pin a look on her again, wrapping her arms around herself as she shivered. She hadn't been warm enough today.

He looked at her for a moment, before standing up. 'Come on.'

'Where are we going?'

'I'm taking you home.'

She shook her head. 'I can't go home. The press are there.'

'Welcome to my world,' he said dryly. 'OK, then, you can come back with me. But I'm warning you now – I'm going to kick you out before you can run out. I'm not going through that again.'

She stared up at him, a smile twitching on her lips. How had he come into her life, this man? This extraordinary man who commanded armies of fans across the planet but wore the adulation lightly, who tracked her down in a city of millions and made her feel like the only person in it, her guardian angel in black denim, with eyes the colour of olives.

She took his hand. 'Well, I couldn't possibly risk that. You'd better take me home, then.'

He tucked her arm under his so that their bodies were close as they walked down the path. 'You know if you'd just told me, things could have been different?' His voice was low. 'All that misery this week—'

'Yeah, but then you'd have pitied me. No, thanks.' She arched an eyebrow. 'I much preferred being an enigmatic mutant bunny.'

He laughed. 'I don't pity you. It sucks, yes, big time; I can't imagine what you've been through. But if I had to choose between thinking you'd run out on me because you were just up for the glory shag or because you've got to find your missing mum, I'd take the missing mum every time, thanks.'

She laughed gently, joshing him in the ribs with her elbow. 'It's not *funny*.'

'No. But I am glad that it's a clear-cut case of "It's not you, it's me."'

She laughed again. 'Stop it.'

They walked in easy silence, their strides perfectly matched, their shadows long upon the bumpy snow. They reached the railings. 'Do you need a leg-up?' he asked.

'Do you?' she grinned, vaulting over easily and leaving him on the other side.

He looked impressed. 'You're good at that.'

'I'm good at lots of things.'

He landed like a cat beside her, his eyes drawing her up with him as he straightened, as though there was some static charge around him that brought her body into alignment with his. He took a step closer, his hand finding hers again. 'You know I told you I'm going away for Christmas? A friend of mine's got a place in the Bahamas.'

She chuckled softly, dropping her forehead against his chest. 'Oh God, you're talking about Necker, aren't you? I know you are.'

He shrugged, amused by her reaction.

'It's not normal,' she laughed, suddenly worn out, pounding his chest lightly with her fist.

He smiled. 'I want you to come with me. I'm flying out tomorrow night. Seven o'clock. Terminal five. What do you say? You, me, no complications. Let's get away and start over, do it properly, away from all this madness.'

She stopped laughing, the moment's levity gone in a flash. She looked up at him, feeling the usual tension ratchet tightly within her chest, holding her heart in a vice and threatening to crush it. Didn't he understand? How could she leave her father alone at Christmas? How could she leave him ever? She was all he had left in the world now. There was no starting over for her, no escape, no new horizons. This was her life.

His eyes dropped from hers as he saw her answer. 'Yeah, I thought not,' he murmured eventually, finding her hand again and kissing it, before pulling her into a slow walk, tucking her arm beneath his. She could feel the warmth of him as they walked through the chill, and she briefly allowed herself to rest her head against his shoulder. She felt so tired suddenly. Her eyes closed as he kissed the top of her head.

They walked past the bookshop and grocer's, the cafe

and toy shop, turning to walk past the library and then, moments later, the square opened out ahead of them.

They stopped at the very edge, their eyes scanning for reporters.

'Oh.' She wasn't sure what she'd been expecting – a bank of them, lined up by the slide, waiting for the moment she opened the front door? Rows of tents on the grass, like some sort of asylum camp for the press?

'Don't worry. They'll be back again by five,' he murmured, tugging her onwards. 'I know their routines as well as they know mine.'

They walked round to the yellow house on the back edge of the square, her right hand trailing lightly against the black railings. She was sorry there wasn't further to go. She liked walking with this man. It felt good not to walk alone.

They stopped on the pavement outside. The house was dark, the wooden shutters downstairs closed. Jamie turned to face her, his left hand finding her right one. 'So. You're back safe and sound.'

'Thank you,' she replied. She watched as his eyes tiptoed over her features like fairy footsteps.

'What shall we do about tomorrow? I'm happy to run the gauntlet and pick you up. I could be your decoy.' He winked.

She knew how much he hated the paparazzi's intrusive lenses and couldn't decide if she was tickled or horrified by the idea. 'I think that's called fanning the flames,' she smiled, before biting her lip. 'No, you'd better go ahead and do it without me.'

His expression changed. 'Why? It's the last day. You have to be there.'

'I need to stay with Dad.' She saw him go to argue and cut in first. 'He never asked for any of this, from Mum *or* me.'

Jamie was quiet. Even charity couldn't compete with that argument.

'Jules will do it. I bet she was great today, wasn't she?'

He nodded. 'Yeah, she nailed it.' He shook her hands lightly, his eyes on their clasped fingers before he looked back at her. 'I want it to be you.'

'I want it to be you, too.' Her words were a whisper. She knew they weren't just talking about the campaign now. 'But there's too much in the way.'

'No, there isn't. Not if you don't want there to be.'

'But it's not about what I want. If my life was about what *I* wanted, I wouldn't be living in a vacuum in my child-hood home, waiting for a ghost to walk back through the door.' Her voice cracked and she pulled her hand out from his, pressing the back of her hand to her top lip, trying to stop the swell of tears. 'And even if my life wasn't insane, yours is. You can't pretend you're just a normal guy, Jamie. You're not. You cross the world twice in a week. You prob-ably have stalkers! There's no way we could support both our dysfunctional lifestyles.'

'But you should know by now that all that fuss is noth-ing to do with me or who I am. It's hype. It isn't personal. It's projection. You've seen that for yourself.'

It was true: the bigger her stats had become, the less she had felt it had anything to do with her. She had glimpsed enough of the insider's view to know that fame was bigger than the personalities it cherry-picked.

She placed her hands on his chest, able to feel the rapid thump of his heart beneath her palm. 'In my world, people walk out the door and they don't come back again. Your job means you do that for a living. I just can't be with someone like you.'

She stared back at him, unaware of the tear sliding down her cheek as she watched him absorb the futility in her words, the flat argument that would brook no response.

'We can't just . . . buy you a new mum?'

It was a terrible joke, the shock of it making her laugh, but in the next moment he had bent to kiss her, his hands cupping her head, his lips warm on hers, and she closed her eyes, committing the memory to her DNA and imprinting it on her heart. Because this was the end, this kiss, they both knew it now – the full stop to a love affair that had never quite been. Its potential had been colossal – life-changing, world-beating, an electrical storm that charged the air around them and had made anything seem possible.

But what they wanted things to be and how they really were was a breach too wide to span, and she pulled away, turning onto the garden path in silence. And without looking back, she let herself in to the yellow house.

Chapter Twenty-Seven

Her eyes blinked open and stared at the subsidence crack on the ceiling. Christmas Eve. Historically her favourite day of the year. She had always preferred the sense of anticipation for Christmas than the actual day itself – even as an overexcited seven-year-old, running up and down the four flights of the house on her own, driving her mother mad as she pretended to look for the presents, she never wanted to actually find them; on the contrary, she lived in fear of stumbling across them as she pulled out the towels in the airing cupboard and threw the covers off her parents' bed. To find the presents, to know what they were, would be to put a pin in the bubble. It was just knowing that the presents were already there, in the house, wrapped even – that sense of readiness, of standing on the precipice of perfect happiness, that enthralled her so much.

Nettie thought of the pin she'd put in the bubble last night and closed her eyes again. It had been the closest she had felt to that level of excitement in years. Possibly ever. As she had grown up, the big house with the three of them in it hadn't grown smaller, quite the reverse. The older she'd become, the bigger the house had felt. She began to notice the four spare bedrooms – not their generous proportions or her parents' bohemian taste, but the fact that

411

they were never slept in, the water carafes by the bed gathering dust, magazines that had once been put out as a gracious touch now curling and stiff.

And this was how it would always be, this big house and only them in it. Three, reduced to two. Memories and history everywhere, with no sense of the future.

She lay in bed, her eyes on the ceiling, her ears on the gaggle of reporters outside and wondering if this was how *they'd* ever fantasized their Christmas Eves would turn out to be. Occasionally a flash would pop, weak in the morning light; judging by the round of 'thanks', she guessed someone had just done a coffee run.

She got up and walked to the window, peering out from the edge of the curtain.

Nearly twenty, she estimated, feeling oddly flattered that she had garnered so much attention, letting the curtain flutter back into place. She turned her back. Where had they been four years ago, these reporters, when she'd needed them? There hadn't been so much as a sniff of interest then, when she'd walked into the kitchen her mother had just upped and walked out of. How could the same woman's disappearance be of such urgent importance to the national readership now, four years on, just because she'd pulled on a fancy-dress costume?

She leaned against the wall, her eyes on the four walls that had been her kingdom for twenty-six years. It badly needed redecorating. Even if she wasn't going to leave here, leave her father, they still had to adapt. The room still wore traces of her childhood, like morning-after make-up – she could see the grime mark on the walls where the Wendy house had fitted in the corner and where the wardrobe now stood; there was still a sun-bleached ring on the carpet from the rag rug she'd bought in Camden Lock to hide the nail-polish stain, traces of Blu-tack were still visible on the walls from her Justin Timberlake posters. These vestiges of the girl she'd once been clung to the room, mocking the young woman who sat in it still. She thought of the dingy flat with so much potential in Princess Road. Two and a half thousand pounds and she'd have been building a new home instead. And if she had got on that plane with Jamie, she'd have been in an entirely new world.

A creak on the fifth step of the staircase told her her father was up. She grabbed her dressing gown – noticing as if for the first time that it was red velour with pink hearts and kittens on it, a birthday present from him last year – and made her way down to the kitchen. She was shocked by the pervading dimness. The sun had been bright through her thin curtains; but the solid shutters closed in the sitting room cut out almost all the daylight, only a sliver of shimmering white – as thin as the crack in her ceiling – running along the floorboards and up onto the opposite wall, dissecting the print of Picasso's *Child with a Dove*.

She went and stood by the yellow architrave that denoted the wide archway between the sitting room and kitchen. Her father was standing by the sink, the tap running, but his face turned to the sky. A plate of food covered with cling film was standing on the kitchen table, condensation misting and obscuring the contents inside. Last night's dinner. Had she rung at precisely the wrong moment? When would have been better? When was the right time to tell him what still had to be said?

He moved sharply, as though remembering the running

tap, and turned it off. He turned – jumping again to find her standing there.

She smiled. 'Sorry.'

His hand went to his heart. 'I didn't know you were in, love.' He frowned. 'How did you get past them?'

'I came in late. They'd gone.' She rolled her eyes. 'Lightweights.'

He smiled, physically rallying at the sight of her and doing what he always did – soldiering on. 'Breakfast?'

'Let me do it, Dad.'

'Nonsense. I've already started collating a Christmas Eve extravaganza. How does duck eggs, salami and chestnut mushrooms sound to you?'

'Uh . . .' she said dubiously. 'All right, I guess.'

'Good. Because it's all we've got.'

She watched as he fussed at the fridge, piling food high into his cradled arms, closing the door with his foot and staggering over to the worktop.

'So how was it here, last night?'

'Oh, fine, fine.' He shot her a guilty look. 'I took them all a cup of tea at about ten o'clock.'

'Oh, Dad, you didn't! What did you do that for?'

'They'd been out there for hours. It was perishing out there.'

'Good!' she cried. 'All the better for getting them to clear off.'

He tutted. 'I couldn't leave them without any refreshments. Besides, I thought it might reassure the neighbours to see that we're not . . . holed away in here, that we're not frightened by all this. There's a difference between not wanting to talk and having something to hide. Besides, it doesn't hurt to be friendly. You know what your mother always says – there's nothing so bad a good cup of tea can't remedy it. I must say they were terribly grateful.'

She sighed, running a hand through her hair. 'I still can't believe this is happening. If it's any reassurance, I doubt they'll bother staying here past tonight. Who's going to want to do a stake-out on Christmas Day of some random girl who's raised money in a fancy-dress costume?'

Her father opened his arms wide. 'Come here.'

'Why?'

'Just do as you're told.'

She walked into him, his chest and beard soft as he closed his arms around her. 'I am so proud of my little girl. Raising all that money.' He pulled back, a concerned frown on his face. 'I've seen some of the videos, you know.'

'I know, I know, you're worried about the Ice Crush one.'

'You could have been so badly hurt.'

'I know. But it was over before I even really knew about it.' *Not true.* 'Trust me, I didn't do it on purpose.'

He sighed. 'Honestly, those crazy ears . . . flying about,' he chuckled, going back to cracking the eggs. 'Your mum's going to be so proud when she hears.' He snuck a glance at her as he whisked the eggs with a fork, and they were silent for a few moments.

Nettie felt paralysed by his relentless optimism. Even in the face of all *this* – house arrest, national scrutiny – he still clung on to the hope that there was going to be a happy ending. How could she tell him what she'd done? How was she supposed to say the words?

'You know, I've been thinking – what if she sees it, all this hoo-ha, I mean? I know you feel it's private, no one else's business but ours, but what if we could turn this to our advantage, Button? What if it's actually a blessing in disguise?'

'Dad—'

'We could use it to reach out to her, give them an interview maybe? It could be our opportunity to show her how much we miss her, let her know that it's OK to just . . . come back.' His eyes shone.

'But—'

'She's so close, isn't she? She's already trying. This could be the final little push to help over the hump of it all. And it's Christmas! How can she not get home for—'

'Dad!'

He looked at her in surprise, his hand stopping whisking.

She swallowed. 'There's something I have to tell you.'

He came and sat at the table, as she asked. She thought he should be sitting down when he heard what she'd done.

'Yesterday, before all . . . this broke . . .' She gestured vaguely towards the windows. She raised her eyes to meet his. 'I saw Mum.'

'You . . . ?' His voice cracked like a walnut to a sledgehammer, his hand covering his mouth, and she felt the air dissipate in her lungs, the words fall like bricks into her stomach as his dark eyes shone like a teddy bear's beads. It was an age before he could speak. 'Where? What did she say?'

'I don't know . . . I ran away.' She watched him stare at her, the words bouncing off him like rubber bullets, unable to penetrate. 'I panicked,' she said, desperation colouring her voice, thinning it and stripping it down as she saw the disbelief rise in his eyes like a moon. 'She looked so different. Not like Mum.'

He was examining her face, looking for signs that this was a trick, a cruel joke, a nightmare. His breath was beginning to come in chunks, like solid coals, his cheeks growing florid and hot. He pushed himself away from the table, staggering to the sink again, his back to her.

'Dad?' she asked, her voice quavering as she watched. 'Say something.'

Slowly he turned. 'You ran from her? You ran from your mother?' Disbelief hung from his words.

'I'm sorry.'

'You're sorry? She's been alone for four years and the first thing you do is you *run* from her?' His hands were gripping his hair, a frantic look on his face.

'Dad, she's changed.' Panic ricocheted through her like a pin ball as she sensed the battle line being drawn between them.

He blinked, stultified by the comment. 'Of course she has! We all have! Do you think we're any less broken than her just because we have soft beds to sleep in and hot showers every day?' His voice was like a thunder, shifting her world off its axis.

'I didn't plan it,' Nettie cried, hot tears jumping from her lashes. 'I didn't know I was going to see her. It was a shock, all right? I just . . . I just wanted everything to be like it used to be.'

'But if everything was like it used to be, why would she come back? How it used to be is why she left!'

Nettie stared at him, her shoulders heaving as the truth of his words scalded her. 'But we were happy then!' she yelled suddenly, so suddenly her father stumbled backwards, his hands grasping for the counter. 'I was happy! I don't *know* why she left!'

They stared at each other, sheets of tears skinning down her cheeks, both of them shaking.

Her father dropped his gaze to the floor, the life force spinning out of him and leaving just a sagged jumble of muscles and bones. He aged twenty years before her eyes.

'Dad, sit down,' she urged, jumping up and bringing him back to the table, her arm around his. He put his hand out, leaning on the table as he lowered himself down carefully.

She reached for his hand, covering it with hers as he sat in silence, watching the war that was raging behind his eyes. 'Dad, I'm sorry – I didn't mean to shout at you. It's myself I'm angry at, not you. I hate myself for what I've done.'

'No.' He looked up at her, his voice flat and toneless. 'It's my fault. It's because of *me* that your mother left.'

Nettie felt her sinews tighten at the asserted fact, her hand automatically slipping away from his; she dried her tears with the back of her hand, feeling the tension beginning to set in her muscles. What did he know that she didn't? What was he going to tell her – that he'd had an affair?

'When you were not even a year old, we . . .' He blew out through his cheeks, as though this was an endurance test, not a conversation.

She waited.

'We had another baby. He died.'

Nettie blinked. 'What?' Her voice was a ghost of itself. Baby? Died? He?

'He was breech. The hospital advised Caesarean, but

your mother was still fragile from delivering you, love. It had been a long and gruelling labour, and she had found being taken into the operating theatre like that very frightening. I couldn't be in there with her – they wouldn't allow it, so . . . it was a bad experience.' He patted her hand. 'Although, it brought you to us and we were so grateful for that. So grateful.' He shook his head. 'But when we discovered she was pregnant again so soon, we vowed to take ownership of the situation second time round.' He nodded, his eyes lost in the swirls of the pine table. 'She just wanted a natural birth at home; she had prepared for it. We had a special birthing pool and that . . . that whale music. Smelly candles everywhere. She wanted it to be peaceful, that was all.' His eyes met hers, red-rimmed and watery. 'By the time the midwife realized things were going wrong, it was too late. They couldn't get her to the hospital in time and she delivered in the ambulance.' He shook his head. 'There was nothing they could do. The cord had been compressed.'

'Oh, Dad,' Nettie sobbed, her hand clamped over her mouth.

'Your mother – she never forgave herself. Over and over she kept reliving it – if we'd just gone to the hospital, just had the C-section . . . There was no reasoning with her. She wouldn't accept that it was a tragic accident. She had acted with the very best of intentions.'

Nettie stared at him. All these years and she'd never known, never suspected such a thing. They hadn't slipped up once. 'But you never said anything about it to me. Not a word.'

'No. Your mother was adamant. You were too young to understand and by the time you were big enough to be told, she said it would only upset you to know about your brother.' He stared into space. 'She threw herself into being the best mother she could be for you, but looking back . . . she never recovered; she couldn't even bear to hear his name. If it was in a book, she'd stop reading it; on TV and she'd leave the room.'

Nettie felt like she was carved from oak – dense, immovable and ancient. 'What was his name?'

'Benjamin. Benjamin George Thomas.'

She looked away. A brother. She would have had a brother. All those games of make-believe on her own upstairs, all those hours on the slide, waiting for the other kids to finish tea and come and play.

'But you never had another baby?'

Her father looked down again, giving a quick shake of his head. 'I wanted to, but it was too much for your mum. She wouldn't consider it. I don't know whether it was the thought of giving birth again or just loving another child, but she refused to discuss it. She gave everything she had to you instead.'

Nettie was quiet. She couldn't stop imagining how different her childhood would have been, how different she might have been. 'But this can't be why she left, surely? I'm not saying she got over it, but why would it drive her to leave us, over twenty years later?'

'When you came back from university and started looking at moving out, she told me she wanted to try for another baby.'

Nettie's jaw dropped. 'What?' She did the maths in her head. Her mother would have been forty-nine, four years ago.

'I said no. I thought that it was too late. We were too old to be going back to dirty nappies and sleepless nights. Plus, there would be greater health risks to both her and the baby to consider. After everything we'd already been through, I didn't want to risk it – for either one of us. I couldn't go through it again.'

'And that's when she went?'

He hesitated. 'It was several months later, but . . . effectively, yes. She became very depressed. She disappeared on the day Benjamin died.' He dropped his head in his hands, his hands covering his ears. 'If I'd had any inkling she was so desperate, of course I would have gone along with it . . . I hadn't realized how—'

The sob swallowed his words and she took his hand in hers again, trying to warm it up. 'You couldn't have known, Dad. She hid it so well, always losing herself in us.'

The words had been unthinking, automatic, but they hit Nettie with a jolt. That was exactly it – her mother had lost herself in her family, and with Nettie moving out and moving on, it must have seemed to her that that journey was coming to an end.

She fell silent, processing this new information. After four years of knowing nothing about what had happened and why, she now had a location and a reason. The blanks were being filled in, the puzzle forming a picture at last.

She rubbed her temples, trying to press back the emotions that were throbbing to be let out. Would knowing this yesterday have changed anything? Would she have seen the vulnerability her mother had hidden so well? She might have been protective and not defensive, compassionate, not critical.

Maybe Dan had been right about her being angry; she had spent so long trying to fix it – walking, searching, distributing posters – but she'd never had an opportunity to

understand it. And without understanding, how can there
be forgiveness?

'Where were you?' Her father's voice intruded on her
thoughts.

She looked back at him. 'What?'

'Yesterday? Where did you see her?'

'Dad, it's no good. She won't be there. It's the last place
she'll go to now.'

'You don't know that.'

'I do,' she said, fresh tears budding as her own cruelty
shone back at her in the cold light of day. 'I found her and
I . . .' Her bottom lip trembled. She could barely say the
words; she could scarcely believe she had done it, that this
had been her reaction. How often had she dreamed of
seeing her mother again, of feeling her arms around her
and the gaping hole in her world sealing up? Not once,
ever, had it crossed her mind that *this* would happen. 'I left
her,' she cried, pushing the heels of her hands to her eyes.
'Why would she hang around for me to do it again? She'll
know I've told you. She'll know you'll come looking.
She'll be long gone, Dad. She's more lost to us now than
she's ever been.'

What had she *done*?

She sobbed, her heart feeling small and hot and tight.
Her mother knew how to disappear. She would slip below
the radar again, surfacing in some other random pocket of
the city – or maybe not; maybe she'd travel farther afield to
York or Warwick, Bath or Plymouth. Quite literally, anywhere.

Her father sank into the chair again, his hand grabbing
hers now. 'We have to try,' he said firmly. 'It's Christmas
Eve and we have a location for her – someone might know

where she's staying. We can't give up now, not when we're so close.'

'Dad, I *turned my back* on her. Don't you get it?'

'No, Button, don't you? She is your mother. She loves you above all else; she'll understand. Of course she'll forgive you.' He smiled.

Nettie stared back at him. How could he have such faith after all this time?

He shook her hand lightly. 'Tell me where she was.'

She sighed, her breath shaky. 'It was at Clifton Nurseries, Maida Vale,' she sighed eventually. 'But it's easy to miss. You have to look for a—'

'You can show me yourself.'

'*I'm* not coming!' she said urgently, recoiling as her father stood and held out his hand. 'Dad! I'd do way more harm than good.'

'We are a family, Nettie. That didn't stop just because your mother changed address. Now, upstairs and get changed.'

'But—'

'Now.'

Nettie exhaled heavily, pulling her tears off her cheeks with the flats of her hands. 'I can't go past all those reporters,' she said quietly.

'I quite agree.'

She frowned. 'So then . . . ?'

Her father winked, jerking his head towards the back garden beyond the kitchen window.

'You're mad,' she gasped.

'I've begun to think so recently, yes.'

Nettie laughed. It was futile, this, but her father was right – they had to try.

Chapter Twenty-Eight

'She didn't turn up today.' The woman scowled, her gloved hands holding a potted gardenia. 'God knows she picked her day for it. Christmas Eve, I ask you? We've been run ragged all morning.'

Nettie looked around the nursery. Yesterday's snow had thawed to a lace, but it wasn't the white-webbed plants and pin-lit trees her eyes found. She was searching the crowds again – her expert gaze looking for familiar gait and pose, hands or clothes. She would recognize her again in an instant now, having committed to memory from that one agonizing moment the 1970s shag-cropped hair, wary eyes, hunger-hollowed cheeks.

'Well, do you have an address for her?' her father asked in a polite, gentle voice, his entire world resting on this stranger's kindness. 'It's very important that we speak to her.'

Nettie glanced at him, before looking back at the woman who had no idea of the gravity of her words – the fact that lives would be changed by her answer.

The woman looked at them both suspiciously for a moment, clearly wondering who they were – police? Social workers? Debt collectors? 'That's confidential. I can't give out that kind of information,' she replied disinterestedly. She turned to carry the potted plant to . . . *somewhere*.

Nettie put a hand on her arm to stop her, feeling a rush of anger at her diffidence. 'Please.' Her voice was firm, her eyes flinty. 'She's my mother. She's been missing for four years.'

The words had their intended effect – there was no way to dilute them – and the woman stalled like a car thrown into the wrong gear. 'How do I know that's true? You could be anyone.'

Nettie flipped open her purse and pulled out a photo of their little family, taken at a fairground when she'd been ten – her father, mother and herself all sitting on brown hessian mats at the bottom of a helter-skelter, mouths wide with laughter, eyes bright. She watched the woman scan it, her eyes flicking over them both. It had been taken a long time ago – but her father still had his beard; his hair wasn't entirely grey yet. And she wasn't so different, was she? But then again, maybe they had all changed more than they realized?

She handed over the laminate of the 'missing' poster she kept in the purse too – safely impervious to time, ready to be pulled out at a moment's notice on her weekly walks, to show anyone who might know, anyone who might be interested.

The woman considered, her jaw sliding to the right as she looked them over. Something must have come across in their eyes – desperation? Despair? Hope? – because eventually she nodded. 'You'd better follow me, then,' she said with a tiny nod of her head.

Nettie inhaled deeply, smiling at her father as the woman led them towards an office based in the back of one of the buildings, a clematis trailing up one of the walls outside, the bare arms of a summer bower overhead.

KAREN SWAN

They stood awkwardly at the door as she set the gardenia down on a desk – soil sprinkling onto the paperwork like cake crumbs – and opened a grey filing cabinet. The woman paused, staring at the ceiling as if for inspiration.

'Sian . . .' she muttered.

'Watson,' her father supplied.

'Jones,' the woman said at the same time. The woman immediately looked embarrassed at the conflict. She shrugged. 'That's the name she gave us.'

'O-of course . . . I suppose she would,' her father nodded, before taking to staring at his feet.

Nettie took a step closer to him and rested her cheek against his arm, hoping to comfort him. The realization that her mother had taken a new surname was like a hard slap that left their ears ringing. Was it a manifest rejection of her old life? Of them? Or just an alias to hide behind and keep her new life a secret? After all, the police had checked her bank account almost immediately after she disappeared and it hadn't been used since the day before she left. It would have been so easy to trace her if she'd kept her own name.

'Right,' the woman said, scribbling down an address on a piece of A4 paper. She held it out to Nettie's father. 'This is what she gave us. I can't verify if it's real or not.'

'Thank you,' her father replied, taking it with reverence, but he didn't look at it. He was looking at the woman, conveying something of the significance of her actions.

Hope was still alive, a flickering flame.

'I hope you find her,' she said more quietly as they turned to leave. 'She kept herself to herself for the main part, but . . . well, she seemed like a nice lady.'

They walked back through the narrow paths of the

426

nursery, the shadows of the trees passing over their skin like spectres, the sheet of paper a sacrament in their hands.

Not until they were standing on the pavement of Clifton Villas did they read its contents: *19a Shirland Road, W9.*

Nettie looked at him, aghast. 'The same street as the shelter. I would have walked straight past there on Tuesday.'

Her father nodded, smiling gently. 'No doubt – but you weren't looking for an address then – just a person who looked like your mum. You couldn't check every flat in the city.'

A taxi – its light on – turned into the road and her father shot out his hand, watching as it indicated and did a U-turn in the road to idle beside them.

'Where to?' the cabby asked.

'Number 19a Shirland Road,' her father said, opening the door for her to climb in.

'But that's just round the corner,' the driver protested, calculating the paltry three-pound fare.

'Exactly. We haven't got a moment to lose.'

Even with traffic, they were there in under two minutes, the cab pulling up outside a run of forbidding Victorian flats – four storeys high with dirty brickwork, a steep flight of steps up to the raised ground floor and another down to the basement flat, heavy painted lintels like bushy white eyebrows over the windows.

She looked up at the building above as her father over-paid the driver for his trouble. The sash windows were tall and narrow, hung with limp nets or St George's cross flags, the front doors an austere black.

Nettie ran up the steps to read the names on the entry buzzer.

She ran back down again, meeting her father at the halfway point.

'It's "B" to "F" up there. "A" must be the basement flat,' she said, slightly breathless. Was this really it? The moment the past four years had been building towards?

Her father took her hands on the steps, slowing her down, recognizing the haste in her actions. 'Are you ready?'

She swallowed. 'Yes.'

They stood like statues for a moment, poised between worlds – not up, not down, hovering somewhere in the middle. Then holding her hand in his, they walked down the steps to the pavement, turned and walked down to the basement. They stopped in front of another black door.

Her father raised his hand to the door – she noticed how blanched he was – and knocked. The sound echoed inside and out, slowing time. Nettie looked around them. A wheelie bin stood in the corner by the steps, the black bags inside bulging beneath the lid; a slick of brown ice covering the small patch of bald concrete, weeds growing in the cracks of the walls, newspapers pasted to the lower halves of the windows . . .

She turned back to the black door, her eyes scaling the building. But it had a roof, and walls. It was out of the wind, out of the rain, the snow, the ice. She flattened her palm to the cold bricks, grateful.

The door opened.

A slight woman with thin hair, blonde at the tips, dark brown at the roots, stared back at them. Her body was wiry but muscular, as though maybe she'd once been a gymnast, her skin sallow, with dark crescents hanging below her eyes.

'Yes?' She didn't smile, suspicion hovering around her like a scent.

'Is Sian here?'

The woman looked between the two of them, taking in their clean, pressed clothes, shampooed hair, soled shoes, nourished complexions. 'Who's asking?'

'Her husband and daughter.'

The simplicity of the words was unnerving and the woman's grip on the door tightened, her fingertips pressing to white.

'No one of that name lives here.'

Her father didn't argue. He reached into his coat pocket and pulled out the photograph of him and his wife on their wedding day – she was looking up to him, her hands folded across his chest as he said something that made her laugh. The look in her eyes was one of absolute adoration, the bond between them as visible as a golden thread. It had been love, true love. The truest kind.

'Then does this woman live here?' He wasn't going to be distracted with semantics.

The woman at the door stared at the photo, her lips thinning slightly, her nostrils flaring by a degree. She didn't meet their eyes as she span out the lie. 'Never seen her—' she said, just as a sudden crash emanated from inside the flat. 'Oh my God, Charlie! What you doing?' the woman cried, running back in.

Her hand flung the door to swing closed as she disappeared, but Nettie's father's foot was already just over the threshold and it bounced back again.

Without a word or a look to her, he walked in. Nettie followed, feeling her pulse quicken. She had never searched with her father before. In the early days of her mother's disappearance, it had been more important to cover distance and they had split up, each searching pre-agreed areas they had blocked out on maps. As time had passed and their expeditions transitioned from active searches to general looking, they had each taken comfort in the solitude of their lonely walks, lulled by the repetitiveness of putting one foot in front of the other and feeling they were *doing* something. But this wasn't a look or even a search; it was a hunt, and she was both proud and intimidated by her father – quietly determined, polite but dogged.

They found themselves in a single room. The carpet was matted flat and stained, but the room was a reasonable size. A white sheet, which had been tacked up at the window, was pulled back on itself like a sail; three single mattresses were set back against the two side walls, a cot in the corner; and a kitchenette area was set up at the rear, just off the room and partitioned by a break in the carpet to lino flooring.

The woman was in the kitchen, her back to them, and scooping up the fragments of a plastic plate that had been swept off the tray of the blue high chair before her, most probably by the impish-looking child sitting in it and staring back at them, his spoon raised like a sword.

Nettie looked around the room again. Where was her mother in this set-up? She wasn't here now, that was evident, but had she ever been? Had this woman been telling the truth? Was this just a random address her mother had given her employer at the nursery?

The walls were bare save for a Banksy poster of a little

girl releasing a heart balloon. There was a cardboard box at the end of one of the mattresses, filled with neatly folded clothes. Another box contained some toys – a brightly coloured octopus with squeezable legs, a wooden bus, a cloth ball, a plastic doll with one eyelid closed shut.

'Hey!' the woman cried, turning as she stood up and found them standing in the room, assessing her home with ruthless, expert eyes. They knew how to look. 'You can't bloody come in here! Get out!'

'We're just trying to find Sian. We know she's been living here. The nursery gave us this address.'

'*Who?* Listen, I don't know what you think you're playing at, but you can't go around barging into people's houses like this! Get the hell out or I'm calling the police.' Hostility shimmered around her like a heat haze, a jagged edge of plastic plate held in her hand.

But Nettie's father didn't move – not an inch forward or back. 'I know you recognized her. I saw it on your face when you looked at the photograph.' His voice was calm, quiet, unthreatening. Nettie kept very still, even though her heart was fluttering like a wild bird trapped in a cage, only her eyes moving and taking in the patch of damp on the ceiling, the cracked cornicing . . .

'You're delusional, you are. Get out!'

'We only want to see her, make sure that she's all right.'

'And I've already told you – I ain't never seen her before.'

'She's missing, you see.' Her father drew his own laminated copy of the 'missing' poster from his coat pocket, refusing to listen to her lies, to be drawn into her heat and shout back. 'Four years last month. And we miss her very much. We love her very much.'

The woman snorted suddenly, contempt in the gesture, her eyes landing on Nettie for just a moment before she looked away again.

Nettie tensed, understanding immediately. She knew absolutely that her mother had been here.

'Not my problem, mate,' the woman muttered, her eyes on their feet now.

Nettie turned away, her hand to her mouth as she kept the emotions dammed up. It was never going to end, this.

Her eyes found the small postcard straightaway. Though it was small and almost hidden by the way the sheet at the window had been pulled back, its deep blues and greens, that streak of bitter orange, were stark against the neutrality of the room, and besides, she would have known it anywhere. She walked over to it as though drawn by a pulley – her fingers lifting it easily from the damp wall, the Blu-tack no longer sticky.

'Or perhaps it is. Perhaps you're missing too. Maybe there are people looking for you . . .'

Her father's voice sounded far away to Nettie. White noise had filled her head like a wind, her chest as tight as a tin box as she walked back to him and wordlessly pressed it into his hands.

Silence rang out like a gunshot as he looked down at the image of *Child with a Dove* and saw the proof that her mother had been here, and she had run. There was no point in standing here, being here. She wouldn't be coming back.

It was a moment before anyone did anything. No one spoke or moved. The woman seemed to understand that some momentous shift had occurred in the small room.

Nettie felt like she was suffocating as hope was gradually extinguished after all. She couldn't bring herself to look at the woman again; she couldn't bear to see the approbation in her eyes. She just wanted to go.

But her father walked over to the woman; she shrank from him as he approached but automatically stepped in front of the high chair and shielded her son, her arms visibly trembling as she held up the edge of broken plate.

He held out the postcard towards her. 'She always loved this painting. We saw it together at the Tate before it left the country. It was one of the last things we did before she disappeared.'

The woman looked ashen, fear blackening her eyes.

'Take it,' her father said.

The woman didn't move.

He extended his arm closer still, the postcard just inches from her now. The woman flinched, before taking it from him, her body tensed as though she sensed a trick – perhaps fearing he would hit her as she reached out. Nettie wondered if that was why this woman was hiding too. Was there a man – a bad man – looking for her too?

Her father stepped back. 'If she comes back, please tell her we were here. And that we love her.'

He turned and, taking Nettie by the elbow, walked towards the black door.

'She won't be coming back!'

They faced her again. The woman was in the middle of the room now, shaking with anger, her eyes fixed on Nettie.

'She upped and left 'cos of what *you* did.'

What. You. Did. Each word was like a stab between the ribs and Nettie closed her eyes in pain; she knew it was true.

The woman threw her arms in the air, indicating to the squalid flat, her voice broken. 'We had a good thing going till you showed up there and ruined it all. Broke her heart you did.'

'I . . .' But Nettie couldn't finish the sentence; she couldn't even start it. How could she tell this woman she'd been frightened by the version of her mother she'd seen? That it had been her but *not* her?

'Yeah. She said it was only a matter of time before you found her here.' The woman's face had twisted into a sneer, her hatred of Nettie a visceral force, because she knew, she instinctively knew that Nettie's rejection of her mother in that moment had been a rejection of her – and people like her – too. 'Well, you'll never find her now. She said she couldn't just sit here and wait for you to knock on this door . . . She's gone, good and proper.'

Her cruel laugh twisted the knife and Nettie looked at her father. 'Let's just go, Dad.'

Her father looked at the woman again. He had diminished in size since they'd entered the room, as though his ribs had been compressed, a vertebra removed, his spine shortened. 'If she comes back, tell her we love her,' he said with a quiet stubbornness that refused to believe the finality of the woman's words. 'And that we're sorry.'

'Didn't you—'

'Both of us.'

The woman lapsed into silence at his tone, before nodding at him. And grabbing Nettie's hand, he walked them through the door and back out into the light.

Chapter Twenty-Nine

They were almost back at the square when they realized their error, the suddenly remembered prospect of the journalists round the corner a wake-up call to the reality facing *them* at home. They hadn't said a word on the walk back, eyes barely seeing what was around them, sitting in silence in the cafe, their lunch untouched before them as they faced this, the one thing that even a good cup of tea couldn't remedy.

They had sat on the bus in mute shock. Several times Nettie had looked sidelong at her father, terrified of what she might see in his face. He would have every reason, every right to blame her, but she saw only grief, numbness, emptiness – everything he'd managed to hide from her for the past four years. It was all there now, her own desolation reflected right back at her. She'd got what she'd wanted at last, the affirmation that he felt the same despair; that it wasn't just her, alone in this. But there was no companionship in grief; it didn't halve her pain to see his, and she'd never felt more desolate.

They stopped on the pavement, shielded by the corner house and feeling like refugees – frightened, exhausted, displaced. Their home had become a battlefield. Were they to walk the gauntlet past this army of reporters when they could barely support themselves from the day's brutal discovery?

The light had begun to fade, a banner of vivid purple streaking across the indigo-washed sky, and lamplit rooms were beginning to dot the facades of the houses.

'What do you want to do?' she asked.

Her father sighed, depleted of this morning's energy, robbed of this morning's hope. 'I'm fifty-eight. It's not a good look for a man of my age to be shinning garden fences – as my hamstrings discovered to their cost this morning.' He put a hand on her shoulder. 'You go through the back. I'll deal with this lot and open the back door for you. They owe me an easy ride after those cups of tea yesterday.'

Nettie shook her head, taking his hand. 'No, we'll go together. I've got to face them sooner or later. I'm not going to hide anymore.'

'You're sure?'

She nodded. 'It's not like we don't know what they're going to do. They'll ask us questions about Mum and we just have to say, "No comment." Who knows? Maybe once they see they're not getting an interview out of me, they'll push off.'

'Quite right, Button. Fortune favours the brave.'

They began walking again, turning the corner with inflated chests as they took a deep breath each – and immediately stopped walking again.

Nettie couldn't believe it, her eyes so wide the cold air made them water.

'What the devil . . . ?' her father murmured, his feet shuffling beside hers as they took in the sight, walking along the west side of the square. Their mouths were wide open as they walked in wonder, the hairs upright on the backs of their necks, as they tried to understand what they were seeing.

They walked along the pavement, staring at the yellow ribbons that had been tied to every railing on every side, all the way round, a tea light in a jam jar placed on the ground below each one so that the entire square flickered.

Nettie covered her mouth with her hand, eyes brimming with tears.

'Who did this?' her father asked, his voice a croak. 'Why?'

They rounded the corner to their side of the square and saw the quiet huddle of bodies swaddled in overcoats, gloved hands clasping steaming mugs as voices murmured quietly and feet were gently stamped to keep warm. But they didn't belong to the journalists and photographers who'd made camp overnight – in fact, the only evidence there'd ever been there was the bin in the playground overflowing with takeaway coffee cups. These were faces they knew – Mrs Wilkins next door, Fred from the basement flat two along, Sheila who always collected for Marie Curie Cancer Care and knocked every March with her basket of daffodils, the new family with twins at number 18 . . .

Mrs Wilkins stepped forward, either the designated or self-appointed leader of the exercise.

'Sandra?' her father asked as they stopped in front of the group. 'What is this?'

Nettie turned in a slow revolution as the crowd swelled, more people beginning to spill from their houses now that they had arrived.

'We've been waiting for you,' Sandra said.

'You did this?' her father asked them all, his voice split like a log.

'We wanted to show our support,' she replied, placing a hand on his arm. 'The way those animals hounded you from the house, we wanted to find a way to show you that we haven't forgotten what you've been through – and are *still* going through. You've both done so much for the community' – she included Nettie in the comment with a kind smile – 'we couldn't just sit by and do nothing, pretend that it's all OK. It's not OK.'

'I . . . I don't know what to say,' her father murmured.

'How did you make them leave?' Nettie asked.

'We didn't,' Mrs Wilkins said. 'They just upped and left, the lot of them, a few hours ago. Good riddance to bad rubbish, I say.'

'I'm so sorry. It was my fault,' Nettie said quietly, feeling ashamed that her actions had brought this into all their lives. She glanced at the seven-year-old twins. How frightened must they have been? Had they even been able to play in the playground while those strangers had been camped out there? Of course not. 'If I'd had any idea it was going to happen . . .'

'What have *you* got to apologize for, Nettie?' Mrs Wilkins said stoutly. 'All that money you've raised? We couldn't be prouder of you.'

Nettie rolled her lips, trying to keep the tears back. She didn't deserve their admiration. If they only knew what she'd done to her own mother . . . 'I can't believe you did all this,' she murmured, pointlessly trying to dab her eyes with the backs of her hands.

'Well, we can't take responsibility for the idea, but when we heard about it on the radio today, we knew we had to step up for you – just like you have for all these other people.'

Nettie blinked. Radio? 'Sorry, what do you mean? What's on the radio?'

'About the ribbons. Evie heard it, didn't you?' Sandra asked, motioning to the young Indo-Chinese woman who lived in the first-floor flat in number 13. She stepped forwards.

'That's right. Apparently, people who have a loved one missing are putting yellow ribbons outside their houses for Christmas all over the country,' Evie said quietly. 'Look.'

She pulled her phone out of her coat pocket and quickly bringing up Jamie's Twitter page, scrolled through the tweets that had supposedly mobilized this . . . movement. He may only follow eighteen people, but six million people followed him.

'She raised £2m for others in 2 weeks. Time to show some love back. Like and RT #teambunny. If u're missing someone too, tie a #yellowribbon. #lovenettie.'

There had been over four million retweets already.

'Jamie Westlake's been promoting it all day – Radio One, Capital. He's been everywhere. Because it's the last day of the campaign, right?' She put a hand to her chest. 'I've got to say, I've been absolutely loving it. I couldn't believe it when it came out that *you* were the bunny.'

'But . . .' Nettie's head was spinning. If he'd urged everyone to vote #teambunny . . . 'What happened with the song vote?'

'You won! Didn't you know?'

Her stomach flipped. Jamie had hijacked the vote to support *her?* Nettie shook her head, trying to imagine the emergency meetings being held in Dave's hotel room even now. The record label would be going nuts. Coco Miller would be . . . actually she didn't want to think about what Coco Miller would be doing in response to this. Mike would fire her now for sure.

'Did you see the video?' Evie asked, swiping the screen and bringing up a new page. Nettie double-blinked, trying to keep up as Evie handed over her phone again. Her father came and stood by her shoulder as Nettie pressed 'play' on the white arrow and the screen cut to a close-up of Jamie.

His khaki eyes held the camera in place – who could look away from them? Not her. Not ever, even though this was as close as she'd get now. She was back to being behind the glass, a fan, a stranger, her connection with him only extant for as long as she remained one of what Jules now called the Westlake Eighteen. But with the campaign now at an end, there was nothing else for the Blue Bunny to post. The account was closed, the campaign done. Christmas had been counted down, almost £2 million had been raised. It was over.

The camera panned away slowly to show him strumming his guitar, and as the scene enlarged, she saw he was standing on the fourth plinth in Trafalgar Square, the bunny head sitting beside him, empty. It seemed like a statement – that she wasn't there? That not just anyone could put on the suit?

The video cut to him standing on the top of the Shard, and then the O2 – in fact, all the places she'd been, even the postbox in Belgrave Square, him sitting on the top like it was the most natural thing in the world for him to be playing his guitar there. And amid all these scenes was actual footage of her – speeding down that bloody ice ramp, knock-kneed and unable to stand at the bottom as the rabbit head was pulled off, revealing her white, terror-stricken face; batmanning, planking, money-facing . . . all the daft and crazy things she'd done compiled into a sort of greatest-hits film. And then her pièce de résistance – Blake-ing him at the ball, the skit that had almost killed off the campaign, before cutting back to the present again and showing a small copper bath of iced water being upended over him too. But whereas she had almost fallen off the plinth in shock, screaming and jumping around, he kept perfectly still, not missing a word of the song as he raked his sopping-wet hair back with one hand, those eyes never leaving the camera, before picking up the chords and resuming playing the guitar.

Nettie handed back the phone, completely overwhelmed – when had he done all this? Surely they would have been flat out all day to get this filmed, edited and spliced in time, but if he'd been on the promotional trail too . . .

'Popular, is he?' her father asked.

'You could say that.' Evie grinned. 'The song's already top of the charts on iTunes and Spotify, and they reckon it'll be number one by Sunday,' Evie said proudly.

'But why did he do all this for us? Who is this man?' her father asked, baffled and confused as to how this stranger's song had led to yellow ribbons being tied in their square for his wife.

Evie looked at them both, an eyebrow arched. 'You saw the hashtag. Someone who loves Nettie, I should say.'

She stood by the window in the darkness, looking out at the square. The ribbons fluttered in the night breeze, the cluster of candles grouped by the railings opposite their front door throwing a flickering light onto the laminated 'missing person' poster of her mother above.

Downstairs, two flights below, voices and laughter vibrated up through the floorboards. Almost everyone had accepted the invitation to come into the house for Christmas drinks and her father was hastily digging out the mulled-wine sachets buried at the back of the larder, which had probably been there since her mother had left. Fred, from two along, was on a mercy run to the twenty-four-hour shop round the corner to buy nuts and crisps, and Sandra had dashed next door to bring over extra glasses and chairs.

She had texted Dan, Stevie and Paddy, telling them to swing by on their way back from the Engineer, but Jules wasn't picking up on her mobile and Nettie frowned as the call went to voicemail again. Where was she? What was she doing? Was she still with Jamie?

Her stomach fluttered at the mere thought of him. She placed a hand to the glass, staring down at the spot where they had stood in the twilight not twenty-four hours earlier. She wrapped her arms around herself, giving a shudder at the realization of how close she'd come to getting her happy ending – she had almost got her mother back, almost got the guy.

Almost, but not quite. She had jumped for the moon but fallen short.

And now it was too late. Everything he'd done for her today had been but a parting gift. A golden goodbye. The flashing lights of a plane in the night sky caught her eye and she watched it track the earth's curve until it disappeared behind thick clouds. He was in the sky too, right now, already hurtling away from her, like a comet travelling to another galaxy, another star. Their worlds had collided for two short weeks, just a quick bump that was now sending them spinning off in opposite directions, him back to a land of glittering awards ceremonies and models in couture dresses, gigs and after-show parties, glamorous shoots and long days and nights in recording studios. And her? She was back to this house, this small, quiet safe life with her father and the friends she'd known since school. Even the ridiculous bunny costume was assuming a strangely exotic nostalgia now that custard creams in the conference room were most likely out of reach too. Life was correcting itself and they were both back on their proper trajectories.

She dropped her forehead to the glass, appreciating its soothing chill. The day's events had left her feeling feverish – alternately hot and cold. She thought back to the woman at the flat and her accusing stare, the cruel fact that they had missed her mother by hours – or minutes, even? They would never know.

Her phone buzzed in her pocket and she pulled it out with customary haste. Gwen, no doubt, with her usual Christmas Eve message, reminding her of the importance of hope.

'Got something to tell me????? Ems x'

A moment later there was another text.

'Coming over now. With tequila. Prepare to talk.'

Nettie leaned against the glass with a sigh. Maybe she was prepared to talk now. For four years hope had felt like a thumb on a bruise, and while her mother had been absent and yet ever-present, she had been present and yet ever-absent – hiding behind opaque smiles, turning down the colour in her world to something more muted, something

443

more manageable, where the sounds weren't too loud, the feelings too much to bear.

She heard a taxi chunter slowly up Chalcot Road and turn into the square, coming to a stop outside the house. She put a palm to the glass, trying to clear the fog from the glass. Lord, that was quick!

But it wasn't Em she saw stepping out.

She ran from the room, desperate to get to the door before her guest was swallowed up in the crowd and they were forced into polite, public conversation, unable to talk freely about what had to be discussed.

'Hey,' Jules said, taken aback by the sight of Nettie, wild-eyed, flying towards her down the stairs as she closed the front door behind her. She looked through to the filled kitchen and sitting room – hesitant for once. 'I didn't realize you were having a party.'

Nettie looked into the rammed sitting room. There were so many people they were standing with their elbows pinched in to their waists, Nat King Cole singing about roasting chestnuts from the speakers above their heads. 'No, no, no, it's just a last-minute thing,' she panted, coming back to look at her friend. 'Where've you been?'

'Where've *you* been, more like?' Jules said, shrugging off her coat and throwing it over all the others on the stair bannister. 'Hiding out from the press all day doesn't mean you don't have to answer your phone, you know.'

'It wasn't like that. We got an address for Mum.' She shook her head quickly before Jules could get excited. 'No, don't – she'd already gone.'

'Because of yesterday?' Jules asked, and Nettie knew Dan must have told her.

'Yes.'

Jules put her hands on her shoulders. 'You are *not* to beat yourself up. You were shocked, that was all. Anyone else would've done the same.'

Nettie shrugged, but Jules walked in to her and gave her a hug. Nettie pressed her face into her friend's shoulder, but she didn't want to cry here, not now. If her father needed this party to represent anything, it was moving forwards. Onwards, if not upwards.

'Fancy a drink?' she asked, pulling away. 'Dad's been making mulled wine.'

'Oh, is that what the smell is? I thought you'd gone overboard on those cheap scented candles.'

Nettie smiled and went to head into the kitchen, but Jules caught her by the wrist. 'You heard what he did, then?'

Nettie blinked and it felt like an age before she could answer. 'I can't believe it.'

'Neither could anyone, *trust* me. Dave's practically gone bald overnight, and the record company's going nuts.' Jules shrugged. 'Jamie doesn't care. He told them you'd be getting an MBE for what you've done.'

'Oh my God!' Nettie laughed with shock. 'He didn't?'

'Seriously. He reckons you're going to be named in the New Year honours list.'

'Don't be ridiculous!'

Jules shrugged. 'Just telling you what he said.'

Nettie bit her lip. 'What else did he say?' She stared at the ground, suddenly unsure as to what she wanted Jules to say, what she could bear to hear – because was any answer going to make her feel better? Was she going to feel great knowing that he felt as miserable as she did? Was she going to feel relieved if she heard that he hadn't looked back? She scuffed the floor with her socked foot, her stomach in knots. 'You must be really tired. All that running around London, filming and stuff,' she mumbled, losing courage and changing the subject quickly.

'Yeah, Daisy's pulled in every favour she was ever owed, and Caro's almost given her jaw RSI getting the editing done in time. It was really tight, I'm telling you.'

'I can imagine.'

'And Mike's been fired.'

The way she said the words, so casually, it was a moment before Nettie registered their meaning. '*What?*'

'Don't be so surprised. He promised Dave that your song wouldn't win, and it did.'

'But that was Jamie's fault!' Nettie spluttered.

'You know that, I know that, they know that, but they can hardly get rid of their biggest star, can they? Someone's head's got to roll, so Mike got the chop. He was the "team leader", after all,' she quipped, making speechmarks in the air.

'So then . . .'

Jules grinned. 'Yep. I'm your new boss.'

Nettie squealed, throwing her arms around her friend's neck. 'Does that mean I can keep my job?'

'Nope.'

Nettie's arms fell down to her sides as she looked back at her friend in shock. 'But—'

'If you think I'm letting you commit yourself to the slow death of working in a job you hate, you can think again.' She winked. 'Besides, how can you go back to shaking buckets and eating custard creams after what you've just done? You're the Blue Bunny Girl, for Chrissakes. You raised two mill in a fortnight. You'll be able to walk into any job you want now. We couldn't afford you even if we wanted you.'

'But what will I do?'

'What do you *want* to do? The world's your oyster now. It's time to start making your life what you want it to be.' She yawned. 'Sorry, sorry, I'm so knackered. We started at six this morning—'

Nettie blinked in astonishment. Six? But Jamie had dropped her back here after three this morning. Had he not slept at all?

Jules caught Nettie's look of surprise. 'It was the only way to get it done in time – plus it meant Jay didn't have to deal with the crowds. That just would have made it ten times harder and slower than it already was.'

'It's amazing. I just . . . I can't believe you did all that.'

'*He* did all that.' Jules watched her closely. 'He did all that for you.'

The tears bit again as he crowded her thoughts, refusing to be ignored. 'Well, I guess he knows better than anybody what it's like to have the press camped out on your doorstep,' she replied lightly.

Jules arched an eyebrow. 'I *suppose* so, although I don't think that's why he did it, do you?'

Nettie didn't reply. She suddenly didn't want to pursue this line of conversation after all. It wasn't going to make her feel better to know he felt as bad as she did. It wouldn't change anything – she would still be stuck here and he would still be gone.

'So . . .' She inhaled sharply, knowing she couldn't avoid it. She had to know, if only to start drawing a line under it all. 'He's gone, then, yes? I mean, I imagine he's halfway over the Atlantic by now, isn't he?'

'No, actually, he's in the square.'

Nettie groaned. What else did she expect? She had been friends with Jules long enough to know that if you asked a stupid question . . . 'Come on, then,' she said, turning towards the kitchen again. 'We need to toast your promotion. Em's on her way and—'

'*Where* are you going?' Jules demanded, stopping her in her tracks.

'To get you a drink.'

'Did you hear what I just said?'

'Yes, you're my boss now.'

'*No*. Try again.'

Nettie blinked at her, her eyes shifting over Jules's shoulder towards the front door and back to her friend again. 'But . . .'

'That's right.'

She swallowed, feeling her heart begin to bash. 'You mean you're *not* joking?'

'Right again.'

'He's . . .'

'Out there. Yes, and probably frozen half to death by now. We got a cab over here together. I told him to stay out there. Let's face it, he'd start a riot if he just strolled in here.'

Nettie gasped.

'Go.'

'But—'

Jules reached for the nearest coat – not Nettie's: it was man-sized and the sleeves hung past her hands almost to her knees – and put it on her like a mother to her toddler. 'Go.' She opened the door, a blast of arctic night skittering down the hall as she pushed Nettie over the threshold.

Nettie pulled the coat tighter around her, her eyes struggling to adjust to the sudden darkness. She ran down the steps, realizing too late she was still in her socks. She crossed into the square, past the fluttering ribbons and the candles fighting the breeze, her eyes trying to adapt to the dimness after the noisy brightness of the house.

She looked around, but there was no one by the gate, no one on the bench. Was this really happening? Surely Jules wouldn't joke about such a thing?

And then her eyes found him. He was sitting on one of the swings, one arm on the chains as he watched her look for him.

He stood as she ran over on tiptoes, the ground making her feet burn with cold.

'You're still here,' she managed, breathless with surprise.

'Yes.'

'But you were supposed to leave, like, an hour and a half ago.'

'I know, but there's a problem.'

Her heart stalled. Oh God, what? 'There is?' she asked, stepping side to side on the frozen ground.

He looked down, seeing her socked feet. 'Come here,' he tutted.

'Why?' she asked suspiciously, walking closer but not wanting to get too close, not daring to risk it. She wanted to know what the problem was first. How badly was this going to hurt her? Just looking at him was painful.

'Stand on my feet.'

'*Huh?*'

'You'll freeze standing on the ground without shoes on.' He grinned at her as she looked up at him, baffled. 'Come on.'

She stood carefully on his feet, their bodies touching, his hands holding her by the elbows to keep her balanced on his boots. 'That's better.'

It was more than better. His face was only inches from hers, the one she'd thought she'd only ever see behind glass screens again.

A sudden whine of brakes made them both start and he looked over her shoulder to see a taxi draw up outside the house. Em? But to her surprise, she saw Daisy and Caro pile out, Daisy tugging down the hem of her body-con dress whilst Caro paid the tab, a magnum of champagne balanced between her legs as she rooted in her bag for change. Jules must have told them to come over to celebrate the end of the campaign (and quite possibly Mike's sacking too), Nettie realized, feeling a twinge of regret that she had missed out on today's glory after all her hard work.

But when she looked back at Jamie, she saw their previous moment's levity had gone, and she forgot her colleagues in a flash again. Everything paled beside him.

'When I left here last night, I didn't think I'd see you again. I know you can't leave your dad alone. I know why my lifestyle couldn't be a worse fit with yours.'

He fell silent and this time it was her turn to frown.

'But . . . ?' she prompted.

He dropped his voice and a look she'd never seen before came into his eyes. 'But none of that takes into account the fact that if I go anywhere from here, from you, then you'd be *my* missing person.'

The world spun a little faster. 'I don't want to be anywhere you aren't,' he said quietly. 'It's as simple and straightforward as that.'

'But . . .' She didn't know what to say.

'I know, I know. Nothing's changed. Your mum's still missing.' He nodded, squeezing her arms. 'But *you're* found, Nets. I found you and I don't want to lose you. I won't.' His fingertips brushed the coarse wool of the huge overcoat and he frowned. 'Even though you appear to be shrinking.'

She laughed, resting her forehead against his chest. 'Oh, Jamie,' she said quietly. 'Of all the girls you could be with . . . I am *not* the easy option.'

'I'd be disappointed if you were.'

She stared back at him. 'Are you sure? I mean, you could have anyone.'

He frowned as though her words made no sense. 'But why would I want *anyone*? I want you – you in all your crazy, mad, ridiculous, and yes, sad glory. The whole package. What does it say about my life that a girl in a bunny suit could feel more real to me than any other person I know? And anyway, it's not like I've got it all figured out, you know.' A smile crept into his eyes, enlivening them, and tugging a smile at the corners of his mouth. 'I don't have anywhere to spend Christmas, for a start.'

She grinned, surprised. 'Well, if you'd like to spend Christmas in Primrose Hill, I'm pretty sure we'll have enough turkey to go round. Dad usually completely over-orders and gets an eight-kilo bird for the two of us. He's still not up to speed with the metric system.'

Jamie chuckled lightly. 'Great. It's about time your father and I met.'

'You make it sound like I've been keeping you apart. We've only known each other for two weeks,' she laughed.

'Exactly. Enough dithering.' His hands squeezed her arms and she shifted position on his feet.

'Is he scary?'

'Very.'

'Scarier than Dan?'

She grinned. 'Much.'

He missed a beat. 'Who's his team?'

She laughed, remembering how easily Dan had been 'won over'. 'It's going to be tougher than that, I'm afraid. Where do you stand on electronic shifting?'

'Come again?'

She shook her head, feeling light-headed with happiness. 'Don't worry, he'll love you.'

He didn't say anything but the implicit question – did she? – hung between them, and she felt herself blush in the moonlight.

'Although if you're going to gatecrash our Christmas, you should know that he'll insist that you wear the paper hat from your cracker,' she said quickly.

He blinked. 'Really?'

'Mm-hmm. Think you can handle it?'

He cocked an eyebrow. 'Well, do I get a say in the colour?'

'None whatsoever.'

'And this is a deal-breaker, is it?'

'It is.' She nodded firmly, doing her best to suppress her smile.

He bent down and kissed the tip of her nose. 'Then consider it done.'

Chapter Thirty

She knew it had been snowing again from the light in the room. Everything was diffuse and soft as though seen through a white rainbow, a thick, pillowy silence blanketing the usual sounds of London life. But she wasn't remotely interested in what was outside; she may have wanted a white Christmas when she was a child, but all she wanted now was him. She shifted position to get a better look at him, to check he was still here and real, even though his arm was as heavy around her as a log.

He looked back at her with one eye. 'Stop grinning,' he grinned, his voice deeper with sleep.

'I'm not grinning,' she grinned, resting her head on her hand and gazing down at him. He was the most beautiful man she'd ever seen. She kissed his eyelids, his lashes, the tip of his nose, his temples.

'I'm glad you got the rider,' he murmured. 'That is exactly how I like to be woken up.'

'Hey!' She nudged him in the ribs and he curled up with a sleepy grin, somehow sliding her arm out from under her and flipping her round, scooping her into a ball with him. She nestled deeper, marvelling at how perfectly they fit one another, as though they'd been moulded as two halves of a single whole. She smiled sleepily, reliving in her head all the wonderful details of the previous evening. 'Oh,' she gasped, remembering something particularly juicy. 'Did you see Daisy dirty-dancing with Jimmy last night?' The party had had a second act later in the evening, when the neighbours had politely – and reluctantly – made their excuses at ten, leaving Jules and Em, Daisy and Caro, and the boys from the pub. Jules had made a booty-call to Gus and when he'd turned up with Jimmy in tow, they had jammed on their acoustic guitars, revelling in the yellow house until the small hours.

'Nope.' He kissed her neck.

'I wouldn't have thought he was her type at all.' She twisted slightly. 'And I thought Caro and Stevie were getting on well too.' She smiled with euphemistic stress on 'well'.

'Not as well as Dan and Em,' he murmured into her hair.

Nettie gasped. 'What?'

'They were all over each other in the kitchen.'

'Dan and Em were?' she echoed.

'Yes.' He pulled back to look at her. 'Why? Is that a problem?'

'No,' she scoffed, smacking his arm lightly. 'I just . . . I just never thought about it before, that's all.' She fell quiet for a moment, imagining them together – both so tall and lean, she had to admit they would look striking as a couple. And Dan's easy-going attitude was the perfect antidote to Em's ambition. If she could get him to focus on what he really wanted to do with his career, rather than just drifting through, and trying to wind up his mother . . . 'You know, now that you mention it, I can totally see it.'

'Really? All I can see is you,' he said, making her smile,

and she reached her arm up behind her, raking his hair with her hand.

She closed her eyes as his hand stroked her thigh. 'And to think I could have been slumming it in Necker,' he said into her hair. 'Thank God for the gentlemen reporters of the press.'

'What do you mean?' she asked, trying to twist to face him, but he pinned her wrist down on the mattress, holding her there.

'Well, if they hadn't uncovered your identity, I never would have known why you really ran out on me.'

She considered this for a moment. 'I guess when you put it like that,' she sighed, stretching her neck to allow him closer in still, his hands beginning to wander. 'Hey, I don't suppose you happen to know why they all miraculously disappeared from the front of the house yesterday, do you?'

'Might do,' he mumbled, and she sensed she was losing him to his right hand.

'Tell me,' she said, wriggling her hips free so that he was forced to pay attention. He rested his chin on her right shoulder as she looked back at him.

His eyes worked their magic again, making her go limp in his arms. 'I held a press conference, promising to answer every question they asked me on the condition that they left you alone.'

'You did what?' she gasped, trying to turn to face him, but he still had her pinned down. 'But you never give interviews.' She tried twisting, but he was too strong.

'I know, but it's all a game. I do something for them; they do something for me.' His voice tickled her ear. 'I know how it works, but . . . you're new to this. I thought you had enough to deal with.'

She turned and this time he didn't try to stop her. She faced in to him, her ankle hooking his, one hand on his cheek as they stared at each other on the pillow.

'Happy Christmas,' she whispered.

'Happy Christmas,' he whispered back, kissing her on the mouth.

'I didn't get you a present,' she murmured, grazing her fingernails down his chest. What was she supposed to get him? The man who literally had everything.

He tipped her chin up with his hand, his leg pushing between hers. 'Oh yes, you did.'

They tiptoed downstairs two hours later, their silence to no avail. Her father was already up and dressed, a cold pot of tea on the coffee table as he grappled on all fours with a vast, bushy green Christmas tree in the corner of the sitting room that was standing at a seventy-degree angle.

'Dad!' Nettie exclaimed, rushing over and trying to correct it before it fell completely to the floor, taking the contents of the mantelpiece with it. 'What are you *doing*?'

Jamie took it from her, more easily able to hold the tree upright with his longer arms.

'What does it look like?' her father asked breathlessly, pine needles densely knitted in his hair and beard. 'We can't have another Christmas with that dratted sapling on the table. It's too bloody depressing.' He got up off his knees with a groan, shaking himself out like a Labrador and looking down sadly at all the needles on the floorboards. 'Shame I couldn't get a non-drop, though.'

'But *where* did you get it? It's Christmas morning.' Nettie laughed, incredulous. 'Nowhere's open.' She spied a dusty box that hadn't been out of the loft in many years – their old Christmas decorations.

He winked. 'The old fella selling them at the garage had just left behind what he hadn't sold. No one else is going to buy one now.' He nodded. 'I mean, admittedly it's a bit wonky.'

A bit? Nettie and Jamie laughed. One side of it appeared to have been shaved off.

'Here, Nets, I'll hold it upright if you tighten the screws at the base,' Jamie said, correcting the tree to its proper ninety-degree angle and taking the weight.

'Tch, I wanted to have this all ready for you for when you woke up,' her father said disappointedly as she set to work.

'Dad, it's fantastic!' she exclaimed from under the tree. 'I love it. A proper tree.'

She crawled out again and looked up at him, beaming.

'Well, it's about time, wouldn't you say?' her father said. 'We've been holding on to the past too tightly.'

Nettie stood up and put her arms around him, listening to the steadfast plod of his heart beneath her ear. Her father pulled back first and turned to Jamie.

'And last night wasn't the time to say it, too many people about . . .' he said solemnly.

Nettie smiled as she remembered everyone's faces when they'd walked hand-in-hand into the house, a hush falling over the gathering within seconds. Jamie had dealt with it with his usual low-key languor, doing his best impression of someone 'normal', as Em had immediately corralled Nettie in the kitchen, scolding her for keeping her alter ego a secret, before timidly asking in the next breath whether she'd visit the children's wards in costume on Christmas Day. Nettie thought she'd never felt so proud.

' . . . But what you did – you've shown us that we need to start trying to move forwards.' He held out his hand and Jamie shook it. 'We are in your debt.'

'No, you're not. Nettie's given me far more than I've given her, Mr Watson.'

'Please – Gerry.'

Jamie nodded with a smile. 'Gerry. My life was becoming pretty jaded. I thought I'd pretty much seen it all until your daughter burst into my life.'

'Actually, strictly speaking, you burst into mine,' Nettie corrected as she began picking pine needles out from her hair. 'There I was, perfectly happy—'

'Dressing as a giant bunny and careering down ice tracks?' Jamie grinned.

'I suppose that's one way to get attention, Button,' her father sighed. 'Although I've always thought you had such a lovely smile that—'

'Dad!' Nettie groaned, placing her hand on his arm. 'Shall I brew a fresh pot of tea?'

Her father beamed. 'Superb, Button. You go put the kettle on, and Jamie and I will get the lights on this prickly monster. Tell me, do you ever cycle, Jamie?'

She wandered happily into the kitchen. There were still empty bottles and half-full glasses and bowls of crisps and olives from last night's party.

She quickly loaded the dishwasher to capacity and put it on. She was pulling the milk from the fridge when there was a knock at the front door.

'Oh, can you get that, love? It'll be Dan!' her father called. 'He's dropping off a spare fairy for the tree.'

She pattered down the hallway, wondering whether to tease him about Em, glancing in on her way past at the sight of Jamie and her father standing on tiptoes and unwinding the cord of lights, passing it between themselves like a weaving shuttle, each trying not to be jabbed through their shirts by the sharp needles.

She bit her lip as she opened the door. 'Hi, Da—'

'Love, what is it?' her father called from the sitting room a few moments later, hearing the distinct lack of conversation or of doors closing.

'You did your hair,' Nettie whispered, almost wanting to laugh as she heard the words out loud; of all the things she had fantasized about what she would say to her mother when – if – she ever saw her again, 'You did your hair' wasn't it.

'Yes. It needed doing.'

She could see her mother resisting the urge to pat the newly styled crop, which had an elfin charm, the fresh hazelnut tints almost gleaming in the snowlight. Her clothes were different too – better than the other day, although still not how she'd remembered her mother dressing: straight-leg jeans, a pair of trainers, a black polo neck beneath a trendy but cheap olive parka.

Nettie felt her chest inflate as shame filled her. 'I'm so s—'

'Sssh.' Her mother held a finger to her lips, but Nettie could see from the way it trembled slightly that her mother was also struggling to hold back her emotions. 'You have *nothing* to be sorry for, you hear me?' she said sternly. Maternally.

Nettie nodded, feeling her breath like a rolling sea inside

her. She couldn't keep it all in, this; it was uncontainable. She didn't know what to do, how to let it out. She wanted to run to her mother and throw her arms around her, to lock the door behind her and throw away the key; she was so close now – on the step, within touching distance – but Gwen's sober warnings resounded in her head: how difficult return was, how overwhelming for the missing person to accomplish, rarely done in one go, or at the first attempt. She could just as easily turn away and disappear again. This could be as good as it got; this might be as close as she got.

She didn't know what to do; she didn't want to mess it up again. 'Do you . . . do you want to come in?'

She saw her mother's eyes slide behind her, then, and she knew her father was there. She could hear the vacuum of air in the hallway, as though a black hole had opened up behind her and threatened to suck her into it, far away from here.

'Well, that depends on you,' her mother said slowly, her eyes on her husband.

'Of course we want you to come in,' Nettie gasped, the words in a rush. 'There's nothing we want more, isn't that right, Dad?'

Her father nodded, but the movement was jerky and reflexive, like a marionette's.

'Have you seen the ribbons? In the square? They're for you, Mum. All for you.'

'I know . . . I heard on the news last night. They're beautiful . . .' Her eyes shone at the dismay that she knew came from their private family tragedy becoming an oh-so-public news story. 'But it's not that simple, love.' Her mother's voice was small, contained, as though she'd put it in a box.

'It is!' Nettie cried, feeling her calm begin to crumble, sensing her mother recede. 'Having you back is all that matters. You're all we want. We've missed you so much.'

But her mother just shook her head. 'It's not just me, you see.'

Nettie reeled, stepping back as though the words were pushing her over. What? She had . . . another husband? Another man?

She whipped round to face her father, who still hadn't said a word. He didn't look like he'd taken a breath in all that time.

'Dad?' Nettie asked, making to move towards him, before noticing suddenly his eyeline. The angle of it. Tears rising like moons in his eyes. Understanding dawning.

She turned back again, feeling the spin of the earth slow fractionally. For there, at the bottom of the steps, behind her mother, was a little girl – thin but rosy-cheeked in a puffy hooded snowsuit. No more than three years old, she guessed.

'This is Molly,' her mother said, but her voice had changed again, thin to the point of translucence, weightless. 'And I understand if . . . I understand . . .' The emotion she had kept in check till now – the courage she had mustered to get to this doorstep – broke free like wild horses and she dropped her head. Nettie noticed her hands were balled into fists, the sinews in her neck straining like she was lifting a weight far heavier than she could bear.

'Mummy sad?' the little girl said in a voice as high as a piccolo, and with it, drawing from her father the sound that had been lost till now – an anguished yelp, like a dog with a pin in its paw, a man with a break in his heart.

Nettie couldn't take her eyes off her sister, remembering the doll she'd seen in the box at the flat yesterday.

'I know what I've put you through. I know what I've denied you, Gerry. And I've missed you so badly, more than you could ever know. But I didn't know how to . . . to say it . . .' her mother said, the words drifting into silence. Nettie and her father were unmoving as they stared at the little girl they had never once even thought to imagine.

'When I walked out that day, I had no idea I wasn't going to return. I just . . . had to walk. And think. I'd come back from the doctor's and I didn't know how to tell you I was pregnant again, not after the conversation we'd had. But then I walked so far I didn't even know where I was or how long I'd been walking. I'd left without my bag and I realized I had no way of getting back – I couldn't catch a bus or train or taxi. I felt so *stupid*, so *guilty*, knowing what you must be going through to come home and find me gone.'

Neither Nettie nor her father replied. It was a day neither one of them would ever be able to forget – or, possibly, forgive.

'And yet, the next morning, my absence made it all seem somehow easier. My mind felt clearer. I knew I wanted the baby and so it seemed obvious, suddenly, what I had to do. I'd been so broken. At some level, I think I thought you'd be better off without me.'

'How could I ever be better off without you?' Nettie cried. 'You're my mother. I needed you.'

'But Molly did too, and I didn't think I could have you both,' her mother said quietly. 'You were so . . . independent, finding your place in the world. You'd got a job, found your first flat, were settling into a relationship.' She shrugged hopelessly. 'You'd grown up. I didn't think you needed me anymore.'

'You were wrong,' Nettie whispered bitterly, feeling the tears smart at her eyes as she stared down with a stony heart at the fledgling child. She had been abandoned by her mother for *her*? She had always wanted a sibling – but not at this price.

'I know that now. And I'm so sorry, darling.'

Molly staggered up the steps, seemingly not aware that her legs bent at the knee, and making her mother smile through her tears as she bent down to scoop her up. Nettie was surprised to realize she had laughed too.

Her mother looked back at her, the child on her hip, terror in her eyes. 'Nettie, this is your little sister, Molly.'

Nettie blinked as the little girl looked straight at her – guileless, brimful, innocent. They had the same almond eyes.

'Would you like to hold her? I've told her all about you.'

Nettie bit her lip, recoiling slightly as she checked her instinct to reach out. The silence behind her was becoming oppressive, like a choking fog seeping towards her. 'Dad?' she asked, half turning to him. She couldn't abandon him after everything they'd endured together.

He came to stand behind her, his hand on the door, knuckles blanched white and an expression on his face she couldn't read – joy marbled with grief, relief with betrayal, surprise with dismay . . .

'Gerry?' Her mother's voice wavered and Nettie understood this was it. The final chance. She stood still, braced for either the silence or words that would confirm the path their lives would follow once and for all. Could her father forgive this? Could she?

She closed her eyes as she felt him step back, a rush of air gathering behind her as he stepped away from the door, retreating into the shadow of the house, and desolation barrelled through her. It was too late; he had been pushed too hard, for too long, his wife's secret a step too far—

'We're just making some tea,' he said.

There was another pause, and Nettie's gaze tangled with her little sister's as they waited, both of them, for their family's fate to be decided, negotiated.

'A good cup of tea?' her mother asked back, a light beginning to shine in her eyes.

Nettie caught her breath as she heard the refrain that had echoed throughout her whole life – the remedy for any problem, no matter how terrible.

She watched as her father slowly smiled too. 'Yes. We're going to have a good cup of tea.'

Acknowledgements

A person going missing is uniquely sad. In the course of my research into the subject, I read many historic stories of people going missing that articulated the lingering despair of the families left behind who are not only left wondering where their loved ones are, but also whether they are even alive and safe. Missing People is an excellent charity that provides support to both the people who go missing and their families, and the lyrics you read in the St Martins-in-the-Field scene are taken from a song 'I Miss You', written especially for them by a father whose son went missing twenty-six years ago. Should you be so inclined, it's well worth taking the time to listen to it, as it's hauntingly beautiful and the £1 download fee benefits the charity. www.missingpeople.org.uk/imissyou

As someone whose working day involves spending eight hours alone in a room, making up worlds in my head, the more niche machinations of big corporations are outside my immediate sphere of knowledge, so I'd like to offer big thanks to Sarah (@sesp) who volunteered her expertise from the Twittersphere – rather appropriately given the topic of this book. I had never heard of CSR before our first ssages and I'm so grateful for her patience in advising

Also, as ever, I'd like to thank the teams both personal and professional that support me day to day in getting my books written, finessed and published into these beautiful, sparkling products: Victoria Hughes-Williams and Caroline Hogg, thank you for your insightful and incisive edits; Natasha Harding, your military-grade organizational powers; Katie James, ever-smiling and ever-optimistic on my behalf even though my life is unfailingly boring for editorial purposes; Jodie Mullish and Amy Lines, doing things that I will never understand with computers (meta-what?) but that somehow mean the most beautiful posters of my books are flagged up on walls and screens around the country; Daniel Jenkins, Stuart Dwyer and Anna Bond for securing dazzling subs that mean bookshelves (both nationally and internationally) are groaning under the weight of Karen Swan tomes; James Annal, for such a lovely cover – again; Eloise Wood and my copy-editor Laura Collins for enduring my appalling grammar; Holly Sheldrake for the alchemy that turns my word document into beautiful book-dom; and Jeremy Trevathan and Wayne Brookes for seeing the big picture. I'm so grateful to you all.

To my family – all of you – I couldn't make you up. You're better than fiction.

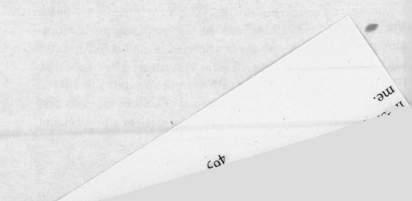

Prima
DONNA
by
Karen Swan

Breaking the rules was what she liked best.
That was her sport.

Renegade, rebel, bad girl. Getting away with it.

Pia Soto is the sexy and glamorous prima ballerina,
the Brazilian bombshell who's shaking up the
ballet world with her outrageous behaviour.
She's wild and precocious, and she's a survivor.
She's determined that no man will ever control her
destiny. But ruthless financier Will Silk has Pia in
his sights, and has other ideas . . .

Sophie O'Farrell is Pia's hapless, gawky assistant,
the girl-next-door to Pia's Prima Donna, always either
falling in love with the wrong man or just falling over.
Sophie sets her own dreams aside to pick up the debris
in Pia's wake, but she's no angel. When a devastating
accident threatens to cut short Pia's illustrious career,
Sophie has to step out of the shadows and face up to
the demons in her own life.

Christmas at
TIFFANY'S
by
Karen Swan

Three cities, three seasons, one chance to find the life that fits.

Cassie settled down too young, marrying her first serious boyfriend. Now, ten years later, she is betrayed and broken. With her marriage in tatters and no career or home of her own, she needs to work out where she belongs in the world and who she really is.

So begins a year-long trial as Cassie leaves her sheltered life in rural Scotland to stay with each of her best friends in the most glamorous cities in the world: New York, Paris and London. Exchanging grouse moor and mousy hair for low-carb diets and high-end highlights, Cassie tries on each city for size as she attempts to track down the life she was supposed to have been leading, and with it, the man who was supposed to love her all along.

The Perfect
PRESENT
by
Karen Swan

Memories are a gift . . .

Haunted by a past she can't escape, Laura Cunningham
desires nothing more than to keep her world small
and precise – her quiet relationship and growing
jewellery business are all she needs to get by. Until
the day when Rob Blake walks into her studio and
commissions a necklace that will tell his enigmatic
wife Cat's life in charms.

As Laura interviews Cat's family, friends and former
lovers, she steps out of her world and into theirs – a
charmed world where weekends are spent in Verbier
and the air is lavender-scented, where friends are wild,
extravagant and jealous, and a big love has to
compete with grand passions.

Hearts are opened, secrets revealed and as the necklace
begins to fill up with trinkets, Cat's intoxicating life
envelops Laura's own. By the time she has to identify the
final charm, Laura's metamorphosis is almost complete.
But the last story left to tell has the power to change all
of their lives forever, and Laura is forced to choose
between who she really is and who it is she wants to be.

Christmas at
CLARIDGE'S
by
Karen Swan

The best presents can't be wrapped . . .

*This was where her dreams drifted to if she didn't blot her
nights out with drink; this was where her thoughts settled if
she didn't fill her days with chat. She remembered this tiny,
remote foreign village on a molecular level and the sight of it
soaked into her like water into sand, because this was where her
old life had ended and her new one had begun.*

Portobello – home to the world-famous street market,
Notting Hill Carnival and Clem Alderton. She's the
queen of the scene, the girl everyone wants to be or be
with. But beneath the morning-after make-up, Clem is
keeping a secret, and when she goes too far one reckless
night she endangers everything – her home, her job and
even her adored brother's love.

Portofino – a place of wild beauty and old-school
glamour. Clem has been here once before and vowed
never to return. But when a handsome stranger asks
Clem to restore a neglected villa, it seems like the answer
to her problems – if she can just face up to her past.

Claridge's – at Christmas. Clem is back in London
working on a special commission for London's grandest
hotel. But is this really where her heart lies?

The SUMMER WITHOUT YOU

by
Karen Swan

Everything will change . . .

Rowena Tipton isn't looking for a new life, just a new adventure; something to while away the months as her long-term boyfriend presses pause on their relationship before they become engaged. But when a chance encounter at a New York wedding leads to an audition for a coveted house share in the Hamptons – Manhattan's elite beach scene – suddenly a new life is exactly what she's got.

Stretching before her is a summer with three eclectic housemates, long days on white-sand ocean beaches and parties on gilded tennis courts. But high rewards bring high stakes and Rowena soon finds herself caught in the crossfire of a vicious intimidation campaign. Alone for the first time in her adult life, she has no one to turn to but a stranger who is everything she doesn't want – but possibly everything she needs.

Christmas in
THE SNOW
by
Karen Swan

In London, the snow is falling and Christmas is just around the corner – but Allegra Fisher barely has time to notice. She's pitching for the biggest deal of her career and can't afford to fail. When she meets Sam Kemp on the plane to the meeting, she can't afford to lose her focus. But when Allegra finds herself up against Sam for the bid, their passion quickly turns sour.

In Zermatt in the Swiss Alps, a long-lost mountain hut is discovered in the snow after sixty years. The last person expecting to become involved is Allegra – she hasn't even heard of the woman they found inside. It soon becomes clear the two women are linked and, as she and Isobel travel out to make sense of the mystery, hearts thaw and dark secrets are uncovered . . .

Summer at
TIFFANY'S
by
Karen Swan

A wedding to plan. A wedding to stop.
What could go wrong?

Cassie loves Henry. Henry loves Cassie. With a Tiffany ring on her finger, all that Cassie has left to do is plan the wedding. It should be so simple but when Henry pushes for a date, Cassie pulls back.

Henry's wild, young cousin, Gem, has no such hesitations and is racing to the aisle at a sprint, determined to marry in the Cornish church where her parents were wed. But the family is set against it, and Cassie resolves to stop the wedding from going ahead.

When Henry lands an expedition sailing the Pacific for the summer, Cassie decamps to Cornwall, hoping to find the peace of mind she needs to move forwards. But in the dunes and coves of the northern Cornish coast, she soon discovers that the past isn't finished with her yet.

It's time to relax with your next good book

THEWINDOWSEAT.CO.UK

If you've enjoyed this book, but don't know what
to read next, then we can help. The Window Seat is
a site that's all about making it easier to discover your
next good book. We feature recommendations,
behind-the-scenes tales from the world of publishing,
creative writing tips, competitions, and, if we're honest,
quite a lot of lists based on our favourite reads.

You'll find stories and features
by authors including Lucinda Riley, Karen Swan,
Diane Chamberlain, Jane Green, Lucy Diamond
and many more. We showcase brand-new talent
as well as classic favourites, so you'll never be
stuck for what to read again.

We'd love to know what you think of the site, our books,
and what you'd like us to feature, so do let us know.

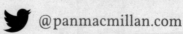 @panmacmillan.com

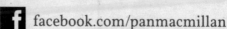 facebook.com/panmacmillan

WWW.THEWINDOWSEAT.CO.UK